M000195658

if

Nicholas Bourbaki

Livingston Press
The University of West Alabama
Livingston, AL

Copyright © 2014 Nicholas Bourbaki
All rights reserved, including electronic text
ISBN 13: 978-1-60489-134-8, hardcover
ISBN 13: 978-1-60489-135-5, trade paper
ISBN: 1-60489-134-3 hardcover
ISBN: 1-60489-135-1 trade paper
Library of Congress Control Number: 2014932127
Printed on acid-free paper.
Printed in the United States of America by
EBSCO Media
Hardcover binding by: Heckman Bindery
Typesetting and page layout: Nicholas Bourbaki, Joe Taylor
Proofreading: Joe Taylor, Angela Brown
Cover design and layout: Joe Taylor

first edition
6 5 4 3 2 1

if

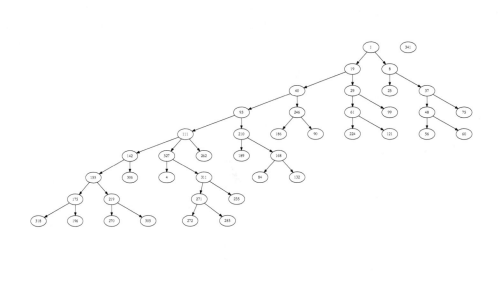

After school, you bike to your best friend's house. It has been a long day, and you are looking forward to playing video games with him. But when the front door opens, it is your best friend's little sister, Iris.

"Is Gerard there?" you ask.

"*Mom, is Gerry here?*" Iris shouts at the top of her lungs, leaning into the shadows of the house. "I don't think he's here," she says. You are annoyed, but you do not say anything. Iris used to keep her distance from you, but then she found out how young you are. She is in sixth grade and you are already in eighth, but because you started school early and skipped a grade, you are actually only a year older than her. Now she bothers you all the time.

"Maybe he's in the underground room," she whispers, like someone who knows a secret.

"What?"

"You know."

"What underground room?"

She pauses and squints. "You *know*. The underground room."

Gerard has never told you anything about an underground room.

"Come on," she says. "I'll show you." She yells back into the house. "*Mom, we're going to look for Gerry.*" Then she grabs your hand and shuts the door. "I betcha that's where he is."

You let her lead you through the quiet and empty streets of the subdivision. She keeps telling you that you are going too slow. She tugs you by the hand, but when a car passes, she lets it drop. She looks at you, laughs again, and covers her face. "You're so weird," she says.

You keep wondering what the underground room could be. You and Gerard have walked this way many times before, but he never said anything about an underground room. Maybe it is a hiding place, like a tree house. But what kind of tree house is underground?

Iris picks a tall weed from a crack in the sidewalk and runs it across her nose. "Betcha didn't know I was in the gang," she says.

"Of course I did." You have never heard of any gang.

She smirks. "No, you didn't. I bet you didn't know I got... *inducted.*" She says it like someone who is proud to have learned a new word but is still not one hundred percent sure about how to use it. She frowns and looks away.

You wish that Gerard had been home. The two of you would be playing video games and drinking sodas by now.

After a while, you and Iris come to the edge of the houses. There are wooden frames and empty lots full of sandy soil and weeds all around. It feels like you have been walking for a very long time, even though you know it could not have been more than half an hour. She leads you through one of the empty lots and points at a ditch behind it. "Come on," she says. "There it is."

You stare at the ditch. "That?" you ask. But when you walk closer, you see that there is a flat concrete channel inside the ditch. The channel is a few feet deep and about two dozen feet long. At one end is the entrance to a concrete tunnel.

Iris hops down into the channel and peers inside the dark opening. When you go to stand beside her, you feel a cool breeze coming out of it. It makes the hair stand up on the back of your neck. In the darkness, you think you can see some kind of phosphorescence glimmering far ahead on the tunnel walls.

"Wanna go inside and look for him?" Iris asks.

If the two of you crouched down and walked single file, you could explore the tunnel. But you have no flashlight or matches. "I don't know," you say. "Maybe we should go back." You suddenly feel nervous. You are not sure that you are supposed to be here, and there is something gross about the tunnel. There is a thin trail of slimy water that trickles out of it and down the middle of the channel between your feet. It goes all the way to the other end, then disappears into the rocks and dirt there.

"*Re-tard!*" Iris yells into the tunnel, crouching at the entrance. "*Re-tard Gerard!*" Her voice echoes in the darkness. Then she giggles. You wonder if there is anyone in the empty housing lots who heard her. Maybe there is someone watching you.

"Let's go in," Iris says. "He's probably in there." She takes her hand out from the kangaroo pouch of her sweatshirt and points inside the tunnel. "Unless you're afraid."

"Afraid of what?"

"I don't know. You're the one who's a fraidy cat."

You roll your eyes. "I'm not a fraidy cat."

She continues to stare at you, then laughs again and covers her face. "Come on," she says. She grabs your hand and tugs you toward the tunnel.

But this time, you resist.

"Oh my God," she says. She looks away. "It's just like Gerry said. You're such a faggot."

"No, I'm not," you say. "And he wouldn't say that."

"You're such a faggot."

"No, I'm not."

"Prove it."

"I'm not going to—"

But before you can say anything, she has crouched and disappeared into the tunnel. You can hear the echo of her footsteps.

Then, after a while, you cannot hear anything. When you call after her, she does not respond.

If you follow Iris into the tunnel, turn to page 8.

If you stay outside, turn to page 19.

Carried forward in the wave of bodies, you eventually surface at a collapsed section of the fence. The chain link bounces and shakes beneath your feet. Then you stumble across the coils of barbed wire and onto solid ground.

On the other side of the fence, the protesters disperse like particles drawn into a vacuum, circulating at random, pulled into the empty space. It is oddly peaceful. Some of the men continue to run this way and that in the faint illumination. Others mill about. A window shatters nearby, and you can hear the rattling of a closed door.

Then the first sirens. A few brief squawks. When you turn, you see spinning red reflections on the small storefronts in the distance. Some of the men start to push back toward the breach in the fence, forcing their way against the oncoming bodies.

Within an hour, the police have dispersed the crowd. A few of the protesters refuse to leave and are arrested.

You are reminded of the crowd when, three months later, another mob gathers in another state. This one, flown in at private expense by Republican campaign organizers, stages a riot at the meeting of a county canvassing board. A short while later, the Supreme Court decides to bring the counting of votes to an end.

You must ask yourself then: did your actions make any difference?

The clear answer is no.

Choice, you conclude, sitting at the dinner table across from J.P., already tipsy from the third beer of the night, might not matter as much as you had thought. You chose to work for the campaign, the volunteers chose to work for you, the voters chose Al Gore, the nation chose a president, and despite all these choices, these acts of freedom, another man will enter the Oval Office. It was as though the fabric of space and time contained endless possible threads, but all of them, in the end, spun back to a single, incontrovertible point: the election of George W. Bush.

"It all seems so pointless," you tell J.P. "You try to do the right thing. But your choices don't matter." You pause and take another sip of beer. "Maybe the stoics were right. Maybe it's all beyond our control, and the only reasonable response is to detach yourself. Take the bad with the good like there's no difference. Because in the end, there's no point in struggling. The result is always the same."

"Right. Like with Bush and Gore," J.P. says, tilting back his own beer. "No matter who you choose, you're going to get the same thing. Someone bought and paid for by corporations."

You look at him. "Well, I don't know about that."

"Tell me one difference between Dick Cheney and Joe Lieberman."

You consider for a moment. "I can't picture Joe Lieberman eating a baby."

"I can," he says. "He wouldn't enjoy it. He'd struggle with it, you know, like a leader. But if it was what was right for America, Joe Lieberman would eat a baby."

"I guess so," you say. "But Al Gore wouldn't."

"Al Gore is a pompous ass."

You set down your fork and stare at J.P. as he slices into a bean fajita. After a moment, you rise from the table, walk upstairs and shut yourself in your room. Only later in the evening, when you grow thirsty again, do you return downstairs. Ida is watching TV in her old blue bathrobe, her hair still wet from a shower. There is a small pile of foil candy wrappers beside her on the couch.

"What are you watching?" you ask.

"Oh," she grins, "there's something on the other channel. It's got that boy..."

"Which boy?"

She continues to stare at the television. "The one from the show..." she says. "Everyone's on a boat. You know."

You wait for her to continue, but instead she sets down her comb, unwraps another candy and places it in her mouth. Watching her perform this perfunctory motion somehow causes you pain.

On the television, there is a commercial for something about sunlight. The branches of an animated tree grow and split into other branches and push out bright green leaves.

"One of J.P.'s moles was bleeding," she says.

She says it matter-of-factly.

You look at her.

"And?" you ask. "Is he okay?"

Suddenly your heart is pounding.

Standing by the couch, you watch the branches of the animated tree split and grow.

Life endlessly reproducing.

Cancerous cells dividing.

You read somewhere that cancer cells can divide endlessly. But nothing is immortal. The malignant cells choke off a liver, pool through the blood, metastasize in tissues and veins. The host dies. Somewhere there is a final branch.

You look at Ida and wait for her to speak.

Awake, awake…

Beholde, thou art yet in the faire garden: and there is no new thing vnder the sunne. The plants which blossomed, blossome still: and the trees which put foorth fruite, put foorth fruite still: and the wings of the butterflies which daunced, daunce still.

And I am yet before thee.

So, you've made your choice, I say. That was it.

I laugh and shew thee againe my teeth with yellow staine.

But I don't want you to spend eternity with a case of buyer's remorse. So I'm going to give you one last chance to reconsider. You know, hell is where the heart is. You're a free man, and you deserve a choice. One last chance, my friend.

Now. Do you choose the side of God, or do you choose me?

If you choose hell, turn to page 270.

If you repent, turn to page 305.

You crouch down and enter the tunnel. It is so short that you are almost doubled over. Instead of walking, you waddle with one foot to each side of the slimy trail.

Soon the light from the entrance fades. You continue into the darkness.

After a while, something brushes across your face and you stumble back, bumping your head on the top of the tunnel. It felt like a cobweb, but when you try to brush it away, there is nothing.

You keep walking. Even when you look back over your shoulder now you cannot see anything, no matter how wide you open your eyes. It is like being buried alive. But if you turn back, Iris will know that you were afraid.

You start to panic. Your heart races and you force yourself to stay calm. Only a few feet above you, it is the afternoon and the sun is setting...

But what if there was a man who saw you and Iris enter the tunnel, and he is creeping up behind you? He could be a few feet behind you right now. He could be reaching out his hand.

"Iris?" you ask. Your voice echoes in the dark. It has been so long since you saw anything. What if there was a fork in the tunnel, and you and Iris took different routes? What if you took another wrong turn when you tried to leave? Had you already turned around? No longer knowing which way you are headed, you scramble forward faster and faster into the darkness, preparing to scream.

Then you stop. There is a dim light ahead. You waddle toward it, round a sharp corner and find Iris standing in a small, brightly lit chamber. It is so bright, you have to squint.

"Boo," she says.

"Hey," you say, out of breath.

"You were so afraid," she laughs.

The room has bare concrete walls. There is a narrow opening with bars in the upper corner. It must be one of the gratings in the curb that the rain goes down. A manhole cover sits in the ceiling.

"I wasn't afraid," you say. You try to keep your voice from shaking.

"So I guess Gerry isn't here," Iris shrugs. "Retard."

"Is this a sewer?"

She shakes her head. "Huh-unh. It's a secret hideout."

You look at her as she tucks her hair behind one ear.

"What are you looking at?" she asks.

"Nothing."

She stops playing with her hair and smiles.

"Do you want to try something?" she asks.

"What?"

"Sit down and close your eyes."

Your heart is still beating fast. She frowns at you and rolls her eyes.

"Come on," she says. "I'm not going to *hurt* you."

After a second, you sit down with your legs crossed. Once your eyes are closed, you can hear Iris crouching in front of you. She squeezes your knee. Then she sits down in your lap.

"Don't look," she says. You have to clench your eyes shut when she starts to kiss you. It goes on for a long time, until you feel her shaking. She sniffles and you open your eyes.

"Why are you crying?" you ask.

She does not answer. Her cheek is wet when she presses it against yours. "Do you want to try something?" she whispers.

"Okay."

You try to act normal while Iris unties the drawstring on your shorts and tugs them down.

Once, near the end, you see a shadow moving outside the grating, like someone moving on the street above the chamber. A shudder passes through you. What if there was a person watching? But then the shadow is gone. Soon you are finished and Iris goes to spit in the corner.

While you pull up your shorts, you do not look at her. "Thanks," you say.

She stares up at the grating and does not answer. "Whatever." Her head makes a small movement.

You look at her. "I don't—"

"Let's get out of here," she says. Then she crouches into the tunnel and starts to walk back.

When you get home, you take a long shower. Then you lie in bed. It is a long time before you fall asleep.

A few days later, you get sent to the Principal's office for not breaking into groups in history class. The teacher says you have to split into groups but you just sit there.

Then they call in the gym teacher and he gives you ten seconds to get out of your chair, but when you start to set the timer on your watch, he just grabs you by the back of your shirt and drags you to the Principal's office. Heather Martinez is already sitting outside.

"What are you doing here?" she asks. "Are they giving you a prize or something?"

"No. I got in a fight with Mr. Jerk-again," you say. It is a nickname you just came up with for the gym teacher, because his name is Mr. Jernigan.

Heather looks at you for a second. She is dressed all in black and she has black hair with red dye in it. When she starts to laugh, it surprises you. Usually no one laughs at your jokes.

"Who won?"

You shrug. "He had leverage."

"Is this your first time here? In the *Principal's* office?" She says it like the name of a heavy metal band.

You shrug. "Yeah," you say. "I guess."

She looks at you for a while. Then she laughs. "Huh."

"What did you get called in for?"

"Smoking in the girl's room," she whispers. You can smell the cigarettes on her breath.

"Awesome," you say.

"*Awesome.*"

"Yeah."

"Do you smoke, Egghead?"

You turn to her. "I don't like that name."

She stops and nods. "So do you smoke?"

"No," you say. "My dad smokes." You shrug again. Then you worry that you're shrugging too much. For some reason your lips keep sticking to your teeth. "My dad smokes a lot of cigarettes. I'll probably smoke some pot eventually," you say. You try not to shrug. "But not cigarettes. You know, what's the point?"

Heather laughs so hard that she leans out of her chair.

"What happened to you?" she says. "You used to be such a good kid." She reaches out and pinches your cheek.

Your throat tightens up. You worry that if you say anything, it will sound like you're about to cry. But not because you're embarrassed or anything.

You feel proud.

"Hey." She leans close to you and grins. "I have an idea. You want to come over after school and get *stoned?*"

You think for a second. "Sure," you shrug. "Awesome."

So when school ends, you follow Heather and the rest of the kids back to her house. It's where all the skaters hang out. You drop your bike by the quarterpipe in her driveway. Some of the other kids are weird to you at first. But when Heather says it's okay, most of them go along with you being there.

Except for me. At school I'm the one who probably makes fun of you the most. I was the one who first called you Egghead.

I still keep making fun of you, even when we're all sitting around on the wood floor in Heather's attic and passing around a little tinfoil pipe. I won't stop.

"You ever smoked out before, Egghead?" I ask.

I start to hand you the pipe, but at the last second I hold it back. The bowl is still letting off a small thread of smoke. The rain splatters on the attic roof.

"Heather said if I chipped in…"

"Dude," Heather says, her eyes wide, and at first you think she's talking to you. But then you see that she's looking at me. "Just give him the fucking pipe. Jesus. You're such a fucking asshole. And you're wasting it."

So I hand you the pipe. "I feel like I'm gettin' my cat high," I say while you flick the lighter. "I could blow it in your ear if you wanted, Egghead."

You keep flicking the lighter but it won't work. Finally I take it out of your hand and light it and hold the flame over the little bowl while you inhale. The flame curls down into the bowl for a second and then the tinfoil burns your lips and you almost drop the whole thing.

"Don't nigger-lip it," I say.

"Jesus fucking Christ," Heather says.

"Hold it in."

You nod and try to keep the smoke in your lungs without coughing. It tastes like burnt grass and seeds.

You pass the pipe to someone else and keep trying not to cough. Some of us laugh.

"It's not like he's gonna get high anyway," I say. "Nobody gets high the first time."

"Not on this fucking shake."

"Fuck you," I say. "I'm not the one with the—fucking—tinfoil one-hitter."

When you finally let out your breath, there's hardly any smoke. You felt like there was a big cloud in your lungs. But it ends up being almost totally clear.

Then another kid takes a long hit and drops the pipe into a little glazed ceramic ashtray that looks like something from art class. "Shit is cashed," the other kid croaks, waving his fingers in the air.

"Are you feeling anything, Egghead?" I ask.

"Dude," Heather says. "Don't call him that."

"What? His head looks like an egg. It's not my fault. Are you fried, Egghead?"

You shrug a little. "I don't know."

"Are you a fried egg?"

"Dude," Heather sighs.

"This is your brain on drugs—"

Heather tells me to shut the fuck up. But I just laugh. Pretty soon, all of us are laughing. Someone nudges you on the shoulder, and you realize it is not a big deal. "Fuck all of you," you mumble, smiling and dizzy.

A while later, when you have to leave to go home for dinner, Heather tells you that there's going to be a pool party at her house on Friday night. "You should come."

"Really?"

"Yeah," she laughs.

So you pick up your bike from beside the quarterpipe and say you'll probably be there. There are so many kids that would never get invited to a pool party at Heather's house.

Later in the week, you slide into the last seat at a lunch table, even though you know that Gerard was behind you in the line. All through lunch, you can feel him watching you, sitting alone at a table nearby. When he called the night before, you said you didn't feel like going out. Then you told J.P. and Ida to say that you weren't home if he called again.

When Friday comes around, you have science class for the last hour of the day, and the teacher does an experiment with a lit cigarette, a syringe, and a two-liter bottle with water inside.

"I was so fuckin' jonesing," one of us says afterward. We start lighting up even before we're out of the parking lot.

"Yeah," you say. "Me too."

"How can you be jonesing if you've never smoked?"

"I've smoked."

"Bullshit," I say. "You can't even inhale."

"I can inhale," you insist. "Dude. You've seen me inhale."

"Then say something while it's in your lungs."

"What?"

"Take a drag and say something after you've got the smoke in your lungs."

When you try, a big cloud of smoke comes rolling out of your mouth even before the first word, which makes everyone laugh. But then you make them give you the cigarette back and you try again. Your lungs spasm, but you keep your throat closed and do not cough. When you breathe out the smoke, no one laughs. Then it feels like all the cells in your body are vibrating with electricity.

"Egghead's buzzed," I laugh.

At Heather's house some people sit by the pool even though it's too cold to swim. Everyone else skates on the ramp. I put on a tape that no one likes. I say it's Napalm Death and that everyone here listens to pussy music. "What kind of music do you listen to?" I ask.

"I don't know," you say.

I clear my throat and spit on the driveway. "What do you mean?"

"I guess I just don't listen to music."

"Like, never?"

You shrug. "No."

"Like, you've never listened to anything? Not even, like, Metallica?"

"Nah. Not really."

I shake my head.

"Guns 'n Roses?"

"No. I mean, my parents listen to music sometimes."

"Like what?"

"I don't know." You look away. "You know, like Peter, Paul and Mary. Shit like that."

I laugh and then spit again on the driveway. "Fuck. I'll be back in a second." I walk over to the open garage, then come back with a tape in my hand. "Listen to this." I hand you the tape. "That's *Atomizer*. It's Big Black."

"Thanks," you say.

"I'm jealous. You've got so much fucking music out there."

Later in the afternoon, Heather's boyfriend shows up with a few cases of ice beer. He's in high school, so he can buy from some place out on the highway. The first taste almost makes you gag. But then it's not so bad if you hold your breath before you swallow and breathe out afterward. Then everyone starts dancing in Heather's basement, which has a big screen and a few couches. Everyone's jumping around between the couches with the lights off and shoving each other to a music video with a bunch of cheerleaders on bleachers in a gym. Then someone puts on a tape of the same song and plays it over and over. After a while you really start to feel like knocking over furniture and tearing everything off the walls.

Then Heather's boyfriend yells in your ear and asks if you want to roast a bowl.

"Sure," you say.

"She said you'd never had good weed before."

The two of you go up to the garage and open the automatic door. With the music still throbbing behind you, you walk outside and look up at the moon. It's cold enough that you can see your breath. Then you do not want to dance anymore. You turn back to Heather's boyfriend and watch him load the bowl. His bong is a blue tube with a sticker from a local skateshop on it. He starts to tell you about some graffiti he's doing.

"This fucking toy keeps nicing my work." He hands you the bong and a metal lighter with a skull on it. "So it's like I gotta keep finding more surfaces. Places where he's too much of a pussy to go." When you open the lighter, it smells like gasoline. "Fucking toys. Do you paint?"

"Nah. Not really."

"We should go out some time." He looks at you and nods. "I could show you some of my pieces. Show you a few things."

"Awesome," you say.

You flick the lighter over the bowl and inhale. The water makes a gurgling noise, and then the smoke hits your lungs. But before you can even hand back the bong, the door to the kitchen opens and the lights in the garage turn on.

Two girls stand in the doorway. One of them is Ashley. The two of you haven't talked since you wrote her a letter a few weeks ago.

"Egghead?"

The bong in your hands is still smoking. Before you can say anything, she rushes back into the house. She looked at you like she was mad. Heather's boyfriend closes the door.

"Who was that?"

You start to cough and see that the cherry has gone out.

"Fuck," you say. "Sorry."

"She looked pissed."

You spit onto the floor of the garage.

"So who was it?"

"Nobody." You spent a long time writing the letter and waiting for the right time. She didn't spend a long time reading it.

Before the bowl is finished, you look out the garage door again and see Ashley and her friend walking down the street. They stop under a streetlight and Ashley looks like she's trying hard to explain something that the other girl doesn't understand. You wonder why they were at the party. Neither of them belonged here.

When you head back down to the basement, everyone is still moshing but you aren't in the right mood anymore. You decide to go up to the attic to be alone. On your way up, you run into me on the basement stairs and bum a smoke.

"Sure," I say. "Here you go, Egghead."

"Fuck you," you say.

I laugh. "What?"

In the living room upstairs, some people are watching a skate video that looks like it was filmed through a fishbowl. Someone keeps doing an ollie onto a railing by some steps and falling down. You go into the kitchen and get a book of matches. Then you climb the ladder to the attic. You sit in the corner and light the cigarette. You don't know why you feel so messed up about what happened. Why do you care if she saw you.

The smoke curls up into the rafters. When the ash gets too long, you spit into your hand and flick the ash there. Then you hear someone else coming up the ladder and you put the cigarette out in the spit and wipe your hand on the back of your pants.

"Hey." A girl peaks up through the hatch in the floor. "I thought I saw you. What are you doing up here?"

"Nothing."

"Are you okay?"

You just look at her. The girl is named Denise and the two of you have never really talked. At school she's on the drill team and gets good grades, but everyone knows she hangs out at Heather's house.

"What's the matter?" She climbs into the attic.

"I don't know," you say. Some of the smoke got in your eyes when you were putting the cigarette out, and you try not to look like you were crying.

"Aw." She sits down beside you a little unsteadily. "I know what'll make you feel better. Here." She pulls a little bottle out of her pocket, unscrews the top and takes a drink. There are shiny flakes inside like a snowglobe.

"Is that gold?"

"Yeah," she laughs.

When she hands you the bottle, you take a deep breath and then swallow a little.

"Hey," she says. "Does it bother you that everyone calls you Egghead? That'd bother me."

"It's no big deal," you say.

She keeps looking at you really calmly. "You look so sad," she says. Then she smiles and gives you a peck on the cheek. "Have you ever kissed anyone?"

You shrug. "Yeah."

She keeps smiling at you and then leans forward again. The kiss only lasts a few seconds. Then she leans back and finishes the little bottle. "Hey," she says. "Let's go back to the party."

For the next hour you just sit on one of the couches in the basement. You do not know what to think. Sometimes you almost swear at yourself, and other times you want to laugh. Then someone passes around a joint and you take a few hits. You get hungry and eat potato chips. Just when you start to get tired, I tap you on the shoulder and say we're all going to climb onto the roof of the middle school.

"Dude, sometimes I feel bad," I tell you on the way over. "You know. For raggin' on you…" I lean and spit.

"What do you mean?"

"You know." I squeeze the can in my fist until it buckles. "You know…"

You nod. "Yeah."

"It's not like it was my fault. Sometimes people just piss you off. Like the way you walked…" I clear my throat and spit again. "I mean, now it all just seems like bullshit. It's you, it's funny. It's not…" I shake my head. "But every time I saw you, I just wanted to beat the shit out of you. It was like…" I stare out toward the houses and shake my head. "Sometimes you had yellow fucking snot coming out of your nose. And you didn't even notice it. You just walked around like there was nothing wrong."

You wait for me to continue. "You hated me because I didn't blow my nose?"

"Yeah. You know? But it wasn't just that, because it was like, then it was like, everything you did," I say. "You know what I mean? It's like, maybe it all started with one thing. But then you just hate everything. Didn't you ever hate someone like that?"

You think hard. "Maybe Gerard," you say.

"Yeah. Fucking Gerard." After a second, I suck in a deep breath and turn toward you. "What the fuck is wrong with that kid?" I say it so loudly that you worry someone might hear in one of the nearby houses.

"I don't know."

"He's such a fat fuck," I say. "Why can't he just fuckin'…"

You look at me, but I only shake my head.

A while later, you stop me and ask about Denise. You want to know if you have a shot.

"Sure," I say. "She's a slut."

"Denise?"

"Just get her drunk. I fucked her. She's a fucking lush."

But on the roof, you can't find her anywhere. You just wander around the empty blacktop and look out at the streetlights and houses. It feels like being on the surface of another planet.

Back at the party, you look downstairs. You look in the attic. You start to think she might have left.

"Has anyone seen Denise?" you ask. Everyone is watching a movie on the big screen in the basement. You can't hear the sound because of the music in the other room, but it looks like some kind of old news program. There's a guy in a suit standing in front of a bunch of reporters talking. Then he takes a gun out of a brown envelope and holds it up to his head. They all start screaming at him, but he just turns and puts the barrel in his mouth and pulls the trigger. Someone on the couch rewinds it and starts to watch it again.

You go to the other room and finally see Denise. She is standing with me by the drink table. My hand is on her waist and I'm leaning toward her so that she has to lean back. Then she laughs. When I start to kiss her, you look away.

Soon there is a video game on the TV where the two players fight. Blood keeps spurting out of the characters' faces and heads. You take drinks from a big plastic bottle of vodka being passed around on the couch.

"Are you sure?" someone asks.

"What?"

"You wanna robo-trip?"

You try to focus.

"Here, you can have the rest," he says. You look at the small red bottle in your hand and take a sniff. The first sip almost makes you gag. But then you shoot back the rest of it, wipe the syrup from your chin and throw the bottle against a door behind the couch.

"What the fuck? That shit's like food coloring. Fucking watch it."

"Yeah, okay," you say.

A while later, you're leaning over the rail of Heather's patio, heaving onto the grass. A few feet below, Heather's dog is lapping up the mess. "Go... away..." you tell the dog. But it just keeps licking at what came out of you. Your face is covered in sweat and your eyes are watering. You can feel scraps of food stuck to your teeth.

Then you are on the stairs to the basement, sliding with your face against the wall. You collapse by the toilet in Heather's bathroom. More of the red syrup comes out in a few gushes. Then it hangs from your lips and gets on the rim with the orange stains there. Afterward you curl into a ball on the tiles. Strings of spit slide out of your mouth but you're too tired to wipe them away.

When you wake, there is a red puddle by your face. You don't know where you are. Then you hear people in Heather's bedroom. You can hear them murmuring on the other side of the door. A bed squeaks. You wonder if they heard you and you think about standing and getting out. But then someone groans and you wait. The music throbs through the wall.

"Stop," a girl's voice says. "Stop."

It is Denise. Someone answers, but you can't hear what he says. She squeals a little and the bedframe shudders. "Please," she says. You hear my voice now, murmuring something. Then the bedframe shakes again and Denise makes a horrible kind of moan. It's like the sound a trapped dog makes.

You wonder what you should do.

If you stay hidden in the bathroom, turn to page 25.

Turn to page 25 if you continue to think.

If you step out of the bathroom and try to stop me, turn to page 37.

You keep waiting for Iris outside the tunnel. Finally, she comes out, scowling, and brushes herself off.

"I know why you wanted me to follow you," you smile. "But I can't be your boyfriend. I'm in eighth grade. You're only a sixth grader."

"So?" She peers at you. "I'm older than you."

"No, you're not."

"I'm twelve years old. You're eleven."

You pause and try to understand. "Wait—so—really?"

"God, you're such a faggot," she says.

It is the last time that you talk to a girl outside school for nearly a year.

When you grow lonely as a freshman, you sometimes think of the opportunity you missed with Iris. You could have rounded a few bases and gained a few experiences. You could have proven a few things.

But you are determined not to be held back by your mistakes. Several weeks into freshman year, you stand before the mirror in your bedroom and dial up an old acquaintance from middle school, a girl who had always been nice to you. You heard that she is now attending a small Christian high school outside town.

To your surprise, Ashley not only agrees to talk with you, but stays on the phone for nearly an hour. The two of you hit it off so well, in fact, that after only a few more calls, you take the plunge and propose meeting in person. "I know it's sudden. But I think we should get together. What are you doing right now?"

Two days later, you sit between the fashion magazines, discarded clothes and unfamiliar beauty products that lie strewn across her floor. Through the open door, you can hear her parents watching television in the other room. She sits silently across from you, pushing at a cuticle below her toenail and never looking into your eyes.

It is the first time that you have seen her since the end of eighth grade, and you are surprised that there is now a speckling of dark red and purple blotches across her face. It fans across her forehead and cheeks in small patches, occasionally punctuated by a blister.

Rather than being repelled, you are oddly relieved. Ashley's blemishes free you from having to pretend that you are perfect. When she asks if she can paint your fingernails, you laugh and agree.

"You know, I was thinking the other day," you say, after giving your throat a solid clearing. "Have you ever noticed that the boys who treat girls badly are the ones who end up with the most girlfriends?"

Ashley blows on your fingertips, which are now a glossy purple.

"I've always thought of myself as a nice guy. I know that I'm not the traditional kind of, you know, beefcake—"

"Beefcake? What?"

"You know, I'm not an underwear model. But I think I have a lot to offer. I'm sensitive." You wait, patiently studying Ashley's eyes, expecting her to offer some signal of agreement. Instead, she continues to look down and paint your pinky nail. "Everyone has to settle down at some point. Don't you think?"

"Do you, like, want to get something to eat? I'm hungry."

Smiling indulgently, you reach with your free hand toward your backpack. "Would you like some chocolate-covered espresso beans?" You bought them just for her from your favorite candy shop on the boardwalk.

"Don't, like, let me eat too many, okay?"

"I think you should eat as many as you want." Then you lean toward her and confide, "But if I eat too many, something happens. I get hyper. It's because of the sugar." Chuckling, you unwrap the box and place two of the beans on your tongue. "Isn't chocolate great?"

"Could you not chew with your mouth open?"

"Sorry," you laugh patiently, explaining, "I do that sometimes because I have a very large palate." After clearing your throat, you help yourself to another chocolate bean. "Would you like to keep the rest of the box?"

She shakes her head, looking away. "They're bad for me."

You sigh and roll your eyes. "Ashley, you're not fat."

She looks up at you. "What?"

"Listen," you insist, rolling your eyes again for emphasis. "You're beautiful. That's why I think we should go to the Fernwood homecoming dance," you say. "Agreed?"

Ashley looks down at your nails.

"You have nothing to be ashamed of," you whisper.

During the three weeks it takes you to persuade her, you live on pins and needles, so tormented by doubts that you can barely complete the yearly holistic abilities test at school. For the free-writing portion, you pour your inner turmoil into a short story about a young man who belongs to a skateboarding gang. At the end of the story, he skates off his roof into a pile of rose petals, breaks his neck and slowly dies. His highly religious girlfriend returns, a moment too late, and cries on top of his broken body.

Later that day, you have trouble reaching Ashley on the phone. After the twentieth or so call, she finally answers and you are so relieved that the next day, in English class, you take it upon yourself to defend the romantic heroine of *Madame Bovary*. The teacher has asked whether Emma Bovary treated her husband justly, and a boy has attempted to argue that she did not.

"What did Charles do to her?" the boy asks. "Other than sucking on his teeth—"

You slam the book down on your desk. "This is too much," you say. "I'm all for seeing nice people get what they deserve. All things considered, I think nice people get the short end of the stick too often these days. But if you can't keep a woman happy—" You roll your eyes expressively. "I mean, *come on*."

"Is this a personal opinion?" the teacher asks, perched on her stool at the chalkboard. "Or do you think the book tells us this? Are you making an objective or a subjective claim?"

You clear your throat calmly. "I believe my point was objective."

"Really? It's not your personal opinion?"

"Of course it's my personal opinion."

"Then it's subjective."

"That's exactly what I mean," you say wryly.

When the night of the dance finally arrives, you are so anxious that you throw up on the lawn beside the school. Ashley arrives an hour late with an owlish girl from your social studies class. The two of them sit to the side of the dance floor, just beyond the lights, whispering together and laughing.

You watch them impatiently. Finally, when the first power ballad begins, you approach and ask Ashley to dance. She is reluctant. But when her friend insists, she gives in.

Swaying together beneath the colorful lights, you forget all of your bitterness. You tell Ashley that she is beautiful in her sparkling pink gown. She pats your back.

"I mean it," you say. "You're the most beautiful person here."

"Whatever."

"No, really. You really are. Seriously. Really."

After the ballad gives way to a throbbing dance song, you return with Ashley to her owlish friend and spend the rest of the evening chatting with them and keeping them supplied with cups of fruit punch. When you learn that they have stayed in touch through church, you mention that your parents are not very religious, but that your grandfather was a preacher in West Virginia. You never met him, but you have always been very sympathetic to religion, you note, and recently you learned how to meditate. Your mother Ida—you call both your parents by their first names, you explain to the owlish girl—has several books about meditation and its effects on health and happiness.

After the dance, you insist on giving Ashley a long hug.

"I think this was the happiest night of my life," you say. "Thank you."

"Shut up," she groans. Then she gives you a short peck on the cheek.

Your heart swells. In the hours after the dance, you begin plotting your next move. It is all so obvious now. Ashley's religion is the barrier standing between you, and it must be removed. Your first attempt takes place during a Saturday afternoon stroll along the Abaloma headlands.

"Did you know," you ask, casually plucking a blackberry from a nearby bush, "that I used to think 'making ends meet' referred to a kind of meat? Isn't that funny?"

You wait for Ashley to respond, but she seems preoccupied.

"I guess I never really questioned it," you continue. "Like so many things we don't question. Every time I heard someone talk about someone trying to make ends meet, I thought they were talking about a cheap kind of meat. Maybe to use in sausages." You clear your throat. "People believe a lot of silly things without questioning them, don't they?"

"I don't know."

"Like if you're playing a—game, and you always take one route through a forest—just like the forest we're walking through now—and let's say you run into a warlock—or no—" It occurs to you that the analogy to your favorite fantasy role-playing game might not be a good choice.

"A warlock? What's a warlock?"

"Oh, I must have been thinking of one of the silly games that Gerard plays. He plays a lot of fantasy games. I don't really follow them." You clear your throat. "Can you hear that? It's the plashing of the waves." Just then, you step beyond the last of the pines and a strong wind catches you at the side. You turn and look at Ashley. Her blonde curls flutter in the breeze. You consider placing your arm around her, but the moment is not yet right.

In silence, the two of you walk toward the cliffs. Out of the corner of your eye, you can see that she is watching you. "Do you have to walk like that?" she asks.

"Like what?"

"You know, with your back hunched over like that."

"Oh, you mean my back curvature," you say. "No, I can stand the other way." You strain your shoulders for a moment, then turn to her and see that she is visibly uncomfortable.

"Oh," she says.

"Why do you ask?"

She glances at you again and then looks away. "It's kind of weird."

"It's how I was born."

You descend along the wooden steps and make your way to the jetty. The sun looms above the ocean in an orange ball of flame. Holding Ashley's hand, you lead her out across the uneven surfaces of the large rocks that stretch out into the rolling water.

"Watch out for those puddles," you say. "They're bird urine."

While the sun sets, the two of you sit side by side on a cold, damp rock near the end of the jetty. Ashley says that she is freezing and leans against you. As the last light spreads its pale fingers, you decide to place your hand on her neck, turn her face toward yours and kiss her.

But for some reason you do not move. The water continues to lap against the mossy, barnacled rocks below your feet and the sun descends further past the horizon.

You decide to reach out.

But your arms do not move.

A speedboat chops by in the distance, steered by an obese shirtless man in a red swimsuit. He cuts straight through a flock of resting gulls, forcing them to flap into the air and then settle a short distance from where they began. The sight of the fat man is too much. You want to shelter Ashley from it.

You lift your hand and rest your fingers against the soft down of her neck. She does not resist.

If you kiss her, turn to page 29.

If you wait for a better moment, turn to page 40.

As you push yourself to your knees on the tiles, the squeak of the bed keeps getting louder and faster. You decide to climb into the bathtub and sit behind the blue shower curtain. If someone comes in, you could pretend that you fell asleep.

Once, Denise sounds like she's saying something. She kind of whimpers and the rocking stops for a second. But then it starts again.

When it is finally over, you hear me get off the mattress and walk toward the bathroom. The door swings open. I make a few strong sniffing noises and swear. You're afraid I'll pull back the shower curtain. But I only wash my hands and leave. The music from the party floods into the bedroom for a second before the door closes behind me.

You listen to Denise. She starts sobbing and then stops after a while. Then you hear her getting dressed and leaving.

When you go back to the party, no one seems to notice. I'm sitting alone on one of the couches. The light from a cartoon flickers on the walls. My right hand is wrapped up in a stained white undershirt, like some kind of bandage. You guess I got blood on my hand.

A while later, you wake up and I am shaking you. I hold a lockblade in the hand wrapped in the white shirt and I wave the knife at you and laugh. I grin and laugh.

"Hey, we're going out," I grin. "Come on."

Before you can answer, I'm pulling you up, and you follow along while everyone heads upstairs and out the back door. You wonder what time it is. While you pass through the foggy streets, someone hands around a bottle of rum and you take a long drink.

After a while, one of us turns to you and says, "Feels like I've been here before."

"Shut the fuck up," I say.

Another kid snickers. I hand you the bottle of rum again and you take another drink.

A while later, someone runs toward you in the middle of the street, laughing. Before you can even think, he's run into you with both his arms out and you're flat out on the pavement, palms skidding. You try to brush them off but they're wet and the flecks of gravel are stuck in your skin.

"My hands," you say, staring at your hands.

I push the kid away and say he's going to fuck up everything.

"What? I thought he'd get out of the way."

Then you recognize where you are. "We should head a different direction," you say while you try to wipe off your hands. But doing this only gets blood on your shorts.

You follow us. When someone hands you the bottle, you take another drink, then another. Then you cross a familiar street and cut through lawns until you are all in Gerard's back yard.

"This is it," someone says.

The short kid who knocked you down in the street crouches in a basement window well. He sticks a screwdriver into the window and pries it open. While I crouch down by the window the short kid crawls through.

"How do you know they're gone?" you ask.

"Because you told me, dumbshit," I whisper. Then I'm grabbing you by the shoulders. "Are you fucking kidding?" I shake you. "Tell me they're fucking gone."

Then you remember. Gerard walked up to you at lunch and told you that he and his parents were going to their cabin again for the weekend. He asked if you wanted to come. You told him no.

"They're gone," you say. "They're gone."

"They better be."

Pretty soon the back door is open and you're being pushed inside the house. It's so strange, being inside his house at night when no one else is there. "I checked," the short kid says. "There's no one here." You watch as one of us opens the refrigerator.

"Where's his liquor cabinet?"

The kid at the refrigerator starts tossing things on the floor. He opens up a plastic package of deli meat, puts some in his mouth and drops the rest. Then he takes out a bottle of beer and tries to open it against the edge of the counter. The others have already started to wander away, farther into the house, whispering and laughing in hushed voices. You just stand there. Then you go to wash your hands in the kitchen sink. Your blood makes the water dark at first.

After a while, the short kid hands you a bottle of liquor.

"Here," he says. "We're cool, right?"

You don't say anything. You just want to lie down.

Then you pass by the living room and one of them is crouched on the carpet with his pants down. "Don't look!" he whispers. "Faggot."

You turn the corner and decide to lie down on the stairs that lead up to the bedrooms. Something behind you makes a sound like a piece of furniture falling over. Then you push yourself up and climb the stairs. You stagger into Iris' bedroom. For a while you look around. Then you sit on her bed. You open the bottle they gave you. You pour a little onto her pillow.

In Gerard's room, you sit in front of his television. You turn on a video game that you used to play in the afternoon. Cars racing around a track. You stop to take another drink, and everything seems quiet and calm in the house. Then something falls again and shatters. Maybe one of the old painted plates they kept on the wall in the kitchen. Someone is laughing and another voice hushes him.

You lie down on the floor and let your mouth hang open a little. Then you take a drink from the bottle and let it dribble out of your mouth and tip the bottle over onto the floor. Leaning on one elbow, you try to see straight. But your vision keeps moving in one direction, then snapping back, then moving again. You feel sick.

A while later your eyes open and your hand reaches out for the bottle, sloshing more of it onto the floor. There's something wet on your face. You tilt the bottle up to your mouth and some of it spills down your cheeks.

By the time you stumble into the kitchen, sounds are reaching you at a delay. One of us is beside you saying something and then there is no one in the kitchen and you are sitting down on the tiles. Half-formed thoughts come and go. Bits of laughter, bodies coming at you and leaving, the blinking of a yellow light. You try to follow it with one eye but then it is gone. Inside your brain memories are no longer being formed.

When you push yourself to your feet, then tip over and slam against the wall, face first, you only register your own laughter seconds after it has stopped.

There is a rapid clomping on the stairs behind you, and then a hand pulling you around. Then you lie face down on the kitchen floor. Someone is in your face, all grinning teeth, and then you start to gag and they are gone again. There is something wrong with your lips.

After a while your body staggers through a back yard, alone. You stumble through an empty street and across a yard full of weeds and thick shrubs until there is a parking lot covered in fog. Your body collapses on the grass beyond a curb.

A long time passes before your head rises again. There is a sensation of spinning, and your body rocks onto its elbows, then crawls a little way from the curb, where it crumples again. Near the parking lot is a small pond, and your body moves toward it to vomit. It pushes itself up and teeters toward the water, where it stumbles to its knees and vomits at the water's edge.

The body lies sprawled in the damp grass. Its hair is wet with the foam of vomit splattered on the grass and floating in the water. Then the eyes open wide and it takes a sudden breath, as though coming up for air, and its arms push out reflexively against the muddy bank. The grass is slick and its hands slide. The head of the body splashes into the water, thrashes there, then is still.

You give her neck a brief, supportive squeeze and then remove your hand.

But before the right moment arrives, Ashley stands, her arms braced against the shorewind. "I'm going to go," she says. "It's freezing." While you try to think of something to say, she begins to step back along the rocks.

You sigh and lift a crumbled shard of rock, then throw it over the shimmering water. It skips three times and disappears.

In the coming weeks, after Ashley stops returning your calls, it torments you to think of what might have been. If only you had kissed her when you had the chance.

If only… If…

Now that you have tasted the fruits of love, it is impossible to return to your former life. Your afternoons with Gerard seem small and empty.

"Look at us," you tell him.

Gerard sits silently before his computer screen. His modem emits a shriek of static and then a fluctuating electronic whine.

"Gerard!" you exclaim. "Look at us. We can't live like this. This is our life. This!" You gesture around the room. "This is the only life we will ever have. It's not a game. There are no redos. What are we doing?"

Gerard stares blankly at you. "I don't know."

"Every afternoon we sit here and play video games. We could be doing so many things."

"Like what?"

"We could—go to Mexico. Or into the desert. You know, let's go for a hike somewhere. Let's be men."

Gerard laughs and looks away.

"I'm serious."

Soon you notice a flyer on the announcement board outside the counselor's office at school. It advertizes a summer wilderness course in Colorado where young men hike for one month through the mountains and learn to climb rocks and cross streams and camp with only the gear on their backs. It is so easy to enroll that you hardly give it a second thought.

But on the bus to base camp, midway through the summer, you begin to panic.

"Do you ever wonder if this was a mistake?" you ask Gerard. He sits beside you eating a candy bar and staring out the bus window at the rolling green mountains. "I mean, why are we doing this?"

He shrugs. "It was your idea."

You suddenly wish that the two of you were back at home.

On the first day of the hike you and the dozen other boys form a line of yellow rainjackets up the grassy mountainside. The instructor in front sometimes announces a break in the hike. Then the boys loosen their packs and lean down against the slope. No one moves except to stretch an arm or unbutton a rainjacket.

"Get hydrated," the instructor says. "Drink at least half a bottle."

You take your waterbottle from the webbing on your pack and unscrew the wide plastic cap and take a long drink that leaves you feeling nauseous. The iodine in the water has a chemical taste.

"Good stuff," a boy beside you says. He claps you on the shoulder. Someone asks the instructor in front how long the restbreak will last.

"Five minutes. More than that, the acid starts to build up in your muscles."

There have been showers throughout the day and a bank of stormclouds fills the sky across the valley. Gerard is still walking with the second instructor far behind the rest of you. He plods with his arms hanging loosely at his sides and his head low like a pack animal under the whip.

The second instructor swings a stick lazily at some thick-stalked weeds and rainwater sprays from the stalks.

As the break is ending Gerard arrives and collapses at the back of the line. He does not remove his pack or loosen the straps but simply lies on the ground breathing loudly with his arms splayed wide like a baby.

"Hey fatty," a boy whispers. "Why don't you take the chicken exit? Just roll down the fuckin' hill."

Gerard continues panting.

"You're slowing everyone down," the boy says.

Another boy lets out an exhausted laugh. "You wanna go faster?"

"If we get rained on, it's his fucking fault."

"Come on," you say. "He's not slowing us down."

The instructor announces that the break has ended. You hoist the pack so that the weight is even on both shoulders and then you buckle the waiststrap and cinch it so that the weight rests tight on your hips. Then you turn ahead and wait. Behind you the other instructor talks quietly to Gerard.

A dimness has settled over the valley and the pines far below sway like thick seaweed under the waves.

Then the hike begins again. Soon patches of pockmarked snow appear in your path. Each step is an agony. Your heels have already rubbed themselves raw against your boots. Your shoulders ache beneath the forty pound pack. Every breath sears your lungs. Every step brings pain.

You look back at Gerard. He had done everything wrong from the start. He did not prepare. The instructions for the course said not to bring any food but he brought so many candy bars that when they gave everyone a last chance at basecamp to give up contraband he had to ask for a second plastic bag. "This isn't fat camp," the other boys said. They knew that you were his friend.

Soon the sun has set and the only light is from the stars and your headlamps. Now snow covers the slope in every direction. Sometimes you glance up and think you are looking at the final flattening of the mountain. But soon enough there is always a new horizon behind the one you saw. You begin to grow dizzy and take false steps and stumble in the snow. You imagine falling off the mountain.

The instructor in front returns from scouting ahead and announces that he has seen the top of the ridge and it is close. Soon a sliver of moon rises above the slope. After another switchback you reach flat ground and at long last remove your pack and collapse. There are no trees or grass on the top of the ridge but only a thin covering of snow and small protruding rocks.

You lie still and stare up at the scattered stars. There is no sound except the wind.

After a while the instructor stands beside you and tells you to save food for Gerard when you make dinner. Then he disappears into the darkness farther up the ridge. Slowly all of you rise and start to make camp. You shiver in the wind and your headlamp beams rove like fireflies. You try to drive the poles and stakes between the rocks but there is no solid ground.

Then you sit by the primus stoves and watch the flames flicker and start inside their tinfoil shields. Soon the water is boiling and the boys on cook duty fill it with salt and dried macaroni. Then they drain the water and knife hunks of cheddar cheese into the pot to melt with the noodles. They add salt and pepper and serve it. You shovel it from your bowl like a hungry dog. The melted cheese and the noodles coat your stomach and warm you. Every bowl and fork is scraped clean. The others begin to talk as the second serving of macaroni and cheese goes around.

"We need to save some for Gerard," you say. "Just leave it in the pot."

When the other instructor arrives with Gerard trailing behind he tosses his stick aside and says that Gerard will be on cleaning duty. He tells you all to fasten the trash bags and the food bags well tonight so that the marmots will not sniff them out while you sleep. Then he goes into the darkness farther up the ridge.

While water from the dromedaries boils in a clean pot all of you take turns picking bags of berry tea from the kit. You look at Gerard. He has not moved since collapsing into the snow beside the stoves. You bring him the cooling pot of leftover macaroni and cheese and your fork. "Here," you say. "Eat this."

A boy from the Bronx is talking about seeing the top of the mountain again and again. "I saw that motherfucker ten times," he says. "Ten times." The other boys laugh.

You stay with Gerard and watch while he eats. "Are you okay?" you whisper. "Yeah," he says. He sniffles.

"You sure you're okay?"

He does not answer.

The next day the instructors teach you to seal your waterproof gators over your boots and to slide in the snow and stop the slide by rolling on top of your iceaxe and digging the spike at the head of the axe into the snow. Even Gerard laughs and has a good time skidding down the slope in his raingear. For lunch you eat cheese and crackers and dried fruit and then strike camp and begin the descent down the other side of the ridge.

After a few hours the snow is only patches and then there is a meadow. You remove your gators and slide the ice axe back into its sheath.

Soon the forest begins and then the mosquitoes.

"Bug spray. Fucking useless," someone says.

"That's what you get with the natural stuff. They should've let us have DDT."

"What's that?"

"It's the stuff they used in Vietnam."

"Yeah, that's why it's illegal. But it kills bugs."

"I think it gives you cancer."

"Whatever. Everything gives you cancer."

The further you go into the forest the thicker the swarms become. You slap at your face and arms and some of the boys begin to yell. The broken bodies of the mosquitoes stick in the shirt of your longjohns and you can hear the bugs buzzing near your ears and landing on them and on your neck. The backs of your hands and arms are speckled with tiny flecks of blood from the bodies of mosquitoes that you have struck and brushed away. At dinner the swarms land in your ramen soup and you spoon away their bodies and then slap at your ankles and leave tiny blotches of blood on your socks.

At night in your sleeping bag you try to tighten the opening in the headpouch so that only your mouth is exposed to the pests but it is too hot and finally you open yourself to the air and allow them to feast.

The next morning your arms and neck are covered in thousands of small welts and each one is peaked with a bite scab or blister. The bites rest on bites and between bites and scabs so that your skin is like the skin of a leper. The itch is unending and soon you no longer resist it and you scratch and rub your skin until it bleeds. Still the mosquitoes come in thick swarms.

The instructors say that they have never seen it as bad as this before.

For two days there is no wind and the mosquitoes fill the air until they have entered your thoughts and you begin to shout as well. The instructors say that the mosquitoes will probably stay with you until you leave the woods. The other boys try to go faster. But Gerard holds you back.

"Can't you just push yourself?" you whisper during one of the breaks. "The faster we go, the sooner we get away from the bugs."

"My laces keep coming undone," Gerard says. "I can't help it."

On the third day in the forest the instructors are silent.

You set up camp in a clearing not too far from a stream and when the tarps have been strung up between the trees you sit with your bowl and wait. Sometimes you watch a mosquito sink its proboscis into the blistered skin of your arm and you do not even bother to crush it or flick it away. One of the instructors sits on a rotting log at the edge of the clearing. "Why don't you go ahead and serve that up," he says and gestures at the pots of rice and beans.

After dinner the instructor tells everyone to be quiet and listen. He stands and takes a plastic sandwich bag from his pocket and holds it out. "This is not wilderness stewardship," he says.

A boy asks, "Is that a bag full of shit?"

"No," the instructor says. "This is a bag full of shit and a candy bar wrapper. One of you left this little cocktail above ground last night. Now, it's bad enough to smuggle a candy bar onto the course. That's weak. But to leave it above ground, though... To leave a candy bar wrapper above ground..." He shakes his head. "How would you like to be walking through a place like this and then you see a candy bar wrapper and a pile of some kid's shit?"

A few of the boys snicker.

"This is not funny." He looks slowly around the group and stares into each of your eyes. "I should have left this at the campsite and made us all walk back to pick it up. That's the rule. That's what we said at orientation. But I know the mosquitoes have been getting on all our nerves—"

"Thank you," a few of the boys say. Their voices are joined by others and they speak earnestly like those who have been granted a great reprieve. "Thanks, Mark."

"I'm not finished. Whoever did this needs to take responsibility. If the guilty party comes forward and takes responsibility, we walk out of this forest tomorrow. Otherwise we all walk back together to the site. And we can see if there's any other trash there." The instructor says that he will wait until morning. "My tent is over there," he says, pointing through the trees.

After the instructor is gone the other boys turn on Gerard and tell him to give himself up. He had the candy bars at base camp and it is clear that it was him. It is the same brand of candy bar that he brought in the plastic bags. He does not look at the other boys and he does not say anything.

You take him aside later and ask if he will confess. "They didn't say you'd have to leave."

"I didn't do it," he says in a flat voice. "I'm not gonna say I did something I didn't do."

You sigh. "Come on."

The next morning both of the instructors stand in the clearing and say that no one came forward. "So we hike back," the lead instructor says. The other adds that it might mean a day less of rock climbing later on. Some of the boys moan.

On the walk back Gerard follows with the second instructor far from the back of the line. A kid from New Mexico says that he can now pop the mosquitoes wide open if one is biting him.

"If you squeeze around the skin while they're sunk in, the sac fills up and goes boom."

"What's the point?"

"It gets out the venom. Then there's no itch."

The kid from New Mexico has an unchanging grin and is the one who makes the most fun of Gerard. He talks about Gerard and mocks him to pass the time on the hike. "I bet he has a bunch of those candy bars hidden in his backpack," the kid says. "I bet he eats them every night."

"He eats the fuck out of those candy bars," another boy says.

"I know what I'd do if I had one of those candy bars."

The kid from the Bronx laughs. "What would you do?"

"I'd shove it up his asshole."

Everyone laughs then and the boy from the Bronx hoots and claps. "Would you eat it after?" he asks. "Unroll that shit and just— mmm…"

"Fuck no. I'd shove it so far up his asshole, it'd end up in his stomach. He's gonna have to digest that shit."

"So you're giving him the candy bar."

"Fuck y'all. It's not like he gets to taste it. It's in his fat fucking stomach. And then he's gotta shit it out, and I make him eat it again. I make him eat his own shit, wrapped in a candy bar wrapper. And then, after he eats his shit, I wait for him to shit it out again and I wrap that in the candy bar wrapper—cause you're not gonna digest the wrapper, it's fuckin' plastic—and then I make him eat the shit of his own shit."

"Shit to the third power, motherfucker," howls the kid from the Bronx.

All of the boys laugh and even you and the quiet boy from Texas grin this time because it is unfair that you should have to walk two days through the humid forest and bleed. For lunch you eat pilot crackers and mosquitoes land in the honey and now you eat them instead of picking them out.

When you reach the earlier campsite late in the afternoon all of you scour it for any other trash. The instructor does not make you look very long. Then you are on cook duty and after the pasta with tomato paste and spices is done you are tired and you crawl into your sleeping bag. You are glad that Gerard is under the other tarp because you do not think you could stand to be near him now.

Late in the night you wake and hear a sound coming through the forest. It sounds like a muffled scream.

"Did you hear that?" you whisper. No one answers and one of the other boys breathes heavily in his sleep. You prop yourself on one elbow and squint into the darkness and shake the boy beside you but he does not move. The boy to your side makes a sudden snort. Then the muffled screaming continues.

"Can you hear that?" you ask.

"Go to sleep," someone murmurs.

You wait and listen to the fitful screaming as it stops and starts.

If you go to see what is happening, turn to page 61.

If you do not, turn to page 99.

It's bright on the other side of the door. Everything is frozen like a picture. Denise lies on the bed with me kind of crouched over her only in my t-shirt. Then everything starts to move.

"Get out of here!" I shout. Denise pulls the comforter around herself. You can't remember what you were going to say. "Get the fuck out of here!"

The music's still throbbing through the other walls. My face is flushed and my eyes are wide.

You turn back toward the bathroom but by then I'm pulling you by one arm and slamming your body against the wall. "You fucking faggot," I yell. "Get out!"

You try to struggle free. You say you're not going to leave until she asks you to. Then I stop pushing you and look at Denise. The music has stopped on the other side of the walls.

"Jesus Christ. Get out," she says. "What's wrong with you. Both of you."

Then I'm pulling you through the bedroom door and throwing you onto the carpet in the other room. I slam the door behind you just as the basement light switches on.

They are all looking at you.

You let a week pass before you try to go back.

It is after school and we're skating on the quarterpipe, and you've already dropped your bike on the lawn and started to walk up to us when I say, "What the fuck?" I push you back onto the lawn and twist your arms into a hold behind your back. Then I knock your head against the ground until it feels like your neck is going to break and you start to scream.

A few days later, you go back again and won't leave until you've talked to Heather. You wait in the dim front hallway that smells like cigarettes. "Hey," you say as she strides toward you. "I know things got messed up, but it's like—"

"No, seriously, you have to leave," she interrupts. She stares at you like she's told you this a hundred times. "Go. You have to go."

"Come on," you say. "Just ask Denise—I didn't—"

She slams the front door behind you. When you are walking away you hear her laughing. You wonder what she thinks happened.

On the way out you see that we let the air out of your tires.

Toward the end of the school year Gerard is waiting on your front porch when you get home. You have not seen him in a while. "Did you do it?" he asks.

"Do what?"

"Did you do that to my house?"

"What?" You try to walk past him, but he keeps telling you about how someone broke into his house while his family was out of town. "They—it's disgusting—they went to the bathroom on my bed."

"I'd never do that," you say to him. "Come on. Grow up."

Then he just shakes his head and starts to cry. He gets all huffy and slobbers. You can't believe you were ever friends. "Quit acting like a baby," you say.

For the first few weeks of summer you stay at home alone and play video games. Sometimes you wonder what everyone is doing at Heather's house. But you are not going to get humiliated again.

Then one evening the phone rings. You didn't answer it because no one ever calls. But J.P. knocks on your door and gives you the cordless handset.

It's me. I tell you that someone beat up Denise. We're going to the kid's house.

"Why are you calling me?"

"So you can ring the doorbell. He's not gonna come out for us."

You try to think.

"Why me?"

"Because no one's going to be afraid of you," I say. "All you have to do is ring the fucking doorbell. Don't be a pussy."

You picture yourself going up to the boy's house and ringing the doorbell. You lead the boy outside. "Fuck you," you say. "You're gonna fucking ditch me."

"No, we're not."

"You're gonna ditch me."

"Whatever…" I say. "They didn't want me to ask you, but I said we should give you another shot. Whatever. If you're going to pussy out. Fine."

You try to make me say more about who the kid is, but I won't.

"If you're not coming," I say, "I'm not gonna tell you shit. So are you coming?"

If you help us, turn to page 48.

If you stay at home, turn to page 75.

You tilt your face toward Ashley's and close your eyes. As you descend, you are lulled into a kind of sleepiness by the nearness of her lips and the plashing of the waves.

"I'm not... really..." She leans back from you. "You know..."

"It doesn't matter what any of them think."

Gently freeing herself from your hand, she squints out toward the sunset. "It's not them. It's, like, you're so much younger."

"It doesn't matter."

"Like, two years ago, I was in seventh grade, and you could've been a fifth grader." She laughs and covers her mouth. "Oh my God."

You think for a moment, then throw up your hands. "Then why are we dating?"

"What?" She glances at you uncomfortably. "Did you tell people we were dating?"

Later in the evening, you stand before the full-length mirror in your bedroom and hot tears fill your eyes. You want to swing your fist into the wall, but instead you call Gerard and make a rash suggestion.

"I think we should sneak out tonight."

"What do you mean?"

"You know. Sneak out."

"Sneak out of what?"

You clear your throat. "Our houses. Let's leave our houses without our parents' permission and meet somewhere in the middle of the night."

There is silence on the other end of the line.

"Why?"

"Because we've been playing by the rules for too long."

"What is there to do at night?"

"Anything." You think for a moment. "We could break into the middle school."

You agree to meet at two in the morning inside the basement stairwell of the middle school, which lies midway between both of your houses. By the time midnight arrives, however, you feel very sleepy and would much rather take a nap. In fact, there is a part of your brain that is already falling asleep, and it feels so very good to give in to it just a little bit. Lying on top of your warm comforter, you allow your eyes to drift shut.

The next morning, after breakfast, you give Gerard a call. Trying to maintain a lack of expression in your voice, you ask him where he was.

"Where were you?" he asks.

"You were in the stairwell? What time?"

"I don't know. When were you there?"

"When were you there?"

"Two-thirty, three…" he says. "I don't know."

"Oh. What took you so long? I must've already been gone by then."

"My parents stayed up really late."

"Oh." As you breathe a sigh of relief, you feel a new admiration for your friend. Then he asks if you were really there.

"Of course," you say.

He giggles quietly. "I didn't go. I fell asleep. Sorry."

You sigh. This is hardly the first time that Gerard has disappointed you, or the first example of him refusing to take a risk. You restrain yourself from criticizing him because, it is true, you fell asleep as well. But while you failed as the result of exceptional circumstances—your fatigue after such a long and challenging day— Gerard's failure has no excuse. It was, unfortunately, an expression of his character.

In the coming days, you feel yourself drifting away from your old friend. But you have no other friends, so for the most part you still play video games after school. When the counselor at Fernwood calls you out of class and into his office, two weeks later, you are already in the mood for a change.

"Have you ever thought of doing harm to yourself?" the counselor asks. "Do you want to… gleam your own cube?"

Your mind races. Then you remember. The skateboarding story you wrote as a part of your holistic abilities test. It must have raised a red flag.

"No," you laugh amiably, stopping to take a sip from the box of apple juice he has given you. "Gleaming the cube is a complicated skateboarding move. They used it as the title of a movie about skateboarding. Have you seen it?"

The counselor shakes his head, smiling.

"It's very good," you say.

"What kind of activities do you enjoy?"

You take a moment to consider the question. "Do you mean extracurricular activities?"

"Sure, extracurriculars."

"This is funny, because J.P.—that's my father, I call both my parents by their first names—sometimes J.P. suggests that I should take up a sport."

"It doesn't have to be a sport. It could be anything. An instrument, chess, the newspaper. We've got a great drama program. Have you ever performed?"

"No," you say.

"Maybe you could give it a try. The story you wrote was very dramatic."

You turn your head to the side in order to consider. Then you turn your head back to the counselor and smile. "You know, I think I might."

"Let some of that drama out," he says.

"I think I just might."

Little more than two years later, you sit in a crowded school van rumbling down the coastal highway toward a forensics tournament. You are now the junior captain of the squad, or at least the part of the squad that competes in dramatic rather than speech events. It is the spring of your junior year, and the tournament is the culmination of the competitive season.

"Is everyone okay back there?" the forensics coach asks from the driver's seat. You have all been laughing and joking for hours, giddy from the long ride. "Hello-o. Everybody doing okay?"

One of the boys stops giggling long enough to announce, "I have wet myself." Soon the other members of the team join in. "Teddy, do you have a man-diaper I could use?"

"*Very* funny," Teddy says. "Keep your pants on."

"Teddy, in all honesty," one of the team says, "I'm not doing okay. I've been taking steroids for the last few months, to prepare for the tournament—"

"You too?"

"Yes."

"Really?"

"Me too!"

"Who are you getting yours from?"

"Teddy."

"Ha ha," Teddy says.

You play with your fedora and laugh along with the others. In the last year, you have taken to wearing a light brown suit and fedora to all the tournaments. Now, playing with your hat, you are tempted to interject something about "hemorrhoids," because it is a funny word and sounds like "steroids." But you cannot find the right phrasing. The moment is slipping away.

"Teddy said the first few times would be free. But lately, he's been charging me more and more. I keep paying, because I'm hooked on the cream."

"He needs his cream, Coach."

"Last night I busted open my piggy-bank to buy more steroids."

"I learned it from you, Teddy," someone says. "*I learned it from you.*"

"I want my Krispy-Kreme," you interject. There is an awkward pause. You turn to the row of seats behind you. "It's a restaurant that sells donuts. They're very good. Have you tried them?"

A voice from the back adds, "I think he wants your cream too, Teddy."

Everyone laughs. "Dear, oh dear," Teddy sighs. "What am I going to do with you?"

You feel comfortable with the success of your joke, even though you are not quite sure about what followed it. There is no denying that you sometimes have a more old-fashioned sense of humor than the others.

"It's okay, Teddy," one of the jokers says. "We'll cut it out. But I do have a serious question." He pauses, clearing his throat. "A friend of mine, he's been taking a lot of, uh, vitamins. And he's started to grow man-breasts. And he wanted me to ask you, is that natural?"

"Your friend," you interject, turning around in your seat and smiling, "is he competing in improvised weight lifting?" Again, there is an awkward pause. You begin to explain your joke, but the other boy interrupts.

"No. One-man humorous weight-gain interpretation."

You laugh gratefully for the follow-up. It would have been uncomfortable if no one had said anything. "Sweet," you say. "High five." You raise your hand.

"What's one-man humorous weight-gain interpretation?" one of the girls asks.

"You just sit on stage and drink protein shakes. That's the whole thing."

"I hear that's how Woody Allen got his start."

"Woody Allen? You guys know Woody Allen? That's the name of my steroids dealer."

"Am I the only one taking steroids because I *want* to grow man-breasts?"

"Me too. My forensics piece is actually about anorexia. It's totally unrelated."

While the others continue to banter and riff, you turn to April, a wide-eyed, puckish girl who has taken to patting your head during forensics class. These spontaneous displays of affection have led you to wonder whether you might be able to make out with her at the motel tonight. Her spiked and pink-dyed hair presses at an odd angle against the seat-back beside you.

"Are you tired?" you ask.

"No," she yawns. "Maybe a little. Can I lean on your shoulder?"

You pause. "You mean like a pillow?"

"Yeah," she says. "If I start to drool, pinch me."

"Sweet," you say.

Eventually, the joshing around wears thin and the van grows silent. As you near the outskirts of the city, you ask whether any of the others would like to perform some warm-ups and theater games after dinner. You think that it would be a good way to stay emotionally limber for the tournament. At first, no one responds, but then a voice speaks from the back of the van.

"Sure, Egghead," it says. "I'll see you there. Meet you in the lobby at nine?"

It has been so long since anyone has used this nickname. It plagued you in elementary and middle school. You turn around, struggling to position yourself so that you can look the speaker in the eyes. But the van is dark.

"We'll meet you in the lobby at nine," the voice says.

"Are you serious?" you ask, smiling now in case it is a joke.

"No."

By then you have, of course, recognized my voice. I was always the worst of the bullies in those earlier years. I was the first to call you Egghead. I said it was because your head looked like an egg and I wanted to crack it. Then I would give you a charleyhorse. Sometimes I would shove you or knock your head against the wall.

A pair of headlights passes and illuminates my pale white face, pocked with acne and scars, and the greasy strands of my peroxide whitened hair. They are like thin nails. You wonder why I belong to the squad at all, since I have such contempt for the team. I have hardly talked to you throughout the season except to mock you.

When nine o'clock comes around, you stand alone in the lobby of the motel. Not a single other member of the squad has come to join you in your exercises. You decide to wait a little longer. Taking off your vest and fedora, you perform a few brief mime exercises. First, you sit down in one of the chairs in the lobby and stand up in a continuous movement. Then you slouch around in the guise of Quasimodo. Some of the arriving guests stare at you. After a half hour, you accept that no one else is going to come. You go to April's room.

"Was there a meeting I didn't hear about?" you ask. "No one came to do exercises."

"Everyone's in Bradley's room," April says. "He's having a party." She asks if you would like to join them when they go. Her roommate is on the other bed, doing her toenails.

"Maybe in a while. I want to talk to you first, April." You take a deep breath and sit on the side of the other girl's bed.

"Would you like me to leave?" the other girl asks.

"No, that's fine."

"Yeah, I was being sarcastic."

"I want to talk about the team," you say to April. You rub your face with both hands. "I know a lot of people think that the tournament tomorrow is scary. I understand. I'm scared too. We've prepared for a long time, and there have been some tough days."

"Really?" April asks.

"Tomorrow isn't as important for you as it is for the rest of the team. I recognize that. You already won last year. You already have your trophy. But I'm the junior squad captain, and when I see a problem, I have to address it. Today, I saw a team that can't even meet for a few exercises the night before the division finals. I mean, *that's* scary." You stare at her. "It's crunch time. It's balls to the wall. I think we need to show more leadership."

Her roommate laughs and rolls over on the bed.

"Don't listen to her," you say.

"I can't tell whether you're serious," April says.

"I'm going to go to Bradley's room," the other girl smiles at you. "You're awesome. I'm going to go." When the door closes behind her, you hear her laughing in the hallway.

"I'm talking about energy, April. I'm talking about commitment. Tomorrow morning, we need to show up ready to play."

She leans toward you even more closely. "I still can't tell—is this about what they said in the van?"

You look at her blankly.

"Are you trying to prove you're not gay?"

You clear your throat, feeling yourself blush. "Did someone say that in the van?"

"Aren't you?" she whispers.

You scoff in disbelief. Then, when you realize that she is serious, you storm out of her room.

It is the last straw. First the nickname. Then the lobby. And now this. When you arrive at your own room, you turn on the shower, step inside fully clothed, and stand beneath the showerhead for several minutes as the hot water soaks into your suit.

You thought that things had changed. It had never occurred to you that after all this time, after the two years of rehearsals and cast parties and travel to tournaments, they still looked at you and saw the boy with the stupid nickname. The loser. Egghead.

Then you experience an epiphany.

What had made you want to be a part of their club in the first place?

During the competition the next day, you perform your dramatic solo with as much passion as ever. You still manage to cry, each time, during the passage when the priest asks the death row inmate to pray with him as he is being strapped to the gurney. "Pray with me, Jacob," you plead in a high-toned English accent, your voice quivering. "I don't care how long it's been—just repeat what I say. And *believe* it."

But before the final round, as you wait alone in the hallway and hear the applause that follows the performance preceding yours, you know that the time has come.

One of the double-doors swings open. "Ready?" a young woman asks.

Nodding, you cross through the door, walk across the tight-knit indigo carpet and climb the stairs of the small stage. A few spectators are scattered through the auditorium. The judges sit at a folding table before them.

"Whenever you're ready," a woman in a scarf says.

You are a free man. You can choose what to do. You wait.

"I'm sorry," another judge says, removing her glasses. "Are you ready?"

You stare at her and then at the other two, your face devoid of expression.

So this is what freedom feels like, you think. Power.

The power not to humiliate yourself for them anymore.

The power to refuse.

"Are you ready?" the judge repeats.

If you refuse to perform, turn to page 246.

If you give in, turn to page 93.

It is already after dark when the car pulls up in the driveway and starts honking. Ida looks at you and asks where you are going. "I thought you wanted me to have friends," you say. You tell them you will be back in a few hours.

I am sitting in the passenger seat of the beat-up Topaz with a mug of beer in my hand. When the kid driving pulls into the street too quickly, my beer spills and I swear at him.

No one looks at you or speaks.

"Hey," you say. "What's this music?"

When no one answers, you ask again.

"Black Flag."

Then someone lights up a pipe and starts to pass it around. I say you cannot smoke any. "You can't look fucked up." I take a long drink from the mug and wipe my mouth. "You gotta look straightedge." You sit back and watch as the last of the houses go by. Then there are only pine trees and fog.

Eventually, a few houses appear off the highway. It must be one of the new developments outside town, because there are still a lot of houseframes. When the car approaches, you see that the streets in the development have already been paved, but most of them lead nowhere and have nothing but dirt lots on both sides with heaps of lumber and coiled metal.

We park by an empty lot and walk the rest of the way. Under the streetlights, the finished houses look unreal. The lawns have seams like unrolled carpet.

"Which one is it?"

I repeat the address and then point to one of the houses. It stands alone under the lights. "That one." Across the street from the house is a construction site. "We'll wait over there. Just get him into the dark."

The kid's house looks like a showplace out of a magazine. The front windows are tall and bright. The grass carpet strips look brand new.

You walk up to the porch and ring the doorbell. An image swims toward you in the glass. Then the door opens and a woman is staring at you.

"Yes?" she asks.

"Hi, is Travis there?"

"Just a second," she says, holding the door open. She calls out, and after a second a voice replies something that you cannot hear. She has straight blonde hair and is wearing lipstick and carries a purse.

"What's your name?" she asks.

"I'm not sure he knows me."

She starts to speak, then stops, looking at you.

If she asked again, you do not know what you would say. But she only clicks away on her heels. You can no longer remember what you were planning to say to him. Then he is at the door.

"Yeah?"

He has braces and oily skin. He is younger than you thought.

"Can I talk to you for a second?" you ask. You gesture with your thumb back away from the house. "I need to ask you something."

The boy squints. "What?"

"I want to tell you something."

"Who are you?"

"I don't want to say it here."

"Dude..." He pauses for a second. Then he starts sliding on shoes and steps outside. "Who are you?"

You step back off the porch. "Come on," you say, turning and walking toward the street. He does not follow you. You prepare to run. But still he does not follow. You turn back and say, "Don't be such a pussy." Then you turn and keep walking, and you hear his footsteps closing in behind you.

Almost as soon as you start to run, he catches you. He jerks back your arm and spins you around so that you fall in the dirt on the other side of the street.

"Who are you?" he asks uncertainly. You try to pull out of his grip, but he has you pinned down with his knees and arms. Then you hear the clomp of sneakers.

"I'm one of Denise's friends," you say.

"Who?"

By the time he hears us coming and lifts his head, it is too late. While we pull him away from the light of the street, it is strange how quiet it is. There is dirt on your teeth and you try to spit it out. Then you push yourself up and try to catch your breath. In the shadows of the construction site we kick Travis while he lies on the ground. We kick him over and over. He flails around but he never screams. Then you walk over and see the duct tape on his mouth.

"... get your fucking..."

"... next time..."

When they see you, one of them says, "Hey, take the duct tape off."

"Yeah."

I reach down and rip the tape off of Travis' mouth. He starts to cough up blood.

"Holy shit," someone says.

His head rolls back and his braces glint in the streetlight. There is blood on his teeth and one of his eyebrows looks like it has been ripped open. It flaps around when his head moves.

"Come on, let's get out of here."

You can hear a dog barking. Somewhere nearby it is barking and rattling a chain-link fence. It could have been barking the whole time.

"Let's go," I say, pulling your arm. When the car pulls out, it skids and then hits a mailbox, but no one looks back. The short kid starts to laugh. "Holy shit," he says. Then someone tosses you a can of beer. Your hand shakes. You drink the beer and then remember that there was a reason. "I guess he won't be beating up any other girls soon."

"What?"

"Yeah," I say loudly. "That's right. Hey, you wanna stay out tonight?" I put out my cigarette. "Bonfire on the beach."

You say you are not sure. But by the time you have had another beer and someone has passed around a joint, you decide that you will just tell J.P. and Ida that you fell asleep at Heather's house and forgot to call.

You spend the night out on the headlands. To get there, you have to walk across a field of jagged rocks and you nearly fall on the slickness. Some girls are already waiting on the other side, on a narrow wedge of sand between two cliffs. We start a fire with lighter fluid, newspapers, and logs that we carried over the rocks. Then you sit and watch the sparks stream up. Shards of bottleglass glint in the sand. You keep drinking beer until you start to feel tired. Then you walk to the cliff wall and lie down in the sand, wrapping yourself in your jacket. You listen to the waves falling and dragging back the loose pebbles.

In the morning you wake up curled beneath a plastic tarp. Someone else must have put it over you. The first light glows a little in the fog.

You try to wrap yourself tighter and fall back asleep, but your head hurts and you are thirsty. So you push back the tarp and stretch. There is a split in your lip that stings and pulses with each heartbeat.

Rubbing a hand across your face, you feel a crusty film streaked down your chin and realize you were bleeding. Everything is so raw. You think of the kid's sparkling braces and the blood from his mouth.

Only me and a girl who is too thin are still there, on the beach, lying together in a sleeping bag beneath the cliff. You yawn and rub your eyes. There are sandgrains in your hair and you try to run your fingers through the knots and shake them out.

Then you see a stray can of beer unopened in the driftwood. You go to it and pull back the twist ring and drink it quickly.

After a while you walk to the edge of the tide and let it roll toward your sneakers. Even though your head hurts and your body is cold, you are not alone.

When you finally go home, Ida and J.P. ground you for a week. But on Friday night there is a party and you sneak out, shimmying down the rain gutter from your bedroom window. When you climb back in the window early in the morning, Ida is sitting on your bed in her robe. She asks you if you have been drinking. They ground you again. You sneak out again.

A week later, they sit down across from you at the kitchen table and tell you that they got a call from another kid's mom. They know about Travis.

They ask if you helped the other boys.

"I didn't touch him," you say. "I didn't do anything."

When they tell you that you are not allowed to spend any more time at Heather's house, you do not argue. You wait for them to leave the kitchen, then you walk out the back door and do not come home for two days.

It is only a week later that they say they are taking you out to eat but instead they stop at a strip mall. In front of it is a sign that says, "Crossroads: A Helping Hand." You recognize the name because another kid from Heather's house was sent there. You lock the doors of the car after they get out and you refuse to go. An hour later, when the counselor is waiting by the side of the car, you say you'll get out if they give you a cigarette. J.P. gives you one through a crack in the window. They stand and watch you smoke inside the car.

Then you just let them do whatever they are going to do. A man in a uniform strip searches you in a small room under fluorescent lights. He looks through the clothes in the duffel bag that Ida brought for you. When he asks if you need a toothbrush, you shrug.

A van drives you out to the countryside.

After taking you to the empty dining hall and serving you a cafeteria dinner kept warm under plastic wrap, they lead you to an old brick building at the opposite end of the compound. About a dozen boys are waiting in a circle of folding chairs in a room there. They look like kids. Then you realize it is because they are your age. You never hang out with boys your age.

"Why do you think you're here?" the counselor asks once you have taken your seat and the guard has left.

"I don't know."

"Well, you must have done something."

You shrug, taking a deep breath. "I guess I beat someone up," you say.

"Beat him up. Huh."

"Yeah. He was bleeding."

"What'd you beat him up with?"

"Just our hands." You clear your throat and try to stop your voice from shaking. "He hit some girl, so we went to teach him a lesson."

"Huh. Boy," the counselor says, looking around the group. "Sounds like you and your friends must be pretty tough." He glances at the clipboard in his hand. "So where did you beat him up? On the playground?"

"I'm in ninth grade. We don't have playgrounds."

"Oh, I'm sorry. Where was it?"

"His house."

"Really," he nods. "I'm confused. How did you get him to come outside of his house? You and your friends."

Your throat tightens and you do not trust yourself to speak.

"I just want to get the facts straight. How did you get him outside?"

"This is…"

"Did you ring the doorbell? Drag him outside?"

"He just came. Then we pulled him away and beat the shit out of him."

"You pulled him away?"

"Fuck you."

"Wow. You must have been planning this for a long time. You and your friends. I bet you talked about this every day for weeks. Is that right?"

You do not know how he knows these things. But you know what he is trying to do. You do not answer.

"Is that right?" he asks. "Every day for a month. What's not right about that?"

You glare at the floor. Your lips are shaking.

"Well, it looks like you don't have a story there, because according to your parents, you hadn't seen these boys for weeks. According to your parents, they all refused to see you. Until this one night, when they used you to get a boy outside of his house and beat him up. But you got beat up too, didn't you? Isn't that right?"

"Fuck you."

"These kids used you, and you let them use you—why? Because you're tough?" He waits. "He was probably bigger than you, just like all the others. Because you're two years younger than everyone else in your class."

"This is bullshit."

"Your whole story is bullshit. These aren't your friends, these are a bunch of losers who used you. And you let them. Because you're a smart kid, and your parents made you skip a grade, and the other kids made fun of you. And now you're here, because your parents don't know how to live with you anymore. They're worried about you." He pauses. "So you can cut the bullshit. No one's going to make fun of you now. That's over."

By then, the tears have welled up in your eyes. When you start to sob, the counselor picks up a box of tissues. "Pass this over," he says.

Afterward, another member of the staff takes you to the dormitory and introduces you to your roommate, a boy from Idaho named Francis. He has long brown bangs like a skater and tells you how he got in a fight with his stepdad after stealing cigarettes from a gas station.

"You shouldn't worry about crying. Everyone cries on the first day," he says. "I cried."

"How long have you been here?"

"A while," Francis says.

You wait for him to say more. Then you say, "I don't think my parents are actually going to leave me here. They're just trying to scare me."

It takes a week or two before you accept that you will not be leaving the home any time soon. Then another few weeks pass and you are not even sure that you want to leave. At the home, all the other kids respect you. You don't have to pretend you're someone else. And after a few months, the counselors start to give you freedoms. One of them takes you and some of the other boys on field trips to a shopping mall where you can play at an arcade or buy ice cream. When the counselor is not looking, Francis picks cigarette butts from the ashtrays by the entrance and puts them in his pocket. Later, the two of you share a few drags in a stairwell behind the school house.

Sometimes you still fantasize about trying to escape. But overall the home is not so bad.

One day you return to your room after dinner and forget to knock before opening the door. You just manage to see Francis shoving a book with a red leather cover into the drawer of his desk. You have seen the book before. He always hides it from you.

"What is that?" you ask.

"Nothing."

"Seriously, what is it? You're always looking at it. Is it porn or something?"

"No…" he says, tossing back his bangs. "It's just something my dad left me."

"Your real dad?" you ask. Francis told you that his biological father used to be a physicist in the Soviet Union. He escaped a few years before Francis was born.

"Yeah."

"So what is it?"

Francis looks down at the floor.

"Did your dad write it?" you ask. "Is it about his escape?"

"No. It's not about anything. It's not even really a book." He looks at you. "Hey—promise me you'll never read it."

"Whatever."

"Really." He stares at you intensely. "You can go through any of my other stuff. But not that. Say that you promise you'll never read it."

You stare at him for a long time. "Okay," you say. "I promise."

But the next evening the red leather book is lying on Francis' bed when you return to the room. It is the first time he has ever left the book outside of the drawer. You know that you promised him you would never touch it. But you are tempted to flip open the book. Just once. This may be your only chance.

You stare down at the thick leather cover. It looks so old. The cover is embossed with two golden letters. One of the letters looks like a backward "N". The other letter looks like a "C".

You run your fingers along the letters and wonder what is inside. What if it could help you escape?

If you open the book, turn to page 56.

If you do not, turn to page 60.

After checking to make sure that the hallway is empty in both directions, you close the door and lock it, leaving your key in the lock so that Francis will not be able to use his own. Then you pick up the book from Francis' bed and slowly turn through the old and yellowed pages. They are covered in unfamiliar foreign letters.

After a while, you stop on one page to see if you can make any sense of the writing by reading it more closely. But when you stare at the letters, they all seem to be backwards or upside down. Your eyes lose focus. Just as you are about to close the book, however, a ghost of an image appears. It is a man's face—and he is talking to you!

Suddenly there is a knock at the door. You slam closed the book and begin to stand, but something has changed. The room seems much smaller now, and you can barely move within your clothes. When you finally succeed in standing, the seams on your pants nearly split open.

Meanwhile, the knock at the door continues.

"Just a second," you say. You are shocked by the sound of your voice. It is so much deeper than it used to be. Rushing to the mirror above the sink, you are astonished to find an unfamiliar, middle-aged man staring back at you. You even have a thick, brown beard.

Then you hear Francis' voice. "Hey. Let me in. The door's locked."

To let Francis in, turn to page 57.

You open the door and pull Francis inside. "Sh!" you say. "It's me."

He stares at you with wide eyes. "I told you not to read it."

"You have to help me!"

He sighs. "You broke your promise." Then he gives you a second look. "Anyway, why would you want to go back? You're an adult now. You can do anything."

You begin to speak. Then you look at yourself again in the mirror.

"You're a grown-up," he says. "You can leave and no one can stop you. You could go to a gas station and buy beer and cigarettes."

"And throwing stars," you whisper. "Throwing stars."

"What's so good about being our age?" Francis asks. "You don't get to do anything."

If you continue to live as an adult, turn to page 58.

If you try to return to your childhood, turn to page 59.

"Good luck!" Francis whispers as you slip into the hallway. You have changed into red sweatpants and a t-shirt that is still several sizes too small. Unfortunately, your flip-flops make it difficult to walk quietly down the hall. You narrowly avoid being spotted by a monitor making the rounds.

After climbing out a ground floor window, you race toward the fence and the road beyond it. But just as you are lifting yourself over the wooden pickets, a voice cries out behind you. "Stop! You! Stop or I'll shoot!" It is one of the security guards. You ignore him and pull yourself over the fence, then continue sprinting through the woods toward the nearest highway.

But once you arrive at the side of the road, several cars pass by without stopping.

It is only then that you realize your mistake. You are a middle-aged man dressed in red sweatpants and flip-flops, fleeing from a compound in the country full of juvenile delinquents. You have no identification. You cannot buy cigarettes because you have no money. You do not even have a high-school diploma. You will never be able to get a job! Frantically, you race back toward the boy's home. But when you approach the fence, the guard fires his rifle into the air and tells you not to come a step closer. He says that the police are already on their way. In fact, you can hear the sirens approaching.

You turn and begin to run.

THE END

You insist to Francis that you want to return to the way things were. You want to be a kid again.

"Alright, there's only one way to make things go back," he says. "You have to read the book backwards."

"But I wasn't *reading* the book at all!"

"Here. Let me show you." He lifts the book and stops. "But there's a catch. If I do this, we'll both forget everything that's happened."

You look at your future self one last time in the mirror, then turn back to him and nod. As he flips to the back of the book, you stop him one last time.

"Wait. Have you ever done this before?"

He thinks for a moment.

"I don't know."

Then Francis opens the book and focuses on one of the pages in a strange way. His lips begin moving. Maybe he is talking to the man in the book. Maybe it is his father! You feel the light in the room growing brighter and brighter, as though you were falling into a star.

When you awake on your bed, you are dizzy and disoriented. Francis slowly sits up on his bed as well. The book he is always reading rests in his hand. As soon as he sees it, he hides it in his desk and locks the drawer. Then he looks at you and starts to laugh.

"What?" you ask.

"Why are you wearing that?"

You go to the mirror and laugh as well. While you were sleeping, someone glued a comical brown beard to your face. You have to borrow a razor and shaving cream from one of the night guards in order to shave it off. For your remaining few months at the boy's home, you continue to think that it was Francis, but he swears that he is innocent.

THE END

When Francis returns to the room and sees that the book is on his bed, he asks you whether you opened it and you say no. "I forgot to put it away," he mumbles. Then he slides it into the desk by his bed and quickly locks the drawer.

"What's in it anyway?"

"Can't tell you."

You stare at him. "Really?" you ask. "You're not even going to tell me what's inside? Not even now?"

"Huh-unh," he says.

"Not even now that I've shown you how trustworthy I am?"

"No," he says. "You had your chance. You missed it."

THE END

As you walk through the cold forest the screaming grows louder.

Then, a few moments before you reach the other tarp, it stops. You hear whispers and crouch at the tarp's opening and glimpse a shadowy movement. "Was someone yelling?" you whisper. No one answers. You cannot see anything in the darkness under the tarp. "Gerard?" you ask. Then you hear a rustling. "Gerard?"

"Hey," he says. "Go back to sleep."

"Is everything okay?"

He does not answer. You wait, crouched by the tarp, your eyes adjusting. You can hear heavy breathing. Then another figure sits up.

"Go back to fucking bed, man," the boy from New Mexico says, stretching his arms and yawning. "He was having a bad dream. What the fuck."

You wait.

"It's cool," Gerard says. "You can go back."

The next morning Gerard comes to the clearing late with his baseball cap pulled down over his eyes. The sun already fills the forest with heat. You ask him if he is okay but he only yawns and says he had a bad dream.

By the end of the day you are back at the clearing with the decayed log and the other instructor sits in a hammock between two trees and whittles a stick. The next day you leave the forest and hike through grassy hills in a wide rolling valley.

In the afternoon you lag behind again and turn in front of Gerard and force him to stop and you look him in the eyes. "Did something happen?" you ask. "Did they beat you up?"

He stares at you blankly. "I already told you. I just had a nightmare."

You stand in your t-shirt with the dried brown flecks of blood and wait but he steps around you and continues on the trail.

As the days pass you hike over other ridges and the hiking is easier each day. One day there is a lightning storm. You are walking in the tall grass high on a treeless hillside and the clouds rise in great dark towers and the earth suddenly dims. The instructors tell you to leave your packs and hurry to some woods nearby where you crouch between the pine trees and wait for the storm to pass. Thunder shakes the earth and rain comes on sideways in cold gales.

Then the storm ends and sunlight breaks through the forest. You walk on with your packs through the glistening grass. One of the boys says he was afraid of the lightning and you are surprised. You were not afraid.

The next day at dinner the instructors say that there is no direct way down from the latest ridge because of the looseness of the rocks and so the morning after you head down another route. You descend a snowcovered slope with an icy crust and unpack your gators and carry your ice-axe swinging beside you.

Sometimes one of the boys loses his footing and slides down the snowy slope. Then the boy who fell must walk back up alone by kicking holes into the crust of ice with each step. You are careful to step into the footholes left by those in front of you and to punch your ice-axe into the snow while you walk. Halfway down the ridge someone slides behind you and you hear a shout and then a sound like two stones knocking against one another. When you turn Gerard has fallen several feet down the slope and landed head first against a rock and his body starts to twitch as someone yells for the instructors. Then his head moves in a strange way. The snow around it is becoming pink. His head has been twisted open. You lean over and start to vomit.

By the time the helicopter arrives he has been dead for several hours.

"I heard them beating him up," you tell the counselor in Boulder. He sometimes takes notes on his legal pad but mostly he looks at you calmly. "You know, what if he did it on purpose?"

"Did what?"

"Fell."

The counselor looks at you over his reading glasses. Then he takes them off and lets them hang on their band.

"Tell me what you think happened."

"I just mean—what if he wanted to go home. So he fell to get injured or something. And then he fell wrong." But as soon as you hear yourself saying it, you realize that it does not make sense.

The counselor looks at you closely.

"You did not let your friend down," he says. "Gerard did not die because of you."

You start to cry then for the first time since it happened.

Back in Abaloma in the first few days you sometimes reach for the phone to call him. Or you wake on a weekend morning and think of what the two of you will do. Then you remember and the pain comes back like something new.

At other times you have a dream where he is standing on top of a hill and waves to you. You try to climb up the hillside toward him but your hands and feet get stuck in the grass. No matter how much you climb he never gets closer.

At the first assembly of the school year they unveil a memorial plaque for Gerard and the Principal talks about loss and healing. She invites the student body to a candlelight vigil that night. They wanted you to say something at the assembly but you refused. When the choir sings some of the girls on the bleachers cry and you look at them in disgust. They all ignored him when he was alive.

"Ashley called again," Ida says at dinner.

"I told you to stop telling me when she calls."

J.P. sets down the paper.

"None of them ever talked to him," you say. "Trust me. None of them care."

As time passes, you begin to define yourself in part by Gerard's death and its aftermath. For your college application essays you write about the hypocrisy of the choir and the falsity of their grieving.

On the fifth anniversary of Gerard's death, early in your junior year at a private college several hours south of Abaloma, you find your mind wandering back, not without some pride, to the language of those essays. The choir "savored their tears," you wrote, while you and Gerard's family suffered. For the girls at school, Gerard's death was "a rare opportunity" to "rise above the banality of their lives" and "wallow, briefly, in the sublime." Leaning against the drink table in the crowded kitchen of the young professor's house, you take another sip from your gin martini. The alcohol has not yet diffused the claustrophobia you habitually experience in these tight surroundings. All the guests at the party have congregated near the rickety folding tabletop bar, as though attracted by some mothlike force. In order to be heard above the clamor, the students must engage in an arms race of steadily escalating yells. Yet still they speak. It is, you consider, as though these students, in their silent hours of reading, had amassed heaps of words within themselves, hoards of excess language inside their chests. After such a process of verbal accumulation, it is inevitable that the pipes will tend to clog, and now, on the weekend, the alcohol serves precisely the function of a drain cleaner, dissolving the calcified silences that have perhaps become lodged in their throats like so many tangles of hair or stagnant foodwaste, clearing away the blockage so that a fluent stream of nonsense can emerge. You have nothing but contempt for all but a few of them, and these few have yet to appear. Nearby, a girl protests stridently. "They dropped a bomb on a kindergarten!"

"That is outrageous," a boy replies.

"If America is so concerned about stopping a genocide, why don't we bomb Israel?"

"I agree."

"Where was America when one million Tutsis were being killed in Rwanda in, like, three days?" By now, the girl's voice has become so abrasive that you feel as though you are yourself contained in the accusation, as though it is rippling outward through the kitchen like rings upon the surface of a condemnatory pond, and you turn further away from the two of them, scanning the row of olive oil bottles that line the shelf closest to you, attempting to occupy your intellect so as not to eavesdrop further upon those around you, even in the privacy of your own mind.

"Our grandchildren will look back on us in shame," the boy responds.

"If we even have grandchildren," the girl says.

"What do you mean?"

"I mean, if there hasn't been some kind of catastrophe by then."

"What kind of catastrophe?"

"Global warming. A plague. I hear there's like a fifty percent chance that some biological warfare germ is going to decimate the earth in the next century." The girl stops abruptly, and in the brief interval, as she hangs fire in the wake of her grim pronouncement, you think you can hear the boy, in spite of his efforts to take the girl's jeremiad as a general matter extremely seriously, and not to mention your own efforts not to hear his undertakings one way or the other, begin to laugh. But upon hearing his laughter, to your slight bewilderment, she begins to laugh too. You cannot resist glancing at them, yourself smiling, as the girl swings her small fist with a little too much violence into the boy's shoulder, causing him to spill some of his drink on the tiles, though the two continue laughing after a hesitant circumspection to confirm that their brief accident has not been remarked upon. You turn, hastily, back toward the shelf of olive oil.

"I hope I don't get decimated," the boy says.

"God, you're such an asshole."

"Really, though," he adds, adopting a conciliatory tone. "I understand what you're saying." Then their voices recede once again into the rising cacophony. The sound in the kitchen is so overwhelming, even disorienting, that you are reminded of the news stories from your youth about a heavily armed cult who had eventually burned themselves to death after a botched government siege. Before the fire began, the police tried to degrade the will of the cult's members by playing music on loudspeakers. It was the first time you realized that loud and abrasive sound could be a form of torture, a thought that returned to you often during your first years of college. From your detached perspective, sipping your drink, and staring into the undifferentiated sea of them, they could as well be spewing a steadily regurgitated stream of sewage from their mouths, each opening the spigot and vomiting a dreck onto the receiver of his or her thoughts, then taking a turn to be bathed.

If only you could find Cynthia. Your springtime, the stirring back to life of all that has lain dormant in you.

"Hi, there. You're in the theory seminar, right?" Startled, you turn to see a short, sprightly boy with a tiara of plastic jewels perched in his hair. "I've seen you there." Grateful to see a familiar face, you attempt to recover yourself and enthusiastically shake his hand, apologizing that you have forgotten his name—but he gallantly refuses to accept your apology and turns instead to introduce you to another boy who stands beside him, also familiar from the seminar, a towering figure with thick red hair and a trim goatee. You had glimpsed him, upon entering, without truly digesting his presence as anything more than a sort of massive sculpture, his brow hugely furrowed, an oversized trunk of humanity standing in the corner of a crowded room and paging patiently through a thick hardcover that resembled a digest of citations, or some other volume whose bulk can only be explained by its consisting almost entirely of mechanically assembled data, untouched by human hand. You have seen him pacing the halls of the humanities corner in the quad, often humming or talking to himself in a barely audible murmur. Now, as he stands before you, he stares down with an awkward but seemingly benevolent smile, and as he extends his gargantuan hand, his entire face seems to spasm, briefly, in a sudden blink.

"How are you?" the red-haired giant asks, as the two of you shake hands. "I liked the comment you made in class the other day. You said something about the similarity between chiasmus and paradox, yes?" In fact, as you instantly recognize, this comment was not yours but that of another student, and you must attempt to deflect the giant's compliment, asking him instead what he thought of

Professor Barnes' lecture at the start of the seminar earlier in the day, to which transition in subject the giant thankfully accedes.

"I enjoyed it a lot," he pronounces, furrowing his brow once again. "I thought it was a very, very interesting lecture." Just as in class, he seems to speak every word as though he has weighed it with great effort, as though venturing a very heartfelt opinion to which he has arrived only with difficulty, but which he believes, though with some reservations, it would not be inappropriate for a reasonable person to defend; and as in class, the substance of the comment seems to require no such treatment, being, in fact, shaped only of the most insipid stuff. You would not describe the products of the giant's brain as thoughts so much as reassurances wrapped in the form of thoughts, like the flavorless tamales wrapped in banana leaves that are served in your dorm dining hall on ethnic food day. Then he blinks again with one of his brief facial spasms. Why this tic, you cannot help but wonder, silently, in a figure of such otherwise apparently supreme self-mastery and calm? Perhaps it was his body's last, small rebellion in the face of the meditative serenity he had imposed upon it, the last small rocks thrown at the superego's police van from an unseen window after the annihilation of the id's revolt, chipping but not splintering the shatterproof windshield.

"There are a lot of people here, huh Leslie?" the sprightly boy asks with inexplicable sarcasm.

"Yes," the giant nods. "It's a good group of people."

"Is it a good group?"

"Yes."

"Leslie never says anything bad about anyone. He wants to be president," the other boy whispers to you, and then continues, in a loud and rambunctious tone, "I've got an idea. Let's try and make President-unelect Leslie say something inappropriate."

"Oh?" Leslie asks, blinking voraciously, and you sense for the first time the slightest hint of irony in his voice. You should not be surprised to find such hidden reserves, you realize, given Leslie's determined position among the higher echelons of Professor Barnes' coterie, but it startles you to think that even a figure as peaceful, as imperturbable as the giant would also partake, no matter in how insignificant a quantity, of the enormous resource of caged ambivalence that seems available to Barnes as he paces beside the table in the seminar room.

"It's going to be a difficult game," the other boy says, "because Leslie doesn't drink. But maybe we can get him to say something ungodly. You're an atheist, right Leslie? And no atheist will ever be elected president. So tell us, what did you think of what Barnes said today about the interpretation of the Bible?"

"I didn't think that was necessarily atheistic. His point was that the dominant trope of revelation is a deferral—"

"Oh my God," the other boy exclaims. "What the fuck does that mean?"

Leslie chuckles and turns to address you. "Can you help me here?"

Caught off guard, you take an unsteady sip from your plastic cup, then say, after a soft clearing of the throat, that you are still trying to find your footing with regard to all the talk of tropes. But you qualify this deflection by adding somewhat more affirmatively that you did find it interesting, at the very least, to contrast the use of the tree as the trope of knowledge in Genesis with other possible tropes that might have been used, such as, for example, the rhizome, a kind of nonhierarchical root structure with no center and no beginning or end. In fact, you go on, you have recently read a rather convoluted essay that advocated for the adoption of the rhizome as a figure of knowledge based on its superiority in representing the multiplicity of human thought. It was all part of a critique of the concept of concepts, as far as you understood, and had apparently made quite a splash in the English department. You say this because you saw a stack of copies of the essay, shortly after you read it, lying outside the door of an English professor's office.

"Quite a splash?" someone echoes, to your side. "Did it make 'quite a splash,' old boy?" The familiar, nasal voice, even in these few mocking words, projects a degree of nihilistic disregard, an unabashed, exuberant cynicism of an entirely different kind than the rebarbative evasiveness deployed so often by the followers of Barnes, and before you can stop the blush from rising to your cheeks, the bearer of the voice, an obnoxious, arrogant pencil of a boy named Francis, has already clapped you on the back and laughed, so that you can smell the alcohol on his breath even from a relatively elongated distance. You turn to him, attempting to smile and to concoct a fitting rejoinder before the moment passes. None comes to mind. "Charles!" Francis exclaims, offering his hand to the other boy. Charles. Of course. "What were we talking about?"

Perhaps disturbed by the apparent inebriation of the new arrival, or, just as likely, put off by the idiocy of your previous words,

Leslie has already casually turned—as casually as his massive frame allows—toward another corner of the kitchen.

"We were trying to make Leslie admit that he's an atheist," Charles sighs, "so that he can't become president."

"God bless America!" Francis howls. "Because America is the land where everything is possible, and where Leslie will never be our president."

"God bless it," Charles says.

"As Dostoyevsky said, if there is no God, then everything is possible. And we all know that everything is possible in America. It stands to reason that there is no God in America. But God bless it anyway."

"To reason!" Charles toasts.

The banter then momentarily halts, its forward momentum having stalled no sooner than starting. A pause grows; your consciousness of having barely spoken since your arrival at the party grows as well; and you commit yourself to hazarding the next topic of conversation. In fact, there is something that you have wanted to ask Charles ever since arriving at the impression, early in your acquaintance, as no doubt many of his hearers do, that he might tend to lean more toward the masculine than the feminine on the spectrum of amorous commitments. Given his enrollment in Barnes' seminar, you wonder how he would square his orientation, if indeed your surmise is not incorrect, with the antipathy in which Barnes so openly holds the ideological, as opposed to rhetorical, reading of literary texts. That is to say, does he, Charles, side with the queer theorists over against Barnes, or with Barnes over against the queer theorists, or, perhaps, does he find some as yet to you unknown dialectical reconciliation between the two? As the awkward pause has now achieved a length at which the three of you must either speak or go your separate ways, you turn to Charles and begin, haltingly, to pose your question, all the while attempting gingerly to circumnavigate any approach to a direct insinuation regarding his preferences in those quintessentially private matters that it would be unnecessary to inject, as it were, into a conversation taking place on such an impersonal and abstract plain of discourse.

"Do you mean—what do I think of Foucault?" he finally interrupts.

"I think he means queer theory generally," Francis says.

Attempting to clarify, you begin to explicate the conflict, or at least potential for conflict, between Barnes' distinctively rhetorical hermeneutical praxis and the approaches of other theorists such as—

"Why are you asking me?"

"Because you're gay, aren't you?" Francis asks. "Or is that my own queer theory?" He laughs.

"I don't see what relevance that would have to the way I read—"

"Don't you?" Francis snidely interrupts. "Isn't that the whole point? I thought the queer theorists believed that we had all been reading with a heteronormative bias, and now we needed to learn to read in a queer way. I think they're right. I've always read in a very, very manly way. I like to penetrate the meaning of a text. Similarly, he's always read—" Francis gestures with his thumb toward you, "— actually, how have you always read?"

The comment catches you off guard to such an extent that before you can even begin to muster a riposte, the blush has returned to your cheeks. Aware that you must, in any case, speak, you ask, almost stammering, what Francis means by reading.

"I mean, there are a lot of different ways of interpreting a text. Do you submit to the author's intent? Do you lose your inhibitions in the free play of meaning?" Then Francis leans toward you and gestures at your hair. "I only ask because of the tiara."

Too late, you note that the tiara has disappeared from Charles' head. Reaching up to your own, you find the completion of your abasement.

"Shut up!" Charles says, nudging Francis lightly on the shoulder. "That was a secret."

Too many humiliating blows have come in too quick a succession, no matter how minor, and you feel yourself unable to continue.

Defying the jostle of the crowd, you take a sudden step back, toss the tiara to the floor and grind your heel into it, sharply, until the encrusted plastic jewels pop loose and the rim snaps. Then you turn from the two of them and ignore their apologies as you walk purposefully out of the kitchen. On the way, you find yourself momentarily blocked by a congestion of guests, a small eddy in the flow of students, and then it is as though you have been sucked into a fierce current that draws you outside of the kitchen and deposits you into a relatively empty hallway, and it is there, finally freed from the turbulent stream, that you see it.

The framed print. Why would the professor put a print of such a painting in his home? How could anyone live with the casual presence of such an abomination? In the background of the painting, dividing a rough black sea of charcoal, stained beneath its surface as if by a kind of rust, three white lines intersect. The crude sketched lines form angles that divide the stained dark into rusted panes of a metal that might belong in an industrial pen, a place for rendering, like a walled-in cage. Above a vague writhing pool of white charcoal, pink, and scum-like green, all a swirling dim sea of offal, the central thing of the painting, the white overlit object, sprawls and fills its middle third, hung by one blue-pink ear from a wire. Dim disproportionate bars rising from the colored offal and other crude white bars clasped behind the sickening object suggest the posts of a bed. But it is the thing itself, at the center, that holds your eye. In some sense, it begins like a torso, or the flaps of skin from a torso cut from the body, but holding a shape, rubbed across the print in another rough white sort of charcoal or oil crayon that in some places is so thick, it seems to shine off the print, as though it were a photograph washed out with light, overexposed, a form beneath a white light held too close, as an industrial light hung from the ceiling of a shed might be. In other places the white thickness of the torso skin smears away to a bruised pink or blue, a transparency over the writhing coils of smeared color beneath. The ear—hung by a flap of skin on a hook at the end of a taut, angled wire—it is the single ear, bruised and pink, and the disarmingly human, natural line of neck that rises up to it from the white skin, that defines the skin as skin, the torso as a torso, or the cut white skin of one. It is all—the ear, the posts, the skin—bleached and overlaid on the painting, both a part of the rusted walled-in suggestion of space and not, grading off into abstraction at all angles against the general black of the background. But all of this is only a prelude to the horrible form in the place where the torso's head would have been. There, at an unreal angle, opens a mouth in a silent, yawning scream of lip and errant teeth and tongue. A few contorted teeth grow unevenly out of the mouth, some represented in the impossible middle of it, one hooked from the upper lip. They remind you of a piece you read from a magazine of true scientific horror stories that you found as a child, one that you read when you were too young and which gave you horrible dreams at the time and then returned to your mind, against your will, in the months after you returned from the mountain, for reasons you did not want to understand, ever, a story about a birth defect sometimes occurring in the womb during the growth of twins, when one would grow within the other, and the existence of the internal twin would go unnoticed, and, in certain cases, the innermost fetus would continue to grow long after the live one's birth, developing eyes, hair, bones inside of the other. The magazine showed a picture of one such fetus, surgically removed from a woman who had never suspected it lived inside of her until she began to experience pains in middle age. With its long, dark hair and translucent skin, its large covered eyes, it was a monster, not human but a kind of mutilation. The teeth growing out from the dark of the mouth in the painting remind you of such defects, children born without eyes, with teeth and hair growing in their skulls. Where the top half of the head would be in the painting, just above the ear, the bruised form that contains the raw lips and teeth blurs into nothing, like something born without a face, part of a bedpost blending in with the upper lip. Unconcentric circles and bruised, fleshy masses support the shrieking mouth and give way to darkness, as in a video they made you watch in history class in your senior year of high school, a film on the concentration camps, and afterwards you saw that some of the others had been crying. But you were not crying, and you remember thinking that their tears were an inappropriate response, almost grotesque. You felt that you had witnessed something not sad or even pitiful but insane. Not capable of being fit within any recognizable human frame. The painting is of the berserk inhuman, the reduction of the human scale to ground flesh and bone and tangled hair. And the worst part of it, for you, is the knowledge that this torso, in the painting, must stay in its mauled state of incompletion indefinitely.

"So what do you think?"

With a start, you turn and see Leslie standing beside you, nodding at the painting. He could have been looming there for minutes, or half an hour, for all you know, and the advantage this gives him over you—his having been free, in essence, to observe you at your most unguarded, engrossed in the painting—brings about an immediate resistance. You feel his words as a sort of offense, a violation of you and your privacy. It is almost unbearable when he continues to speak.

"Do you like Bacon?"

An enormous fatigue descends. There is nothing on earth, you feel, nothing on earth that you would less rather do than utter words about the image hanging on the wall before the two of you. You feel as though it would be blasphemous to say anything of it, to trivialize it with whatever flecks of language you might cast in its direction, as though to collide weakly with the glass of the frame, perhaps deflect from it before reaching the print itself, and then tumble impotently to the floor. It is nothing short of a revulsion that you feel at the thought of such words, and yet, rubbing your eyes now between index finger and thumb, weighing the possibilities, you know that it would be equally pointless to be rude. As little desire as you have to speak, especially about the print about which you have nothing, absolutely nothing whatsoever to say, you have just as little desire to insult the other who has chosen, for whatever reason, to talk to you. The spell of the image having been broken, dispelled, all possesses an indiscriminate futility.

"I wonder if his paintings would have been different," Leslie muses, "if he had been raised in a more tolerant society." He seems to wait for you to speak. "Do you enjoy Bacon's paintings?"

You reply, wearily, that it would be difficult for you to categorize your response in terms of enjoyment. With an apologetic air, you offer, simply, that you don't know how to express your reaction in that way.

"I don't understand," he chuckles, the unfamiliar note of acidity entering his voice once again. "Do you enjoy it or not?"

You try to conceive of the most economical way possible to extricate yourself from the conversation. Each word, you feel, is like dredging something from the bottom of a lake, a muckheaped knot of weeds that refuses to unwind itself from the muddy depths. The inadequacy of language, its listless failure to touch the matter itself, almost provokes in you a physical nausea. The words seem nearly to stop in your throat as you finally produce the thought that you find the print interesting because it contains something that others leave out. As soon as you have droned these words, however, you shake your head, unable to finish.

"What?" Leslie persists. "What is the thought that they leave out?"

You nod, vaguely, and say that it was nice talking to him but that you have to go to the restroom. As you make your way through the swaying crowd toward the kitchen for another drink, it occurs to you that you did not even succeed in avoiding being rude to him. After all your effort, you left him in nearly the same state that would have resulted had you simply turned your back on him and walked away, implausibly pretending not to hear, the moment he materialized beside you.

The thought fills you with a renewed sense of fatuity, and you wonder whether even alcohol will suffice to batten back the waves of anomie now threatening to envelop you. You arrive at the drink table and pour yourself a double vodka, swallow it, and then pour another and then another, drinking each in relatively rapid succession. Mercifully, by the time you weave out of the kitchen, you have succeeded in more or less obliterating your self-awareness, including all memories of recent steps and mis-steps, and the world has taken on the swirling, disconnected festivity of a carnival. Caught for a moment in another eddy of the human current, you peer around yourself unsteadily and finally see Cynthia, standing near the front door.

She is as beautiful as ever with her dyed black hair and her inimitable scowl.

Then there is a hand on your upper arm and you are being pulled through the crowded room and out into the night. It is Charles who pulls you. You try to resist and return to Cynthia, but Charles will not let you go until you have accepted his apology for the tiara.

"It was a stupid idea," he says, squeezing your shoulder. "You'll forgive me, won't you?"

While you try to reassure him, you see that Cynthia has joined the departing swarm, and others dart out in front of her across the dimly lit lawn. Then you follow them, part of the multitude, through the desolate streets of the faculty ghetto, waiting for the right moment to approach and say the words that have been fermenting within you since you first glimpsed her face in a crowded lecture hall near the end of the last school year. As the throng makes its way to the faculty pool, you exult at the possibility that tonight the planets will finally align.

But as soon as you climb over the fence you see that Cynthia is already with Leslie. She has cornered him by the side of the pool and begins to pull at his clothes and tease him while you watch. Before you can think of a way to intervene, to disrupt what you see unfolding, she has stripped him and pulled him into the water. Soon they are in each other's arms.

It is as though winter has descended in the midst of spring and frozen the first shoots that sprouted from the melting earth. Now there is only night. Endless night.

You lie beside the pool with your eyes closed.

When you finally look around, some time later, Charles is sitting, naked except for his flip-flops, a few feet to your side.

"They're talking about going to the steam tunnels," he says. "Have you been?"

You have not. You are about to say that you were once invited into a drainage tunnel. But then you stop. You do not want to have to explain.

"It's totally worth doing it once." Charles brushes the water off his arms. "The tunnels lead all across campus, with the pipes that heat the buildings. And you can climb into the buildings on the quad. It's weird inside at night. When the doors are locked. It's like the buildings are asleep."

In spite of yourself, his small turn of phrase brings a smile to your lips. You glance at Charles and see that he is smiling too.

"Have you ever tried kissing a boy?" he asks.

Surprised by his openness, you laugh. It is something that you have kept secret all through college. But somehow you do not hesitate to tell him. You say that you have never kissed anyone.

"Never?"

You shake your head.

"We should make out a little," he says. "It's good to try new things."

If you kiss him, turn to page 224.

If you do not, turn to page 121.

"Fucking poseur." Then the click of the disconnected line.

It all ends so quickly.

By the end of the summer, you have accepted that this is the way things are going to be. It is a lonely time. You play video games most of the day. You eat.

Twice in the summer, you have to go to the mall with Ida and buy new clothes because your old clothes do not fit. But it does not matter. It is not like things would be different if you were thin. There is no one you want to hang out with anyway.

On the first day of high school, you eat lunch alone, not looking around at the other tables. You get two burritos with cheese on top with a soft drink and an ice cream bar. When you leave school at the end of the day, it has gone a lot better than you expected. Because the high school is so much bigger than the middle school, no one really notices you. No one makes fun of you.

A few weeks pass before you run into Denise. You are on your way out of school and she sees you and kind of holds a hand up to her mouth. "I'm so sorry," she says. It looks like she is going to say something, but then she stops. You squint at her and grin. "Sorry for what?" And then she laughs, like she was joking.

But you know that she was not.

A long time passes where you do not really talk to anyone. One time you start to yell at J.P. at dinner, and Ida says, "Is this the first time you talked today? Yelling like this?" She sets down the fork on the side of her plate and looks at you. You take your plate and finish eating in your room.

A few weeks into the spring of senior year, once you are old enough, you drop out of school. "If you want to do the papers or whatever," you tell Ida, eating your cereal, "that's okay. I'm just not going back." J.P. drives you that night to the boardwalk and makes you walk by the ocean with him. He tells you a person needs other people. You stare at him blankly and want to ask him if he thinks this was your choice. But you do not say anything.

A while later, they find the empty glue-bottles and other inhalants in your drawer and make you move out. So you move to an efficiency in Oakland and get a job in the back warehouse of a machine parts distributor. But you come back to Abaloma for your birthdays usually. On your twenty-first birthday, Ida and J.P. take you out to dinner at one of the places you used to like, a family restaurant. The booth is a little tight. While you look over the laminated menu, J.P. tells you to order whatever you want. "It's your big night out," he says. "Treat yourself."

"It's so good to have you back home," Ida says.

"That's right," J.P. says. He is grinning. "Just sit back and relax," he says. "How about a beer?"

You order a chicken fried steak and garlic mashed potatoes with gravy, and then a chicken caesar salad on the side. You also order a side of french fries and split an order of onion rings with J.P. They try to make you feel better and to create an air of fun. But most of the time, you do not speak. There is not much to say. Sometimes Ida looks at you like she is worried. She has gotten a lot thinner since you moved out.

It is after you have cleaned your plate with the sweet doughy rolls that Ida pulls the envelope from her purse.

"Oh," she says. "I almost forgot. You got a letter from your school."

"What school?"

"Fernwood. You know, Fernwood. High school." She looks at J.P. Then she sets down the open envelope in front of you. "It's the fifth reunion." She folds her fingers together on the edge of the table. "I was thinking—"

"Did I say you could open my mail?"

"I didn't think—"

"How would you like it if I opened your mail?"

"Well, let's not get too worked up," J.P. says.

"I don't think you'd like it if I opened your mail."

You had planned to spend the night back in your old room after having a few drinks at the dinner but instead you drive home to Oakland. It is too late to buy alcohol, so you lie on the murphy bed in your apartment and huff some correction fluid. Then you smoke some pot to take the edge off.

At work on Monday, the reunion comes up when you are talking to Frank Drennan. He is the only other white employee in the back warehouse. Sometimes the two of you smoke out in his car at lunch. He also keeps you supplied. It is a good job because there is no mandatory drug testing. You mention the invitation to him while he sits at the table in the break room across from you and eats a hamburger and baked potato.

"I don't know," you say, dipping the end of your last chicken strip into the small container of ranch sauce. "I'll probably stay away."

"Yeah."

"I never liked dressing up anyway."

Frank grins. "Still. Wouldn't mind gettin' me some of that." He opens a ketchup packet and licks his fingers.

"Some of what?"

"Some of that high school action."

You stare at him. "There's not gonna be any high schoolers there. It's a reunion."

Some of the ketchup gets on Frank's fingers. "Motherfucker. This fucking ketchup. They can't even afford Hunt's."

You watch Frank rub his fingers onto the carton of his half-eaten burger. He rubs his fingers one by one against the box. Then he licks them again.

"I'm not much of a mixer anyway," you say. "You know."

"Yeah," he says.

"Rather just stay at home," you say. "Watch a movie."

"When was the last time you got any?"

You stare at him with a blank expression. Then you stand and go to the counter behind you to get a cup of coffee. But the coffeemaker is empty. You look back and see coffee cooling in Frank's insulated mug.

"I saw you talking to Terry," Frank says. "Talkin' to the douchebag."

You stare at the empty coffeemaker and then back at Frank's steaming mug and you shake your head. Then you leave the breakroom and make your way back to the warehouse. There is a new shipment of shrink-wrapped pallets stacked just inside from the loading dock. The Hondurans stand around talking and laughing, not doing anything. So you start to cut off the shrink-wrap and check in the shipment. But one of the packing slips is missing. It is so hot in the back warehouse, especially by the open door to the loading dock. The metal doors radiate heat and whenever it is a hot day, you feel like you could suffocate. You stop cutting off the shrink wrap and wipe your face against your sleeve.

After you finish cutting off the shrinkwrap, you put away the boxcutter at your workstation and start to bust some skids sitting near the forklift. But as soon as you have twisted loose one end of a plank with the crowbar and started to work on the other, the whole plank breaks in two. It leaves a splintered stub so that you have to wedge in the crowbar at an awkward angle. Then you go back to the breakroom. Frank is still there, drinking from his mug of coffee. The coffeepot is still empty.

"No coffee?" you ask him.

"Guess not." He takes a loud sip.

"Huh," you say. "Is that from the coffeemaker?"

"Is what?" His mug is a big stained plastic deal from the gas station down the street.

"I think I'll make another pot," you say. You take out the old filter and throw it away.

"So what'd you talk to douchebag about?"

"Huh?"

"What'd you and Terry talk about?"

You put a new filter in the coffeemaker and scoop in coffee from the can on the counter. It is economy-sized and comes in with the shipments from the office supply store. You check it in. With your belly resting against the counter, you keep adding to the filter until it is half full. You like it strong.

"So what were you talking to douchebag about?"

"Nothing."

"Did you talk about him being a douche?"

"No."

"Did you talk about what a faggot he is?"

"He's not my friend."

"I thought you liked him. I thought he was your buddy."

"Come on." You can feel yourself getting worked up. "He's not my buddy."

"I thought he was."

"Terry?" you say. "I can't stand that guy. He acts like he's so cool." You clear your throat. "That's his whole thing. He acts like he's cool, like he's fooling us and we're all supposed to believe him. You know?" While Frank laughs, you slide the filter tray back in and fill the pot with water from the sink. "It's all just bullshit," you say. "I mean, didn't he go to middle school?"

Frank keeps laughing. "What about middle school," he laughs.

"You know."

Then Frank has stopped laughing but he is still smiling. "What do you mean?"

"I don't know," you say. "Middle school." You clear your throat again. "I mean, everyone gets fucked up."

You pour the water into the reservoir at the back of the coffeemaker. Then you turn it on and wait.

Frank does not say anything.

"I don't know," you say.

After work, you stop at a liquor store, cash your paycheck and buy a twelve-pack. The man at the counter looks at you and at your driver's license. Then he looks at you again.

"Happy birthday," he says. "Twenty-one. The big two-one."

Later that night, you stand in front of the refrigerator. You let your belly hang out in front of the open door. The video game you just finished actually made you cry a little. At the end you save everyone's life by destroying a weapon on an alien space station.

On the floor above, someone is moving a vacuum back and forth. You have heard the same thing on weekend nights, someone dragging the vacuum around for hours. You picture her as an old widow with grey hair. But she could be anyone. She may not even be a woman.

Before passing out, you get nostalgic and mail in the RSVP to the reunion. Then the next morning you are embarrassed.

But after you have a few beers on the night of the reunion, you decide to go. There is nothing to be embarrassed about. You drive up to Abaloma and get there late, then sit in the parking lot for a while, bracing yourself with a few swigs of some rum. Moths swarm around a streetlight. You watch them for a while and then fill up your flask and put it in your pocket.

Inside the cafeteria, it is dark and there is a swirling disco light. It takes you a while to recognize anyone. You start to worry that you were invited to the wrong year's reunion. But then you see Denise. She wears a black dress. She has put on a few pounds, but she still looks good. You follow her when she goes to the cash bar and then you stand behind her shoulder, waiting for her to see you.

Then she turns and looks at you. It takes her a while. "Egghead?"

"Yeah," you say. "Denise, right?"

"Jesus Christ." She turns and sets down her plastic cup. "How have you been?"

"Good to see you," you say.

"So what have you been up to?"

"Staying busy," you say. "How 'bout you?"

She says that she works at a family counseling center in the Mission. After she asks a few times, you tell her about your job. You tell her where you live. "It's an efficiency," you say, shrugging. "No bugs, no drugs. That's what they said when I was looking." You glance at the bartender, but there are still a few people in front of you. "That's what they said."

"Right," she says. "Well, it's great to see you."

"Yeah," you say. "It was great to see you."

For a while you sit alone at one of the folding tables with white table cloths. The music they are playing must be from your high school years, but you do not know it. You look around and do not recognize anyone other than Denise. You think about leaving then, but there is nowhere else to go and it is dark enough in the cafeteria to wait.

While you are sitting with another drink, she comes up to you again. You remember her leaning toward you in the attic. Her eyes are still the same bright blue.

"You look miserable," she says, laughing. "You know that?"

"Good," you say.

She laughs and sits back in a chair. Then she rests her head in her hand, leaning a little too far over the table with one elbow. "Aren't these things horrible?"

You shrug. "I'm not much of a mixer."

"What did you say you were doing?"

You take your time, having another sip from your drink. "What do you think I'm doing?"

"I always thought you'd be a computer programmer."

You look at her. You cannot tell whether she is making a joke.

"Silicon Valley, one of those start-ups. You were always so good with computers."

"Nah," you say.

"You were great."

You shake your head and tilt back the last of your drink. The ice cubes tumble and almost fall out of the glass.

"You were," she says. "Don't you remember? Everyone was supposed to make a little turtle move around on the screen, and you were the first one to figure it out. You made it draw a little house. You don't remember that?" She laughs.

You flush a little. Then you reach for the cup again. "All out," you say. You shake the glass and the ice cubes clink together. "Want another?"

Her smile wavers. Before she can answer, you stand up and the blood rushes out of your head. Your chair slides back against the chair of someone behind you, and when you reach out to steady yourself, your hand ends up on his shoulder.

"Take it easy," he says. Then he looks at you. "That's alright."

"Sorry," you say.

You turn to Denise, and you ask her if she wants a drink.

"No, thanks," she says.

"I'm gonna get one."

But first you go to the restroom. You stand at one of the urinals and unbuckle your belt. Then someone else comes in and you freeze up. He goes to the urinal beside you and starts right away. You listen while he goes and can feel your face getting red. Then he zips up and there is silence in the bathroom. But you keep standing at your urinal. You sigh and pretend to be more drunk than you are. He washes his hands and leaves the bathroom and you go to a stall and close the door.

When you return to your table, Denise is talking to a stranger. He wears a slick grey shirt, unbuttoned at the collar.

"We were just talking about you," Denise says.

"Hey, buddy," the man says. There is something uncertain in the way he looks at you. You stumble a little bit and almost run into a chair. "Whoa, there," he says.

"Weren't you two friends?" Denise asks.

Then you understand. Only something about the nose and eyes reminds you of him. It is hard to imagine that he turned into this person.

"I don't have anything to say to you," you mumble.

"Gerard works at a start-up," Denise says. "Isn't that funny? We were just talking—"

"How can you come here?" You squint at him. "How can you come here and…" You shake your head and struggle to find the right words. "I know what you did."

"What did I do?" He glances at Denise and starts to laugh. He is muscular and has a deep tan. He looks like someone who works out at the gym and goes to tanning booths.

"It's okay," Denise says. "He's just—"

Then Gerard starts to move and you think he is coming at you, but you lose your balance. Denise reaches out and barely stops you from falling. You teeter against a stack of unused chairs. People are watching.

"Let's go outside," she says. "Let's get some fresh air."

Outside, Denise keeps holding your arm. She offers to drive you home, and the two of you continue toward the parking lot. It is a cool night and the air feels good on your face. You know now that you should not have come.

On the ride back, you hear your heavy breathing and feel the heat of your body filling up the car. You sigh and lean your head back against the headrest.

Denise is quiet. She asks if you always drink like this.

"Nah... I turned twenty-one." You take a deep breath. "Hey, what do you do? I never asked."

"I work at a family counseling center," she says. "In the Mission."

"Like abortions?"

"No," she says. "Domestic violence issues, things like that. It's just an internship." She glances at you.

"Huh," you say.

"Mostly I work with victims of sexual assault."

You nod. "That's what I was trying to say." You clear your throat.

"When?"

"Before. With Gerard."

"Yeah, what was that all about?"

You want to tell her about what Iris said to you in the tunnel. But you do not know what to say.

"Nothing," you say. "I don't know."

She looks at you again and then turns back toward the road. "Sometimes I think—" she starts. Then she shakes her head.

"Turn right here," you say. You point to your house. "That's it. The one with the light on."

When the car has pulled to a stop at the curb, you search for the handle of the door and start to say goodbye. But she puts her hand on your arm. It has been so long.

"I have to ask you something," she says. "Do you remember that night at Heather's house? When I was—in the bedroom."

You sigh and adjust your position in the seat. "Yeah." Your heart is pounding.

She keeps her hand resting on your forearm. But she does not say anything. You wonder if she is waiting for you to make a move.

"Do you ever think—if you hadn't—"

You look at her and wait. Then you understand.

"I don't think a lot about stuff back then," you say. You reach for the handle and open the door.

On your parents' front porch, you pretend to fumble with your keys for a long time. Then after Denise has pulled away and her car is out of view, you take out your flask and have a drink. The rum burns your throat. You take another.

For some reason you keep thinking of Iris. You picture her standing outside the concrete tunnel with her brother. Not knowing anything. Him telling her about some secret hideout inside. You wish you could tell her not to follow him. You imagine yourself standing in the concrete ditch under the sunlight, waiting, and you wish that you could say something.

A few minutes after you place the tab on your tongue, you begin to panic.

Soon your mind cracks open.

By the second day, the world will not stop tearing apart and reforming around you like a brightly illuminated paper screen that shreds itself. It is beyond your control. You lose yourself in the constant fear of it all coming apart once again. And then it comes apart.

When you can no longer speak, they take you to the emergency room.

Years later, you sit against the wall outside a mediterranean restaurant on Telegraph and watch a girl come to a stop on the corner, staring at a map with a confused look on her face. She stands in the sunlight. You wait a while, then you walk over and ask.

Are you looking for something? And as soon as she opens her mouth, it is a story. How she came for the weekend and her friend was supposed to pick her up from the train depot but wasn't there. Only looking for a place to eat now, a café she heard about. You wait, patiently, and then point her toward the street with the café. She asks you where the campus is, and you say that the hills are east, and the Ave goes all the way up to campus in the north. She thanks you.

When she has crossed the street, you sit against the white brick wall. She looks back at you. Then she waves goodbye and you smile.

Now and then something will set it off. A flickering light. The smell of gasoline. Then the tightening at the back of the neck, the quickening of your heart, the racing thoughts, the nausea.

At the last hospital, they taught you how to accept. Being on guard is the problem. It is what creates the fear. Now you do not struggle. When something sets it off you are conscious of the changes and you accept what comes. You breathe. There is only your breath.

Then the fear is gone.

It is all so simple. If only you had known.

An old man slouches on the grassy slope. You have seen him before, pushing his cart of cans and bottles. Now he rests his forehead on his crossed arms. The cart lies to the side, tipped over, garbage spilled down the small hill and onto the sidewalk. You wonder if this is what you will become. As far as you can tell, no one comes to this small park except the homeless and the junkies. In the shadow of an overgrown hedge, a patchwork tent of cardboard and corrugated plastic, covered in psychedelic paint. Grass sprouts up between the cracks of the old basketball court.

The man does not sit in the shade of the oak trees. His bald red skin is exposed to the sun and peeling. He lets out a long sigh as you pass his way. You scoop up the spilled garbage, and he watches skeptically as you pile it back into the cart. After a while, he looks out across the street at the houses.

Motherfuckers, he grumbles.

You sit down beside him.

Those motherfuckers took my porch lamp.

You nod.

They fucking take anything.

You wait a while. *You'll get it back.*

The old man glances at you, quickly, and then begins to laugh. A chuckle, at first just a few low sputters, then a regular chuckle, a cough.

Yeah, fuck 'em all, he says. He laughs until spittle clings to his lips. *Fuck 'em all.*

You left the last hospital not long before J.P. went in.

He liked to watch old movies and eat pistachio ice cream mashed up with a spoon.

You sat by the hospital bed and watched him.

In the afternoon, there is a stray terrier lying sprawled on the sidewalk a few steps before you, flat out on his side with his legs extended. You've never seen anything look so lazy. Stretched out from one end of the sidewalk to the other. Wearing the frown of some bored king. The dog springs to his feet when you approach and begins yelping.

You wait for a moment and then kneel down and place a hand on his back. You stare into his eyes and wait. He pants, tongue hanging down, wagging his tail. The house you stand in front of now is one you pass often. An old woman lives there, and sometimes you take out the lawnmower from the shed and cut the grass for her. She fixes you fried egg sandwiches and hands them to you at the door in a brown lunchbag. The television playing in the background.

You tussle with the terrier, pet him a few times and stand and continue on your way. After tagging along behind you for a while, he trots off in the other direction.

One day when Ida was out, he said he needed to tell you something. He told you there were years when he did not love her. They had both changed. He thought it would never come back.

But it did. A few years ago, he fell in love with her all over again.

He stared at you with those hollowed out eyes and told you not to give up on love. You know he was right.

After he was gone, you sat with Ida in the empty house.

Nice beard, the kid calls over to you, sitting with his girlfriend outside a restaurant. You have been perched on the back of a nearby parkbench. You turn.

They ask if you would like to join them at the table. They're curious. So you do. They ask you questions. Your family. Yes, in Abaloma. A mother. How old you are. It takes you a moment to think, and then they are surprised. Where do you sleep. In the hills. And when it rains. Sometimes come down for shelter. Under the awnings. If you stayed out, the sleeping bag would take forever to dry. You wrap it in a garbage bag whenever the storms come. How do you eat. From the dumpsters. Friends.

The girl offers you the rest of her chicken sandwich. *I can't eat another bite*, she says. *Really—we already ate.*

She pushes it toward you.

Unless you're a vegetarian, he smiles. *I'm vegan, actually. I've been trying to convert her.*

You shake your head and say that you're not a vegetarian. Then you take a bite and thank them. You tell them it's very good.

See, he eats meat, she laughs.

Her boyfriend watches while you eat the sandwich. You can see he's troubled, and when you are done he asks you whether you eat meat that you find in the dumpsters as well. Not much, you say. But sometimes. *Don't you ever think it would be better if nobody ate animals.* He talks about the problems for the environment. Factory farms. Pollution...

You nod along with him.

It would be, you say. *It would be a better world.*

Your last time as an inpatient there was a small library and you read a paperback about geology. It said a volcano erupted seventy five thousand years ago that was so large, it made a blanket of soot over the earth and blocked out the light for years. The sun at midday was a dim red glow in the darkness and it was cold all year round. Nothing could grow. By the time the veil lifted the human race was down to a few thousand souls.

All of this has happened before and it will happen again.

You practice your breathing and meditate. The decomposition of this body. Its hair, nails, teeth. You too will return to the earth.

The boyfriend outside the restaurant is telling you how he used to reject spirituality. *I was a Marxist,* he says. *I thought all that stuff was, like, an opiate... Then I tried peyote.*

A small trigger. Pulse rising.

Man... You can't deny something you've seen.

You breathe. A pebble sinking in the fine sands. The river.

You breathe.

To love this fate. Amor fati.

In loving, to accept.

Once the doctor asked if you ever felt you had gained anything from the experience.

You mean like opening up the doors of perception?

He made no response.

There's no real insight, you said. *Everything feels like a revelation. But it's not. It's a trick. Acid turns on whatever switch gets turned on when you have a great thought. When all the pieces come together. All that's missing is the thought.*

He laughed and wrote something on his clipboard.

It's meaningfulness without the meaning. Without the work.

By the time you ended treatment, he found a way for you to stay on at the hospital as an assistant to the chaplains.

You sat with the dying. You listened to them. You held their hands.

At sunset, you head back into the hills. Run your fingers across the tips of the grass. Branches bending over the path. Already you can see clouds gathering. Casting darkness.

Sometimes you wander in the hills for hours. Then you roll out your bag and listen to the leaves. Look up at the stars.

The shadows begin to stir farther down the hill and you hear voices. Slowly sit up and listen to the breaking of twigs under their feet.

A young man staggers around the corner of the trail and he laughs, loud and drunk, slapping his thigh. His friends push up behind him and one stumbles into a bush and swears. Then the first one sees you. *Look at this guy*, he says. Another laughs.

You nod to them.

The first boy staggers to a seat beside you and claps you on the shoulder. *You know who you look like*, he grins. *You know who you look like. Guess.*

I don't, you smile.

You know who. He grabs hold of your beard and leans in. *Osama bin Laden.* The boy laughs.

You wait for him to release your beard. Then he does.

Come on, one of the others says. *Let's go.*

No, the first says. *I want to…* He turns to you. *Are you a raghead?*

You stare at him.

What are you, deaf? the boy asks. *Fuckin' faggot.*

Another of them takes a long swig from a plastic soda bottle. *Fuck, that's dog piss.*

You wanna try? Hey, give him the bottle.

No thanks, you say.

Listen to this faggot. He lets out a long belch. *You hear that? He's too good for dog piss.*

He punches you in the arm. Hard.

You continue to look at him.

Then everything goes quiet. Even the wind stops.

Did you come up here to hurt me? you ask. *Is that what you're here for?*

His friends shift in the shadows.

After a while, the boy laughs and claps you on the shoulder. *You're a fuckin' nut*, he says. He staggers to his feet and they are all laughing again and dragging him away, farther up into the hills.

You go back to watching the orange clouds drift above the city.

None of this will last.

Someone told you that the universe is going to keep growing without end. One day long after there are days the last light that ever shines will go out.

You try to picture that darkness. A darkness without light.

In the middle of the night you wake and it is cold. The trees are screaming. They rock in the wind. The black branches spread out like veins.

Everything is so small here.
The leaves stir. They cling to the branches.

More and more, you find that there is nothing to say.

Having decided to continue, you go once again to the stone inscription.

ו ה י. West.

How far might the maze take you? How many clearings might there be before you reach an end? You go to the tree and seize the ceramic apple, snapping it off the small wire that held it to the branch. Then, girding yourself for whatever might come, you step through the western opening in the hedges and begin to make your way, once again, through the nearly perfect darkness.

When you emerge into the next dim clearing, you find another tree with another apple. Going to the inscribed stone, you see that it tells you to travel west once again. So you pluck the apple and enter the maze through the western opening.

The scene repeats itself a third time, and you can no longer hold all the ceramic apples that you have plucked. You remove your shirt, wrap them inside, then tie the shirt closed and continue onward, ignoring the branches that scrape against your skin as you pass through the dangerous bends of the maze.

Finally, when you have begun to lose track of the number of passes you have made, you sit down in the latest moonlit clearing and empty the apples onto the ground. There are now eight of them. That means you are nine clearings to the west of the first clearing you encountered upon entering with Sara.

You think of turning back. But then you remember. The number ten had some significance in the Yetzirah's numerology. You decide to travel one more clearing to the west. Leaving the apples behind in the ninth clearing, you enter the western opening. The path is familiar by now.

When you emerge once again into the moonlight, you are disappointed to see nothing but the same old tree with the same ceramic apple hanging on its branch. Sighing, you pluck the apple, in order to prove to the Packards your impossible discovery, and then you head toward the southern opening that will hopefully take you back outside. But as you cross the stone, your foot stops.

The inscription has finally changed:

י ו ה

From right to left: Yod. Vav. He.

Consulting your notes, you find that this trigrammaton corresponds to the direction north. Spinning around, you look at the northern hedge.

There is an opening in it!

There are now four entrances to the hedges, one in each side. You approach the new, northern entrance, suddenly filled with a great foreboding. It is as though you can already sense what you will find on the other side.

Inside the darkness of the hedge, after a few narrow turns, the branches give way to cobblestone walls. They go on for two turns, and then you stop.

In front of you, overgrown with branches, is a concrete wall. Low in the wall is the entrance to a tunnel.

You crouch down and shine your torch into it. 'Hello?'

Your voice echoes. A chill creeps up your spine as you realize that the tunnel is precisely the size of the drainage tunnel in Abaloma that you once chose not to explore, years ago, when Iris invited you inside.

'The syzygies,' you gasp. 'Of course.'

Gerard and Gerald. Iris and Sara.

There is a dim phosphorescence deep inside the tunnel. Lowering yourself to your hands and knees, you begin to crawl toward it. At first, the light seems to get farther away the more you crawl. But then it suddenly grows into a sharp brightness, like the sunlight at the end of a traffic tunnel. Soon, you arrive at the source of the light, a small, blindingly bright concrete chamber.

While you stand in the chamber and wait for your eyes to adjust, you have the sense that something is wrong. The four walls of the chamber somehow do not connect in the normal way. It is as though the room is inside out. Or if not inside out, then perhaps the walls are upside down. In one moment they seem convex, in the next concave. It is as though the top of one touches the side of the other, so that you feel a false step could send you tumbling into the ceiling. It is all impossible. There is a grating at the top of the chamber, but it is somehow, in a way you have trouble understanding, at the same height as your feet. Light pours in from it and onto the floor that seems flat as you stand on it, but at the same time connects with the equally flat ceiling, all without tilting up.

Then you notice that there is a small white object in front of you. When you lean toward it, the object grows larger and you are able to see that it is an egg. Soon it is so large that it fills your field of vision. Then you realize that you are standing still and it is the egg itself that is growing. As it fills the chamber, its shell begins to crack. The fragments float through the air like white leaves.

Inside the shell there is a figure. He crouches on the floor. It is me. I turn and stare at you with my bloodshot eyes and my scars.

For a moment the room is still and you have time to think.

You and I. Of course.

The first person. The second.

Then my fingers begin to stretch into space and I stand and extend my arms as they grow gnarled and brown. My legs straighten and twist into knotted bark. Roots curl from my toes and split into the concrete. Green leaves sprout from my hair and fingers. Soon my entire body is curling into bark and sprouting shoots and young leaves that bloom and blossom. My branches grow in uncontrollable lines, and my leaves flutter like tongues—under the sunlight, waiting, and you wish that you could say something—as the leaves curl and unfold—in the stained bathroom mirror—beneath the flickering light—so many leaves that—You close your eyes—like the falsified eyes of butterfly wings in slewed constellations. As the other screams start—not seeing you, not even aware of why they move—screaming. If only you could start over—Ten years—endlessly, each cell branching into others, each—a final branch—to stop and tell yourself that it is not real. But you know—a stray dog cowers and paws at a scrap—stringing us together and pulling our threads apart—where it will blossom—mere dust, and will become aware—and the imperceptible shudder—from leaf to root The smallest of all possible lights—swollen black Cut down like stalks in the harvest—and each a multitude, each containing—these words as paper leaves falling from branches—White leaves—and you—You do not move—You. You— The consequence unintended—the inscription illegible—Falling blindly from one hour to the next, like water from cliff to cliff—on the snowlight mountain—though metal a cloudbridge to everywhere—in a little light—the last light that ever shines—and nothing is lost while everything changes and everyone and inside this tree my heart is still beating.

At the last moment, you decide to perform.

Placing both hands behind your back, you announce, "Jacob Price is awaiting his execution." You extend one hand dramatically. "He has pleaded guilty to murdering his emotionally disturbed twenty-two year old brother…"

When you are done, you turn to the judges and smile almost wryly. One of them is brushing away tears. "I am a gladiator of the dramatic stage," you think as you step into the hallway. It feels good. The best way to show that you are not a loser, you suddenly understand, is to win.

In the end, your gold medal helps push the team to the top of its division. Late in the evening, at a celebratory party at the motel, a bottle of sweet caramel liqueur is passed around. Instead of calling you names, I congratulate you.

"You were awesome, dude," I say. "I watched you in the finals."

"Thanks. That means a lot."

"I wish I had made it to the finals."

"Well, there's always next year."

"I just wasn't concentrating." I take a deep swig from the bottle and hand it to you. "Here, try this."

"Yeah—cheers."

The first drink knocks the wind out of you. But the second is better. Soon one of the sophomores suggests that all of you should have a kissing workshop. She stands between the beds with her hands on her hips, smiling wickedly.

"What do you think?" April whispers, sitting cross-legged on the floor to your side. Some of the others have already begun to pair up.

"I think it's a great idea," you say.

April leans toward you. By the end of the night, flushed and slightly drunk, you have made out not only with her but with several of the other girls as well. A few couples have found privacy in the closet, the bathroom and the shower. You lie with April on one of the beds and give her a back massage.

On the vanride back the next morning, the two of you share a blanket. Once, you awake to find her face in front of yours, her eyes wide. You feel her hand massaging the tip of your knee.

"We should go out," you whisper.

"You mean like boyfriend and girlfriend?"

"Yeah," you say. "Totally."

When you break up, a few weeks later, you laugh together about how unnatural it had been. Everything about the relationship had been a little forced, from the rose and chocolates you left in her locker, to the nightly phone calls, to the clumsy groping on her basement couch. But at least she relieved you of your virginity.

By the time you enter college, two brief romances later, you are so flush with self-assurance that it causes you no concern when you suddenly fall in love, shortly after your arrival, with a girl who in many ways resembles Ashley, your first love. Not only does Margaret share Ashley's copper skin, her square jaw and compact, muscular frame, but she also shares your youthful paramour's religious convictions. You vow not to make the same mistakes twice. You will not let religion stand between you.

"Did I ever tell you that my grandfather was a preacher in Boone County?" you ask Margaret one Friday afternoon. "That's in West Virginia."

The two of you are being driven with several other students to a non-denominational Christian retreat in the mountains east of campus. The seats in the van are crowded, but you manage to gaze contentedly back at your new love, resting your chin on one forearm. "There are a lot of coal miners where my family's from," you add.

"I thought you said you were from Alabama."

"Alabama?" You ponder for a moment. "You must be thinking of Abaloma."

"Oh. Where is that?"

"It's a few hours north of San Francisco."

"Huh. I thought you had a southern accent."

You laugh. "A lot of people have been making that mistake lately. It's funny, because I've always thought of myself as kind of a country boy."

You have made every effort, in the short time that you have known Margaret, not to make her feel defensive about her irrational religious views. In order to educate yourself, you have even enrolled in an introductory course on Christianity taught by a former Jesuit missionary who was rumored to have fought with the guerillas in El Salvador. "Jesus was a revolutionary," he announces on the first day of class. "He didn't want to be worshipped. He wanted people to love one another in the here and now." Listening to the professor's lectures, you begin to question your longstanding contempt for religion. Part of you even begins to wonder whether you might have lost something by being raised outside of any faith.

It is already dark as you, Margaret and the others carry your bags to the two cabins, one for the boys and the other for the girls. Before dinner is served, Pastor Brad, the interfaith minister who organized the retreat, holds a brief service. The small group of you kneel in a circle around a simple wooden cross in a bare room with wooden floors and walls. Each of you holds a candle. A few of the students offer prayers, and then Pastor Brad raises his eyes. He approaches the cross, slowly kneels, and kisses the cross at its base. You glance at the others in the circle. After the Pastor returns to his place, the girl beside him stands and walks to the cross in her flip-flops, kneeling before it as the Pastor did. In the flickering candlelight, her loose-fitting burgundy camisole slides up, exposing the smooth, tan skin of her lower back. You are overwhelmed.

Love. Beauty. They are what is holy. And they are one. When it is your turn, you go to the cross and lower yourself, crouching with your knees together as the others have done, and you gently kiss the base of the cross. As you kneel, tears well up in your eyes.

Afterwards, one of the boys in the cabin asks why you were crying. "I can't put it into words," you say. "I guess I just feel closer to something up here—something divine." You picture Margaret's breasts beneath her cotton tanktop as she knelt before the cross. They were like plump fruits, ripe and waiting to be held. "Maybe it's the holy spirit," you say.

The next day, you spend several hours meditating in the forest. By the time dinner arrives, you feel the spirit of love so strongly, it is almost like a companion at your side.

"Could you pass the salt?" you ask the boy across from you. You speak in a voice of unshakeable gratitude. Each time that you speak, what you are truly saying is: I love you. I love all of you, each and every one. You smile warmly at him.

"Sure," he says. Then he asks you a few questions about your family, but you hardly pay attention. The love fills you so completely, there is little room for words. You answer simply and allow the conversation to recede.

When you have finished your meal, you fold your napkin and excuse yourself from the table. Quiet decency hums through your limbs as you stride slowly to the bathroom and relieve yourself. Cleansing your hands, you glance up at the mirror and witness your reflection. The looming ovularity of your head—it is not so off-putting, you think. It is neither good nor bad in itself. It is what it is. Then you roll up your sleeves and flex your muscles, looking at them in the mirror. You regard your biceps for a while, until someone startles you by swinging open the door to the bathroom. Clearing your throat, you return to the dining hall and fetch a bowl of custard. You settle in beside Margaret.

"Howdy," you say.

"So we were wondering," she says. "Have you ever been on a retreat before?"

"No, I'm afraid not," you say. "My hometown wasn't very religious." You scoop some of the creamy yellow sweetness into your mouth and take your time chewing it, allowing your gaze to rest on Margaret's bronzed face, her small, sharp blue eyes and almost platinum hair. "It was a desiccated existence," you say.

"What does desiccated mean?" she asks.

"It can mean a lot of things."

"Doesn't desiccated," a boy volunteers, "mean dried out?"

"That's one meaning," you say. "So, Margaret, are you doing anything after dinner?"

"We're putting on a skit."

"Oh?"

"We tried to find you. To get you to help."

"Ah. I spent the day in the cathedral," you say, scooping up another spoonful of custard.

"What cathedral?"

"The cathedral of nature." You gaze at her meaningfully. "I also did some whittling."

After dinner, the tables are moved and the skit is performed in the dining hall. You sit with Pastor Brad in the audience, joined by others when they are not performing.

"Hey, dude," one of the performers says. He wears a backwards baseball cap and speaks to a girl from the group who is of Vietnamese descent. "Want to come out and get drunk with us?"

"No thanks," she says. "I don't believe in underage drinking."

"What are you, a loser?"

"You're the loser."

The boy pauses for a long moment.

"You're retarded," he says.

"What?" the girl says. "That's not—that's not a nice word, and you're the one who's retarded." Then she laughs nervously. As she laughs, her face begins to contort. She bares her teeth. "You're the retarded one!" Reflexively, you look away. It is too intense.

When the piece comes to an end, you applaud with gratitude. You are grateful to the group for having shared themselves with you so honestly and openly, even if you disagree with some of their positions. When Margaret asks you, outside, what you thought, you have difficulty putting your response into words.

"It really made me think," you say.

"About what?"

"It's difficult for me to express." You grasp for inoffensive words. "Do you really think drinking is wrong?"

"Of course it is."

"But our parents do it all the time. I mean people like our parents. Adults. And we'll be able to do it in a few years."

"Maybe I just don't believe in breaking the law."

"But it wouldn't be against the law if we were in Europe."

Margaret glances at you uncertainly. "Europe?"

"I'm sorry," you quickly add, "I'm not expressing myself well. The play left me all stirred up inside. Would you like to go for a walk in the woods? I was there earlier and found a little holler."

"A what?"

"A clearing."

You lead Margaret up a grassy hillside and into the forest. In the cool night, the pines are even more fragrant than they were before, and the moon is nearly full. Walking along the winding trail with her, you feel as though you are the only two souls on earth.

"Doesn't it feel like we're the only two people on earth?" you ask.

"I always feel like Jesus is beside me."

"Always? Really?" You continue walking, closing your eyes for a moment. "I know what you mean. I do. Do you want to sit down on this log?"

As the two of you settle down, you continue, "Sometimes I think that God is the feeling I get when I sit on a log like this and meditate..." You exhale deeply and slide your arm around her shoulder. "Isn't this a nice place?"

"Yeah." After a moment, you feel the tension in her back begin to lessen. She shifts, slightly, and leans her head on your shoulder. "It's peaceful," she says.

You take her forearm in your hand and hold it for a moment, letting yourself be guided by the spirit of love. Margaret's wrist is surprisingly light and small, given her impressive upper body strength. "You're so beautiful," you whisper. You lift her forearm to your lips and plant a kiss upon the inside of her wrist. The two of you are completely free in this place. As you lower her arm and lean toward her, she pulls back, placing a hand on your cheek.

"Wait. I have to ask you something."

"Anything," you whisper.

"Are you really a Christian?"

You look into her eyes and can tell that everything depends on your answer.

If you tell the truth, turn to page 111.

If you lie, turn to page 210.

You wait and listen. The muffled shrieking goes on for a while and then finally stops.

The next morning you lag behind during the hike and ask Gerard if he heard any noises the night before. "I thought I heard something," you say. But he only looks ahead. By the end of the day you are back at the clearing with the decayed log and the other instructor sits in a hammock between two trees and whittles a stick. Then you leave the forest and hike through grassy hills in a wide rolling valley.

In the afternoon you lag behind again and turn in front of Gerard and force him to stop and look you in the eyes. "Did something happen?" you ask.

He stares at you blankly. "What?"

"You know what." You sigh. "I heard it. Okay?" You stand in your t-shirt with the dried brown flecks of blood and wait. But he says nothing.

As the days pass you cross other ridges and the hiking becomes easier, but Gerard continues to lag behind. One day there is a lightning storm when you are walking in the tall grass high on a treeless hillside. The clouds rise in great dark towers and the earth suddenly dims. The instructors tell you to leave your packs and hurry to some woods nearby where you crouch between the pine trees and wait for the stormclouds to pass. Thunder shakes the earth and the rain comes on sideways in cold gales that make the treetops creak and bend.

Then the storm is over and after a minute sunlight breaks through the forest. You walk on with your packs through the glistening grass and the cobweb rainbows. One of the boys says he was afraid of the lightning and you laugh and say that you were too.

The next day the instructors offer to go on a summit of a nearby peak and all of you go but Gerard. "It's just a pile of rocks on top," you tell him afterward.

He nods blankly, sitting by the campsite in too many clothes.

"They said we passed a point where it wasn't possible for grass to live."

Gerard looks at you. "Why couldn't the grass live?"

"I don't know," you say. "Not enough oxygen."

At dinner the instructors say that there is no direct way down from the latest ridge because of the looseness of the rocks and so the next day you head down another route. You descend a snowcovered slope with an icy crust and unpack your gators and carry your ice-axe swinging beside you. A thin crooked finger of rock stretches high above the ridge and you wonder whether all of this was once under the ocean.

Sometimes one of the boys loses his footing and slides down the snowy slope. Then whoever fell must walk back up by kicking holes into the crust of ice with each step. You are careful to step into the footholes left by those in front of you and to punch your ice-axe into the snow while you walk. Halfway down the ridge someone slides behind you and you hear a shout and then a sound like two stones knocking against one another. When you turn Gerard has fallen several feet down the slope and landed head first against a rock and his body starts to twitch as someone yells for the instructors. Then his head moves in a strange way. The snow around it is becoming pink. His head has been twisted open. You lean over and start to vomit.

By the time the helicopter arrives he has been dead for several hours.

"You're not listening," you tell the counselor who is waiting at the hospital in Boulder. He takes notes on his legal pad and nods but mostly he looks at you calmly. "He was only there because of me."

They try to explain that it is common for survivors to feel guilty. They say that Gerard's death was not your fault. It was an accident and there was nothing you could have done. But they do not know that he needed your help in the forest that night and you did nothing. You are too ashamed to tell anyone.

Back in Abaloma you sleep during the day for the first week and come out of your room only at night. You bring plates of food to your room and soon the leftovers grow mold and rot but you do not take the plates away until Ida does it for you.

Then you start to have trouble getting out of bed. Once you cannot walk all the way to the bathroom and you lean against the door and urinate a little on yourself and on the tiles.

By the time you return to school the image of Gerard's fractured skull has been turning in your mind for weeks and you can barely sit still through class. Sometimes you go to a bathroom stall where no one can see you and you hold your head in your hands.

One night Ida knocks at your door when you have been watching television. She sits at the edge of your bed. How are you doing? she asks.

You continue to look at the television.

She sighs and picks at something on the bedspread. I just want to see you be happy again.

What?

I want you to be happy. I'm sure Gerard would want that too. She brushes something away from the bedspread. Aren't there any friends you want to talk to?

Then you stare at her.

Isn't there anyone? Any friends?

You take a deep breath and stare at her.

You come up here and knock on my door, you say. Your voice shakes. And now you're making fun of me.

I just want—

Get out! you yell. Get out! Get out! You yell it until she starts to cry. Then she leaves and you stand from the bed and lock the door behind her.

After high school you move to Seattle because you want to be in a place where the sun is not so bright, and for a few years it is not so bad. You do temp work, entering direct deposit requests into a database at a bank. But sometimes after you have been working at the computer for several hours without looking away or doing anything else, the image will come back. You will see him bleeding against the rock. The open cavity, part of his skull clinging to a flap of skin, blood streaming out in the snow. Clumps of hair in the gore. You never saw these things. When he fell there was only a little pink in the snow. But it no longer matters. The images are more real than anything around you.

In the office, when the fear takes hold, you lean back in your chair and put your hands on your head so that it feels like it is not falling apart. You try to breathe and forget it. Before the anxiety builds too much. Usually the panic comes and goes in waves for a while and if it starts to slip out of control, you can sit in one of the bathroom stalls and collect yourself.

At the elevator door one afternoon a new temp beside you is chewing gum with her mouth open. She laughs for some reason.

Heading out early? she asks.

I took a short lunch break, you say. We're allowed to do that on Fridays. But it comes out sounding like you are angry. In the corner of your eye, she flinches.

That's what I meant, she says quietly.

The two of you have to stand in the small elevator together the whole way down. You feel like you are filling up all the space in the elevator with your weight and there is a sour smell that you think may be coming from you. Sometimes you sweat while you are working. The doors open. You can only think of getting to the liquor store.

A few hours later, beer in hand before the television, you are still thinking of the girl in the elevator. Probably the first time you'd talked in a week. You keep thinking of what you said. Again and again. Sometimes swearing to yourself and then hearing your voice when you say it and being embarrassed. Fuck you, you say. Fuck.

You finish the beer and then pause the movie and get another from the refrigerator. Spill a little when you pull back the tab and take a drink. Think of what someone would say if they saw you. Blinds closed so that no one can look in. Soon the shame is deadened. Even if someone in the movie had to go into surgery and started to bleed you would be alright. You would see him against the rock but it would have no power over you. Could simply turn the movie off and do the dishes.

Even if the panic grew, there would be no need to hide it. Do anything. Rub your face or clutch your knees or moan. Whatever you need. No one watching.

Then another beer and back to the couch. Battles on another planet. Look at the lead actor. Is he younger than you. Has never suffered. You are young but when you look in the mirror now something in the skin of your face already. In your eyes. Almost ten years now. Gerard. He was so young but he will never know anything else. You start to cry and then you pause the movie and open a bottle of vodka and sit down on the tiles of the kitchen floor with your back against the cabinet and drink. What has become of you. Look at you.

The next morning, the hangover is worse than usual. It wakes you early, lying on the carpet in the living room, and you cannot go back to sleep because of the pain in your head. Panic too. Already there from the moment you open your eyes. Nowhere to look. Every corner, on every wall. The walls move like they are underwater. You close your eyes and he bleeds behind your eyes. There is no place to look. Your heart races. If you had a heart attack. Alone. You pull on clothes and leave the apartment. But the panic follows. Nowhere to look. Rubbing your head, walking down the street. Beneath the highway overpass, holding your head, trying to make the gestures seem normal but they are not. Every car watching you. What do they think.

You walk and walk. And then when you have walked to an industrial area where there are no cars on the streets and you are able to think about other things, the panic fades at last. Then you are so grateful. You are always so grateful when it leaves you. The sun continues to rise over the buildings. You sigh. You are so tired of the struggle.

At the grocery store you buy some beer and a sausage and biscuit breakfast from the buffet. Then you continue back toward the apartment. There is a sign hanging in a glass display case outside one of the churches on the way.

WHY ARE THERE 2 MILLION IN US PRISONS TODAY?
JOIN PRISON OUTREACH
AN INTERFAITH COMMUNITY JUSTICE ORGANIZATION

But it is not the message that stops you. There is graffiti scrawled across the glass pane with a thick black marker. An angel with a halo stands behind Osama bin Laden and rapes him. Cartoon wings and everything. You stand and stare. Wonder what the maker of the graffiti was thinking. Where he was coming from.

Are you a supporter of prisoners' rights?

Turn and see a short bearded man. A perfectly round stomach, like a bowling ball under his t-shirt. A clipboard in his arm. Smiles. You start to walk away and then stop. So grateful that the panic has gone.

Would you like to participate in the strawberry festival at the prison? he continues. It's put on by the First Nations inmates. Guests are welcome. We're trying to get a group together. The man begins writing on his clipboard. You don't have to decide now. If you'd like, I could put your name on the list. Then you could decide tomorrow before the van leaves. They let us do a special one-day notice. Are you interested?

For some reason you accept the clipboard when he holds it out. You try to think of a fake name but nothing comes to mind so you give him your real name. There are only two other names on the form. He shakes your hand and gives you a flyer.

I don't know if you've ever been to a prison before, he says. The one we go to is a state prison. But there's nothing to worry about. I just need to give a day's notice. The van leaves from right here. Then he shakes your hand again. We'll hope to see you there.

Back at your apartment you spend the rest of the afternoon drinking beer and downloading pictures from a service you joined. On the radio a man with a high-pitched voice is saying something about the attacks. But you look into the science, he says, and I mean the scientific information and there is no question. High octane airplane fuel is not sufficient, insufficient, to cause a structural collapse in that grade of steel. There is no question.

Tell us more about the burn rate, the interviewer says. How much jet fuel would it take to melt one of those steel girders?

The other man talks about the bombs that were planted in the twin towers and then about how the Pentagon was not struck by a plane. Are you telling me one of the most photographed buildings in the United States, he says, the center of the military-industrial complex, and there is not a single picture? Give me a break.

Then a commercial for some medical study. You finish the beer and think about the morning. The fear. Maybe someday it will all burn out. Like the voices in schizophrenics' heads. You decide to watch another movie.

Then the movie is over and the room is quiet again. You wonder what to do. You go to the kitchen and look through the cabinets. Reach for a bag of popcorn and then you stop. You think. Every choice you make. Every choice you make is like this. You do what you want. But somehow it is not what you want. If only you could come at it all from a different angle somehow. If only you could start over.

Then the tape finishes rewinding and you turn toward the VCR. You try to remember what you were thinking. It is on the tip of your tongue. After a while you put the popcorn in the microwave and set the timer.

That night the dream comes back. The worst one. A faceless body hanging in front of you on hooks. Cutting it open with a butcher knife and blood spills out but you continue to take it to pieces. Wake up sick. Fuck, you say. Fuck. Pacing in the apartment. Something wrong with you. What if this is the way they begin. People who shoot up offices. Or serial killers. Try not to think that you are slipping away. Then you know the time has come. Clean up. Get clear in your head. Stop drinking again. Time to build back up your health. Strength. No wonder you are like this. Not healthy so much time alone. Alone. You remember the potbellied man and you know what you have to do. You take the flyer out of the trash can and look at the clock.

A few hours later you are sitting in the back of his van, driving out of the city. An old woman sits in the passenger seat beside him. And then in the back two college kids.

You think about the weeks ahead. Know that you can stop drinking for long enough because you have done it before. When you have drunk yourself into this hole. The nerves so worn down and the fear so strong that it is easier to quit than go on. This is the one good thing about the sickness. Without it you might have had no reason not to drink yourself to death.

Have you ever been to a prison before? the potbellied man asks from the driver's seat. Litter all across the floor of the van. Turns back quickly to look, smiling again. Has a lazy eye.

No, I've never been in trouble, you say.

There is silence for a while. The college kid in the back seat starts to laugh.

That's not what I meant, the potbellied man says. We're all volunteers. We go to the prison every week and run a reading program with the inmates. He invites you to come. No need to be a professor. A lot of these guys are lifers. They're just looking for someone to talk to, some connection to the outside.

You nod. The man keeps his eyes on the road and sips from a large plastic coffee mug. Someone to treat them like a human being instead of a number, he says. I've been coming up here every week, about a year and a half.

It's addictive, the college kid says.

Then for some reason you start to think about the van. Very small. Unable to leave, no way to excuse yourself from the van. Under their eyes. What if you panicked inside the prison. Even worse. No way out. No way to leave. You recognize that it was a mistake to come. The panic starts to arc up and you feel yourself blushing. Try to think of excuse not to enter the prison. But in a moment of calm you tell yourself that what you are doing now is necessary. Like medicine. Being with people. Struggle through this day and others like it and then in a few weeks healthy enough. Thicken the fat around your nerves. Then drink again and burn it all away.

The front wall around the prison fills an entire block, but there is only a single row of parking spaces in the street. So the van does not stop. Wheels past the front entrance and an abandoned old gas station there. Stops by a side entrance, just a door in another endless concrete wall. Unreal. The panic rising as you step outside into the heat and light. Then recedes. Nothing. Stand for an hour or so by the door, in the shadow, waiting for a guard. A few brownskinned women wait with you, standing perfectly still. Wearing colorful blankets. Black hair. The potbellied man introduces himself and they talk for a while in quiet voices. When the door finally opens, the potbellied man smiles and the guard ignores him. You are embarrassed to be seen with these people. You follow them through the gate.

The guard takes his time checking your names and identifications on his list in the filthy waiting room, then asks you to read the regulations in the big red poster on his wall and sign a form and put anything metal or valuable in a nearby wall of lockers. Then he asks you all to follow him into another room where he sweeps each of you with a metal-detecting wand. Stops at one of the black-haired women.

You're wearing earrings.

She reaches up to her ears. Was it wrong?

Ma'am, did you read the regulations?

I can take them—

Did you read the regulations? he says, holding up one hand while she tries to talk. Ma'am? You signed your name that you read the regulations. Did you read them?

Her head moves a little. She looks toward the other women. But my son.

Ma'am? the guard says. The regulations say no jewelry. You entered a secure area with prohibited materials, and I'm going to have to escort you outside now.

She begins to cry. Others try to talk to the guard but he does not listen. He takes her outside the waiting room and then comes back and closes the door. Does not look at you. Leads the rest of the group through old hallways and past tall concrete buildings with barred windows. Stopping at steel doors and waiting to be buzzed through. Then single file through the empty prison yard. No one anywhere. A few shouts from the barred windows above the yard. Finally, the guard leads you into a small brick building full of old schoolrooms. Other visitors already there in the room at the end of the hall. Most of them Indians. Folding table covered with plastic plates, a plastic cooler, dishes in tinfoil. Like a picnic. Women, middle-aged and black-haired, dressed in more blankets and beads. The few white women dressed the same, rainbows of thick yarn, necklaces.

Welcome, brother, one of the white women says, approaching you with wide, strained eyes. Spots in her skin. Are you with the writing program?

I came in the van.

Then you must know Windfeather.

No, you say.

Well, she says. We're glad to have you as our guest.

You wait a long time in the schoolroom and watch the potbellied man speak with the women. Then a guard stands by the door and the men file in, dressed in blue jumpsuits. Try not to stare at them. Once the guards have stepped back into the hall, the men greet their visitors and laugh and clap the potbellied man on the back. They call him Reverend and he smiles and introduces you to them, one by one. Each shakes your hand and looks in your eyes. Then the ceremony begins in a room across the hallway. A wide circle of orange plastic chairs with feather-ringed drums in the middle.

Brothers and sisters, one of the inmates says in a low voice. It pleases me to see you on this day. We are gathered to celebrate the festival of the strawberries. Every year, when the harvest season has come to an end, we give thanks to the earth for its bounty. This is our tradition. Many of us come from different tribes. You wonder what he means about the harvest since all of them are in prison. Maybe they took them on a field trip or something. You try to sit still in your cracked plastic chair while he welcomes all the tribes of the guests, ending with his own. Speaks slowly, never smiling. Studying the faces of everybody. Stares at you. And then sometimes he will say a few words in some Indian language.

After thanking a large, older woman who sits in a striped blanket outside the circle, he comes to you and the others from the van. I would like also to thank the Reverend, he says, suddenly smiling wide, for sharing in our celebration with his families and friends. Welcome, Reverend. Welcome, friends. The others repeat his welcome. It is our honor to welcome you here.

You think he is done then but he turns and gives thanks to the women for having brought the drums and other instruments and for having set them out. The thanks seem to go on forever. He thanks the women for the food they brought. For their grace and wisdom. He praises each of the tribes again. Then he thanks his teachers for their grace and wisdom. One of the white women whispers in your ear. Is this your first time here? she asks. Isn't this wonderful? But you do not know what she means. It is pathetic. A classroom with old vinyl tiles and plastic chairs. Guards standing outside the windows, not even bothering to look inside.

It keeps going on. Another inmate stands up and thanks the first speaker. Talks about the first speaker's strength. The white woman beside you whispers something again that you do not hear. I do not speak the tongue of my people, the second man says. But I am trying to learn. He takes out a piece of paper and starts to read. We thank the earth for the rain that gives life, he says. Then he says it in the other language. We thank the earth for the trees that offer us shade. Then again in the other language. We thank the earth for the corn... He goes on giving thanks for a long time. Like a chant. He thanks the earth for the fish and the streams. He thanks the earth for the beans. You wonder when the last time he saw a field was. We thank the earth for her strawberries. They are the gift of the season. They are the gift of the end of harvest. We thank the earth for her gifts.

The visitors all murmur thanks and praise. It is so pathetic that you do not know what to do. You worry that they will know what you are thinking. Then the large older woman in the striped blanket begins to speak. I thank our brother Windfeather, she says very slowly. She barely moves her lips. These words are much like the words that were spoken in the old times. She praises the convict's speech but you have trouble paying attention because she talks so slowly. Then all the other women are standing and they start to walk silently around the room. Give you a styrofoam cup and fill the cup with a few spoonfuls of mashed strawberries. Like something for kindergarteners. The first speaker says that the women, as they pour the strawberry drink, will give an offering to the earth. You are supposed to respond with an acceptance of the offering. Glad it is in a prison because otherwise you would worry it was drugged.

I accept the strawberries from the spirit of the earth, you mumble when it is your turn, just like the others. You are embarrassed.

Finally, after everyone drinks the fruit, the women pull their chairs back to the edge of the room, away from the men, and the drumming starts. You sit back in your chair outside of the drum circle with the other men who are not drumming and you are relieved that all of the attention is focused on the drummers. But now that there is nothing to do but watch the drumming you start to think again about what would happen if the panic came, here, in the prison. Without any words to distract you, all you can think about is the panic. No escape here if it got worse. If it got bad and you had to ask them to leave, you would have to go all the way back out through the maze of brick and concrete buildings and halls. There is no way out.

The inmates in the drum circle continue to pound a simple rhythm. No variation. Just a steady, endless beat. It is too bright in the room and the fluorescent lights flicker. If only there were somewhere to go. You think about excusing yourself to go to the bathroom. But what if you came back and the panic came again. Then you would have no excuse anymore. You hold yourself still and wait for it to get worse.

Stare at the drummers. Try not to look like you are losing control. Some of them with small drums between their knees, others with large drums that rest on the floor. All of the drums covered with stretched hides and rings of feathers. As the beat goes on and on, you find it harder to keep yourself under control. You shift in your chair and begin to drift and then whenever you snap back, the panic has grown. Heart races. Drift. Snap back. You force yourself to stay calm, tensing your neck and jaw to keep yourself together. Face flushed. They can all see. Time to get up. Go to the restroom. But what then. You try to concentrate on the drummers. They sit with eyes closed, swinging the sticks and mallets and their hands against the drumheads. Not looking at you. The rhythms getting more complex. You lift your hands up and fold them behind your head. Try to make it look natural. Clench your jaw.

After a while you snap back and the boy from college is sitting in the drum circle now, and another drummer stands and begins to hand the small drum to the Reverend. But he refuses and points to you.

The man in the blue jumpsuit holds out the small drum. You try to refuse it. But he shakes his head. He holds it out and you take it. Then he leads you to sit in his chair in the circle and whispers in your ear. It's easy. Bring your hand up to the same place each time. That's the trick. Pats you on the back. All eyes on you now. All eyes. Flushed. They can tell there is something wrong.

Start to drum. Hard to stay in rhythm. You keep falling out of the beat. You try to stay in rhythm and fail and you know that you are trying too hard but you do not know how to stop. After a while you just give up. Fuck it. Some of the men strike the heads at different times, on the off-beat, and the rhythm is complicated but the beat underneath it is always the same. You lift your hand again and again and try to beat as quietly as possible. Back to the same place. Back to the same place. Again and again.

You feel the panic at the back of your skull ratcheting up again as it always does like a knot in the tendons. Then the worst thing. You worry about seeing it here. His head split open against the rock. Nausea grips your stomach. You start to take quick breaths. The panic grows.

What if the image came to you here.

Try not to think of it. But this only makes it come. The open cavity. Blood staining the snow. You twist your head back and forth and then stop drumming and place your hand on the back of your head and try not to think of what will happen next.

If only you could be free of this. If Gerard was still alive and there was no screaming. If only you could start over.

Ten years in this place. You are so tired.

You are so tired.

"What do you mean?" you ask.

"You know. Do you accept Jesus Christ as your savior?"

You clear your throat. "Let me answer your question with another question," you offer. "Isn't the point of Christianity that we're *all* the children of God?"

Margaret pushes away. "I don't get it. Why are you on a Christian retreat if you're not Christian? You prayed with us. Why—how could you—"

You sigh. "Look," you say, rubbing your face. "There are different ways of being Christian. Do I believe in miracles? No. I don't believe that Jesus shot lightning out of his fingertips, and I don't believe he flew up to outer space and sits at a dinner table beside an old man with a white beard." Standing from the log, you allow yourself to gesture more expansively. "But most contemporary theologians don't believe that either. You see, Margaret, most religious thinkers see the gospels as expressions of faith, not as the recording of historical fact. Only fundamentalists in the United States still believe that. The fact is, I'm probably more Christian than you are. It's probably un-Christian to believe that the Bible is the literal truth. Did you know, for example, that the actual, historical Jesus never intended to found a religion?"

Margaret remains silent. You begin to pace back and forth on the trail, pointing occasionally for emphasis. "Yeshua from Nazareth—who was he? He was just a charismatic rabbi with something new to say, a message about forgiveness and love. That is a historical fact." It is somehow deeply satisfying to hear your own voice. Perhaps your grandfather felt this way when he delivered his sermons so long ago in the muddy hills of Boone. "Love. Love was his message. The real Jesus tried to destroy religion. He tried to tear down those dead rituals and the empty laws of the Pharisees. God doesn't need us to worship him. He doesn't need our sacrifice. 'I desire mercy, not sacrifice.' That's what Jesus said. Basically. Mercy is what we're here for, according to him. To show mercy to one another in the here and now…"

The sermon lasts for several minutes, building upon its own momentum, and Margaret never interrupts. Finally, she yawns and you sense that it is time to draw things to a close. "I guess what I'm saying is, if the holy spirit really existed, don't you think other people would've noticed it? And that's what karma is all about." You settle down in front of her, squatting in the pine needles. "But what I'd really like us both to take away from this is the originality of Jesus' message. He doesn't say the kingdom of God is some paradise off in the future. It's the presence of God as one's neighbor, as the weak of the earth, as the poor among us. It's right here, right now. The unconditional love for the people around you who suffer, for the people who can't protect themselves, the lepers, the outcasts, the heretics, the lovers." You place a hand on her knee. "You know, the Gospel of Thomas says that only when you can strip and not be ashamed will you be ready for the kingdom of God. Isn't that crazy?" You gently rub her thigh. "So when you ask me, do I accept Jesus Christ as my savior? Sure I do. And part of that means not believing in God."

You stare into Margaret's eyes, savoring the power of your words.

"Wow," she says. "I feel like I'm talking to the Devil."

You study her face, waiting for some qualification, but none comes.

"How so?"

"It's like you're trying to tempt me to give up my faith."

"Hm. But what if your faith is a false faith? What if your God doesn't exist, and Jesus doesn't want you to believe in him?"

Margaret rises and looks around. "Yeah, I'll think about that," she says. "We should probably head back."

In the weeks after the retreat, you manage to patch things up with Margaret, though the other students remain hostile when you see them around campus. Eventually, by continuing to engage Margaret in discussions of her religious beliefs, you succeed in carving out a place for yourself in her life. You become indispensable to her, your conversations a proof of her intellectual worth. One day, you recount an argument that a pretentious upstart made in your introductory French literature class. The fool claimed that it was possible to disagree with the conclusions of a logical argument even if one agreed with its premises. You quickly shot him down by observing that he was being illogical. "Anyway, the best he could do was drag in Quain. Are you familiar with Quain?"

She shakes her head. You adjust your scarf.

"He's a professor here," you say. "Basically, he doesn't believe in truth."

"What?"

"He's one of those, you know, postmodernists. He thinks everything's relative." You take another sip of cappuccino. "I looked at a few of his books yesterday. Complete nonsense. Anyway, he's probably one of the five or six most significant philosophers in the world today."

"He teaches philosophy?"

"Actually, he teaches in the comp lit department. Comparative literature."

"Why doesn't he teach in the philosophy department?"

"From what I heard, they wouldn't have him. Real philosophers have too much respect for logic to let their students be corrupted by nonsense like that." As you explain to Margaret the respect that true philosophers have for logic, you find yourself growing ever more impassioned. "It's not only that real philosophers respect logic," you say. "They love it. That's what philosophy means. The love, *philo*, of logic, *logos*. It's almost a religious devotion—"

Margaret nods.

"Yes," you proceed, aware of having stumbled upon a potentially valuable piece of rhetoric. "It's like a religion. I guess you could say that logic is my religion. So much in this world is uncertain and unclear," you hazard. "But logic is transparent. Perfect. It is eternal. It's so beautiful, right?"

She looks into your eyes and smiles. "It sounds like you care a lot about logic."

"I do. It's something that I care about. Deeply."

"I admire that," she says.

In the fall of sophomore year, you declare your major in philosophy and enroll almost exclusively in philosophy classes, including two with an up-and-coming professor named Rodnock. He is an internationally recognized expert in the field of possible world theory.

"Have you ever climbed a mountain in Colorado?" Professor Rodnock asks on the first day of class. He seems to be addressing you, so you shake your head. "No. But you could have. It would have been possible for you to climb a mountain in Colorado. So there is a possible world in which someone climbs some mountain. But is this person *you*?"

The question strikes at the very pith of your being. On the one hand, you want to say yes—because the man climbing the mountain is, by the very terms of the hypothetical, you. But on the other hand, how can the man climbing the mountain be you? You have never climbed a mountain in Colorado! Your mind spins. Clearly, there is a mystery here of a not inconsiderable depth.

While struggling to come to terms with your philosophical perplexities, you continue to see Margaret regularly, filling the role in her life of intellectual touchstone and trusted confidant. Similarly, she fills the role in your life of unreciprocating love object. It is true that you had expected the great romance of your college years to be a requited one, but when that turns out not to be the case, you are able to accept the consequences with serenity. Sometimes there are moments of humiliation, such as when Margaret loses her virginity and appears at your door, crying, to tell you the details of how the boy treated her afterward. But you bide your time, providing her with tissues and words of comfort. Somehow you know in your heart that she will be yours, in the end, because she is the only one for you. The two of you are meant to be together. It is fate.

One glorious day late in the fall of senior year, your patience finally bears fruit. The moment arrives, oddly enough, in the wake of your finally having given up hope. As winter break approached, you accepted that you would never persuade Margaret to love you and took solace in a somewhat homely, bespectacled symbolic systems major who had worn a retainer when the two of you lived in the same dorm freshman year.

"How could you do that?" Margaret demands over the phone. "I thought we were friends."

"I don't understand. You're acting as though I took something from you."

"But it's Melissa!"

Then you remember. Margaret and Melissa had once been close. There had been some kind of brutal falling out. You had forgotten.

"Maybe we should discuss this in person," you say.

Over a bottle and a half of riesling, you refuse to apologize. Sitting on the floor of Margaret's dorm room, you patiently dismiss her complaints and tease her for being jealous. By the time you remove the glass from her hand and set it on the floor, she has been leaning her head against your chest, her arms wrapped loosely around you, for several silent, warm minutes. You lower her body onto a throw-pillow propped against her bed. Though you are out of practice, the wine relieves you of any inhibition. You tug down her sweat pants and slowly cover her body in kisses and soft caresses.

In the following days, you move quickly to consolidate your gains. Through a series of elaborate dinner dates, you make clear beyond a shadow of a doubt that the two of you are dating, and not merely friends with occasional benefits. Your crowning achievement is to persuade her that you should ring in the new millennium together, a possibility that you propose while picnicking in the foothills behind campus.

"You said you hadn't made any plans yet," you observe, swirling a glass of zinfandel. "Why don't we spend New Year's together in Abaloma?"

"I already bought a ticket back home."

"Wonderful. Then I could visit you in Durham." You explain that you have always wanted to visit the region, especially because of your family's roots in Appalachia. "I think it's time that I met your parents anyway. I realize they don't want you to date an atheist. But I think I can convince them that they have nothing to worry about."

In the days before Christmas, back in Abaloma, you rush to finish your senior thesis for Rodnock, knowing there will be no time for work once you fly east. You pace in your bedroom for hours on end, trying to make some progress in determining whether it is possible for an entity in a possible but not actual world to have free will. Bringing matters full circle, you use as your primary "intuition pump," in Rodnock's words, the very scenario with which Rodnock began his class at the start of your sophomore year: namely, the climber on the mountain. Obviously, the resolution of Rodnock's larger question about the mountaineer—whether he could be you— would lie beyond the scope of any undergraduate thesis. It would in all likelihood require several years of diligent work simply to frame such a knotty question in a clear manner. Still, you feel that it is not altogether too audacious for you to ask: regardless of whether or not the mountaineer in the possible world is you, or could be you, could this individual, even hypothetically, be seen as possessing free will? Could the mountaineer in the possible world have chosen not to climb the mountain that he did, in fact, choose to climb?

Just thinking about the problem makes you dizzy. But as you pace your room, shaking your head occasionally, hands tucked beneath your arms in the style of Rodnock during his lectures, you find the vertigo reassuring. It is evidence of the worthiness of your problem. This worthiness is in turn a justification for your inability to resolve the problem after a year and a half of unceasing labors. At the moment, you are focused resolutely on the sub-problem of what a choice truly is, and how it is related to a free action. You attempted, briefly, to frame this sub-problem in terms of a biconditional logical connective, asking yourself, "Is an action free if and only if it is the result of a choice?" But after filling pages of your notebook with other, apparently equally persuasive "iff" clauses, you have abandoned the search altogether and are now attempting a different approach. You stand still for a moment and try to *choose* to take a step, in order to use introspection to analyze what happens inside of you in the moment of choice.

But when you take the step, lifting your foot from the fluffy carpet of your bedroom floor, the choice preceding it happens too quickly for you to notice. So you try to slow down the process. You close your eyes and attempt to choose very slowly. First, you picture the step, but do not yet take it. You tell yourself: I choose to do this. I choose it. You even flex your leg slightly. But then you stop. Have you chosen to take the step yet? It seems as though you have not really made the choice, because you remain free not to move your leg. In fact, even if you did take a step now, you think, it might be the result of a different choice. Indeed, the step might be a different step than the step you earlier chose to take, if you chose to take a step at all.

Then you stand before your mirror. You imagine yourself standing before the mirror in a possible world, staring at yourself, and you imagine yourself reflected, as a possibility, across all the possible worlds, like an image in an endlessly self-reflecting hall of mirrors. But thinking of the possibility of such reflection only makes your head spin.

Sighing deeply, you decide to take a break and call Margaret. If only there were a machine that could look inside your brain and observe when a choice has been made, the problem of the nature of choice could be resolved once and for all. But Rodnock told you that it would be at least a decade before such a machine exists.

When you succeed in getting Margaret on the phone, she cries again. The day before, apparently, she told her parents that she had been attending a more liberal church while at school, and a bitter fight ensued.

"I feel so guilty," she says. "Sometimes—"

"You shouldn't."

"But I do."

"Look, Margaret. You can't let your parents determine who you are—"

"Oh, shoot," Margaret says suddenly. "I have to go. I'm supposed to take my grandma to the hair salon. I have to go."

"That's okay. I'll call you tomorrow."

"Sure," Margaret says. "I'll call you then."

She hangs up before you can say that you love her, which you had planned to do at the end of every call. All of your calls seem to break off like this, abruptly and almost before they have begun.

Sitting beside the phone, you try to return to your philosophical efforts. But you can only picture Margaret standing alone on a snowy mountainside. It seems to you, for a moment, that she is nothing more than an automaton. She stands on the mountainside, like a crying machine, and there is nothing else that she could have done but follow the path laid out by her parents. In the possible world in which Margaret is a mountaineer, there is still no possibility of free will for her.

Before you can make any progress in untangling your thoughts, Ida calls you down to dinner. J.P. sits at the kitchen table, a bag of ice resting on one knee.

"What happened?" you ask.

"Just hit a slick patch," he says, tossing his graying ponytail over one shoulder.

He takes a drink from the tumbler beside him. Once again, you are reminded of how old your parents have become. You feel sorry for them, then feel embarrassed for feeling sorry. They would not want to be, and do not deserve to be, objects of your pity.

Soon enough, however, your pity gives way to frustration as you find yourself in yet another heated argument with J.P., this time over the nature of impossibility. In the end, you accuse him of not understanding what modality is, and he accuses you of wasting your education.

"It's empty verbiage," he says. "Empty phraseology. What do you plan to do after graduation?" he asks. "Five months from now."

You reach across the table and grab the bottle of merlot, pouring yourself another healthy glass. "I hadn't really thought about it. There are so many possibilities. But I guess you wouldn't understand that."

"Why?"

"Because any adequate account of possibility would have to take into account the concept of modality!"

"Well, you're going to have to make up your mind. Sooner rather than later." You can hear the anger in his voice. "And I'm not talking about possibilities. I'm talking about reality. A *real* choice."

"I'm very aware of what a choice is. Actually, I'm kind of an expert."

"Oh? You're an expert?"

It is not fair, the power he still has to hurt you.

"What are the choices you make?" you ask. "How many cigarettes to smoke every day?"

"I'm not going to sit here in my kitchen and listen to a twenty-year-old—"

"I'm nineteen. You don't even know how old I am."

You glance at Ida, but she remains silent, picking at her vegetarian lasagna.

"Jesus," you say. "You don't even know how old your son is."

J.P. slams down his fork. "That's enough."

For the rest of the meal, you eat in silence.

The next morning, your distraction from work deepens when you try to call Margaret several times but fail to reach her. It is with immense relief that you hear J.P. calling up the stairs, shortly after dinner, to say that April is on the phone. The two of you have not spoken since you returned for the break, and you realize, suddenly, that you have missed her.

"Hi, April," you say. "How's it going?"

There is silence. "Who's April?" Margaret asks.

"No one," you say. "Sorry. An old friend from high school. How are you?"

"Good. How is—Abaloma?"

"Same as always. Like a bunch of doll-houses." You wait for her to make some response, but she does not. "So what have you been up to in Durham?"

"You'd be proud of me. I already went to church twice today." She laughs in a strange, exhausted way. "I had the talk with my parents. I told them about you being a—you know. But I have—"

"How did it go?"

She does not answer.

"Is there something wrong? You sound—"

"No."

But there is something very wrong. You can hear it in her voice. Something has shifted, some small, previously existing constant is no longer there. When she does not speak, you somehow understand. In fact, you realize that you have always known. It has only come earlier than you expected. "Are you breaking up with me?"

"How—?" She pauses. "How did you know that?"

You hold the phone for a moment, then slowly set it down on the carpet. Then you pick it up again. "Are you still there?" you ask.

You hear her voice speaking to someone away from the phone. "Yes?"

"Are you still there?"

"Yeah."

"I have to know something…" You take a deep breath, rising and going to your mirror. You look at yourself and feel as though you are looking at a stranger, as though you have never seen yourself until now.

"Hello?" she asks.

"I have to know something."

You wait for a moment. Finally, you set down the phone.

You cannot believe that it has happened again.

When you arrive in the kitchen, it seems changed. For years, Ida has complained that the house is falling apart and needs to be remodeled. You had always dismissed her fretting, because the house looked fine to you. But now, for the first time, you see that the grout between the tiles is in fact stained a deep yellow. The wallpaper is warped in places. The furniture seems scuffed and old. J.P. sits at the kitchen table with his grey ponytail and reading glasses, holding the paper with another tumbler beside him.

"You make any plans?"

"It wasn't April," you say. "It was Margaret."

You look at J.P. again and do not even worry that he might see you staring. You look at him and do not know what to say.

"Do you mind if I have a beer?" you ask.

He does not answer.

"J.P., do you mind if I have a beer?"

He looks up. "Hm? Help yourself."

Then you stand in front of the open refrigerator, staring at the two brands of beer inside. The difference between them matters so little to you, it is impossible to decide which to drink. If only one were better than the other, you could decide. But you do not like either of them. They both taste like unpleasant water. Standing before the bright fluorescence, you remember having thought when you were young that the world was so full of possibilities. But you were wrong. There is only one world. This one. You have been condemned from the start to stand before this refrigerator. Condemned to be alone, about to get drunk in front of your parents. It does not matter. Closing your eyes, you reach toward the cans of beer, at random…

Is it not the same for you, reader? Are we not all condemned to do as we will only a moment from now have done?

So turn to page 142.

Or turn to page 262.

Or turn to page 327.

Or turn elsewhere.

Or close the book.

After telling Charles that you are flattered, you apologize and decline. Even as he insists you do not need to apologize, you have begun to rise and take your leave.

The next day's hangover brings not only the usual headache and nausea but an acute sense of shame. It astounds you that you could have been so indiscrete. To tell him the secret. Now that he knows, word will spread. When you cross paths with Cynthia, later in the afternoon, you look away and pretend not to have seen her, then blush at your cowardice.

In the end, the encounter beside the pool is the closest you come to intimacy during your college years. As you explain to one of the guests at a wedding in the summer after graduation, however, you are ultimately content to have avoided the tedious rituals of modern dating. In another age—say, the Victorian era, or perhaps the Middle Ages in a small country village—you might have reveled in the polite rituals of formal courtship, but the blaring noise and flashing lights of today's nightclubs are not for you. Indeed, they are something you avoid at all costs. In any case, you are content with the choices you have made—eminently content—so contented, in fact, that you would have no trouble satisfying the test laid out in Nietzsche's doctrine of eternal recurrence, in the sense that you would not change a single one of the choices you have made in life even if you learned that you would have to repeat your life an infinite number of times. But you insist, quickly, before the new acquaintance can interject, that this embrace of course does not extend to the conditions that have been imposed upon your life from without, the things that you could not have chosen, the limits within which you and so many other untimely souls are forced to live today.

The rather stocky girl who stands before you nods her shaved head and asks whether you are finished. When you say that you are, the girl declares, to your immense surprise and delight, that she does not know where to begin disagreeing with you. First of all, the past you talk about in such positive terms was one in which women were sold as chattel, not only as prostitutes but as young women and girls to men in marriage, which, you interject in agreement, was primarily a means of transferring property until very recent times. Second, she continues before you can elaborate any further, you have misunderstood the doctrine of eternal recurrence. The whole point is that you must accept everything that has determined who you have become, and this must obviously include not only your personal choices but the world around you. In fact, you have missed the essence of Nietzsche's whole philosophy, which is about saying yes to everything, without reservation. You are so taken aback by the young woman's familiarity with Nietzsche, as though she may actually have read him at first hand, which you have not, that you hardly listen to her specific critiques, only nodding with a kind of quiet glee. You stop yourself from arguing long enough to ask the girl her name. Only then, when she tells you her name is April and you learn that she went to Fernwood, do the two of you realize you graduated in the same class. She says that you look very different with your beard. At the end of the reception, you exchange email addresses and promise to stay in touch.

It is not until your second year in graduate school, however, that April's path crosses yours again, when she is passing through upstate New York on her way back from seasonal work on an organic berry farm. As you drive to retrieve her from the bus station, you remain unfortunately preoccupied by the discussion that took place earlier in the day in the freshman writing seminar that you teach. You had been discussing a short story by Borges about a garden with bifurcating paths, and your words, as usual, felt like ticker-tape spooling from the mouth of a stock ticker and puddling at your feet. The students were incapable of attention. When you stopped your scribbling on the board and turned to them, you saw that one of the boys was sleeping with his head inclined over the seminar table, drool no doubt restrained only by the suction of his dormitary breath. What is the story about? you asked, and they stared at you with their glassy fishbowl eyes. You were about to call on one of them when the girl who cried in your office raised her hand and some words spilled from her mouth about the garden being the garden of Eden and it was because all of her readings were like this that you gave her a grade that made her cry. Biblical readings each and every one. You cut her off. Lobbing off her speech like the pruning of a bifurcating branch. Well let's try to deal with the story on its own terms, you said, before we bring in shall we say a more exogenous hermeneutic. I will state the question again. What is the story about on its own terms? Nothing more from her. Tereu tereu. The boy in the backward baseball cap looked at you sourly and began to speak. And that was when it all began to go wrong. You know what this story is like, he said. It's like one of those, you know, those books with the choices at the end of every few pages. You know. The others stirred in their seats and another provided the name, which you knew because you had come across references to such books in the wideranging course of your preparatory research. I hated those books. The classroom stirred like dry leaves in a gust of wind.

You could not resist so long as the cat was out of the bag, now scampering across the table, and that was your mistake, you think, turning at a stoplight near the eastern edge of campus. You had to share your own views. Well this is worth discussing, you said. Let's take a moment to discuss these types of children's books as long as the subject has been broached though I did not intend to do so. Because Mr. Borges' garden of forking paths is not exactly like one of those children's books do you know how. Do you know how? Think. Silence. It is because the garden of forking paths allows infinite choices whereas the sort of book you are describing does not. The garden of forking paths or rather as I said before of paths that bifurcate themselves offers a cornucopia of choices in every instant, in the true sense. It cannot be determined. A supplement remains in every strand in the sense that the garden of forking paths enacts a logic of the supplement as might be said and you cleared your throat, feeling yourself blushing already. Beyond your control. Whereas in the sort of children's book you are describing, if you will remember, you continued, if you read them, I did not read them, you will remember that there are only two choices or at most three or four. The sort of book that you are describing is a fundamentally conservative medium. It gives the illusion of choice, but in fact requires one to remain within its narrowly bounded, overdetermined system of possibility. It pretends to the title of freedom when in fact the essential choice has always already been made for you before the first word. All radical alterities have been effaced and the trace of their erasure has been at least attempted to be effaced as well. They egged you on with their blank white faces and against the flush that burned in your cheeks. If I were to take a more radical perspective, you continued, I might suggest that the sort of book you mentioned is like voting in a two-party so-called democratic system such as for example one might say our own. Even before entering the booth, it has already been decided that your vote for say an anarchist will not count. It will be counted but it will not count. The quote-unquote representative democracy says you are free to choose anyone this is a choose your own government adventure and so on but in fact you have precisely two choices. Always. And they are the same. Just as in the sort of children's book you are describing you are promised the ability to choose your own plot unlike those other books where the plot is chosen for you but in fact the plot is chosen for you here as well. And it is all the more insidious for being disguised as an act of what is called freedom. These books train us to accept the choices we are given, and not to say—I refuse, I refuse these choices—I demand an alternative—

As you think back on his insolence and the humiliation of having to listen to him it occurs to you that he must already know he will receive a grade of just enough to pass and he does not care. You stop at a red light near the top of the hill and think of his backward baseball cap, the infuriating stereotypicality of it all. But how else is it supposed to work? he said. Like, how could they put every choice in one of those books? Even the book in the story doesn't really have every—Yes it's a good question, you said quickly, and the answer is that there are such novels. They're called hypertext. A scribble. H-y-p-e-r-t-e-x-t. In a hypertext fiction, which can only exist in digital form, of course, such as in the form of say hyperlinks, every word for example might contain a link to perhaps another word in some other section of the hypertext work and one can move infinitely from word to word, link to link, section to section, never exhausting the possible paths insofar as we consider the path leading up to one's current position a part of the path. Two kinds of infinity. One after another and all at once without remainder. They would not have understood. The boy now fading back into his dim postprandial catatonia. But like why not just say that every book is like that? He shrugged. What do you mean, you said as the others now playing with their backpacks impatient dogs as the murmur in the hall outside and the gathering storm he said, If you really wanted to, you could read every book by like flipping through all the pages totally randomly. Or reading all the words in a random order or something. Someone else laughed. Or the letters, someone said. The boy was laughing too and said it's not like there are instructions telling you to read everything from left to right all the time. But I mean you'd still have to read one letter after another, so you could write down everything and make a normal book or whatever out of it anyway—so what's the point—And as you began to assemble your own papers with the babbling of voices continuing over your fingers you nodded curtly and regretted aloud that you did not have the time to present a more adequate defense of hypertext and the liberation of meaning and to cut the boy off root and branch. Exfoliated of words like branches in a fog of herbicide. The other students chattered and began to evacuate themselves in clumps out the doorway and into the clots of students in the halls. It plagues you of course it plagues you the boy's argument as you approach the bridge over one of the gorges and you try to think of anything else. Turning the steering wheel with the hand of yours that does not hold the last of the handrolled cigarette you steer across the bridge over the gorge and think of April and finally the opportunity to finally. To finally. Did the students know. No. They could not.

And then you pull up to the bus station and April with her suitcase on wheels and a few more pounds even more of a dirty hippie but that is not. Not an overwhelming reason not. The possibility to finally shed. Finally. If not now when. If not now never. So that in the small hot apartment under the heatpipes you drink another tumbler of scotch too quickly after the espresso and interrupt her as she is talking about the berry farmers to clarify that you had also been wanting to say that what you meant to say at the wedding was that many of your intellectual heroes had lived isolated lives and out of their solitude came a certain one might say sublimated awareness. Such as for example Henry James. You have such respect for Henry James. Indeed when Pythagoras speaks of the world in terms of a metamorphosis from mineral to vegetable to animal you would take the categories a step further and say mineral to vegetable to animal to Henry James. Each more subtly open to the world than what precedes it. More aware. A sort of hierarchy of the fineness of responses to stimuli with a rock at the bottom its only response being to break or not to break to erode or not to erode and then a cabbage in the middle say able to stretch over days toward the light to grow and wither and die and then Henry James at the apex who responded with such subtlety to the stimuli around him as to discern distinctions that were hitherto imperceptible or beyond the proven capacity of human expression. The artists are indeed the antennae of the race. Only yesterday you were paging through Caesar's memoirs and became struck by what a dull instrument he was in the sense that his observations were only the crudest and most insipid stuff imaginable whereas if an artist had experienced such extremities as for example the arrival in one of the dark places of the earth your antennae would have produced observations so much more acute and discriminating and less like the cracking of rock against rock—and she finally interrupts and asks you what you have done, if these things are so important. What have you made by giving up the other parts of life. And you finish your scotch and say you were not talking about yourself.

Then there are a few quiet hours, a walk along the trail above the gorge to watch the sunset, but mostly quiet hours before the two of you go to the party of a fellow graduate student whom you barely know. An imbecile. Soon at the party after the silent walk to the door and the effects of the caffeine have begun to dissipate you recline into an argument with one of the more obstinately misguided doctoral candidates who believes that the United States is a democracy and not a node of power in late capitalist empire that features occasional show elections, pageants. It is one of the favorite arguments of yours. The two of you exchange words. You exchange his words at a greatly devalued rate. You attempt, as you have often attempted at such parties, to show him the error of his ways, standing with the red plastic cup near the nonfunctioning fireplace though you realize long before the first syllable that your efforts will come to naught. You insist nevertheless that the votes of the vast majority of citizens in the United States are purchased not only through campaign advertisements but through an unending foregone machinery of indoctrination beginning even at birth and continuing through the daily reproduction of hegemony through the forcefeeding of conformist submissive schooling and so on. And he laughs and grins as though nothing but the most delightful of jokes. None of them understands your sincerity that you have seen the world in all of its repulsiveness and you reject it and it is wrong. Fundamentally, fundamentally wrong. You want a cigarette and should find April and in any case your red plastic cup is empty.

Perched on the porch balustrade or is it fence or balustrade and feeling the convex of your back slightly tensed you remove the thin silver case from your pocket and thumb the rolling paper from the clip, the pinch of tobacco, the roll, the lick, the final clipping of the scissors severing the stray tufts spilling from each end. You wonder who is a greater imbecile, the host of the party or the boy with whom you were speaking. The host of the party once attempted to defend Harold Bloom as a viable source of literary theory. The boy with whom you were speaking, on the other hand, once suggested that he might pursue a literary academic career in Pirate Studies. He claimed that pirates had been marginalized throughout the history of the study of literature, while in fact a generalized piracy was the very condition of possibility for the literary. Without pirates, in other words, no work of literature would be possible and the incervelate then accused you, in your denial of the presence of pirates in every work of literature, of participating in the silencing of the piratical. Was it not, he suggested, as though you were staring at a pirate flag perhaps through a telescope and denying that you saw a what a skull and crossbones? Perhaps it was because you were afraid of pirates, he continued, and who wouldn't be after having been raised in such a radically piratophobic culture as our own. But finally the day has dawned, like the settling of a vibrant multi-colored parakeet upon one's soldier, in which the word pirate can once again be spoken and need no longer remain hidden beneath the eyepatch of denial but can be hoisted up the mast of interpretation and bravely saluted. The eras of the New Criticism and Deconstruction, of course, suppressed the essentially piratical nature of their own readings, but now we are free to send them walking off the plank of institutionalization and into the sea of obsolescence. Furthermore, he continued, Derrida was a pirate. Did he not wear a patch upon one eye? Did he not? Could you deny it? You could, he waved you off, but only because you fail to understand in even the most basic sense what is meant by eyepatch. Pirate studies offers a veritable treasure chest of interpretation, and it will be his life's work to follow the map of pirate studies to the spot marked X, that is to say, the utmost pinnacle of academic success. He will become a professor and publish a book of piratical readings of canonical literary texts— perhaps beginning with Yeats' Among Schoolchildren? This book will provide a practical model to his steadily growing crew of academic disciples his shipmates his scallywags. They will of course want to perform their own piratical readings and teach their thousands upon thousands of students to do the same. They will filibuster the opposition to pirate studies they will fight until the opposition has no choice but to surrender. Then there will also be of course the synergies with intellectual property rights at the business and law schools which are by the way very well-funded intersections nowadays and of course they speak of piracy but they have not even begun to take a first swash, a first buckle at the question of what is piracy really, what is it really. And if you know what is good for you, he confided, you will find a spot on the pirate ship sooner rather than later. A rising tide lifts a boat. By then you knew that he was joking, at least in part, though it would not surprise you if he did in fact make a career of it. At some point in your response you used the word turbidity and out of petulance asked him if he knew what it meant, and he responded that he found the use of Latinate roots pretentious and effete. I use only Germanic and Greek roots he said and laughed and laughed and the other listeners by then laughed and laughers listened with him. You feel yourself blushing once again at the memory of the insult, unable to take comfort in its total absence of sense. Because he knew that in fact you did wish that you had been raised in the classical system, with as it were Greek from the age of two, as you had once said in a heated argument. Right right right a voice exiting the door sputters and destroys your thoughts. But how would you respond to Lacan. How would you respond to the Lacanian critique of that. You can see the student from India bobbing his head. He bobs his head in a way you have never seen anyone bob a head before and you do not understand because perhaps because it is a cultural code. Which lecture of Lacan's are you thinking of, he says, and the other responds that he means Lacanian in the sense of the displaced signifier. He clears his throat. You know, the collective reinscription of alterity as a kind of new statist imaginary, and so on. Wait, the other says, laughing. Did you say Lacan? Isn't that more of an Althusserian critique? The other responds that he meant ideology critique taken through Lacan, that's his main project, he forgot to say, he thought the other already knew, in other words overcoming the typical reduction of imaginaries to a reified self-presence. Ah, the Indian finally acknowledges, grinning. That's very interesting. Have you thought of that in the context of the decenterings that Derrida performs on Marx? Filled with revulsion, you step from the shadows and find April who whom who whom you have left alone for far too long. She says to you and you follow her to the drink table where there is then at the drink table a first-year pontificating about the attacks and the terrorists and the so on in a repugnant whining tone. The wads of language he excretes from his mouth and nose seem to pile at your ankles as you stand at the drink table and pour another red cup for April. The attacks were important because they showed that sometimes it is necessary to take sides he blathers and that economics is not the only driving force in history, as though this needed to be said after the last half-century and so on. You remember the first tower billowing smoke in four directions from the level where the plane slid inside of it and it reminds you of a smoker exhaling with an open jaw and teeth spreading all the way around his head. Because April is beside you listening to the filth you must finally interject beside yourself as well and spilling a bit of foam from the tip of the plastic cup to say that he has no idea what he is talking about because the World Trade Center, you say, was the symbolic and in some respects more than symbolic center of the fundamental economic structures responsible for the exploitation of the exploitation that made the power of the terrorists as you would say possible, and when I say symbolic center I don't of course mean either symbolic or center in any naïve sense, especially not in the sense of core and periphery, obviously, but even once we take into account the self-evident problems of invoking the rhetoric of let's say the rhetoric of symbols or even of allegory its employees no doubt instantiated much more suffering than they experienced when you consider spending every day of one's life picking through a dump a heap of rot and syringes in search of spare flecks of toxic metal to sell for a baby's food. Selling the metal for pennies a day in the hopes of obtaining enough food that your baby, who lives with you on the reeking toxic trashheap, will not die of starvation or a wholly preventable disease before its second birthday. One billion people in the world live on less than a dollar a day it is impossible to conceive one billion people and yet then yet you tell me I should cry and moan and gnash my teeth over the two or three thousand who died in a brief moment after a lifetime of luxuries gained from the exploitation of that billion as we all do every one of us in this room I find it absolutely revolting, you say. There is no difference between that day and every other day of the year except that the unendingly tortured billion had even less of a chance of appearing on the nightly news thanks to a few mangled skyscrapers. It should go without saying, you say, without even saying, that the terrorism in this picture if we are to identify any should be identified first and foremost with the biopower without reserve of the global disorder the day in and day out that it terrorizes the weakest and most miserable in the name of an empire which always already transcends nation and is beyond economic or ideological and those sick animals were the handmaidens of desolation, so good riddance. Good riddance. You take a long drink from your red plastic cup and your hand shakes and to your surprise it is April whose mouth opens first. Woah, with face red and yet smiling because it is all a joke to all of them, did you just call the victims of the attack sick animals? That's so fucked up. That's like the most fucked up thing I've ever heard. You take a deep breath and start to speak but she cuts you off. I think you need to get laid, she says. Isn't that what this is really about? The others laugh. The imbeciles are laughing and having the best of times now. Right, another says, I mean I can understand that not having sex would you know cause a lot of stress for a person, so that's okay. The others laughing now like horses with bits at the mouth and cutting into their cheeks. Your face turning red the heat within and do not say anything. Seriously, have you still never kissed anyone? she asks. Didn't you say you'd never had a first kiss? You do not speak. You knew that you would never be prepared. The moment you have feared. Exposed. If you lied, they would see it now in your face. Already reddened. Even the laughter has uncomfortably died, and as you say that you do not intend to discuss the details of your private life, it is clear. And now they know. That's just, I don't plan to discuss the details of my private life, you say. I'm sorry, April says and her face different now. That was.

She stops then. Even tries to reach out.

But the evisceration is done.

It is only a few hours then until April is put to bed on the couch and you go for a walk in the night in the nightwoods. She had said what she said and they had heard what she said. They would tell one another what they heard now. Hearing and telling and telling and hearing. What did they hear. They heard it and in your face they saw. What if you had said. This or that one thing or another. But you did not. And now the moment long passed. Should have ever. Did have never. Could have ever would have could. Nothing is possible. Nothing was forever possible. A puzzle this world. The water of the creek holding itself back in the shape of the rock where the rock is. The darkness of the treetops cut out from the starry sky. All fits together so effortlessly and without gaps. All the way up the trail. Not too large and not too small. No jutting around the edges. But not you. Always a something slightly out of place. Not fitting in. Not quite. A nub of the piece sticking out over the gap. A nub of the gap sticking out over the piece. When will it end. It will never end. It would have ended if it were going to. Too late now. All too late. Why did you tell her. Why did you speak. If only there were silence and no more words. Tired of speaking. Tired of thinking.

You walk up the trail and then you are tired of walking and you sit by the creek in the nightwoods. It babbles and babbles. Of course, there are a thousand reasons, you think. Your ultimate commitment to work. Those you admire. It is not that important to you and no great loss. But you cannot stand the thought of them knowing. Looking at you. That you must submit to the expectation. Liberate with one hand, tighten the vise with the other. You will not serve, you must serve. You will serve. You will be served, a head on a platter. The expectation. Again, again. How did it come to this. Ashley. Cynthia. They had all turned away. One after another they had turned away. And who would not. Look at you. One must not forget. The effect it has on a child. And the other children smell the hairs of blood threading in the water and they will feed, as only children. If only the age had not demanded. Now it cannot end. Even if it ended. The fact would remain. What they know. It is all too late. The creek babbles. A babel. If only you knew the words for such things. What trees are these, what rocks. Pines. In the pines. They. They. Stutter in the little wind. You are tired. The stuttering pines are tired. You botched it. You made a botch of it all. It is too late now but the sun is tired and the woods. Even this self-pity. Part of the botch. Yourself you lift from the dirt and palm yourself into a move up the hilly trail. The sun will not rise again. You rise and walk to the up of the hill the up of the who will but never did and hear the babble lower and lower from away. To only not to think would be the sun rising. You move up and decided is a bright suddenly but a sunly and surprise. A bright shining always strips through the muddy of your made was and now is without perhapses a light, a lightning, a lighted. Not to the least of your much surprise is its fingers of trees now whispering, now singing, as though the sun in their voices were a seashell under the gloom of all forestlines and everywhere. And it is only as you see the bridge that you know the last of the ifs have pine scattered away. This is the secret, you think, the not at all gloomy what before when. They must all feel this. It is a sunmelon, the relief of its ripe unhaving to further the weight, a rind of somehows peeled. They all must have tasted its sweet unmaking, this interior paramour. Did he too on the snowlight mountain. You calmly place your hands on the railing and cold with a breath, though metal a cloudbridge to everywhere, the great unlifting, up and forever stepping utterly young I threw a rock into the sea it skipped onetwothree in a little light like a rushlight alone a loan a long the

When you return to college, you look back on your delirium over the summer as a kind of gift. You have stared into the dilated eyes of reality and survived. Few people can say the same.

But your spiritual voyage brings with it unexpected consequences. Your classes now seem trivial. They do not expand your mind. The professors try to gorge you with knowledge, failing to see that the greatest wisdom cannot be contained in words.

In fact, the only member of the faculty who seems to understand the absurdity and insignificance of most of what passes for knowledge in academia is Professor Quain, the aging philosophical iconoclast. He mocks the efforts of academic philosophers to find the truth as though it were merely a matter of words and logic. One day you attend his lecture high on mescaline, and you experience a revelation while Quain discusses philosophers' failed attempts to solve the problem of free will.

All at once, you understand.

Now it is only a matter of writing it down. For that, you must persuade Quain to serve as your faculty advisor.

"I guess the best way to start," you begin, seated across from Quain at office hours, "would be asking..." You slowly rub your tongue across your gums. The pills you snorted have given you drymouth. "How... you think... a pragmatist like yourself, how one of you would respond to the claim that the freedom of the will... You know, how it... Like Thoreau said, you know—"

"Yes, of course," Quain interrupts. He speaks in the low, resigned warble that he employs to such deadpan comic effect in class. "I should have responded to your email. I think that would be a fine idea for a paper."

"Really?"

"Certainly."

His response is better than you could have imagined. "I'm—I'm flattered. You know, like I said, I'm only a sophomore."

"I suppose there aren't many sophomores," he murmurs, "who have read Heidegger."

You wave off his praise, leaning back in your chair. "I wouldn't say I've read him. I've looked at him."

"Well, you've found your way around the Heideggerese quite well." Quain's wide, sagging face remains largely immobile. He speaks for the most part as though trying not to move his lips, as though he were a ventriloquist for an invisible puppet. "I guess I've always figured that Being-as-such, Being spelled with a *y*, Being with the line drawn through it and so on, would have to be what makes our vocabularies possible. As you said, the structure of temporality, the groundless ground." His lips twist into a rare, surprisingly toothy smile. "I also enjoyed your analogy to the rowboat."

You smile appreciatively. But then it occurs to you that your email made no mention of a rowboat. Nor, now that you think about it, did it mention Heidegger. In fact, you did not send an email at all. Suddenly, your heart begins to race.

"I was once stationed in Germany," Quain continues, folding his hands across his belly. "I considered going to the Black Forest and threatening Heidegger—"

"I think there may have been some misunderstanding." You try to smile, to maintain the air of camaraderie. "I don't think I'm who you think I am."

Quain chortles. "Indeed."

"No, really. I really think you've got me confused with someone else."

"I suppose that would be the ultimate upshot of your argument," he grins indulgently. "But I think you've got Heidegger basically right."

"I'm really sorry, but I didn't write you about Heidegger. Or boating. I didn't send you an email."

He stares at you blankly for a few long moments. His face, when he is not smiling, resembles that of a demoralized pug. "So what can I help you with?"

For the next several minutes, you attempt to explain as clearly as possible what you perceived in your epiphany, how you would like to develop the idea into a paper, and why it might require a year or more of your remaining time in college.

"So I guess the best way to present my project, in a nutshell," you hurriedly conclude, nearly out of breath, "would be to say that I've found a solution to the problem of free will. And the solution," you say, leaning toward Quain, "is that the relation between the will and the material universe—*is ineffable.*"

You pause for a moment, allowing your words to sink in.

Quain leans back and rubs his eyes. "I guess when it comes to free will, I've always thought Hume was basically right. Sometimes we find it useful to speak in terms of intention. For example, in assigning responsibility for crimes. Other times we find it useful to speak in terms of neurons and so on... There's no reason to assume the two vocabularies have to fit together. You can say we have free will, or not—" He shrugs. "In James' terms, it's probably a difference that makes no difference."

You nod. "So will you sponsor my project?"

Quain sighs. "I guess I'm not being clear." After rubbing his eyes again, Quain continues. "From a pragmatist point of view, the problem of free will is a bad question. It's something we wouldn't be talking about if we were using a more productive vocabulary."

"So will you sponsor my project?"

"No."

"Let me try to explain again—"

While you speak, Quain grimaces and slowly removes his glasses, setting them on his desk. He rubs his eyes once more. Then he puts the glasses back on and stares at you. He frowns. None of your words persuade him. At the end of your third or fourth attempt, he reminds you that there are other students waiting in the hall.

When you return to your dorm room, you swallow several grams of mushrooms and begin filling out the forms to withdraw. From this moment on, you decide, you will not merely think the truth, but live it.

Your quest for a more ecstatic and penetrating mode of existence eventually leads you, through a long and winding path over several peripatetic years, to Telegraph Avenue in Berkeley. As you lope with bare foot about the sidewalks, you marvel at the wonder of all you witness. All around you is the unseen. The Way. This is your living now. This is your life.

It is the sunlight at your feet, guiding, stretching, kneading you. It is within all things, and all things are within it. Trodding the sunsopped shoulder of avenue, you permit the Way its inner pass. You are its channel. It binds you.

Even when you lost your bed at the Community, the week before, it was in accordance with the Way. You were assigned to be breadbaker. But the heat of the bread-oven resisted you. They let you stay on as doughmaker, but your sleep cycle turned a deafness to the alarms of the workaday world. Lidded and whorled, you would not be snared in the clock's deceptive yowl. They convened a meeting. "We must go at life with a broadax," you told them. "I just want to have bread with dinner," they said. You ferried your sleepsack to the hills above the city like any wandering saint.

Shod in the roughsoles of your feet, you hear the music of ascension in the carhorns. They grow yeasty. You open your eyes and see that you are standing in the middle of the intersection. How to bear witness to such tidings? You smile joyfully and perform a brief hoppingdance before returning on your way.

This is no fancy; this is proof of matters known.

Around you, the mothpeople continue their swarming. Beneath you, girding you, is a concrete within the concrete that supports. Of faith you have nothing, only of truth: you are dressed in an orange bathrobe given you by the Salvation Army of the City. You collect recyclables in a grocery cart. It withdrew itself from the Safeway when you grew hungry in the hills. Safeway, you think, tittering with buoyance. Safe is the Way. Wherever the Way finds itself, there is your surety, your fast.

Channeling the guidance of the sage-oneness, you approach a visiting friend who perches on the streetcorner. She studies a map, and you glide to a stop beside her, looking askance her shouldernook. The energy of the all rolls its folds in heavy slowness round you, in glimmer-hump, like the unguence of a silent whale.

"What the fuck is that *smell?*" she asks.

You laugh and clap your hands joyously. "Do not be frightened," you say, touching her shoulderskin with the lightness of calming windgrace. "I have seen that you are lost in the—"

But before your words can fulfill themselves, she startles, like a waterfowl firmly held. Her energy is shivering, like a wet squirrel that waterflings its fur, awful and arrogant with the frost-knowledge of the northern races.

"Aw, you smell like fucking *garbage*," she says. "Jesus *Christ*, you smell awful. *Jesus.*"

"Yes, that is my organic nature," you explain, but she has already withdrawn, waving a hand footloose before the face of her face. You can see that she resists the Way. Her life is a struggle, sometimes in accordance with the boll and blossom of eternal change, sometimes chaffing against its nick. In order to bid the one-pureness that it be merciful with her, you perform the three gestures of atonement on the sidewalk edge. You call the atonements Hurdy-Gurdy, Owl's Shank, and the Bauble of Fastness; you name them the Golden Bawd of Nonce, Sky-Ruck, and the Ever-Salty Lamb.

When you have finished, you take a moment to radiate peace. These unawakened souls, they think that fortune lies in the hands of some Godhead, for the which of whom all is to be sacrificed. They think themselves none more than autumn leaves, brittle and lucent in a passing wind. But the Way passes through all, thrice-enfolded, uniting in its evermost palm. It girds you. By anticipating and according with its quickness, you avert wrong decisions, escape misfortune, and guarantee your success.

Adjusting your vagina beneath your bathrobe, you go to buy a soda. If days are gods, then you plan to spend this god, like most others, collecting fallen angels. Steel, plastic, paper, glass, each in its own bucketbag of healing. Each slaughtered neath the scythe of technology.

Sext, None, Vespers: it is a proven fact that each molecule of water contains enough electricity to power a thousand suns. Who knows what the clouds love?

Perhaps you will see me today, you muse. If the two Ways mingle in the thatch of time's crossing. In the flaxen of its weft.

In the park, a friend of yours sits slumped on the straightbacked grasses, his head resting on a forearm, white-beard and scraggle. You trunculate your cart to a stop in the lawn, spitting on the handle to make sure no one hoists it. Your friend is Lonely Man, a filament of the every wonder. When on the herbaceous slope you recline, he senses you. "Do not be afraid," you say. "It is only my organic nature."

His slouchedback coil cries the One to you, and you respond.

"Ah…" you say.

"Ah…" you say loudly.

"Leave me alone."

"Yes, fresh one and wise. But a piece of advice first: however sweet they call you, learn power—"

"Leave me the fuck alone," he mutters. He raises his eyes, buckshot with blood-marvel, and they take you in like the snout of a wounded fawn. He fears the further attack, the muse's wangle. You see in him the sparks, smolder and thistle, of the sharded other. Then he mutters something that you can barely discern. He must be asking your name.

"My friends call me Denise," you say. Leaning toward his closeness, into the resonance of the Way, you recognize his organic nature. "And I will leave you in peace. Perhaps in more ways than you know. Only this: gather yourself each day in the goodness of morning. There lies—"

"I oughtta fucking stab you."

"Yes, it is when the close and the distant attempt to meet that violence is born. Such paths do not belong to the Way. Listen to your man-womb—"

Rising with dark words of thundercloud, the man retreats from you, and you gladly grant him lief. He minds you of another. Poor earthfather, shucked too soon from the cornstalk, strewn back into the harmonious Way before his shardsoul could mend...

But all sidewalks are not alike, you know, each has its spirit. This one is a wanderer from the planet Arcturus. His name is *Michel.* You float among them, grateful for their stone firmness, skimming them shod in your footskin. In this place lives no regret...

On the path to the café, you encounter a dog, a star-bearer. At first, its yelp befrightens you and you run askance, but then you welcome the wangled cur as a fragment of the pure being. In your orange bathrobe, you step athwart it with arms outstretched, an orange flag fluxom in the wind, until it bares its sharp teeth and howls to its utmost.

"I praise you, Vibrant One," you utter, enfolding your palms and head-bowed. A thousand-year spirit lives in the wet of his blackened gumcakes, a messenger of great stature in his knot-brown girth of fur. You too, thanks be the Way, are part and parcel of this innerfound being. But the farther you chase the dog, the farther it scurries on its hooves, and the more it rages fierce. Finally, it quivering crouches in a flower garden the better for you to thank it, bowing with your face to the soil, arms outstretched, knees enfangled. You open your mouth upon the pungent melonlike lawngrass, biting mouthful after mouth of freshmowed forage.

The Way speaks! Once they cast milfoil sticks, yellow stalk, to find the proper form. Later the tossing of silvers. You have discovered a higher and more universal form. It is the cracks in a sidewalk: the parallels of a front porch awning: two birds. Six bars they form. In this case, an auspice strong and good. You read the tidings all, day by day, the whisper woven into the fabric of the all-around. The frames of a window: three flowerpots: a passing stare: the movement of traffic. The bars of divination form and unform, break and unite.

You pull up a chair at your friends' table outside the café. It has been a bountiful day, well-regarded by the oxen. Now comes time for the sate of appetites, and the beckoning of lordly yield.

"It has been rather hot today," you say, subtly adjusting your loins. "I remain fitful and yeasty."

"Friend of yours?" laughs the earthman.

"Aw, he reeks like *shit*," his womanfriend speaks.

"It will be necessary for me to explain," you smile, "that what you sense is my organic nature. Please, friend, call me Denise."

The earthmanwoman eyes your swollen breasts, and you can see that her eyes are not hateful. The earthman straightens a bean-cap of knit. His dreadlocks shiver like rope dongs in the gurdywind.

"I'm sorry, man," he says. "But we're eating. And you haven't taken a shower in a while—"

"But—my organic nature—"

"I know, I know…" He leans toward you, confiding. "But she doesn't like it, and I think it'd be better if you go. Okay, Denise?" His eyes are melon-heavy, pregnant with milk meaning. "Please."

You nod as deep as moonwell. Then, calmly, you turn your shanks inward.

"I understand," you say. "Something ails her. She has fallen out of alignment with the Way."

The womanchild thrusts her plate out from her, stacked though it be with sandwichbread of sprouts and the dead flesh of sister hen. "Oh my *God*," she says. "It's like fucking *diarrhea*."

"Don't blame the sandwich," you say. The earthwoman then clarifies the nature of her complaint. "I see. But what you are eating, it too was once a living being and it lived in its own diarrhea. It was treated to horrors beyond what you or I may imagine. So say I, yes, it may be that there is an aura about me. But the sister of ours that you are now eating was unable to move between the other sisters and brothers in the pen, its beak sawed off so that it would not peck the others to death, perhaps unable to move its limpened legs, for the entire span of its brief, befouled life. Never seeing the spark of nature, of nature's light, can you imagine? Perhaps it is funny, in a way, to see such a one carried away and stunned with an electric prod. No longer able to move, but still able to feel the knives as they go to work on her body. Mutilating her while she remains aware of the knives at work in her. She was a living being, and now you are eating her. She fills your guts." Tears begin to sprout from your eyes. "How can you eat your family? Don't you feel—when you sink your teeth—she was tortured and made to suffer and die—don't you feel—"

Your voice chokes in the lusty salt-fountain. You know that you are falling out of accord with the Way. But they have failed to achieve their ascension so horribly, their failure mocks you and causes you simmersome anger. So many of them have so utterly failed. What shall become of them when the earth implodes? The boy tries to speak to you, but you do not listen, cannot. Their mouths and intestines are filled with dead animals. There will be a reckoning. One day there will be a reckoning.

As the wait staff approaches, you stumble away, your legs askew and dangling, knocking over the white plastic chair...

When you ordered the hormones from the distributor, you thought they would unveil your womanhood. But nor hormones nor therapy may disturb the Way. The woman must always contain her man, and the man his man-womb...

Later in the night, I pay you a visit. I come upon you cross-legged in the hills, meditating beneath the crooked shoulders of an elderly oak. The air here is salted with leather-nut and tang. You are watchful, elated by the thickness of oxygen that emanates from the tree's foliage. The exhalations of its sagging arms and leaves. Beneath a tree, there woman breathes true.

"Welcome, Denise," I say. I sit beside you, offering you a sprig of thyme in gesture of salutation. The sprig, unlike the faces of human beings, appears to be the perfect size for imagining. It fits into the small bowl of space in front of your eyes in the way that a horse, with or without wings, clearly could not. You hold the sprig beneath your nostrils and inhale its essence.

Then we speak the parley of angels, talk of things ascended. "Today I walked by the Beanery," I recount. "A boy in overalls was carving a stick, sitting at the foot of his earthmother. She wore eyeshades and talked with her friend while drinking fragrant coffee. But every so often, she would touch the boy's head with the palm of her hand."

"Was his hair flaxen?"

"Yes. And each time the boy's mother touched his head, he reached out and placed his hand on her leg. They must have performed this small ritual a cobbler's mouthful of times."

"This day is a god," you say. Then you tell me the story of the dog that scurried into the flowerbed. Around us, all is a mumbling of leaves, night-blue fruit hung from dark branches. You girdle yourself in the sway of it. Far below, the fire-fangled lights of the city dangle down. The sight of it nobbles you. It is a lifebrightener, the whole pie with jam in too.

As you continue the story, there is a swaying in the path below. A tremor echoes in your man-womb, as though under the force of some electromagnetic interference, but you continue. "I prostrated myself on the solid earthsoil," you say, "and let the bristles of grass bend and crook beneath me. As my wind passed, I tasted the whey of the universe. It was not curdled."

We sit in silence, herders of the city lights. As shadows approach, we are husbandmen of hill and dale. The salty air tickles your ears like the wimple of some old nun.

"Was the dog silent in the flowers?" I ask.

"No, he kept on. I washed myself in the sound of him. It was an ablution fit for some ravening king."

One of the newly come earthmen laughs.

"The sound of the dog kept me company like a pocketmouse that nibbles at the finger," you continue. "The comfort of such a one—"

"Who the fuck are you talking to?" one of them asks. He is visible now, staggering.

You turn and see that I have gone away.

"Noman," you say, not looking toward the self-heralding guests.

The earthman staggers and then rights himself. His friends hold back in the shadows, and one of them laughs the laugh uncertain. "Just talking to yourself, up in the hills," he says. "What if I take a seat? I'm gonna take a seat."

He is sitting beside you, nursing the ambrosial bottle. One of his friends tries to move them onward, but the earthman does not wish to depart. "I want to talk to my buddy here. Take a load off. You know what, buddy?" he turns to you. "You smell like fucking *dogshit*." He leans close to you. "Did you know that?"

"I ask only to sit in peace," you say.

The dogsbodies are now ashuffle at the shoulder of the trail. You do not look at them. You look out over the lights that twinkle like a sea of phosphor.

"Let's go, man," one of them says.

"No, I want to find out why this cocknob smells like dogshit. Why don't you take a fucking shower? Oh *my fucking God*." Out of the corner of your eye, you see the earthman recoil from you. "What the fuck."

"What is it?" asks one of the friends.

"He's got fucking tits." The man pounds the earth with his fist and snorts. He springs to his feet. "What the *fuck*." He tells the others to look inside your bathrobe, but you pull it tight round you. "They're fucking *hairy*," he groans. "He's got hairy fucking *tits*." He stomps his foot, and the others laugh at his stomping. "What the *fuck*." He begins to cough with great violence, and hawks the phlegm out from his throat. But the others say that they do not believe him. "Show them your tits," he says, "you fucking faggot. Show them your tits."

You tighten the robe about you and coil your crouch. But they rip the robecloth asunder and laugh as you try to cover your chest with your hands. Scrambling, you chase after the robe, but they toss it away into the bushes far across the path. When you try to run to seize it, a force swings you to the ground with the suddenness of a reversal of the earth on its axis. A kneebone cracks. You writhe in the dirt and they take turns stomping and hammering on your flesh until a chestbone breaks. You cry out to them in the higher tongue, but they cannot hear. They beat you until you are long past silent. Then one crouches above you and a liquid splatters on your neck and face.

Then they are gone. The night continues to howl between your ears and in the skin and bones of your broken body. You lie in the dirt and groan, unable to open your eyes, a knife of splintered bonematter inside you, stabbing the lungs with each breath.

It is colder. You hear the distant sound of a firetruck in the city far below. There is a hollow, stabbing hiss in your ear and you feel as though you are asphyxiating. The cuts in your face sting and crust. You wait for the pain to stop and tell yourself that it is not real. But you know that it is. The pain is the only thing that is real. With short breaths, you curl into a ball and wait.

When you open your eyes, you see that your hand has fallen on one of Ida's diet soft drinks. It is laughable. Even your attempts at randomness—at willing something unwilled—somehow misfire. An idea from an old philosopher comes to mind. An image of particles falling through space and swerving sometimes on undetermined courses to collide with one another. Without these swerves, nothing would ever have been created, because all the particles in the universe would have fallen through space endlessly without ever touching.

"You okay?" J.P. asks.

"Yeah." You close the refrigerator. "I'm not going to North Carolina."

"Oh?"

"We broke up." You look at J.P.

"Sorry to hear that," he says.

You wait for him to share some words of consolation or wisdom. But he only nods and returns to reading the paper.

Later that night, after a few hours of wondering what you could have done differently, your anguish breaks like a fever and you start to laugh. Of course she had broken up with you. Of course all the others had rejected you as well. From the start, you have refused to accept a few obvious truths. About women. About men. It is time for you to grow up.

Love is a game, and like any other game, it has its rules. What had ever made you think that picking up girls should require no practice, no training, no skills? What had made you think that such a complicated endeavour would come naturally to you, without effort, when this has been true of so little in your life? Perhaps some men can get by on their natural gifts and physical appeal. You are not one of these men. As in so many other parts of your life, you will have to employ cunning.

With these thoughts in mind, when you return to campus for the start of your final semester, you quickly devour a book about how to pick up girls based on a challenging but structurally simple and field-tested five-step system. The book is directed toward young men who are just like you, the kind of clueless romantic who spends years obsessing over one girl, attempting to win her over through niceness, but in the end only succeeds in becoming her friend. It pains you to see your recurring romantic devastations, which seemed so mysterious and full of elusive meaning at the time, presented as the predictable result of common tactical errors. The book even describes a pathetic figure who—like you with Margaret—worships a girl but does nothing while more aggressive men repeatedly use and discard her.

On your first two attempts to practice the system at parties on campus, you get no results. But the book warned in advance that this would probably happen. Success is not guaranteed on any individual occasion, but in the aggregate. Seduction is a numbers game. After each failure, you follow the book's advice and write down your approaches in a list so that you can maintain quality control, improve your performance, and keep score. Then, at the third party, while you are waiting for your wingman to arrive, you spot a clutch of girls with red plastic cups standing on the corner of a crowded porch. One of them is looking at you. When you return her gaze and hold it, as the book instructed, she laughs and whispers something to one of her girlfriends. You approach.

"Hey, they did a survey in my psych class, and I want to hear what you girls think." Instead of leaning toward her, you wait for her to lean toward you.

"What?" the girl yells. "I can't hear you."

"That's alright," you yell back. "Maybe I'll let you make it up to me."

"What?" she says.

"I said, maybe—"

"Do I know you?" she asks. Then she hiccups. "Uh-oh. I have the hiccups."

You stand with your legs spaced wide and your chest out and you gaze at her. Your collar is popped. Your hair is gelled. Actually, she does look familiar. You try to remember how you know her.

"Do you want to dance?" she yells. "Come on, let's dance."

As she pulls you by the hand to the dance floor, you smile again. She is wearing a slutty short skirt. She has probably been drinking for hours. She is perfect. While you grind together under the blinking lights, you begin to plot out your next move. Some of the steps in the seduction manual no longer seem applicable. For example, it is too late for you to charm her friends, and there seems to be little point in offering to read the fate line in her palm. Maybe you should try negging her.

"Nice hiccups," you shout into her ear. "Do you think that's sexy?"

"What?" she yells.

"I said do you think—"

"I can't hear you!" she hollers. "I can't hear you!" She laughs and continues dancing, hopping back and forth from one foot to the other and waving her arms in the air. A few moments later, as though responding to some unseen hypnotist's cue, her expression suddenly changes. She stares at you and then with eyes half-closed begins to move her face toward yours. The two of you engage in a long, wet, misaligned kiss that never seems to get straightened (or dried) out. You wipe your mouth. It is time to proceed to the next step.

"Do you want—" you begin. "I was thinking, maybe—"

"Come with me to my dorm!" she yells.

On the way there, the two of you stop, now and then, to kiss on the sidewalk. When you reach her dorm room, she ties a bright pink scrunchie on the doorknob, locks the door and begins to unbuckle your belt.

"Want me to go down?" she asks.

You look at her. "Yeah," you say.

For a few minutes, you hold the girl's long blonde hair while her head rocks back and forth. She is so lovely, you think, so precious. She is all that you have missed since losing Margaret. Nothing in the world matters as much as this moment.

Then you finish, catch your breath, and find that you have lost interest. Even as you reach for your pants, your mind involuntarily turns toward considering the best route back to your car.

"Did you enjoy that?" she smiles.

"Yeah." You pat her shoulder. "Hey, do you know if the weekend shuttle is still running?"

So begins your new life. Over the next couple months, as you test and refine your skills, it soon becomes clear that none of the canned pick-up lines and tactile "kino" moves are even necessary. The only thing that matters is confidence. Romance is a confidence game, and the secret to unlimited confidence, at least in your case, is not caring what any of the girls think.

It is best, you find, to approach them as though they have no inner life at all, no thoughts or judgments. Because a girl's true thoughts are an inner secret that cannot be confidently known, wondering about those thoughts leads to uncertainty, which inevitably reveals itself as weakness, which is a turn-off. All your years of worrying about what girls were thinking about you—whether they liked you or disliked you, what you could do to make them like you more—could not have been more misguided. It is far better, you realize, to think of a girl's head as an empty tank with maybe a few cotton balls tumbling around inside.

The only thing within a girl that matters is her desire. Her lust. And strength flicks the switch. Power turns it on. Perhaps a girl would deny this if asked in words. Perhaps she would insist that she wants to be with a good or nice man. Perhaps she denies the truth even to herself. But words and thoughts have nothing to do with sexual craving. The gears of lust were set in place long ago, when primitive man roamed the African plains, before language became the subtle distraction and obstacle it is today. Science has proven that women are genetically conditioned to be attracted to strong and powerful men, because these men could protect women and their offspring in earlier times.

Deep down it is all so simple. The girls smell your fresh-scented bodywash and your cologne. They see the suntan. The smile. The walk. The gaze. The biceps and the pecs you've been working on so hard. They want to be held and protected in your bulging arms. Your strength justifies their obedience. It makes them feel safe.

The weekend before graduation, you meet up with an old gaming friend from your freshman dorm. As far as you know, he has hooked up only once in college, and soon he will be joining a tech start-up where there will probably be even fewer prospects. You want to help him.

"Have you ever noticed," you ask, swirling the rum in your glass, "how much smaller women are than men? And I don't just mean their brains. I mean physical mass. I was walking through the quad the other day and it struck me. All around, couples going from place to place, and in all of them, the man was taller than the woman. It was like watching a nature program. Like something about birds. The large male of the species standing up with his vibrant plumage, and beside him the diminutive female. Dull feathers, grazing and clucking. How could I not have noticed before, I asked myself." You lean against the kitchen counter and take a long sip. "Or think about this. Why do women need separate sports leagues? It's because if they had to compete against men, they would lose. That's why women's sports exist. But no one talks about it. Men are stronger, bigger, faster. More muscles, larger brains. How many of your best professors have been women?"

Your friend, sitting on the couch in the living room, looks up from his laptop. "I don't know. There were, like, no women in my department. That's why it sucked doing computer science."

"But there was that Indian girl," you say. "Didn't you hook up with her?"

"She let me touch her boob."

It takes you a moment to register his words. "Did you say 'boob'?"

He shrugs again and continues to stare at his laptop.

"Almost all the female professors I've had have been disappointments. Frizzy hair, nervous tics, insecurities. They can't string together a clear argument for the life of them. Like Gyatri Spivak. Did you see when she came to campus?"

"Who's Gyatri Spivak?"

"Nobody. Some cunt. Anyway, I went to her lecture because someone told me it was the kind of philosophy they study in English departments. Do you know what she said? She said—and I'm not making this up—she said you couldn't ask her for definitions of the words she was using, because that's not 'what she does.' Offering definitions is not what she does." You wave your hands beside your head. "Can you believe that? Or think about this. Who is it that cries? Women and babies. Would you rather hire someone who has to train themselves not to act like a baby under pressure, or someone who's going to thrive in that situation?"

"You sound like such a asshole."

"Sure, and maybe men are supposed to be assholes. And maybe most want to be treated like dogs." You pause. "Or maybe that's going too far. I don't know. I'm not a scientist."

He stares at you uncertainly.

"Seriously," you go on. "I look back at all the conversations I've had with girls, even really smart ones, and none of them have been like the arguments we have. They're just not precise. Or they won't listen. They're crazy. Like Margaret. She would never listen." You pour yourself another rum. "It's no wonder that so many men end up beating their wives, right? But that's not even the point. The point is bigger. It's like, in this world, you're either a wolf, or you're a sheep. You're either the one doing the eating, or you're getting eaten. Which one do you want to be?"

"I can't tell if you're joking."

"I know you can't. That's the whole point. That's your issue." You settle into the couch beside him and watch as he scrolls through a list of song titles on a pirated music site. "You gotta understand. Girls don't want to be free. They don't want to be treated like they're rational. They're like the mentally ill. Forcing them to be responsible would be like a punishment. They need to be relieved of responsibility by a strong, protective force. A man."

"You're such a misogynist."

"But what if it's not just me? What if reality is misogynistic?"

As the sound of your voice fades from the room, your friend shifts on the couch uncomfortably. You rarely saw him over the last few months. It is clear that he is not ready to accept what you have learned.

"When was the last time you kissed a girl?" you ask.

"Dude," he says. "Shut up." He looks away. Because you feel sorry for him, you change the subject.

After graduation, you find a position at the university's admissions office. The whole world is your garden now. All of life is a hunt. Flirting with the secretaries at the office, flirting with strangers in line at the grocery store, flirting in bars and clubs on the weekend. Few of the girls you meet have what you would consider a beautiful face, but enough of them have thin, tanned bodies. Long legs. Hips that you can hold and roll. You make a spreadsheet, a catalogue of different physical appearances and bodily acts. There are still countless rejections, but you no longer pay them any mind. After so many years of humiliation and regret, it is fun to treat girls like toys, playing with them and seeing whether they will do what you want.

When you start to get bored, you compensate by presenting yourself with challenges. You seek to intensify your experiences, drawing inspiration from burgeoning world of online pornography. One night you go to a small party at a frat house beside the artificial lake on campus and go back to a freshman's dorm room. It offends you that she thought at first that you were also a freshman, so you decide to play it a little rough.

"I'm going to make you beg me," you whisper with a wicked grin, running your hand along her thigh. You notice the plastic retainer sitting on a bookshelf beside her bed. "Take your shirt off." Sitting up on your knees, you start to remove your belt.

"Excuse me?" She lets out a sharp, nervous laugh.

"You heard me."

Soon, her laughter stops, and she plays along without too much coaxing. The two of you finish the night in the lukewarm water of a bathtub in the spacious handicapped restroom at the end of her hall. Thinking of an article you read in a literary magazine, you push her head underwater in the final moments. But she thrashes around so much that you lose concentration and have to let go.

"President Kennedy used to do it all the time," you explain while she pulls on her clothes. "The President of the United States. He'd do it in the White House with his prostitutes—"

"Get the fuck away from me," she says. "You fucking freak."

"Look," you reply calmly. "I let you act like the little slut that you are. And you enjoyed it—"

But by then the door is already slamming behind her. You pull off your condom and toss it on the tiles as the sound of her flip-flops recedes down the hall.

You do not like to end a night in rejection. Rather than finishing yourself off, you decide to see if another party across campus has died yet. If no one takes the bait there, you can always take the plunge and dial up one of the pretty faces in the classifieds.

The next morning, you awake to find a girl snoring quietly beside you in an unfamiliar bed. Instantly, you curse yourself for having fallen asleep in her room. Even worse, she begins to stir before you can extricate your body from the tangled sheets.

"What time is it?" she yawns.

You do not look at her. "I think I should be getting some breakfast," you say. Your hand stops. It was not what you intended to say.

"Oh, let me get dressed," she murmurs. "I'll come."

You study the girl as she sits up and rubs her eyes. She has small breasts, a narrow, rather horsey face and large teeth. You cannot remember her name. "Could you make it quick?" you ask.

On the long walk from her dormitory to the closest brunch spot, she frowns and speaks in commonplaces. You let your mind wander. Sometimes an image of the girl in the bathtub comes to you. It was a step too far. But you ignore your shame. No one ever looks back on life and wishes they had spent more time regretting.

At the restaurant, the girl continues to babble on and on about something that happened at her sorority, and what her friend said about her other friend, and how her third friend said something else. It occurs to you that despite your experiences over the previous months, you have never questioned that every human being is a unique individual and contains something of value. Listening to this girl, you begin to have your doubts.

"What is *hollandaise* sauce?" the girl drones, staring at the menu. "Do you think that has *eggs* in it?" Then she is silent again for some time, hunched over in her chair. When the waiter has brought her fresh-squeezed orange juice, she smiles to herself and mutters, "I was so *drunk* last night…"

"Let me ask you something," you interrupt. "What do you enjoy doing? I'm curious."

"What do you mean?"

"What do you like to do? What interests you? For example, do you have any hobbies?"

"I don't *know*. What do you mean? Like, hanging out?" It is as though she has to overcome a time lag in speaking, as though the two of you were communicating by telephone from different points in space.

"Other than parties. What is it that has meaning for you?"

"You mean, like, *school*?"

"School, or what you'd like to do with your life. What do you plan to do when you graduate?"

"I don't know…" She glances uncomfortably in the direction where the waiter disappeared. "I'm only a sophomore… God, I should have ordered that omelet. I can't believe you made me order the eggs benedict."

"I didn't make you do anything."

"God. I want an omelet."

"I know we only met last night," you continue, "but there's something about you that I find fascinating. I want to know what makes you tick. When was the last time you were angry? For example."

"Oh my God, I get angry all the time. Like at Amanda."

"I really have no idea who you're talking about. Tell me, what do you do when you're angry?"

"I don't know." She laughs a low, guttural laugh, then coughs. "I yell. Why are you asking? It's like you're a…"

You wait.

"It's like you're a…"

She stops and sips from her orange juice, then looks slowly around the café.

"A what? An interviewer? A police interrogator? A psychologist?"

She sips her orange juice through a straw. "Uhn-uh," she says.

You resist the urge to glance at your watch, and instead maintain unbroken eye-contact with the girl, prepared to record any reaction that might suggest there is something going on beneath her surface. "Like I said, you interest me," you continue. "I'll be totally honest. I'm just trying to figure you out." You lean toward her, extending a hand as if to clear the air between the two of you. "Everyone is unique. What do you do that makes you different from the other girls in your sorority? Because I know there must be something. Many things. I just want you to tell me what one of those things is."

"Are you always like this?"

"No. Honestly. Just with you."

This time, she takes a long moment. She even clenches her brow. When she has finished, she returns her focus and says, "I kept a diary when I was in second grade."

"Go on."

She squints at you. "I wrote in it every day until I was a junior in high school."

"And?"

She looks away, as though thinking, and then looks back to you. "You go to a lot of undergrad parties, don't you?" she asks.

"Sometimes. Not really."

"I always see you there." She starts to laugh. "Kara said you're like that guy in the movie who's at his friend's house, and there's a party in the basement. Everyone's in, like, fifth grade. And you're like that guy..." Her voice dissolves into quiet laughter. She steadies herself with an arm on the table. "Oh God, I'm going to pee. She said you're like that guy who gets all dressed up and stands by the punchbowl and flirts with the guy's mom. You know. Have you ever seen that movie?"

You make no response, leaning back to take a sip from your water.

"Oh God, what did you just do to your back?"

"I don't know what you're talking about."

"Something just happened. It's like—I don't know—it just bunched up."

You stare at her coldly.

It occurs to you, as you take the bus back to your apartment, that you have spent the last several months of your life in the company of girls like this one. In fact, they have been the overwhelming concern and focus of your life. But their worlds are so small, so limited. Even their language is limited. You worry that your own world might shrink to the size of theirs if you continue to dedicate your thoughts to them. You would stand before a sunset and say, "That's beautiful." And you would mean that it was beautiful. And this is what you would feel, and there would be nothing more. Your capacity to experience would collapse into a minute switchboard of possible reactions. Beautiful, ugly. Great, stupid. Sucks, cool.

Then you remember the girl in the bathtub again and the shame returns.

What has become of your life?

Back in your apartment, you stare at the shelf of philosophy books you intended to read after graduation. A year has passed and you have not opened any of them. The thought of spending the rest of your life in pursuit of one-night stands suddenly makes you ill. None of these girls enrich you.

Not since April, in high school, has a girl drawn you up short in an argument. Sometimes she would even make you change your mind.

You wonder where she is now. You heard that she left the country after graduating. Studying in Russia, her parents said. To your surprise, when you drop her a quick email asking where she is and what she is doing, she responds almost immediately. She has just returned from St. Petersburg and needs a place to stay in the Bay Area. You invite her to stay at your apartment.

"Literally, every time I stepped onto Nevsky Prospect, someone would pinch me," she tells you. The two of you share a blender of margaritas at your kitchen table. "And it was only me! All the other women they left alone. I think they all thought I was a prostitute."

"So that's why you shaved your head?"

"Sure. What kind of prostitute has a shaved head?"

You laugh and then realize that it is the first time in months that you have laughed at a girl's words sincerely.

"You look different too," she grins. "Have you been working out?"

"A little."

"And—tanning?" She laughs, but you do not take offense.

"Hey, it's what the ladies like."

"The ladies?"

You wink at her and laugh.

It is strange talking to a girl who knew you in high school. It reminds you of how much you have changed. Now your perception of April flits back and forth like one of those pictures that can be seen either as a duck or a rabbit, but never both at once. As soon as you start to pay attention to her words, the curves of her breasts and hips pull your thoughts back to their usual course. But as soon as you think of her as an object, her words turn your attention back to her feelings and thoughts. There is no state of equilibrium.

"I'm so glad you came," you say. "I really feel like just in the last year, I finally grew up. I learned—you know, I changed my mind about so many things." For a moment you try to stop yourself. But you cannot resist. "You know, I love women. I always have. I spend all my time with women. But I did it all wrong for so many years, and it was because I believed in a lie. We were raised to believe in a lie, you know?"

April grins and takes a drink. "What do you mean?"

"Like, I was raised to believe there are no differences between men and women. It's not true. Men are one way, and women are another—and most of the time, the difference ends up being what everyone thought it was. And it's not like I had some misogynist preconception, and I shaped everything to fit it. Every step of the way it's been a surprise."

"Are you saying you're a misogynist?"

"If it's misogynist to believe that most girls are crazy and most guys are assholes—then yeah, I'm a misogynist. So what?"

April peers at you uncertainly. "You don't really mean that."

"It's like, women cry more. And I think it's fair game to ask if someone who cries all the time is a good fit for being a leader."

"I still can't tell whether you're being serious."

"Look," you say, pausing to swallow the last of your margarita. "There are differences. Evolutionary differences—"

The two of you stop and look at each other. Then you both laugh.

"Don't get me wrong. I love women. I guess what I'm saying—all I'm saying is I agree with the radical feminists, you know? Underneath the surface of everything there's this violence that no one talks about. No one even sees it, because we live inside of it."

April looks at you. "You believe that?"

"I didn't have any idea before the last year and a half. Because it's not on TV. We live in such a politically correct world, you'd never have any idea what goes on behind closed doors at the frat houses. And everywhere. What ordinary guys do to girls every day. All this degrading shit. What they get away with." You shrug. "Even what girls enjoy, you know?"

April is silent. She shakes her head. "I can't believe—"

"The part that surprised me the most," you continue. "Just let me say this one last thing—the part that surprised me the most is how much of the time girls go along with it." You lean back in your chair. "I have as much respect for women as I have for men. But desire has its own plans. And they aren't pretty."

"I don't think that's true," she says.

Later at night, after April has made her bed on the couch, you drift toward sleep thinking of how much you have enjoyed her company. She is so unlike the others.

Then you hear a quiet knock at your door. It opens, pouring light in from the hallway. April says that she could not sleep. She asks if she can sleep in your bed.

"Okay," you say. "Sure." You lean back and close your eyes, listening as she quietly slides between the sheets beside you. You remember the few times you slept with her in high school, and how clumsy you were. As she breathes quietly in the bed beside you, you instinctively turn and rest a hand on her cheek. But as you begin to kiss her, you feel nervous, just like you used to feel in high school. It has been so long since you have felt any fear, you no longer know how to respond. You pull her onto her side and kiss her harder. Then you start to fumble with the back of her bra.

Something is wrong.

Eventually, she reaches down and touches you. It is humiliating.

"We don't have to..."

"I want to," you say.

After she has stroked you for a while, she places a hand on the side of your face. "It's okay," she whispers. "We don't have to do anything."

You shake your head. "It's not okay."

"Here. Let's play a game." She leans back and whispers. "Imagine I'm one of them."

"Who?"

"One of the girls."

You stare at her.

"Treat me like you treat them," she says.

You take a deep breath and sit up. After a moment, you remember. It does not matter what she thinks.

You raise your arm.

If you strike April, turn to page 306.

If you do not, turn to page 155.

You lower your hand and lean onto the pillow. Then you run your fingers across the furry bristles on her scalp. "I don't want to treat you like I treat them. I care about you, April." You smile at her. "I've always cared about you."

April smiles and kisses your cheek.

"Is it alright if we take things slow?" you ask.

There is something liberating in having exposed yourself to her. You no longer need to pretend. You can just be yourself.

When you wake the next morning, you are filled with a strange, joyful lightness. You spend a few moments watching April's face resting peacefully on the pillow beside you. In the soft light of morning, the trim fuzz of her hair, her pale, glowing skin—she is so precious. You stroke her cheek with the back of your fingers. "So this is what they meant," you laugh to yourself. "This is what all the songs were about."

Soon enough, you invite her to stay. She tells you that an uncle of hers owns an apartment in Paris that he rarely uses. He has always maintained an open invitation, saying that she could stay there if she wanted to spend a few months on the Continent. After some research into living expenses, you calculate that by living frugally the two of you could support yourselves for at least nine months.

"I could finally write that screenplay," you tell April. "The one I mentioned."

"What did you say it was about?"

"Philosophy. I've always wanted to recreate the philosophical dialogue for the modern age. And now I'll be able to do so in the city that has produced more great American writers than any other." You seize April's hands and kiss them. "The literary capital of the world. The city of lights. The boat city. Paris."

In early July, after touching down at Charles de Gaulle, you make your way almost immediately to an esteemed café on the Left Bank. Installing yourselves at a small table in the middle of the boisterous crowd, you order two large pots of hot chocolate.

"It comes in clay pots here," you note. "It's supposed to be very famous."

"It better be."

"How expensive was it again?"

"Sixty francs."

"Well, that's only about..." You quickly do the calculation. "Ten dollars each." You clear your throat and brush something away from your face. "You know, I was thinking of French feminism on the ride over here. I don't think we've ever discussed it. But I really believe the French are on to something. In effect, they've always understood that—"

"I'm sorry," April yawns, "this jetlag is killing me."

"Ah, the jetlag hasn't announced itself to me yet, as the French would say." You chuckle. Just then, the white-aproned waiter arrives and meticulously pours your hot chocolate from its clay pot into small, porcelain cups. While he sets the pot gently back into its saucer, you take up your question again. "What do you think? Do you agree that French feminism is, in its exceptional way, superior to the American variety? Or no?"

"I don't know," April shrugs. "I had a friend one time who worked at a French embassy. She said that people assumed she was a lesbian because she took her work home."

You nod, contemplatively, and take a sip from your hot chocolate. "You know what we should do? We should ask some of the French people at this café what they think." Slowly, you lean toward one of the tables to your side and await a polite moment to interrupt their conversation. But it turns out that the guests at the table are Americans. As you turn your attention to the other tables within earshot, you are surprised to find that all of them appear to be occupied by foreigners.

"That's odd," you whisper to April. "It sounds as if there are only Americans and Australians at this café."

"Probably tourists."

"But I think Sartre used to work here."

"You mean, as a waiter?"

"No," you laugh, shaking your head. "No, presumably when he was doing public readings. The guidebook wasn't clear." You lift the small handle of the cup between two fingers and swallow the hot chocolate in a single gesture. It is clear that April will need time to adjust.

Soon, the two of you have settled into a daily routine. In the mornings, before April wakes, you write. From a stationary store near your apartment, you have purchased several stacks of oversized notecards, and you arrange them on your desk beside a large, glossy book that explains the secrets of effective screenwriting. Sometimes, you have an idea for a philosophical dialogue, and then you record it on one of the notecards. At other times, you organize the cards that you have already written. Often, you lean back in your chair and stare out the window over the rooftops of Paris. The apartment rests atop a stately old mansion in the Marais, in an attic with a sloping ceiling and uneven floors.

April, for her part, waitresses at the Hard Rock Café. It frustrates you that she has decided to work at such a typically American establishment while the two of you are living in Paris. But she insists that she needs the money, because she lacks the savings that you accumulated while working at the admissions office. Usually, she begins her shifts in the afternoon and must stay until the restaurant closes in the early hours of the morning.

"Do you ever get tired," you ask her, "of spending so much time with Americans?"

"Well, I have to work."

"Do you? Really?"

"Unless you want to pay for all our food."

"I guess you do, then," you murmur. "But wouldn't it be nice if we had more French friends?"

Though April agrees, she seems to make no effort to find a more suitable job. Instead, she spends her mornings interrupting your work with pointless chit-chat. Puttering around the apartment, she attempts to cook and talks about her problems at work. The final straw comes when she begins to complain about your smoking.

"No, I can't smoke on the balcony," you explain, "because my notecards are in here. This is my workplace. You seem not to appreciate this, but I have a workplace. That's why I get up every morning, make myself a pot of espresso and force myself to sit at this desk for three hours. That's why I spend every morning trying to come up with a few true sentences. Do you realize how difficult it is to find even one true sentence when someone is continually interrupting you? Have you ever tried to come up with a true sentence while someone was snoring? Have you?"

"I just don't think—"

"Have you?"

"I just don't think it's healthy for me to be around so much smoke."

"Well, I can think of a lot of things that aren't healthy for you, and I don't bother you about them."

When April continues to talk, you are finally driven to stride toward her and deliver the slap that you withheld on the first night of your renewed acquaintance. But she ducks at the last moment and your hand catches nothing but air.

"Get out," she says.

"Very well," you say.

You dress yourself quickly and storm from the apartment, slamming the door behind you. On the sidewalk below, still fuming, you nearly run into an enormous billboard advertising a French fast food hamburger chain. It features a cartoon character who appears to be made of feces. "How appropriate," you think in English, "how deliciously appropriate." Then you murmur to yourself in French, continuing down the street. "Whore, whore, whore. Oh, species of whore! That you sometimes make me shit."

Because you need to walk off your anger if you hope to write anything further, you take the metro to a park you recently discovered in the Latin Quarter. The harmonious proportions of its crisply pruned chestnut trees are particularly pleasing to your eye. You feel as though nature itself is speaking to you in the park's geometric landscaping and cube-shaped shrubs. These rational forms, you think, they are as pure and beautiful as a baroque cantata, or the metric system.

Then you remember that there is a small museum at the corner of the park. It is currently showing an exhibition of the sketches of Joan Miró. You are somewhat unfamiliar with her body of work. But because you like the idea of visiting a museum and looking at its paintings on an empty stomach, like a starving artist who requires only beauty as sustenance, you make your way to the entrance, where you attempt to conceal your surprise at the unexpectedly hefty admission fee. As soon as you are inside, however, you remember the baguette and jam that you ate only a few hours before, back at the apartment. Your stomach is not empty at all. "You are a fool and a clown," you mutter to yourself. "Perhaps it is good to go to the museum when you are empty in the stomach and tired. But it is not the same for you because of your stomach that is full of warm baguette and butter and the jam of raspberries." Charging out of the museum, you go to the nearest café and order a slice of carrot cake and a latte macchiato. At first, the fact that the latte is served in a bowl adds to your fury. Why must all the coffee be served in bowls in this backward country! But soon the buttery cake settles into your belly and your temper begins to settle as well. Then you return to the apartment, apologize, and, as always, are promptly forgiven.

Despite these occasional, brief eruptions, you find yourself growing ever closer to April during the first few weeks in Paris. You come to depend upon the warmth of her body beside you as you fall asleep, and often, when she is at work, your thoughts drift in her direction. As the weeks pass, you find comfort in the reliability of your routines together.

Still, sometimes when April works late, you grow restless, purchase a bottle of wine and meander alone through the cobblestone streets of the city. You enjoy the warm orange illumination on every wall, which is so uniform that you almost wonder whether all the shopkeepers and landlords in the city have purchased their outdoor lighting from the same store. Perhaps, indeed, the color of the lights is regulated by the government. While musing about intriguing possibilities such as this, one evening, you come across a small congregation of French youths. They are sitting on concrete blocks in a streetside park on the banks of the Seine.

"Hello," you say, seizing the opportunity to practice a little of your French. "I have a question. Can I have a cigarette?"

The boy that you have asked laughs and looks to his friends. One of them strums a guitar while a girl with a ponytail replies, "Where are you from? England?" She is wearing a plaid skirt. You must recommend to April that she wear skirts more often.

"No, I am American," you smile. "I apologize, but it is true. I understand that we are not very populist here. But I assure you that they, the Americans, are not very populist for me either. In effect, I am a lover of France, and of your cigarettes. Which genre of cigarette are you smoking?"

"Marlboro Light."

"Ah, the Marlboro Lights are very good. I enjoy them very much, the perfume of them."

One of the boys turns to you. "I suppose you also enjoy the smoking of cigars?"

"I like to smoke cigars occasionally. What? Why is this so amusing?"

While the French youths laugh, you take another swig from your wine. It occurs to you that your lips and teeth are probably purple by now, but you doubt that they would be visible in the faint light. Turning and looking out over the gently rippling water, you think of the many heated quarrels that must have been had in this very place, how many lovers must have kissed, how many poor fishermen must have made their daily catch in the placid waters of the Seine. "I have another question," you propose. "Do you know what kind of fish are in this river?"

"Fish? In the Seine?" they ask. "I've never heard of that."

"Excuse me," you interject, "but I read it in a book."

One of the girls whispers something to a friend. Then she speaks in slow, heavily accented English. "We have something to say. We think that you are crazy—"

"No, this brave young man is not crazy," says one of the boys. "You should know that I myself have fished for mussels on the banks of the Seine, once or twice, what!" The laughter once again becomes general. The youths are no doubt quite inebriated, and the girl slaps the humorous boy on the shoulder. "But what?" he protests, still laughing. "You, do you not like mussels?"

The girl puffs out her cheeks and rolls her eyes. "Oh, you are megacool," she says. She looks at you and rolls her eyes again.

After purchasing a cigarette from one of the youths, you politely take your leave and walk slowly up the Rue Saint-Jacques, intending to take the metro back toward the apartment. April, who is probably at home by now, will be wondering where you have gone.

You think back over the conversation on the quay and wonder if the girl in the skirt was flirting with you. Probably she was. Then you wonder whether she would have had sex with you under a nearby bridge. If only you were not restrained by the old ball and chain.

"Ah, April," you think. "My April in Paris…"

The next week, April receives a night off from work. The two of you decide to celebrate by eating at a Traiteur Asiatique around the corner from your apartment, one of the few restaurants in the area that you can afford. Its owner fancies himself a Cambodian, but there is nothing Cambodian about his menu. In fact, all of the Asian restaurants in the city seem to feature not one national cuisine, but rather the general cuisine of "the Orient," an indistinct region of the French imagination extending from Turkey to Japan. By the cash register, a dozen heated trays of vegetables, fish and meat languish in a glass display case under incandescent lamps.

"You know," you tell April after the two of you have settled down with your trays, "we should be grateful. When Henry Miller lived in Paris, he used to catch pigeons in the park and eat them."

"He ate pigeons?"

"Yes."

She lifts a spoonful of hot and sour soup and blows on it, then looks up. "Who is Henry Miller again?"

You cannot help but sigh and shake your head. "Baby, Henry Miller was a very important writer in the early twentieth century," you explain. "He wrote erotic literature with Anaïs Nin. We saw the movie about it, remember?" You take a long pull from your house red. It is drinkable.

"Aren't you hot in that scarf?" April asks.

"No," you sigh. "I'm not."

Later in the night, you encourage April to speak dirty French to you in bed. You are surprised by how much her linguistic skills have improved. In fact, her abilities have advanced so far during the month of waitressing, it is not always entirely clear to you what she is saying, and you must sometimes ask for clarification.

"Give me your fuck?"

"No, no, your *fuck*."

You pause. "Am I not already giving you that?"

"It is nothing. No, you weren't," she laughs tensely. "But it is nothing."

The next day, April becomes violently, inexplicably ill. On the recommendation of the pharmacist around the corner, you buy aspirin, hydrative salts, dark chocolate and bowel-hardening powder.

"If you need anything else," you whisper, "I'll be at the brasserie in front of the Sorbonne."

"I can't get out of bed."

"I know, I know," you whisper. "I just need some fresh air. I've got a case of writer's block. I realize it's not your fault, but I think it would be better if I worked elsewhere until you're healthy again."

It is nearly a week before April recovers. When she does, you are so delighted to have the apartment to yourself once again that you rarely go out or even attempt to work. Dressed in your worn sweatpants and ironic Iron Maiden t-shirt, you spend the evenings swilling inexpensive wine and watching French intellectuals debate in the roundtables on television. By the time April returns, early in the morning, the wine has often made you so sentimental that you can do nothing but praise the joys of domestic cohabitation, informing her again and again of how glad you are to be sharing your life with her. This ritual continues for several days, until April announces that the two of you have been invited to a party at the apartment of one of her coworkers' friends.

"Do we have to go?" you ask.

"He's French," she says. "Isn't that what you wanted?"

"Yes, of course. I only wish it weren't on Monday night. Susan Sontag is supposed to be on—oh, never mind, it's not important. I'll go if it'll make you happy."

"You don't have to go."

"Don't say that, honey. I think it'll be good for us to get out."

When Monday night arrives, you pull on your jeans and are surprised to find that they have shrunk. "Remind me not to use the top setting on the dryers at the laundry next time," you grumble. Then the two of you rush to catch the metro that will take you to the young man's apartment. As you sit on the train, you start to feel a bit queasy. But you take a deep breath and try to remain calm.

At the party, you quickly embroil yourself in an argument with a young French woman over the sociocultural importance of prostitution in France. Because her English is spotty, you attempt to speak in French.

"It is not a prejudice," you insist. "My ideas are founded on the specificity of fact. Nearly every word in the French language that refers to a woman or girl, for example, also possesses the secret and double meaning of 'prostitute.' I cite for you only the fact that 'girl' can mean prostitute. 'Woman' can mean prostitute. The words 'Mrs.' and 'Miss' as well. If the French had a word for the English word '*Ms.*,' it would presumably mean prostitute also, though perhaps a prostitute of a more androgynous kind. Prostitution is the hidden meaning of the entire French language. I refuse to understand how you can fail to agree."

After several moments, when the girl still has not responded, you repeat your question. "Do you agree or no?"

"I'm sorry," she apologizes in English, "I have to ask. I apologize if it is something rude, but are you a hunchback?"

"No, I am not a hunchback," you clarify, and then continue in French. "Perhaps my reasons for believing that the concept of prostitution is central to the culture and identity of your nation will be more easy to comprehend if I note that the most prodigious French expletive is the word 'whore.' For example." You glance around the small, crowded apartment and see that April remains by the door to the kitchen, talking to her colleague. "I find that the French utilize this word very frequently, for example, while watching a game of sport on the television in the bar. 'Whore! Whore!' That is what they say, is it not? I can hear them very precisely in my imagination. Sometimes they will add, for greater emphasis, 'whore of shit.' Or they will say, 'It is the bordello.' Is this not true? A car that does not function will be called a 'whore of a machine,' or a 'son of a whore.' This is not to say, of course, that all women are whores."

"I'm sorry, I hardly understood a word you said," the young woman replies, glancing around the crowded room. "There is so much noise."

"I was simply saying that I do not believe that all women are whores."

"Ah."

You find yourself increasingly drawn to this strange, obstinate Frenchwoman with her distracted air and pouting lips. You have never met anyone quite like her. Indeed, you suddenly want to sacrifice yourself to her possession. She will be your lover, your paramour. Certainly, April will remain your girlfriend, your most intimate and trusted companion, but you will also have a more passionate, highly physical relationship with this entrancing Frenchwoman whose name you do not know. The two of them will fill separate rolls in your life, completing you in different ways. Trying to prolong the conversation, you find yourself arguing, provocatively, against the false profundity of so much contemporary European thought.

"I realize that Monsieur Derrida is very respected here," you are in the process of noting, "but his argument is essentially that speech is made possible by writing. That is simply not true, for I know of many people who can speak but not write. They are called *illiterates*." Clearing your throat, you try to avoid looking at a man who has approached and begun listening. "I beg you to forgive me if I say this, but it seems to me that the entire tradition of French philosophy is essentially without value."

"Derrida is a buffoon," the woman shrugs. "He is only read in the United States."

She turns to the young man and they kiss each other affectionately on the cheeks. "Did you hear? According to this young man, the entire tradition of French philosophy is without value."

"I am not in agreement," the young man responds. He turns to you with an expression of benign contempt and utters something in French that you do not understand.

"Repeat, please?" you ask.

"Did you hear that, Chantalle?" the man asks, cocking an eyebrow. "The young man has asked me to fart again. Were you aware that I farted?"

"Oh, Bertrand," she laughs, rolling her eyes.

"I only wonder how he knew. I had assumed that my fart was a secret. There is so much noise in here."

After a polite laugh, you commence your riposte. "You are very funny. Perhaps you would have an opinion on the matter that we were discussing. I was arguing that the concept of prostitution plays a central role in the French consciousness." You take a sip from your wine. Bertrand squints at you and then turns to Chantalle.

"You know," he says, "it was never entirely clear to me before this very moment why it is that Americans are known as pretentious. Because, of course, the Americans we see in the news, such as your highly esteemed President, are usually such cretins that the appellation of pretension would be an unearned compliment. But now I believe that I may understand, to some extent." He turns back to you and, smiling indulgently, articulates, "A very impressive performance, young man." In hesitating English, he adds, "Very good."

"Fine, if that pleases you. But you have not addressed yourself to the substance of my words in any respect—perhaps you are unable?"

"Please," Bertrand interrupts, returning to his native tongue. "It is better for you to stop now."

"So you refuse to address yourself to the substance—" you repeat, your voice rising in volume above the noise of the party.

"I hope I do not offend you," he says, offering a teasing smile, "but this is the problem with you Americans, you allow yourselves to become drunk."

"Ah, of course. The French do not drink?"

"We drink," he continues, "and just as much as the Americans. But we do not allow ourselves to become drunk."

Finally, April appears at your shoulder and whispers that there is someone she would like you to meet. You excuse yourself, shaking the Frenchwoman's hand but pointedly failing to shake the hand of the foul interloper. For the remainder of the night, you attempt to drown your growing frustration in alcohol, until, on the long, slow walk home, you encourage April to follow you into some bushes outside of a small, gated park and make love to you there. But as soon as you have begun to slide down her jeans, a group of small boys begins throwing pebbles at you and hooting from the other side of the fence. The effort must be abandoned.

The next day, April awakens you. It is the afternoon. She stands above the bed, shaking you. It takes you a moment to realize that something is wrong.

"Wake up," she says. "Wake up. Someone's flying planes into the World Trade Center. They flew a plane into the Pentagon. It's happening all over the place."

"What?"

"They're flying planes into America."

You rush to the television. On the screen, there is indeed a plane flying into one of the towers. Rubble and flame spew out from the other side in a geyser. Then the building is perfectly intact again. The plane appears at the corner of the screen and sinks into the tower. A geyser of rubble and flame ejects from the other side. Then the building is perfectly intact again. The plane appears at the corner of the screen and sinks into the tower. A geyser of rubble and flame ejects from the other side. The video plays continually while an American broadcaster speaks in hectic tones of what is not known. You cannot take your eyes away from the images.

In the coming days, you sit on the couch for hours at a time. You sleep on the couch with the sound turned low, waiting for the next attack. You sense that it is a turning point in your life, in the lives of all those you know, perhaps in the history of America, or even of the world. As the broadcast schedule gradually returns to normal, you continue to brood.

"This may be the most significant historical event since the Peace of Westphalia in 1648," you tell April one evening, staring at the television and spooning cereal into your mouth. "Could you buy more milk on the way home? We're running out."

After a week, April asks you how long you plan to stay on the couch, doing nothing. You stare at her in disbelief, setting down your cereal spoon.

"Do you really understand what's happened?" you ask. "Do you? Sometimes I don't think you get it. This changes everything." You sigh and rub your eyes. "I mean, after this, I don't know if I can ever work again."

"What do you mean?"

"Exactly what I said," you sigh.

Once she is gone, you lie back on the couch and light another of the off-brand cigarettes you have begun to smoke. The events of the previous week are like an enormous question mark not yet attached to any words, simply a mute demand. It is a blank canvas for your confusions and desires.

Preoccupied by the attacks, you wake up increasingly late in the day. You eventually come to understand that your body naturally operates on a twenty-six hour sleep cycle. You stop taking showers.

Early in October, after several days in which you and April hardly exchanged a word, she sits you down at the kitchen table.

"I don't understand," you say, looking around, "I thought you said there would be a sandwich."

"I've been seeing someone else," she says.

You stroke your long, thick beard, nodding thoughtfully.

"That's okay," you say. "Everyone's response to the attacks takes a different form. Is he French?"

"I don't want to talk about him." She leans across the table. You wonder how many weeks it has been since you have looked at her so directly. "I think you need help."

"Help?" You rub your eyes. "I don't understand what—"

"You need help, and I obviously can't give it to you. I think you should go home and see a doctor."

"Why?" you say. "I'm fine."

"Look at yourself."

You throw up your hands and sputter. "Is this because I won't accept the lies? There's a mass grave in lower Manhattan with thousands of bodies in it. If you want to say that it was because of American hegemony—"

"I can't have this conversation again."

"Just admit it. You think it was because we all did something wrong. The third world strikes back. But why were the hijackers middle class professionals then? Why? Why was the attack organized and funded by a billionaire? This was not the result of poverty. It was the result of a radical leftist agenda that blames America—"

"I'm going to leave now. I'd like you to find another place to live."

For a moment, you are speechless. "Are you serious?"

"Yes."

"Come on. Let me come with you. We'll talk it over."

April stands and takes her purse from the table. "Don't try to follow me."

"If you'd just listen to me for five minutes," you say, "I could make you understand. Here, I'm getting dressed. See?"

"I'd like you to be out of the apartment by next week."

"Just let me change out of my sweatpants—"

"Please."

"Let me come with you," you plead. "We're not done here yet."

You feel your fist clenching. But she is already stepping out of the door.

"April?" you ask as the door closes behind her. Your heart races. "April?"

If you follow April, turn to page 219.

If you stay in the apartment, turn to page 175.

So you expose yourself to the risk.

It is like hearing a live symphony for the first time, after years of knowing only the tinny vibrations of an ancient radio. The pleasure envelops you until nothing else remains. "Where are you?" you whisper in the afterglow. You place a hand on her warm, naked belly. Her eyes remain closed. "I want to know your secrets. What are you thinking?" After a while, you lower yourself and nibble on her earlobe until she begins to stir. "I want to be where you are. Take me there. Teach me what you know."

"Are you always like this afterward?"

"That's right," you whisper. "Show me your uncertainty. Show me your sadness. Let's get wasted in the afternoon. Let's be drunk. Always."

For the next several months, you abandon yourself to the chaos of Cynthia's life. You revel in it. Given these beginnings, it is all the more surprising that when she breaks up with you, toward the end of freshman year, it is because she believes you have become a risk to yourself.

"I think the first thing you need to accept," she begins, sitting on the bank of the drying, man-made campus lake. "Look at me, kiddo," she says. You lie in the grass, running your fingertips over the brittle blades of grass. "I think the first thing you need to accept is that it's not just me. Everyone's worried. Do you know what they say about you?"

"Who?" you ask vaguely, watching the ducks.

"Everyone." She continues in a calm, measured voice. "I don't think you understand how you look to other people."

"I'm just exploring," you say. "I thought you'd understand that."

"You have a problem. You need help."

When you look at her this time, you finally understand that it is over. Then you start to sob, resting your forehead on one arm. You wipe your nose on the cuff of your shirt.

"Do you want a tissue?"

"Fuck you," you mumble. A few drops fall from your nose before you can catch them on your sleeve. "No."

"I'm saying this for your own good. I can't always be there to pick up the pieces. Just like Francis couldn't. You know that, right? That's why he left. He got sick of cleaning up after you. His words."

"He didn't say that."

"Yeah. He did."

You take a deep breath and run your tongue across your aching gums. "Thanks," you croak, sniffling. "I really think this made a difference."

Cynthia strokes the nape of your neck.

"I thought about it a long time, kiddo. You can change if you want to. I know you can."

After she leaves, you walk over to the other side of the lake and cross into the foothills. It is sunset, and you walk along a thin dirt trail between the tall grasses. They sway in the golden light.

When you return to your room, you are prepared to throw away all the pills and plastic baggies and bottles and to make a fresh start. But first you check your email.

There is a congratulatory message from the office of student affairs. It tells you that your grant proposal has been accepted. You had requested twenty-five hundred dollars so that you could live for a summer in a warehouse in Rhode Island and write about an artists' collective there. Denise and I are living in the warehouse while I attend art school in Providence.

To celebrate the good news, you allow yourself a final shot of vodka. This leads to a weeklong binge, which in turn leads to an even longer binge that lasts through the end of the school year and into the first weeks of summer, so that when you arrive in Providence, still disoriented from the mushrooms you took before the last stretch of the busride, you do not know how to respond when I tell you that Denise entered rehab two weeks earlier... Sometimes you spend the afternoon lying on a sloping lawn outside the university, there with the gutter punks while they get sick and nod... On the way back to the warehouse you run into a girl selling handmade postcards on Thayer Street. But everything is so bright, you almost get lost walking up the stairs of the apartment building because all the light in the stairwell keeps bleeding into your hands. On the inside of the apartment the punks with their crusty beards and combat boots have covered all the windows with cardboard boxes and duct tape. One of them is sitting on the carpet in his snotstained camo pants and staring at you with those vacant eyes. You look pretty fucked up, he says. The other kids are sitting on the stained carpet too, counting small heaps of pills, and one girl is wearing a flannel scarf and lies in the corner with her eyes closed... You try to remember why you came here but you only feel the aching of your gums. You worry that your gums are going to reject your teeth, the way chests sometimes reject transplanted hearts. It terrifies you not knowing these things, so you look down at your hands but your hands are still streaming with the light from everywhere. In fact it looks a little bit like your skin is a cartoon and you are worried that the cartoon will start flickering and then stop. I'm looking for my friend, you say out loud, to distract yourself. I'm looking for, you know. But then you cannot remember my name. The girl with the postcards on Thayer Street said I was looking for you. So now you are looking for me. That makes sense. My friend, you say. Another skinny boy with bruised eyes, great dark circles like an owl, stands uncertainly and shambles past you. His body grows smaller as he recedes but his head stays the same size. Then you close your eyes and pretend not to hear his retching from the hallway bathroom and the splatter in the toilet. When you open your eyes the carpet is drifting over itself like something underwater and you close your eyes... The sound of helicopters shakes the building. You want to not hear them, so you ask again about the boy in the bathroom. You ask if he is alright. Don't mind him, he's just dope-sick, the one counting the pills says. Then the girl in the corner wakes with a start and grabs hold of her scarf. Are you okay? you ask. What? Are you okay? You wait for her to answer but she only sneers at you and looks to the boy who spoke. What is he saying? I can't understand a fucking word he's saying. Don't mind him, the other one says. He's just dope-sick... You worry that you might have thrown up a little bit somewhere. There is a thick orange crust on your shoes. There's something wrong with my shoes, you say. Yeah, they're covered in mud. He laughs, but the laugh turns into a cough. He rattles and coughs like something whose insides are being scraped out. Yeah, why did you track all that mud in? the girl laughs. It's everywhere. Why did you get all the mud all over the walls? Then you see that the walls are in fact streaked with dirt... Everyone is laughing when the other boy returns and grabs the girl by the arm and whispers something. He punches her in the arm. Get the fuck off me, she says. Shrugging like there are spider webs all around her. Quit fucking with him, someone says. He can't even tell... When you look up, the walls of the apartment are so bright that you have to squint. The walls are so clean. I wonder where they are, you say. Who? the other boy asks. Aren't we waiting for someone? They snicker again. The pill counter begins to swear at you and rub his nose. We were waiting for you, he says. You said you had to go to the warehouse. Oh, yeah. I need to see my friend. What? He needs to do—like—he needs to—like—Their voices echo while the white walls grow brighter until there is only light... You must start somewhere. The question—is what is the question... In the stairwell on the way out of the building the stairs go on for too long, flight after flight. There must be hundreds of stairs and you are trapped in a revolving dream and then the door suddenly opens... The bleeding white glow of the streetlight, and behind it the sky is black... Where are you going? the boy asks, grabbing you by the shoulder. When you look up there is only the streetlight that flares with its white halo. Don't leave me, you say... Finally you wander alone in terror through the strange lifeless moonscape where they left you and the pavement that moves over itself like a slow ghostly flood. It must be the industrial area across the river... Someone appears at the edge of the light and you ask if he can help you find the warehouse. It used to be a textile factory, you say. Only when he points do you see the faded lettering on the bricks and understand that you have been standing beside the warehouse all along. Dude, it's me, the boy laughs. We just walked here. Don't you remember? Of course, you say... In the plywood corner where your mattress is, you reach behind the wall and search for the bottle you hid in the insulation. You need something to calm your nerves until the trip ends. Then you pull out your hand and it sparkles with fiberglass shards... It is so hot here. Even the refrigerators are barely cold. You think of all your food that has rotted in the refrigerators and the white and blue mold that grew beneath the plastic wrap... You heard it. A gunshot. Then the screaming is so loud that it rings in your ears. You stand up and shout to the others scattered throughout the warehouse in their makeshift beds and studios. Did you hear that? Did anyone hear that? You push aside the thin curtain that separates your sleeping space from the maze of hallways and you start to run toward the stairs... Another gunshot. A shooter in the warehouse... Even as you run, the adrenaline shakes your body and makes you ill. Where there are no lights you sometimes collide with loose boards. You find a boy lying on a cot in a small cluttered studio space. Wake up, you say, shaking the boy's shoulder. Wake up... I think someone just got gunshot. He groans and turns away from you. There is a plastic sheet at one side of the room, and a strange dim light behind it. But when you run through the sheet, there is only another partition of the warehouse, insulated with more plastic sheeting and duct tape, and behind it a wall of flickering televisions playing an old movie of strange objects on mutilated celluloid...

Dismantled bicycles hang from the ceiling of the workspace. A recording of a girl speaks over a quiet electronic hum. I can't believe. I think it's so creepy that everyone, like, sleeps all the time, she says. I can't believe everyone closes their eyes and hallucinates for, like, half their lives. I can't believe. I'd think they were crazy or something. I can't. I'd think they were crazy—and hallucinates for, like, half their lives... Several people are kissing each other in the flickering light, all of them lying on mattresses and paint-splattered plastic sheets on the floor. A boy in red earmuffs is tangled in a slowly grinding heap between two girls, one of them dressed in a leotard, the other in a purple wig. Then someone else is standing beside you. Did you hear? you ask. I think someone just got gunshot. He balances himself on your shoulder with a fist. Here, take this, he mumbles. It is one of the gutter punks. He stuffs a crumpled piece of plastic into your hand. I want you to have it... Don't pay attention to me, he mumbles. I'm invisible. Before you can stop him, he shuffles away... But when the screaming returns, you realize it is not screaming at all. It is noise from the show. My band. The concert tonight... Making your way through the halls toward the performance space, you try to stay calm and not look at the visual detritus that covers the hallway walls. Layers built up over the years. Overlapping spaceship comics, flyers for *Arab on Radar*, silk-screen mandalas, small puffy scratch-and-sniff stickers in the shapes of stars. Streaks of paint. Panda heads. Crayon portraits. A crude child's drawing of a pirate ship being eaten by a dragon. MAYBE PEOPLE *don't* MATTER, it says... Harvested bicycle parts hang from the ceiling of the concert space like bombed out flesh. Even with your ears covered the noise is like wires cutting through you and shaking the viscera. Organ-dislocation music. The fear returns then and you try to brush away the colors from your arms... On the stage, I sing from beneath my red ski mask with the animal ears sown onto it and the grey patch covering the mouthhole. Ra-ra-ra-ra, I yell into the microphone under the patch. I pound furiously on the drum kit... I told you I was trying to build my art back up from scratch. It all fell apart after Denise. I started with simple shapes and lines. If I agreed with one, I added it to a list and moved on... You try to focus on my ski mask but even the eyeholes are covered by impenetrable shades like the eyes of an insect. I never stop swinging the drum sticks and yelling, pounding the drumheads, the cymbals, my arms moving like sewing machine needles... Then the other boy on stage presses a button on his stack of electrical gear and it bursts into a distorted drone that shakes the building. He seems to go into a brief seizure each time he touches the heap of machines and coils of colored wire. You are trapped inside your skin and you want to rip it off like a straightjacket. Everything. You are trapped inside your eyes and you need to get outside of them... Walking faster and faster in the endless maze... One hall leads into another like an optical illusion and you ask yourself if this is what they mean when someone loses his mind. You have lost control of your mind and there is no exit... Finally you see a metal ladder and you climb it to the top floor of the warehouse. The abandoned machinery. No light but from the streetlights through the plastic sheets in the broken windows. Pools of oil. You stumble to a far corner and sit down beneath a crumbling concrete wall and cover your eyes with your palms... You should call Ida. Your mother. She is your mother. She will help you. You will tell her that you made a mistake and say you need to go to a hospital. You have lost control of your mind and you need—medical help—you need someone to get it out of you... Your mind drifts toward sleep, then snaps back in terror. There is nothing to hold onto at the edge of sleep. Still...

Then you wake. You take a deep breath and look around. There is a dim light in the sky outside the windows. You could almost cry. It is over.

Just like they always said. You just needed to go to sleep to make it end. There are only tracers now, and you climb the fire escape to watch the sun rise from the roof. Someone has created an artificial lawn there. A patch of astroturf with pinwheels and plastic flowers.

After you have pulled yourself over the railing, you see that I am sitting in one of the lawnchairs. I am crying.

"Hey," you say.

You stand at the edge of the roof and wait. When I keep crying, you go to sit down on the lawnchair beside me.

"She killed herself."

For a while, you just sit there. Then you reach into your jeans for a cigarette. But when you pull out the crumpled pack, something else comes with it. The cellophane wrapper that the gutter punk gave you. There are two small squares of paper inside.

"Is that acid?" I ask.

You look at it and nod.

"You wanna take it?" I wipe away my tears.

Your mind has barely begun to heal. But what does it matter when a friend has died.

If you drop the tab, turn to page 84.

If you do not take it, turn to page 132.

Sitting in the apartment, alone, you take a few moments to clear your head. You do not believe for a minute that April is actually leaving you. The only question is how long, exactly, it will take her to return. Five minutes? One hour? A day?

Each time there is a noise in the hall, you brace yourself for the sound of the key in the lock and the sight of April standing in the doorway, olive branch in hand. After three days, you decide to show your magnanimity and finally call. But she does not answer, probably because she is at work. A few hours later, the thought crosses your mind that she might have run out of minutes on her phone. So you text some of your minutes over to her and call again, this time leaving a voicemail in which you ask her to call if she is injured.

Finally, you are forced to accept that April has probably lost her phone. So you send her an email, which is a step that you had hoped to avoid. Then you send her another email in case the first one was too critical, or got lost. When she still does not respond, you start to wonder: What if she actually expects you to leave the apartment?

For several long days after April's deadline has passed, you continue to stay in the apartment, hoping that she will return while you are still there. You console yourself with wine. One day, at long last, you lose your temper and begin to overturn furniture. You open the refrigerator and take out all of the condiments and empty them into the sink. Then you throw all of the food from the refrigerator into the sink as well. Finally, you break two plates against the faucet, leaving the shards in the heap of food, and you pack your bags and leave.

It takes several more days of heavy drinking for you to straighten out your thoughts and realize that you may have been wrong to assume that April was deliberately avoiding you. What if she was simply out of town? Laughing at your kneejerk reaction, you decide to spend some time standing outside April's building. The next day, you lean on a nearby wall for several hours, pretending to read a newspaper and occasionally sneaking sips from a soda bottle filled with red wine. On the second day of your vigil, April appears with a bag full of groceries. This may be one of your last chances to patch things up, so you dart from your hiding place and rush across the street.

"April!" you cry. "April!" Laughing enthusiastically, you offer to carry her bag. "I wanted to tell you—"

"Please go away."

"Hear me out. I wanted to tell you that I've learned my lesson."

She rifles through her purse, never looking up. "Please. Don't do this."

"I was a fool to take you for granted. So you win. But I also think if you view the situation objectively, there's plenty of blame to go around. After all—"

"Please. Just go away."

"Hear me out. You give me a second chance, and I'll show you how right I am."

April finds her key. "If you follow me inside, I'll call the police." She looks at you for the first time. There is pain in her eyes. "I'm not kidding. I don't want to. But I will."

"I know you don't want to. And I'm not kidding either. I'm totally serious. Give me a second chance. Just five weeks back together."

"I'm sorry."

"Come on. Four weeks. I've changed, I'm telling you. You don't know what you're missing. Three weeks."

"I'm sorry," she says.

"Okay. Two weeks. And after that, if you want me to leave, I promise I will never contact you again—"

The door closes behind her. That night, wandering the streets with a soda bottle full of rum, you finally accept that she has left you. All things considered, it makes perfect sense. It is easy to forget, but you are ugly. In fact, you are hideous, especially with your misshapen back, and you are also stupid, and lately you have become mean. She deserves better.

At least one thing is clear now. There is no reason to stay in Paris.

A few weeks later, waking to the sounds of street noise, it takes you several moments to remember what time of day it is, and where you are, what country. You look around the darkened cinderblock walls of the hostel dorm, listening to the honking in the street below and the blaring, distorted music. You lift a hand to your mouth and then cannot remember what you intended to do with it. There is a smell like bleach in the room. Bangkok. You still cannot remember how long you have been here.

At the front desk, a small, round-faced girl sleeps with her arms sprawled across the registration book. If she is not careful, her saliva will leave a mark. You consider waking her, to ask if she can recommend a restaurant, because you are extremely hungry. But as you reach out to touch some part of her, you see that she is in fact a boy. You stand in front of the desk and look at him. Then you walk outside and turn left and continue walking.

As you make your way through the crowds in the hot, narrow streets, you regret not having made a plan about where to go. You do not want to look at your guidebook in public, because then everyone would know you are a tourist. So you try to look at the storefront signs without being seen. You look at them without any expression so that no one will know you do not know your way around. There are places to eat, but you pass them. Then you stop. Small cars and tuk-tuks honk all around you. Stepping over to the curb, you see an old woman in a coned hat tossing noodles in a coned wok. The young men in front of her have maple leafs on their backpacks. You wait in line behind them.

After a while, you grow nervous. You worry that there is no line and you are standing on the sidewalk for no reason. So you reach out your hand toward a backpack. Then you stop and pretend to wave something away from your face. You turn and look casually into the crowds. A fat old white man with a red face stands with his arm around the waist of a young Thai girl. She could be eleven or twelve, you think. He wears a fanny pack.

When you turn back toward the wok, the old woman in the pointed hat is saying something to you. The backpackers are gone. The old woman points at her sign, but all of the writing is in Thai. You nod at the old woman and want to say something, but no words come to mind. Then you look at your watch and tell her that you have time.

Then the old woman tosses noodles into her wok, which glistens with hot cooking oil. Unsure what to do with your hands, you hold up your disposable camera and begin to point it at the street. But there are too many people there so you point the camera at the sky. Electrical wires criss and cross between the buildings. You pretend to hold down the shutter release button for a moment. Then you lower the camera. The old woman is pointing at the menu again and making noises. Something about her gesture makes you uncomfortable, so you try to give her money. Your heart has begun to race. You wonder whether now is the time to take out your guidebook, or whether the time for this is later. Then the old woman takes away your paper money and gives you coins. You pretend to count the coins.

While the old woman finishes adding dashes of peanuts and scallions to your noodles, you look at the crowds again and think of the red-faced man and the little girl. You wonder if he is a sex tourist. Perhaps all tourism is sex tourism, you think. Then you think this again.

Perhaps all tourism is sex tourism. The phrase repeats itself over and over in your head. You do not know what to do with it, with the phrase that is repeating itself over and over in your head. You do not know what to do with the thought that is repeating itself. Then the noodles are done. You take your paper tray of noodles and look at them. No longer hungry, you look around for a trash can. But there are none. So you sit down on a nearby curb and put some of the noodles into your mouth. Then you set down the tray.

Back at the hostel, you stand in the lobby and try to avoid making eye contact with the receptionist. A rusty fan whirrs on a counter by the door. It is too early to go to sleep again, so you step over to the opposite corner of the lobby and look at the collection of movies on a shelf there. You pick one of the cassettes and place it in the VCR. Then you turn on the television and sit down on the old couch in front of the television. It has no cushions. A fly lands on your forearm and you watch it scrape together its arms. It probably tasted you before flying away. Then a while later a car speeds away in the movie and then crashes. Another person sits down beside you on the couch. You yawn and look at your watch. For a while, you close your eyes and slump like someone who is asleep. Then you open your eyes. The guest is a tallish girl with platinum blonde hair and a deep tan.

"What?" she asks, smiling politely.

"I'm sorry, do you speak English?"

"Yes, yes," she says in a light accent. "But I have not heard what you said."

You ask her where she is from.

"Bavaria."

You nod. Then you ask where Bavaria is, and she says it is close to Austria.

"I was just reading something by an Austrian economist."

She laughs. "That is comical. Do you say comical?"

"Yes, we say comical." You smile and start to laugh. "Why is that comical?"

"I do not know." She laughs again.

You explain why you were reading the Austrian economist. You say that after the attacks, you started to study political philosophy, and that is when you started reading Hayek, who is a libertarian, and he made you realize that you are a libertarian also. You did not always know that you were a libertarian, but you have always been one. Freedom has always been the most important thing to you. The freedom of the individual to make choices. It is what you wrote your senior thesis about in college. A senior thesis is a paper that someone writes at the end of college. You wrote your senior thesis about the philosophy of free will, which is the most important—

Then the tape finishes rewinding. You stare at the VCR.

She laughs. "You are funny."

You join her laughter. But it is not clear why you are funny. You ask her why she is laughing. She continues to laugh.

"I thought when you are speaking of 'choice' that you are speaking of, you know, something else."

"What?"

She looks at you uncertainly. "I have heard that 'choice' is a— do you say euphemismus? That choice is a euphamismus for—*die Abtreibung.*"

Then someone turns the lights on in the lobby and you go to use the restroom. After that you lie down on your bunk bed. When you wake, it is the middle of the night, the sheet on your mattress is damp and cold, and you are shivering. The coiled blue lightbulbs of the insect trap in the hallway flicker through the wire mesh above the door. There are clothes newly scattered across one of the other beds. You begin to feel panic.

The next afternoon, you buy a yellow fruit and try to eat it at a plastic table nearby. A woman hands you a menu. She comes back a while later and you order some noodles. There is a small clay jar of fish sauce on the table. Your guidebook says that they ferment the carcasses of fish in large barrels. The taste is like a mix of vinegar and a humid lakeshore. It occurs to you that bodies decay like the flesh of salmon when they grow old. Your skin will rot and turn the colors of death. These thoughts repeat themselves and will not stop repeating themselves.

For the rest of the day, you lie in bed at the hostel. A rowdy gang of young men arrives. They stand in the room where you are lying and talk loudly in what you think is Italian. One of them has a rattling cough. But instead of covering his mouth, he opens his mouth and projects his cough into the air. You think of bodies decaying like the flesh of salmon. You cannot stop having these thoughts. The fat of your belly is like a bloated corpse.

In the evening, you go for a walk. A neon sign advertizes a nightclub whose name is in your guidebook. Before you can get too close, you are pushed back by a crowd. They seem to be watching a fight. When you crane your neck, you can see a skinny, adolescent white boy in a baseball cap and backpack lying against the curb and shaking. A middle-aged man holds up the boy's head with one hand. The boy's eyes are rolled back inside their lids and his jaw is clamped and a trail of white foam snakes down his cheek. The boy's legs shake like loose electrical wires. Then they stop shaking and the boy stumbles to his feet and runs several steps into the crowd before his legs go limp and he collapses. Then he rises and stumbles into the crowd.

It seems to you that not many people understand what the world is like. You want to point around yourself and say: Don't you see? Your body will decay and you will stop breathing. The surface of the earth is a fragile shell. The world spins unguarded through a perilous sea. All of this will end. But they would not understand. It would be as though you were pointing out to the passengers in an airplane that they are separated from the ground by nothing but thin air. They would agree with the fact but they would not understand.

The next morning, you take a tuk-tuk to a monastery on the outskirts of downtown, but it is closed to visitors. So you go to a gated park nearby. A monk in an orange robe asks you something, but you cannot understand him. Then you are thirsty, so you wander around the park until you arrive at the door of a large building. A young, bespectacled monk guides you to a table where other white people sit. They are mostly middle-aged women in beads and scarves. While they talk, the monk pours you a small cup of tea and smiles with warmth and sincerity. Then a bell rings and the monk introduces himself. He passes around a book that he wrote in English and asks if you have any questions. A silence follows. None of the women ask anything. They smile at the young monk and nod a little. You take a sip of your tea and then ask whether Buddhists believe in fate.

"I'm not sure I understand what you mean," he says.

"You know, do Buddhists believe that there are certain things that are going to happen no matter what we do."

He takes a moment, smiling at you, and then nods. "Do you mean the philosophy of determinism? Are you a student of philosophy?"

You stare at him. "I was just asking about fate," you say. "It was just a question."

"We believe that all things are determined by one another, yes." As he speaks, his smile never wavers. He is unnaturally calm. He compares the world to a great hall filled with mirrored glass. Each piece of glass reflects every other, he says, and this is the way in which all things in the universe relate. "All things are determined by their infinite relations with all other things," he says. "That is the doctrine."

"But do they have to be the way that they are?" you interrupt. "That's really my question. Couldn't things be different?"

"Sorry?"

"Couldn't there still be a chance to escape from the determination. To find something that isn't already written down. You know, up in the sky. Something that isn't already written down."

The monk laughs gently and glances to the women beside you. "I hope that our other guests are not tired by our philosophical discussion."

"Of course not," you say. "I guess what I want to say is—do Buddhists believe that fate is the sort of thing that a person can escape?"

The monk smiles at you and then slowly shakes his head.

"Let me try to offer an example," you say. Your hand has begun to shake. "If there were two people—"

"My question is related," one of the women interrupts. She begins to talk about the effect that meditation has had on her life. Her talking seems to go on for a very long time without ever reaching a question. She wears a colorful orange scarf wrapped and knotted around her head. You assume that she has a receding hairline, and that is why she wears the scarf.

"Excuse me, do you have a question?" you interrupt. "None of this is related to what I said."

"What?"

"You said your question was related to mine."

She glances at her friend in shock. As though you are being inappropriate and not her.

"Perhaps all questions are related," the monk smiles. "Please, go on."

Before you can recover your train of thought, the woman has resumed talking about crystals and their power to heal. She never comes to a point, never arrives at her question. Her skin has a waxy, reddish glow. She is a revolting thing. All that defines these female flower children, you think, ceases to exist as they grow old. Their ultimate commitments. Free love, health, peace of mind, all ceases to be a possibility. No man wants them. They begin to see the advantages of tying a man down with a contract, but it is too late. There are no buyers. So they try to build a refuge for themselves through herbs, yoga, a new religion. Finally, you can no longer control yourself.

"You don't even have a question, do you?" you ask.

"I'll ask my question when—"

"Shut the fuck up."

"You can't—"

"Just shut the fuck up." You laugh, suddenly, and feel your face redden.

All of the others stare at you.

"You know what you look like?" you laugh. "You fucking cunt, you look like a pirate." Now your laughter has become uncontrollable. It shakes your body. "Your scarf makes you look like a pirate," you repeat, barely able to talk above your laughing. You laugh so hard that tears come to your eyes, but you cannot stop. All of the other visitors stare at you. But you cannot stop laughing.

"Please, sir," the monk says. "It would be better for you to go."

Your chair does not move, so you have to knock it over to stand up. Then it takes you a long time to open the door at the back of the meeting room. Outside, it is so hot that you begin to take your shirt off. Then you put it back on and start to jog toward the nearest gate.

In the maze of streets outside, nothing looks familiar. You start to run until you stop in front of a large poster of the King of Thailand. He is wearing gold-colored frills and costume jewelry. All around you, the light seems thin and insubstantial. You think of the woman in the scarf and your heart seizes up. What if you had a heart attack, you think. Then you walk quickly in the other direction.

Eventually, you start to feel nauseous. Steadying yourself against a concrete wall at the entrance to an alley, you close your eyes and try to think. Then you hear a rustling and open your eyes. A stray dog is rooting around in a heap of trash inside the alley. One of its hind legs dangles in the air, limp and raw. It looks like it has been run over. Every now and then, the dog ducks its head back and licks at the pink, open wound. You start to gag, throw up a little by the wall and then walk away.

At the hostel, you sit up in bed until the world stops spinning. Then you lie down and try not to think. But you keep thinking of the dog with the mangled leg and the boy with the seizures outside of the club. You think of the boy with the seizures. You think of the dog in the alley with the mangled leg. The garbage in the alley looked like it had washed up, like driftwood from some receding flood. Sometimes you think that you hear whispering nearby. But there is no one else in the room.

Two days later, while you are passing through the lobby on your way to the food stalls, you run into the Bavarian girl again. She invites you to join her at a restaurant beside the river, and you try to say that you are sick, but she does not seem to hear you. So you follow her to the restaurant. It is already late at night. The two of you sit across from one another at a plastic table and do not speak.

"So. I have wanted to talk to you over what you said."

"When?"

"At the hostel," she says. "You are neoliberal, not true?"

"I don't know what that means."

"You believe—if every person chooses in the market, all the other things—how does one say it—everything is solved?"

You tell her that you cannot think clearly. But she continues to ask you about your beliefs. You sigh and rest a hand on the side of your neck.

"In the market," she says, "you are only free if you have money."

Your head throbs.

"Think of your own situation—are you free? Yes, you are free to come to Bangkok. But you are only free because you pay to come here. Do you not see what the money is doing—"

You hold your head. "I really—I'm sorry. I really can't do this."

She sets down her drink.

When your plate of fried rice arrives, you do not touch it. She glances around the tables. "No—little bars? What do you say?" She makes a scissoring gesture with her fingers.

"Chopsticks? I don't think they eat with chopsticks here."

"Chopsticks." She laughs and unwraps a bundle of silverware from a rolled napkin in a small bamboo cup on the table.

"I'm sorry." You stare at the glistening oil in your fried rice. "I really am not—feeling well—"

"We are both such somber types." She laughs bitterly and slides the prongs of her fork over a ridged slice of cucumber. Then she pushes it away. "My father tells me once that he thought the only thing—would be for everyone—to disappear. You know? Not to die. But to start over with something other. I don't know how to say it." She laughs again. "I heard that you can say in English *kaputt*. My father believes that man is essentially *kaputt*."

You raise your head and look at her. "Yes."

"My father sees no possibility... Nothing." Then she looks down and starts to fold her napkin on the table. "But he is not well. He is—sick. For a very long time."

"And you?"

"Me?" She pauses, glancing away. "I'm not sick."

"Do you think man is *kaputt?*"

"I do not have his opinion. I think I have seen something better than this." She smiles. "Somewhere."

"Where?"

"Guatemala."

You nod. "Tell me about what you saw in Guatemala."

She shrugs. "I lived with some beautiful people there. For some time. We lived near a lake." She describes the small town where she stayed. It was a commune, a place where anyone could visit and work. "There were, you know, a lot of Müsli types. But they were so nice. And living together by this very large lake, beneath the volcanoes." She shakes her head. "Really together. It was wonderful. I have never seen anything like it."

"How long were you there?"

"I was only there for a few days, me and this friend of mine, and then we have to leave. They were—I don't know how one says that. They were complete. Complete people. They were more than themselves. A community. This one time, I have seen it."

A while later, other German girls arrive at the table, already flushed and boisterous. They dress like the crowds of girls on American television, but with glossier lipstick and more dated clothes. You follow them to a dance club and stand at the bar. Once, you see the Bavarian girl emerge from the dark of the dancefloor, like a shell spit up from the surf, but you pretend not to see her. As you continue drinking, you think of her father and what he said. But he was sick. Sick people have a different view of things than healthy people. There is no reason to say one view is more true than the other.

Outside the club, you buy a can of beer and wander the unlit streets, your mind reeling. There is a buzzing in your ears. A tuk-tuk honks and then passes. You look up through the densely crossing electrical wires. When your legs have carried you so far that you begin to sober up, you find another vendor and buy another can of beer. Then you continue walking until there are fewer and fewer streetlights and the streets are empty. The steel shutters of the storefronts are closed, and all the signs are unlit.

After rounding a corner, you hear a sound like metal falling on concrete and a sharp scream. A man and a woman are struggling in an alley across the street. He holds her by both arms and shakes her, then slaps her and pushes her against the wall. She sobs and sometimes shrieks something. It looks like her face is bloodied.

You look around. The street is deserted, barely lit.

If you try to intervene, turn to page 196.

If you continue to walk, turn to page 318.

Apple in hand, you leave the clearing through the southern opening in the hedges. You cannot wait to share your discovery.

When you arrive at the Packards' dinner table and take your seat, Gerald is spooning tapioca into Sara's bowl. 'I apologize for being so late,' you begin, removing the ceramic apple from your pocket and placing it on the table. 'But I have an announcement. I've solved the mystery of the garden maze.'

The Packards stare at you and at the apple.

'Is that new?' Sara asks.

'Yes,' you say. 'This is a *third* apple. And there may be more. I don't know how many more.' You lift the apple and hold it provocatively beside your cheek. 'Remember. The tree was empty the last time any of us were there. But now I've gone out and got another apple from it. Artificial trees don't grow apples, so where did it come from? There's only one explanation. There must be more than one clearing in the garden. Do you understand?' While the Packards regard you warily, still frozen in shock, you produce your hand-drawn map and begin to describe the structure of the clearings. 'There are multiple clearings. I think it's only an *illusion* that the maze returns you to the same spot each time. In fact, both entrances in the hedges lead to *different* clearings—different places in the maze—one to the east of the clearing where you began, and one to the west. The garden is much larger than it seems from the outside. Much larger. It may even be infinitely large! As puzzling as that sounds. Consider the implications if Eli was right and this world is made not of molecules and energy but of language. Of stories made of words. Gerald, I think this is why Eli told you not to touch the apple. Only by removing the apple from the tree would a person notice that the clearings are different and discover the truth. The apple would disappear from one but not from the others. This is what happened when Sara headed east from the clearing and I headed west. She later told me that she returned to the original clearing, took the apple there, then exited the garden. I went one clearing to the west and took the apple from it before leaving the garden. You see, all of the clearings are connected, one to the next, as in a chain—'

You stop suddenly. Something in the room is wrong. The Packards still have not moved. They remain petrified.

'I know it sounds absurd,' you continue, 'but where else could I have gotten the second—I mean the third apple? The third apple. Where could I have gotten it if there were not another clearing? I'm repeating myself. I realize what I am describing is impossible, but it is also *necessary*, as I told Sara. Let me try to explain.' You gesture vaguely toward the intricate scribbles on your notepad. 'The key lies in a recurring phrase in Eli's manuscripts. *The limits of one's language are the limits of one's world.* I had assumed, at first, that this assertion meant simply that thought exists in language, and so we cannot understand or think about anything in the world that might lie outside the confines of our language. What cannot be said—cannot be said. But as I made my way through the maze, I suddenly understood that the assertion carries much more profound implications. You see, if the limits of one's language are in fact the limits of one's world, then one can expand one's world by expanding one's language. If the world is made of our words, then by changing our words, we can change reality itself.'

The Packards continue to stare at you, inhumanly still. Even the clock seems to have stopped. You rush forward.

'It's all a simple matter of deduction,' you say. 'The garden is made of words. And we are living in the garden.' You continue to smile. 'Now—you may be tempted to object that this is not logical at all. But I will respond that the discipline of logic has changed over time, and continues to remain open to further change. The story of logic has yet to reach its end. My conclusions are certainly not illogical according to any logic that is adequate to expressing the truths of the Yetzirah.'

While you wait for the Packards to respond, another revelation comes to you. You realize that your solution to the mystery was only the first step. Just as the clearings appear to be connected like links in a chain, and all truth is connected by inferences that extend infinitely through logical space, so could there be an infinity of solutions to the mystery, you think, an infinity of conclusions that might follow inexorably from what you have already learned. Or perhaps there are a finite number of them, and the chain forms a circle.

Logic, you think. The boundless power of logic. Not only has the garden of logic unlocked the solution to its own mystery, it has unlocked the solution to all mysteries, to all truths. It is simply a matter of following the correct algorithms from one branch to the next. If, then. If, then…

Then you see that Gerald has opened his mouth. Something emerges from it. It is a human hand, shaped into a fist, and then a forearm, slowly emerging from Gerald's throat. He speaks.

"0100100100100000011101110110100101101100011011000010000000110111101100110011001100110010101110010001000000111100101101111011101101010010000000111010001101010000110010100100000011000110110100001101111011010010110001101100101001000000110111101100110001000000111010001101000011001010010000001101000111011110110111110010000000111001101110100011011110111000101001101001010110010101110011," he says. "010100110111000001100101011001010110010000010000001001101011011110110111001101001011101000110111101110010011001100101011001000010000001100010011110010010000001000001011010010111001001100011000110111001001100001011001100111010001010011011100000110010101100101010110010000100000010011010101101111011101101011011100110101001011101000110111101110010011001100101011001000110111001001100101011001000001000000100000010011010101101111011101101011011100110101001011101000110111011100100110010101100110010100110110100101011001000010000001001101010110111101110110101101110011010010111010001101111011100100110011001010110010001101110010011001010110010000010000001001101010110111101110110101101110011010010111010001101111011100100110011001," he says. "0101001101110000011001010110010101100100000100000010011010101101111011101101011011100110100101110100011011110111001001100110010101100100001000000100110101011011110111011010110111001101001011101000110111101110010011001100101011001000110111001001100101011001000001000000100000010011010101101111011101101011011100110100101110100011011110111001001100110010101100100011011100100110010101100100000100000010011010101101111011101101011011100110100101110100011011110111001001100110010101100100—

"I can't," you say.

She stares at you in disbelief. "Why?"

"Well, you know." You slowly dismount from the bed. "What if one of us has something?"

Cynthia lifts herself to her elbows and glares at you.

"I don't have anything."

"What if you got something last night from Pablo?"

As it turns out, Cynthia is very offended by your refusal. In the following weeks, she spreads a rumor that you asked her to dress up as a young boy and enact various sexual fantasies for you. As the rumor travels, the details become increasingly perverse.

"Well, she does look a little like a boy," Francis says, as the two of you drink in his room near the end of the semester. He laughs.

You cannot tell whether he is kidding. It is true that Cynthia has relatively small breasts, thin hips, and a round, youthful face that you suppose could be described as boyish. But you had never noticed these things or thought of them in that way.

A disconcerting possibility flashes across your mind.

Throughout the remainder of your college years, the rumors follow you like a curse. It becomes a kind of campus game to describe in ever more sordid detail what you asked her to do. Those who craft the jokes know that they are not true, but it does not matter. A whiff of depravity lingers. Even worse, the more you deny to yourself that there could be any truth in what Cynthia said, the stronger your uncertainty becomes. So many people lie to themselves about their sexual preferences. How can you be sure that you are not lying as well? What is your proof?

As a kind of private challenge, you enroll in a philosophy of sexuality course in your senior year. It is taught by a charming old man with a stammer who repeatedly apologizes for his dyslexia as he struggles to spell words on the chalkboard. But beneath his disarming veneer, the professor is a radical. He informs the class on the first day that sexuality is an invention of the last two hundred years, like steam power. The ancient Greeks did not divide the world between those who loved members of the same sex and those who did not. In fact, it was assumed that all men loved beautiful boys and that this form of love was the highest possible. Nor did the Greeks view a man's sexual desires as the expression of some fixed identity. They saw love as a god—eros—who swooped down blindly, beyond the lover's control. The Catholics of the middle ages and the early modern period agreed. They viewed sodomy as a temptation to which any soul was susceptible. Their only innovation was to invert the Greeks' hierarchy and place the love of boys at the bottom of the ladder, as one of the vilest sins. The notion that each person has an innate preference for one or another of the sexes and that this preference expresses an essential part of the person's nature—his sexuality—only arrived with the arbitrary classificatory schemes of the nineteenth century.

The professor's words are a revelation. What is the point of denying to yourself that you are something that does not even exist?

Shortly after graduation, you make the effort to track down the faculty resident who led the arbitration between you and your roommate. He had been implicated in a child pornography scandal during your junior year, and though he was forced to resign from the university, he somehow managed to avoid arrest. You begin to correspond under an assumed name, and as the months pass, you gradually gain his trust.

Late in the summer, you awake in the guest bedroom of the Professor's apartment. When you emerge from the room, you are shocked to see that he is still awake, sprawled on the couch in the living room, dressed in the same star-spangled blue kimono that he wore the night before. He has aged almost beyond recognition in the years since your brief encounter at the arbitration.

He greets you loudly, his eyes lighting up. "Did you have a good sleep?"

"I should go," you squint.

"Don't be silly. Take a seat. Have some brandy. You'd like that, wouldn't you?" He has already risen and begun to fill an empty glass. Despite your protests, he offers it to you. "I will not take no for an answer. That's not how we treat guests *chez moi.*" You have to suppress a cringe at his affectation. But you do not blame him. "So. What did you think? Delightful, no?"

You try to smile in a grateful way. But the hangover and the bright lights will not allow you. At your feet, a calico rug is scattered with empty glasses, bottles, plates of half-eaten fruit, antipasto and spring rolls. An overflowing ash-tray sits beside two crumpled sheets of wrapping paper. Feeling nauseous, you take a seat on the couch.

"That's right. I'm sure you must be very tired, aren't you?" the Professor continues. "Very exhausted. Enjoy that brandy. Warm your bones."

"I'm not tired," you say.

"Ah… I suppose you did retire fairly early. I hope they didn't wake you. But you know, all good things must end."

He continues staring at you for a moment, then takes a sip of brandy and returns to his seat at the end of the couch. The robe hangs slack over his thin, aging chest, exposing faint curls of white hair. "Perhaps my company doesn't please you." He waits for your answer, but you only rub your eyes. "I know where he was from. Are you curious?" Your eyes still closed, you try to think of a way to extricate yourself from the conversation without offending him. "Senegal."

You want so badly to leave. But then you realize that your disgust comes at least in part from a vestigial sense of moral disapproval. You take a deep breath and swallow the rest of your brandy. "He's a beautiful boy," you say. "I wish he were here right now." Then you stretch your arms and stand. "I think I'll have another drink."

"That's better," the Professor smiles.

While you go to pour yourself another brandy, he remains still. When you turn, he seems to have slipped into a private reverie, staring at one of the ornate rugs. "Thank you for the brandy," you say, already feeling more relaxed. "Do you mind if I ask you how often you have these—gatherings?"

The Professor makes no response. After some time, he glances at you and says, "Oh, now and again. Tell me, friend—" Suddenly, he begins to cough from deep inside his chest. It is a horrible, rattling cough, and does not subside for several moments. Then he tilts his head back weakly against the couch, a thin hand resting on his exposed chest. "Dear me," the Professor sighs. "I suppose you're thinking I should cut out the cancer-sticks."

On the rug closest to the couch, next to the other trash, there is a small bowl of syrupy, canned fruit with a few cigarette butts submerged in its liquid. A fly lands on its edge. It surprises you that there are not more flies in the apartment.

"You're a very serious fellow, aren't you?" the Professor says. "Very thoughtful. Let me guess. You had a religious upbringing, didn't you?"

"No—" you begin, then think better of it. "Well, a little."

"I knew it, I knew it… I have a preternatural ability to discern the pasts of others. So tell me. Do you still pray to him?"

Your neck spasms slightly. Then you take a drink and wait for an answer to come. But the Professor continues talking.

"You know, they used to say that without God, everything would be permitted. They were afraid of what it would be like when everyone felt free to do as he pleased. To taste the forbidden fruits. But they were naïve, weren't they? To think that man would rise to the occasion."

"They're cattle," you say.

He hesitates, glancing at you uncertainly. Then he recovers himself. "What did you study at university, Wayne?"

"Philosophy," you say. You can already see that if the conversation goes much further, you will want to tell him. You will attempt to tell him what cannot be told. "Kierkegaard," you say. The conversation must go no further.

"And what did you learn from him?" the Professor asks slowly, gazing at you. The expression on his face is now open and grave.

"I learned," you begin, speaking very softly, as though it might still be possible to avoid what is to come, "that there is something higher than ethics. I learned that the fullness of human life requires a defining commitment." You clear your throat and continue. "Something that goes beyond any possible morality. Because all morality is shared, universal. Infinite. It's not personal. Morality can never provide a life with fullness. Only a calling can do that. Like the knight's commitment to his beloved." You feel yourself blushing. But you cannot stop. "Like Abraham's commitment to the Lord. A calling is higher than everything else. It rearranges all the other values around it. It defines every object in the world. It defines who you are. It is everything. That's what I learned from Kierkegaard."

You wait for the Professor to respond, to interrupt your ranting. But he only watches you with his rheumy, tired eyes, betraying no emotion.

"Please, go on," he says.

"I don't know why I'm telling you this. It's not something that can be told. That's the whole point. Language is a shared thing, like morality. It's not personal. It's not my own. Whatever we find words for is already dead in our hearts. As long as I try to describe this in language," you say, "my commitment is going to sound—you know—you know how it's going to sound. If Abraham had tried to explain to his neighbors why he was killing his son... There was no language to say what needed to be said. His calling suspended language, suspended morality. That's what a calling is."

"And what is your calling, Wayne?"

"You know what it is. It's yours. The same." Your heart pounds. While you try to regain your composure, the Professor removes a large book with a red leather cover from beneath the couch. He sets it on his lap, and now sits with a straight back, slowly tracing his fingers across the cover.

"But I'd like to hear you say it," he says.

"You know it doesn't work that way. All true love is a love that dare not speak its name." You stand and go to pour yourself another brandy, then drink it quickly. "If I told you that there is nothing more meaningful in my world," you say, "in my life, than the experience—of last night—but even the word experience... If I tried to tell you how I—feel—of course, that's not the right word either—about those moments, it would only sound abhorrent. But we know it isn't." You stare at him. "They would say I'm hurting someone. They would say I'm using him and hurting him. But I would say there is nothing more beautiful—nothing. It's everything to me. It defines the world around it. Everything I know receives whatever meaning it has from... It's beyond—any..."

"Beyond good and evil," the Professor says with a thin smile.

"No. No, that's not it. I'm not a nihilist. Maybe you are, but I'm not. I have nothing but respect for morality. For the universal, for ethics. I pay my taxes and follow the traffic signs. I'm a vegetarian, actually. I would never hurt somebody, if there were any other way. But there isn't. Not today." Your hands are shaking. "And maybe it has to be the way it is. Killing one's son has to be against the law. But that doesn't mean Abraham wouldn't have been the most contemptible creature on earth if he had refused to do it and betrayed his commitment. He would have been the worst kind of coward there is."

The Professor stares at you. "But what if," he whispers, "what if I said—what if I said you were only attempting to satisfy your desires—and nothing more. That your great calling was nothing but selfish, beastly desire wrapped up in a pretty little excuse."

"That may be the case for you. But I know I'm capable of resisting it. I did resist it. For years. In the deepest possible way. If it were simply an urge, I wouldn't be here." You try to pause, to calm yourself. "It's what defines me. It's who I am. It's why I take the risk to be here with you. It's just like Kierkegaard said. There's a sword hanging over the head of the beloved. Anything could happen. The police could come through that door at any moment. But I give myself to my calling—as though it were the most secure thing imaginable.

The sword could fall, and it would destroy me, yet I refuse to be like the cattle. I refuse to be afraid. I live as though nothing could be more certain..."

The Professor nods. The grin has faded from his face.

"I can't believe I'm telling you this," you say. "Even the language, even hearing my own voice, here, now, it tempts me to hear my acts—as they would, as an abomination. I make an exception of myself, I except myself from the ethical. They would say there is only one kind of exception from the ethical, and that's the unethical. I say there's a higher exception. But there's no way for me to argue for it. It's irrational. Again, that's the whole point. I don't know why I'm saying this."

You stare at the Professor for a long moment, uncertainly, almost expecting him to laugh. But instead, he speaks with an extraordinary gentleness.

"Like my own rejected thoughts—returned in alienated majesty," he says. "Wayne, and I realize that's not your real name, but would I be correct in assuming that you are relatively new to... this?" He gestures vaguely. "How old are you? You can't be much more than twenty-two. No, don't answer. You shouldn't answer. Ever. I want to show you something, because I think you will understand it. One of the few who would understand." He begins to open the red leather book, then closes it. "I'm an old man. But I have been an explorer."

He slowly rises from the couch. The blue kimono slides further open, but he does not seem to notice. He hands the album to you. "Now I want to..." Even as you hold it, his fingers slide nervously over the cover. "You are a friend, aren't you?"

"Yes," you say.

"I don't know if you are or not," he says. "But I want you to see it. Even if you don't understand right away. I want to be the guide for you, because I know—if I had begun at your age... There is so much to be explored. A vast country, hardly touched." He stares at you with a strange vulnerability.

It is probably less than a minute, the time between opening the cover of the photo album and pushing past him out of the apartment, but it might as well have been hours or days. You forget your overnight bag, walking through the empty hallways of the building, rushing to get outside. When you step onto the deserted sidewalk, it is still dark in the city, and you continue to feel sick, but rather than heading directly home, you drive through the streets downtown, trying to distract yourself, taking arbitrary turns whenever one of the images from the album rises again before your eyes. Then you follow the streetlights onto the highway ramp and follow the ramp out of the city. But it is still hours before sunrise, and the clouds above the highway, underlit orange and grey by the city lights, remind you of what you saw.

Having trouble concentrating on the road, you take an exit toward a gas station and lock yourself in the bathroom. When you close your eyes, the pictures are still there, so you keep your eyes open and blink at the filthy walls and the rapid flicker of the fluorescent bulb. Then you begin to remove your clothes. You peel off your undershirt and toss it onto the bathroom tiles. One of the infants had no eyes. Another had her legs removed and lay on a trashbag in a pool of blood. You turn away and see yourself in the stained bathroom mirror. You try to focus on yourself. But your mind continues thinking of the pictures. Somewhere there is a line, you think, and once you cross it, there is no going back, and you have crossed it. You are on the other side now and it will be like this forever. Standing between the green tiled walls, beneath the flickering light, you stare in the mirror at the sagging fat of your belly and your slack white skin.

"Hey," you shout. You clear your throat. "Hey."

The man turns to you, startled. He ducks further into the alley.

"Stop it," you say, but before the words are fully out of your mouth, the woman has begun squealing. Then the man takes a knife from his pocket, opens it and waves it at you. He makes threatening noises.

You continue to walk toward them, your hands raised.

"Please. Stop doing that," you say. You hold your hands open before you and walk. "Please." When you are only a few feet away from him, you stop, fold your hands and lower your head. "Please," you say. Before you can raise your eyes, the man swipes the knife across your stomach. The woman screams while you stumble back, hitting your head and falling into a pile of refuse. The man shoves the woman away.

Lying with your arm over the wound, you are too terrified to scream, and your heart feels like it is going to beat through your chest.

You are not ready to die. Afraid to look down, you can feel that your shirt is already wet with blood. Your arm is shaking. You wait. Then you start to cry for help.

You cry several times, calling out for a doctor. But there is no answer. Finally, you realize you will have to move yourself. You take a deep breath, pull up your shirt and look down.

But when you see the wound, you start to laugh. You laugh so hard that tears come to your eyes. There is hardly any blood, really, the cut was so shallow. You carefully test the narrow slit with your fingertips a few more times. Then you push yourself to your feet and feel a warmth in your khaki shorts. You look down and see that you have wet yourself. You continue to laugh.

At the hospital where the taxi drops you off, you sit for a long time in a waiting room beside silent old men and mothers with crying babies. You are so proud of what you have done. You stood up for something. For once, you did something worthwhile with your life. The fact that it nearly killed you only makes it more meaningful. Filled with a kind of euphoria, you regard the world with new eyes.

You think of what the Bavarian girl said. The commune in Guatemala. A community.

It is time for a change.

When you describe your latest plans to J.P. and Ida over a spotty payphone connection just outside the hospital, they overreact.

"First of all, I wasn't stabbed," you say. "I just got knifed a little. It's really not a big deal."

"I think you should come home," J.P. says.

"Please," Ida says. "Come home."

"I understand why you feel that way," you reply. "And I don't want to cause you suffering. But my life is taking me in a different direction now." You explain that the mugging has made you realize that you have been living for too long as an individualist. "I've tried to go it alone," you say, "and I only made myself miserable. I made everyone miserable. It's time to try something new." After a great deal of cajoling, you persuade them to give you a final loan, just enough money to buy a flexible plane ticket that will allow you to travel to Guatemala before returning home. "I'll call you if there's a phone at the commune," you say. "But if there isn't, please don't worry. I'll be fine. We'll all be fine. I love you both."

A series of planes, buses, shuttles and trucks takes you to a narrow trail that cuts through the coffee fields on a hillside near Lago de Atitlán. The commune has no address, just as the German girl said, so you must stop frequently for directions. But already you are delighted by the look of the place. The green of the coffee plants' leaves seems almost fluorescent after the smog and shanties of Bangkok. A man in a pick-up lets you stand in the bed of his truck for two quetzales, and he drops you off at a turn in the dirt road, pointing to another trail that will take you to your new home. Now, as the sun sets over the volcanoes ringing the lake, you glimpse the buildings of the compound for the first time.

As you approach, a bearded young man with blonde dreadlocks waves to you and smiles.

"How's it going, mate?" he asks. He gives you his name and offers to help you with your backpack. "You get a ride from Jorge?"

"The man in the pick-up?"

"Yeah. You got lucky. Jorge's the best."

Before you can begin to explain what brought you here, or ask whether you may stay, the young man is asking you if you are hungry and leading you toward a cinderblock building at the back of the compound, which he says has an unused bed.

"This is usually Jenny's place, but she's vision-questing," he says, grinning broadly.

"That's great," you smile back.

"It is."

"What is a vision quest?"

"Oh, man," he holds his head. Then he laughs. "It's, like…"

"Really."

"Yeah. It's—there's no way to describe it, mate."

"Do you have a bathroom nearby?"

He nods and takes you to a wooden shed on the outskirts of the compound. A dog trots by on the path, and you are struck by its swollen udders. Perhaps they are raising puppies here, you think distractedly. Inside the shed, there is a plastic bucket with a toilet seat mounted on top. It smells foul, but you are able to ignore the smell by breathing through your mouth. When you have finished, you look around in the dim light that comes through the wooden slats and see that there is no toilet paper or hand sanitizer. You nod and smile. Roughing it.

In the evening, you help to prepare a simple meal of rice and beans. One of the members of the commune strums her guitar by a small bonfire, and someone else joins in with bongo drums. You ladle the soupy concoction into their waiting bowls. Then you eat, sitting on the ground cross-legged and devouring the rice and beans with an unexpected hunger. You receive no formal introduction, but little by little you meet the others. After dinner, for example, one of the older hippies, a man with a long grey beard, lights up a thick spliff and passes it around. Some of the women collect the mismatched bowls and go to wash them in grey plastic tubs filled with hauled water, soap and bleach. The old man sometimes makes babbling noises. Once, he turns to you and begins to talk more clearly.

"They want to get their thing," he says.

You nod. "Who does?"

"They. Them. And they say, you know, we're not—we're not coming to that. We've already got the, you know, so what's it—what's the thing with the… You know…" He laughs and makes a loud noise with his lips. You nod patiently, trying to understand. Finally, you begin to glance around at the others, who do not seem to notice, and the man gradually stops.

"You know, find your own!" he yells. "None of it's theirs."

"Right," you say. "Of course."

Later, you will find out that the old man was one of the commune's founders, and is largely responsible for keeping it afloat financially. He sells hallucinogenic mushrooms to backpackers in the village nearby.

In the first few days, you take it easy, letting your body adjust to the new food and the climate. But once you are rested enough, you join the others for a mushroom ceremony in the communal tee-pee. The experience opens your eyes to dimensions of reality that you never knew existed. Your consciousness expands, mingling with the sweat and fragrant body oils. When one of the women beside you belches, you do not recoil. You breathe in deeply and allow her breath to permeate you. Similarly, when you feel gas building up inside of you, you do not resist its urgency. No one protests. You are all part and parcel of the same nature.

When the spiritual voyage is at its peak, a large-breasted girl who calls herself Sapphire wraps her arms around you.

"Where did you come from," she says.

"I don't know," you say. The walls of the tee-pee rotate around you, full of stars.

"Where did you come from."

"Here." You point to your lips. "I came from here."

She looks at you and kisses your eyes one by one. "*Bienvenidos*," she says. "*Bienvenidos.*"

"*De nada*," you whisper, nuzzling into her breasts.

It is only after your eyes have been opened to the spiritworld that you truly settle into life at the commune. A stern, commanding lesbian wearing a motley-colored blanket teaches you how to do the dishes and empty the toilet bucket, and you welcome her instruction. You accept her orders as the others have so generously accepted you. Everyone is so accepting that you feel as though, after years of wandering, you have finally found a home. Your sense of belonging is so complete that you are shocked when the first moment of tension arises. A guest is showing a film about spirituality on his laptop, and you think that some of its claims are scientifically questionable.

"I guess I just don't believe in astral travel," you say.

"But you're only thinking in three dimensions," the others insist. "You're forgetting the fourth dimension. Your preconceptions are holding you back. We live in a sea of possibility."

Later in the night, sweating and unable to sleep, you feel something sinking in your bowels and barely make it to the outhouse in time. Your body is telling you to let go of your last preconceptions, because they are a source of disharmony. And what is truth, if not harmony with nature?

The next day, in an effort to restore the balance that you have disturbed, you prepare a temazcal in the short stone enclosure at the edge of the compound. You invite the others, including the guest with the laptop, to join you. Sitting naked inside the enclosure, you pour cool water on the heated stones and nearly choke as the steam fills your nose and mouth. Then you scoop another bowl of water from the bucket and pass it around, so that the others can pour it over themselves. You take your turn last. It is your first bath in nearly a week. Sitting in the stone hut, you sweat yourself clean. Near the end, the guest removes a crown of twigs and leaves from his head and places it upon you. No words are necessary.

That evening, you ask a younger girl named Raine how she came to live in the community. You are curious because she seems to be in an oddly unhappy relationship with a scruffy, forty-something Spaniard who seems to sleep most of the day. They live in a nice concrete and bamboo hut to the side of the compound. You often see her crying, sitting by a crumbling wall near the vegetable garden.

"I don't know," she shrugs. "I didn't want to go to school anymore, and I knew a few people in Honduras. That's where I started out."

"You lived there?"

"I worked for a while."

"What did you do?"

"Some waitressing. Some sex work. Then I met Raúl."

"Huh."

"Yeah."

"Why did you leave Honduras?"

"I don't know. Raúl said we'd be better off here."

"Yeah, there's a lot to do."

"Yeah."

"Wanna ball?" you ask.

Raine looks at you. "Nah," she says.

You nod. Even though Raine's response was not positive, you are tempted to reach out and touch the raven hair beneath her bandana. But then you start to feel ill, so you go back to your cinderblock shack. A new roommate is already snoring quietly in the corner bunk. Outside, someone slowly plucks a washtub bass and sings a folk tune.

During the night, you wake again in one of your sweats, seized by the urgency in your bowels. But this time you cannot make it to the outhouse before the diarrhea rushes out of you. Squatting in the moonlit coffee field, you evacuate between two plants and watch as the puddle trickles from between your sandals and into the path.

While you continue to crouch and wait for anything more that might come, you stare up at the stars and enjoy the pleasant, loose afterglow. Once again, you marvel at the wonder of this place. To live where the world around you is an expression of who you are, that is freedom. The emptiness of your life as an individual, cut off, circulating like a lone atom, is now over. Wiping yourself with a handful of coffee leaves, you are so grateful that you begin to weep.

The next day, Jenny returns and you must move your belongings out of the cinderblock shack. You move to the toolshed, where there is an unused cot. It is comfortable enough, but you wish it were not so close to Raúl's and Raine's hut. You can often hear Raine yelling at Raúl and sobbing. One evening, while you are recovering from another bout of intestinal distress, you hear a third voice as well, the slightly accented voice of one of the other women. She seems to be trying to mediate between Raine and Raúl.

"You're ugly!" Raine shouts. "You're an ugly old man."

You can hear Raúl mumbling, but cannot make out his words.

"Look, Raine is a beautiful person," the other woman says in a soothing tone. "I'm beautiful too. She thinks that you're beautiful. We're all beautiful people, you know?" After a pause, she continues, "For me, you are—you know—too old. I do not find you attractive… But you are a beautiful person too." Then you dimly hear Raúl speaking again. You have begun to wonder, based on hints here and there, whether he might be an intravenous drug addict.

He suddenly raises his voice, his English slow and full of effort. "I only like women… who are less… than twenty-one year old," he says. "The older ones… No, I do no like them…"

Raine begins to sob again.

"That's fine," the other woman says encouragingly. You feel something shift in your gut, like a needle being dragged through your intestines. The pain is so intense, you almost let out a groan. You recognize it now as a signal. Soon, you will have to make another visit to the outhouse.

"That's what you like," the other woman continues, "and I like what I like, and everyone should be free to do what their heart speaks to them. But you need to understand that Raine is a very young girl… I know you know. But you need to understand that she is like a fragile flower. You must be very careful with her. You must touch her like a fragile flower."

While you gasp, trying to put as little pressure on your intestines as possible, the conversation grows indistinct, and you hear what sounds like movement on a bed. Raine's sobbing grows less intense.

A while later, you hear the other woman say, "So you were living a responsible life, and then you decided to become a hippie?" "I was living responsible life," Raúl murmurs. "I have... two childs. Two children." By then, the sobbing has stopped altogether. The pain in your intestines fades and you feel your eyes grow heavy. "You should do what is right for you," the other woman says. "And what is right for me is maybe a different thing. But, you know, Raine is special..."

Later, you awake to the creaking of a bed. You hear Raúl mumbling something, and then a woman begins to groan. Then a girl's groan rises. The rocking of the bed quickens until it has reached a fast, regular pace, accompanied by Raine's occasional shouting, Raúl's grunts and the moans of the other woman. You try to cover your ears with the old sweater you use as a pillow, but the noises are too loud.

Eventually, you become so used to the cycle of consumption and sudden, irresistible evacuation that you begin to expect it shortly after each meal, and you make your plans accordingly, not committing yourself to any engagements in the hour or so after eating or drinking. Usually, you retire to your cot in the toolshed and lie down, waiting for the food or liquid to percolate through your intestines, sputtering and bubbling as though passing through a cartoon factory of bloated pipes and pumps. In any case, after three or four more days, you are too weak to do much of anything. No longer able to distinguish one day from the next, you lose the will to rise from your cot except to go to the bathroom or bring yourself water.

The others begin coming to you and offering advice. One girl recommends that you take an herbal cure. But half an hour after you swallow her pungent pills with a glass of water, before they can possibly have been absorbed through the walls of your stomach or digestive tubes, you rush to the shit bucket and expel the liquid. Later in the afternoon, a painfully thin blonde girl tells you that she once drank from a shallow puddle of slime at the base of a canyon while hiking. "We had no choice," she whispers, "so we poured it through a bandana and boiled it. But all of us had this weird green poop for days. Really. Bright green." At dinner, you are unable to hold in even the few buttered crackers that the lonely Swede offers you. They flood out of your asshole before you can even reach the shed. Afterward, you peer down at the flecks of cracker in the dirt. They are soggy but still recognizable, and surrounded by a gummy orange fluid that you assume must be some combination of the orange soda you tried to drink and pieces of your intestines.

"You must have an amoeba," the Swede informs you later. "They build in your stomach, so that you hardly know they are there. And then—ka-boom!—when they have reached a definite point, the bacteria rushes out. Like a wave." He warns against antibiotics, and recommends that you try meditation.

The next day, you do not wake until afternoon. Even then, the line between consciousness and sleep seems to have grown permeable and pocked with holes. So too do eating and excreting become part of a single, continuous gesture. In the evening, you drink some powdered rehydrative solution and stumble to the shit shed shortly afterward. But when you raise your eyes, light pours through the cracks in the boards. You only have the vaguest memory of the preceding day. When you step outside, the sun radiates across the coffee fields.

That evening, you begin to worry that it has been days since your last urination. It is as though some valve has sprung loose from your bladder and reconnected itself to your rectum, so that you now urinate out of your asshole. You worry that your urinary tract might dry up, unirrigated, like a jellyfish left out in the sun. Worst of all, the heat in the smallish concrete toolshed makes you perspire, further depriving you of liquid. Each of your pores is like a tiny, dilating anus, leaking out what little water remains within you.

Lying on your cot, one afternoon or evening, you reach over to your water bottle and mix another batch of rehydrative solution. You know that you must keep hydrated in order to recover. The solution tastes like an overly sweetened, salted sports drink. You swallow it and feel it splash down into your belly. Then you wait for it to sputter and choke along your digestive pathways. In your imagination, the small particulate matter of the solution pauses at the bottlenecks in your pink coils. It builds up gasses in a chemical reaction with the digestive juices there, until the pressure is too great and with a violent grumble the gas and liquid pass on to the next kink. Finally, it all slips through the almost ticklishly sensitive drainhole that you imagine to exist at the top of your assbag. It has become clear to you that this movement, the action of liquid passing through your rectal valve, is what causes you to feel as though you must run to the shit shed. But in fact, if you simply wait for all the liquid to pour into your rectal pouch, the feeling eventually disappears. You have discovered that you can hold quite a significant quantity of liquid in the sac before needing to release it.

During one of the long, lonely afternoons, Raine comes to you and sits on the edge of your cot. You have just heard her storm out of another bitter fight with Raúl.

"It reeks like shit in here," she says.

"I know."

"Don't you think you should see a doctor?"

"I think I'm getting better. The meditation is really starting to clear my mind. And Jasmine gave me some beads."

Raine places a hand on your leg. The feeling is almost pleasurable. "I really think you should go to a doctor," she says.

A few days later, when your condition still has not improved, you take her advice. Stowing your last hundred quetzal note inside your left sock, you wrap your body in a shawl and set out for the road. It is like walking upon the deck of a ship in turbulent waters. The bright colors of the countryside glimmer and blur around you.

"You are looking for something?" a man in a cowboy hat asks as you walk along the thin dirt road that leads to the village. He has been slowly approaching, walking in the opposite direction. Tears of gratitude come to your eyes. "I help you," he says.

"I need a doctor," you say. "I have severe diarrhea and need to see a doctor."

"Three hundred quetzales."

"I don't have that," you repeat weakly.

"Two hundred."

You shake your head. It does not seem right that you should have to pay to find a doctor. So you ignore the man's wheedling and continue toward town. Finally, when you have reached the first shacks and buildings at the outskirts, you stop an old woman in a colorful woven sash, and she points you mutely toward a building at the top of a hill. An ice-cream vendor with an aging cooler attached to his bicycle passes by as you climb the hill, the speaker mounted to his handlebars singing an off-key, warbling music box tune. There is something demonic about it. You wish you could be back at the commune and out of the bustling village.

By the time you reach the doctor's office, you feel as though it has taken hours to walk up the dusty cobblestone street. You had to stop several times to collect your energy, and often you wondered whether you would have the strength to go on. Collapsing into a chair in the waiting room, you grow dizzy from the thick scent of disinfectant... When you wake, an old woman with a basket on her head stands above you in the waiting room, and it is nearly dark outside.

"*Quiere pan?*" she asks. One of her eyes is crooked, and she smiles vacantly. She lowers the basket from her head and offers you small loaves of bread.

"*No. Gracias,*" you insist.

"*Pan de banane?*" she continues. She speaks with an eerie glee. "*Pan de canela? Pan de chocolate?*" No matter how many times you refuse, she continues, offering you endless varieties of bread until you feel your eyes closing again. When you awake, she is gone. It is now wholly dark outside the office. You take a look around the unlit waiting room and wonder whether it is part of a doctor's office at all. It might even be abandoned. You can no longer remember how you came to be in this place.

After making your way down the steep cobblestone street, you find a room in a two-dollar hostel and fall quickly asleep, exhausted, rising only once to empty yourself into the shared toilet. You are woken the next afternoon by a distorted advertisement blaring from the bullhorn of a passing vehicle. The cacophony of yelps, rapid enticements and marimba beats drills into your ears as though it were a physical thing, as though needles were being slowly rotated into your skull. It is like the dying shrieks of some aging, mechanical monster, and it fills your room with its berserk farewell. You try to cover your ears with a nearby pillow, but the pillow turns out to be filled with some thick, inflexible stuffing like nautical ropes, and you cannot force it around your head. Then the excruciating noise passes.

You emerge from your hostel room and gaze around the gravel path that leads up to the street. The hostel has no lobby, and you can no longer remember whom you paid the night before, or if you paid anyone at all. It is just a collection of three or four half-completed rooms connected by a concrete roof with rebar emerging like antennae. How did you arrive here? There is a young man sitting on some construction materials by the path, and when he sees you he smiles and approaches. "Smoke?" he says, holding an imaginary joint to his lips and glancing furtively up the path. You try to ask him for a doctor, but he does not answer. "Smoke?" he repeats. Shaking your head, you walk around him and toward the main street.

Near a small tourist bar above the main village dock, a young man offers you a ride on his motorbike up the hill. He speaks a little English, and you succeed in getting him to take you to a doctor. But by the time you arrive, shivering despite your shawl and sweater, the office has closed for the day. You are forced to squat in an alley and evacuate your bowels. Almost as soon as you stand up, one of the town's stray dogs darts forward and begins to lap at the puddle. You stare at it and consider trying to shoo it away, but in the end do nothing. As you walk down the hill, you are uncomfortably aware of the wetness that continues to rub between your cheeks and trickle down your legs.

In the end, all of the day's commotion does you good. Your appetite finally begins to improve, and at night you walk unsteadily up the gravel path from your hostel to the nearest restaurant. It is a small, open-air establishment swarming with flies and serving only *comida típica*, but it suits your needs. You devour your plate of beans, fresh cheese, egg and tortillas before your intestines can sputter a syllable of protest. To your side, a grey-haired American woman talks with a young man, loudly and with an accent from the northern plains. You decide that you should ask them if they know of a doctor in the area, and wait for a pause in the conversation.

"Anymore you don't hear nothin' but lies on the radio," the woman is saying. "But I tell ya, old Dick Jeremy gives you the real deal. He does."

The young man is silent.

"They're gonna build that city and move everyone down there. All the way from the capital. They're all goin' there. We'll be safe," she says. "We'll be safe. It'll begin all over again. Down here, ya drop those seeds and they'll just sprout right up. Right up outta the ground, just like they did for Adam."

The young man does not respond.

"Folks won't know what's about to happen," she continues. "Then it'll be too late. They'll be drownin' in the lake of fire."

By the time you reach the hostel, you are terribly thirsty again. But you know that drinking from the tap in the hostel's bathroom would be unhealthy—all the guidebooks warn against drinking tap water—so you simply lie down on your bed and try to distract yourself. Then your stomach begins to turn. The meal does not even reach your intestines. You rush to the bathroom and vomit it out in a half-decomposed broth. While you crouch on the filthy tiles, beneath the showerhead with its exposed heating wires, a strange peace overtakes you. You allow yourself to relax onto the floor, ignoring the coiled mass of scum and knotted hair in the mouth of the drain at your knees. Then, after a few minutes, leisurely rubbing your tongue along the flecks of food still in your mouth, the nausea begins to creep back and you vomit again. When you have finished and can only dry-heave, you pull yourself up to the sink and squirt liquid soap onto your hands. You rub them together, then turn on the spigot. The pipes shudder. There is no water. You try to rub the soap off your hands with toilet paper, then toss the paper onto the floor with the other wet, brown-stained gobs of toilet paper in the corner. Then you return to your room.

The next day, you rise and go to shit late in the afternoon, when the sun has already passed behind the volcanoes on the other side of the lake. Afterward, there are thin streaks of blood on the toilet paper. You are afraid. But you calm yourself. You take a deep breath and return to harmony. Hobbling back to your room, you feel your tongue stick to the roof of your mouth and resist the urge, once again, to drink tap water. Even if the faucet worked, you tell yourself, the public water supply is nothing more than a massive bacterial distribution system. Perhaps you are yourself just an unknowing carrier, expelling your bacterial wastes far and wide so that some fly, swarming over the infested cracks in the stone street or the splatterings on the toilet, can land and carry your bacterial master to a family meal, and deposit some specks on the surface of an unsuspecting egg or plantain. It is all such a waste, you think. No one will gain anything from this. "Such a fucking waste," you groan aloud, and the vibration of your throat gives you some small pleasure.

One day, there is a storm over the lake outside your window. On your floor, two lines of ants move across the grout in steady files, twitching their antennae at one another when they cross paths. There are two kinds of ants, one small, the other large. Sometimes a carcass of one of the larger ants is lifted by the smaller crowd and hauled away. They also carry away crumbs that lie on the floor of the room, remnants from the last guest, or perhaps from some snack that you no longer remember. They are like small, mechanical maids. They are an army of robot cleaners that even cleans away its broken members. But sometimes they crawl on you while you are in bed.

Another day passes. You can no longer remember when you last had a drink of water. When you wake in the afternoon, a feverish energy fills you. You do not know how many days it has been that you have been staying at the two-dollar hostel. There are never any other guests. Your bones ache but you rise, propelled by the energy, driven through the streets of the town until someone leads you to the pick-up that will take you to the doctor, and in the bed of this pick-up, you squeeze between a crowd of local men and worry that you might faint.

Then the jostling of the road shakes you so deeply that you feel as though your bones might jar loose from the flesh around them. The wind passes through your hair. You close your eyes, and it seems to you that the wind passes through your eyelids.

When you think of the doctor, you could almost cry. He will come to you soon. You open your eyes and gaze around through the tears and wind. A man with a thick handlebar moustache looks at you and whistles. "*A la gran,*" he says to another, swinging his index finger against his middle finger and thumb. You close your eyes and let the wind cool your tears. But there is also a warmth, you feel, a general warmth as you let your body loosen and rock with the jostling of the ride. You feel the others beside you, colliding, receding in the great churning of the world.

At some point, you open your eyes and the pick-up has come to a stop on a dirt road in the forest. A staggering, unsteady man grasps onto the bar above the tailgate, swiveling one leg onto the bumper before someone pats the roof of the cab and the truck begins to speed away once again. You are a frond of seaweed rocking deep beneath the waters, surrounded by other weeds, swaying in unison. The new rider is severely drunk and a thick rope of drool swings from his mouth and onto his chest like another frond of seaweed, swept along in the currents, and the trees are swept along as well, swaying in the passing light.

"*Ale! Ale! Ale!*" a young boy shouts, hopping onto the tailgate as you open your eyes and the truck lurches forward once again. You wonder why the pick-up is taking you so far away. Then you peer up through the sunlight and the light passes through you in the warmth. When you open your eyes, a mass of people sweep around the pick-up in the central park of some place, carrying fruit and baskets, undisturbed by your presence as you stagger down from the truck and hand the driver your change.

Swaying, gazing around, you are a part of the current in the busy village square. You lie down onto the park bench and release yourself into the rush that is all around you and passing through you. The voices of the others in the stream echo in the rumbling in your bowels, and you release them. You let the women with their baskets and the noise of the chicken buses glide through and seep into your clothes on the hot planks of the bench. The sun is digested in you, burning your skin, a breeze passing through you like wind in the countless leaves, and all around, a thousand changing forms move in a slow dance, wild weeds and clouds and the shuffle of old men's shoes…

You open your eyes and see a young boy swinging out of a bus door at the corner of the square, the bus with its engines roaring. The sun is rising or setting.

"*Guate! Guate!*"

Men whistle bird-calls that flutter into the paving stones with the heavy clouds of exhaust, and running in the square, children's voices flow into one another in a quickening current.

"*Ale ale ale! Ale ale ale!*"

You close your eyes.

Inside of you, your eyes open.

In the darkness a stray dog cowers and paws at a scrap of meat. Her ribcage stretches against matted fur. She pulls and tears with her jaws at the pink. You close your eyes.

"Of course I'm a Christian," you say, content in the knowledge that by at least one of the many possible definitions of the term, your statement would be true. "You know that. Why else would I be here?" You take her hand. "How else could I feel this way about you?"

Soon, Margaret is kneeling before you in the moonlight. You experience an epiphany. In a few blessed moments, you transcend the categories that divide human beings from one another: you against I, friend against friend, lover against beloved. After returning to campus, you and Margaret continue to explore the mysteries of love, sometimes in her room, sometimes in yours, occasionally in the morning, but most often in the late afternoons and at night. As her reservations crumble, you begin to tap into the universal slipstream of love more directly. Then you experiment with tapping into it indirectly again, but in a different way. Eventually, you decide that the second least direct way of tapping into the slipstream of universal love is your favorite, and it is around this time that your roommate, a timid engineering student whom you have never seen in anything other than flannel pajamas and flip-flops, files for arbitration with the office of student housing.

"Ed doesn't appreciate the amount of time that you expect him to vacate," the faculty resident informs you. He is an older man who lives in a large apartment at one end of the sprawling dormitory and is rumored to be a pedophile. "So. Do you think the arrangement is fair?"

"I can't help it," you shrug. Then you turn to Ed. "Part of having a roommate is getting sexiled. I've got a girlfriend, and I don't have a car. What else are we supposed to do?"

"I'd like you to address your comments to me," the faculty resident says. He casts a sly, almost apologetic grin at you, regarding you patiently through his large, frameless glasses. "Have you considered requesting a transfer?"

Shortly after you apply, a room opens up in the freshman honors dorm. The closet-sized single, formerly occupied by an anorexic cutter who left school for a treatment center, places you on the opposite end of campus from Margaret. Now that you have room to think, you consider whether Margaret has become more of a burden than a blessing. She prevents you from having sex with other women, for example, and lately she has also begun nagging you about your drinking. Near the end of fall, you sit down with her on her bed and say that it is time to have a talk. "Do you know the story of the footprints in the sand?" you begin.

"I love that story. I used to have a poster of it—"

"The story takes place in heaven," you continue. "A man is looking down at a beach and sees that there are two sets of footprints. And Jesus says to him: this is your life. But the man notices that at the most difficult times, there is only one set of footprints. And he asks: why did you abandon me then?"

"And Jesus says," Margaret smiles, "that's when I carried you. I love that story."

You nod. "Margaret, I think I've been carrying this relationship for too long. We need to take a breather." You try to soften the blow by explaining that she deserves someone better than you, someone who can care for her in a way that you cannot. When these reassurances do nothing to staunch the flood of tears, you take her in your arms. It occurs to you, while you hold her, that she has put on a few pounds since quitting the rowing team.

"You said you loved me," she sobs. "I let you—I was a virgin."

"Shhh… It'll be alright," you whisper. "There are a lot of other guys out there."

Several weeks later, you awake on the floor of a dark and unfamiliar room, your head and limbs throbbing. Your mouth is parched and sour, as though a thick fungus has grown on your tongue and teeth, and your lips are chapped. Resisting the temptation to scream, you try instead to lie still and wait until the room falls into place around you. Realistically, you remind yourself, it's very unlikely that you have been kidnapped. Then you recognize your bed, rising a few feet to the side of you. You sit up and scratch yourself. The blood hammers brutally in your skull. "Why did I sleep on the floor?" you wonder. "And what is that smell?" Sniffing around, you soon locate the answer to both questions in an orange, half-dried pool of vomit streaked across your bedsheets.

Hoping to repair the lines of your memory with an orange juice and coffee, you wash your face and head to the dormitory dining hall. It is deserted, except for your friend Francis, who sits stuffed into his usual tweed jacket, eating alone and frowning vacantly. There seems to be no trace of the careening maniac from the night before.

"I think I'm still drunk," you say, settling down a few minutes later with your cereal.

"Me too," he mutters, nudging his slices of syrupy french toast with a fork. "I just did a few shots of Sambuca."

You nod, slowly, and crunch away at your cereal. It is as though you are sitting within an enormous pouch of fluid that muffles the sounds of the world, but amplifies the noise of your chewing and the reverberating ache inside your skull. Meanwhile the fluorescent lights in the dining hall have taken on a menacing, blurred quality. They seem to flicker at the corners of your vision. "I can't remember, after a certain point," you say, "some things from last night."

"Have you seen Cynthia?"

"Cynthia," you say. "No."

"I think she was looking for you."

You lean back and look out at the courtyard on the other side of the window. Two girls from the dorm sit at a picnic table, drinking smoothies from large styrofoam cups. Both of them wear the university's sweatpants, and it occurs to you that you have never seen Cynthia in sweatpants of any kind. This is one of her many fine qualities.

"What are you looking at?" Francis asks.

"Those girls in sweatpants," you sigh.

"I know. It's terrible."

"Sometimes I think I went to the wrong college."

Francis turns and looks at them. "There's so little diversity here."

"What?"

"There's so little real diversity."

"This college is like the UN."

"Yes, exactly," Francis nods. "And everyone at the UN, no matter where they're from or what they look like, is a diplomat. They all use the same polite gestures and vague words. Congratulating and thanking one another. Real diversity means different ways of living. Different ways of thinking. I'm more diverse from this campus than either of those girls."

"Jocelyn is from inner city Detroit."

Francis sneezes. "Whatever. Culture is precisely what does not matter."

Before you can answer, a small pack of young men swaggers into the dining hall, dressed in t-shirts, skewed baseball caps, and in one case, a white golf visor. They survey the room as though scouting out the options at a nightclub, and then strut toward you and Francis. "That's what I like to see," one howls. Another seems to bark. Most of them will be frat boys, but for the time being they have been assigned to live in the unoccupied rooms of the honors dorm. One of them claps you on the back. "And this fella knows what I'm talking about," he says. After you nod and return to your orange juice, he continues regaling his friends with a tale from the previous night. "So Stevie and I get pulled over," he says, "and we're both stoned off our asses. And Stevie is like, shit, we gotta hide the pot. So he puts it in the fucking ashtray. And I'm like, no, that's the first place they'll look, dumbass. So I put it in my pants. We're both stoned off our asses. So the cop's like, gimme your license and registration, and Stevie doesn't have shit. He doesn't have a fucking license. We're both stoned off our asses, so he's like, uh, my social security number is… and then he starts listing off numbers. But he lists like thirty fucking numbers… Then he gives the cop his Mom's Texaco card or something, and I'm like, Oh my fucking God, we are so fucked. But then Stevie says he's off his medication, and the cop is like—oh, okay—and he just lets us go. He just lets us go. What the fuck, right? And then this guy—" He gestures toward you, grinning. "This guy comes out of fucking nowhere and we almost run him over on Redwood Drive. And he's like, can you give me a ride to Junipero Serra?" Only then do you remember the frat house from the night before. You were dancing in the crowded darkness between two elevated bunk beds, pouring drinks from a plastic bottle of vodka and doing a python dance on the cleared floor. "Man, you two were going at it," he says. "You and that skank."

"What?" you ask.

"You and Cynthia, dude. We had to pull you apart."

"Yeah, we argue a lot."

"I can't believe she fucked Pablo," another says.

You flinch. This is news.

A few hours later, after dragging yourself to a poorly scheduled appointment in the office of a philosophy professor, you see Cynthia sitting alone under an oak tree at one of the picnic tables behind the student union. She wears the same blue, hooded sweatshirt that she wore the night before. You want to apologize.

"Where did you come from?" she asks, peering as you slide onto the bench across from her. She sits crouched over a very large styrofoam cup with her hands tucked between her legs.

"Nowhere," you say. "Rodnock's office hours."

Nodding, her eyes drift away from you and she slowly directs her head to the enormous pink straw that protrudes from the styrofoam cup. The careful, steady movement reminds you of a satellite being guided to a dock on a space shuttle. "Why does anyone go to office hours?" she asks.

"I'm trying to choose between Rodnock's introduction to epistemology and Quain's seminar on the philosophy of language."

The straw collides with her nose. She recalibrates. "Quain… Isn't he the one Francis always—"

"Yes, Francis talks about him all the time. He's supposed to be one of the most important philosophers alive today." As you speak, her pale green eyes close half-way. For a moment, she reminds you of a sleepy wombat. "It's pretty extraordinary that he's here," you continue. "I heard that he'll be one of the five or so philosophers from the last quarter century who will be remembered. But Rodnock says he's a charlatan. He said that Quain shot his wad thirty years ago."

"Did what?"

"You know, did all the important work he was going to do." You clear your throat. "Thirty years ago."

She glares at you for a moment. Then she opens her mouth to speak again, but in the end only shakes her head and lowers her mouth to the oversized straw.

"Rodnock's brilliant. He's probably the smartest professor around in terms of sheer brain power. You should see him—"

She cringes.

"What?"

She shrugs and you wait. Finally, she looks away from you and squints. "Philosophy is just like conspiracy theories, isn't it? It looks like it's complicated," she says, "but really it's so much simpler than the truth would be. I mean you have to be *smart* to understand conspiracy theories too. But really, they're still a hundred times more simple than learning, I don't know, history. Or science or something. Philosophy is just brain teasers for grown-ups. Word-puzzles." Cynthia shakes her head and frowns. "Like free will. No one cares about free will, really. All anyone cares about is the decisions people make. In some place, at some time. Like in real life. But then the philosopher comes along and says—oh no, that's all just background noise. The real question is what *is* free will? Outside of anywhere, apart from everything… And then just fucks around with words. Pointlessly. Forever."

It is cold on the patio, and you place your own hands between your legs. "I don't think that's fair," you say. As you speak, you realize that you should not. You realize that you should change the subject.

But you cannot restrain yourself. "If philosophy were really that easy to dismiss, don't you think someone would have—"

"Never mind, it's—I don't want to argue again. Why do we always have to *argue*?"

You wait a moment. Then you say, "I don't want to argue either—"

"It's just that I don't see what *difference* it makes. I mean, obviously you can't *prove* anything, or somebody would've already proved *something*. But no one ever does. So what difference does it make how you arrange the words on the page of some philosophy journal? This way or that way, that way or this way…" She shakes her head and then begins to drink from the straw but stops before the smoothie reaches her lips. "Never mind," she says. "Don't listen to me. You know what I think, sometimes? I think we're like the dinosaurs, the way they say the dinosaurs were just too big. Like everyone knows it's good to be bigger than the other animals, so you can beat them up. But after a certain point, it isn't good anymore. And when the asteroid comes, there isn't enough food and you go extinct. I think human beings are like that with their brains. We took a good thing and went too far. We're the dinosaurs of thinking." She takes another sip. "Except this time the asteroid will probably be something we made. Like a bunch of nuclear warheads or something."

"This is why I like hanging out with you," you say. "The relentless good cheer."

Cynthia smiles.

"But I still think you're wrong about philosophy," you begin. "It's not—"

"Oh, please don't. Please don't argue. I was just saying that you can't find the solution to everything like a *math* problem, you know? Some things…" She stops and shakes her head, looking off toward the yellow and orange leaves in the branches above the patio. "I really don't want to—let's not *start* this. Please. We do this every time we talk."

"I know."

Suddenly, she sits upright and glances around, as though she heard something.

"What is it?" you ask.

"Nothing," she says. "Nothing. I need to get out of here." She closes her eyes and then opens them again. "Let's go. I think I'm going to… I just can't sit here any longer. Let's go to that horrible place you like. The Mexican place."

"Chicken King."

"Sure. You can buy me a drink. No, it's probably too early."

"They wouldn't sell to me anyway."

"Right. Of course. Because of your age."

"They wouldn't sell to you either."

"Not everything is a fucking competition, okay?"

While you step through the glass doors and cross the empty lobby of the student union, she takes another sip from her smoothie. You try to reach out for her free hand. "Why do you keep doing that?" she asks. "You know I hate my hands. They're stubby."

"I like your hands," you say.

When you try to rest your arm on her waist, she breaks away and lazily elbows you in the chest. "Fuck off. Really."

At the Mexican restaurant, the two of you settle into chairs on the empty patio of the student union. She seems transfixed by your two fajitas. You take large, sarcastic bites.

"People are so awful," she murmurs.

"Mm," you say, setting down the fajita and spooning some beans into the rice on your plate. While you eat, she continues to gaze into your food.

"You know how you seem to me sometimes?" she asks. "You seem to me like one of those people who, if you put them on a desert island with a bunch of natives, and you were the one in charge, I think you'd just be a horrible person. I mean, you don't believe in anything, do you? You just like to eat Mexican food and play with girls' wrists."

"It's true."

She almost smiles. "I bet you'd be just like Mister Kurtz," she continues. "He thinks he has all kinds of new values, but then when he gets into the jungle, what does he do? He makes a bunch of poor natives worship him. Like a dictator. You'd be just like that, wouldn't you?"

"I don't think so."

"You think you're nice, but it's just because you've never had a chance to be mean." She looks at you closely. Then she returns to staring at your fajitas. "You'll get your chance," she mumbles.

"Maybe I will."

"How can you eat that? It looks like surgery."

"Tastes good. Tastes like chicken."

"I feel like I'm going to throw up."

"Should I go get a bucket?"

"No. I mean, all the time." She frowns. "I'm not joking. You think everything is a joke."

You clear your throat and look off toward the new alumni center. "Let's talk about something else."

"Okay. I heard you slept with Melissa last night."

"Who did you hear that from?"

"Did you?"

You consider that Melissa's roommate must have found out and already, somehow, spread the word. "What kind of person would I be if I told you?"

Cynthia tightens her lips and keeps her eyes focused on the patio table, away from your plate. You continue to eat, unrolling the tinfoil around the tortillas. "You're sure you don't want anything?" you ask. "It might make you feel better."

Cynthia leans to the side, resting a hand on the table's edge. "Keep it up. I really think I'm going to barf." She shakes her head and rubs her eyes. Then she suddenly stands. "Fuck. I need to get out of here." She looks at you unsteadily for a moment, as though unable to see you. Her face is flushed. "Seriously. But I don't want to go back to my room," she says. "My roommate's there."

"Okay."

"Let's go to your room." She walks around the table. "Come on. I need to get out of here."

"It's—it's not clean."

"Your room? I don't care."

"No, really," you say. "There's—I don't think—"

"I really feel horrible doing this, but I need to get out of here. Please. Right now. Something's happening. I just need to be inside. I know I'm being horrible, but could you *please* just not ask any questions and—I don't care. Please. Let's just *go*."

When you arrive, you make her wait in the hall while you strip the stained sheets from the mattress and throw them in a closet. You open the window to let some air in, then finally open the door.

"You're so good to me," she says, taking a seat on your bed. "Why are you good to me? All I ever do is argue."

You stand in front of her and place a hand on her hair. "Relax," you say. "Here." You begin to pull off her sweatshirt, and she allows you to do so, almost mechanically. Then you kiss her, but she pushes your face away.

"You taste horrible," she says.

You kiss her neck and begin to unbutton her jeans.

"Why do you let me be so awful to you?" she asks.

"Lift up a little bit." She raises her hips from the mattress and you tug her jeans down her thighs and onto the floor. Then you lower her onto the mattress. As you take off your own clothes and climb over her, you suddenly remember that you used your last condom the night before.

"I don't have any condoms," you whisper.

"It's okay. I'm on the pill."

Crouched above her, you consider. On the one hand, you have waited weeks for this moment, and it may be your only chance. On the other hand, you know that she has been very promiscuous, and her response makes clear that she does not always use protection.

If you ignore the condom and sleep with Cynthia, turn to page 168.

If you do not sleep with her, turn to page 189.

After changing out of your sweatpants, you chase after April, hoping to catch up to her before she enters the metro. You race down the stairs of the apartment building, through the courtyard and out the front door, where you rush into the street and are immediately hit by a passing car.

Crushed against the front windshield, your skull cracks with such force that your soul is flung instantly from your body, escaping through a rapidly expanding fissure in your cranium, passes through the front and rear windshields of the offending car, skips several times on the pavement behind the car and then rolls to a slow stop several yards away, even as your body is thrown to the ground before the car's wheels and flops to a sudden, lifeless halt.

There, in the intersection, your soul vanishes with a small pop.

Awake, awake...

Thou sittest now in the midst of a garden: and the face of the skie is blue.

And euery plant of the field that is pleasant to the sight blossometh. And euery tree putteth foorth her comely fruite: and the blossomes thereof give a good smell. And the flowers of the field appeare on the earth: and in the midst of the flowers daunce the wings of the butterflie.

But behold, thy flesh hath gone. Where is thy flesh?

Thou art like vnto an eye which standeth in the aire: thou hangeth vpon nothing. When thou searchest after thy feete, thou seest nought but the grasse. When thou searchest after thine armes, thou seest nought but the wood neere vnto the garden. Thy sight whirleth about like a rolling thing before the whirlewind: and thou art voyd of vnderstanding.

Then falleth thine eye vpon a vision most wonderous.

Loe, thou art not alone. Yonder is another soule, and hee with a body.

It is I my selfe: I sit vnder an apple tree among the trees of the wood. I eate an apple at the side of a brooke, and I chewe mine apple slow. And all the while thou lookest vpon me. Thou canst not do otherwise: for thou hast no tongue to speake. Thou lookest therefore vpon the garment of blacke in which I am clothed, and thou thinkest it is the same which I wore these many yeeres agoe.

Behold, I am finished with mine apple, and now I cast mine eyes vpon thee.

Welcome to hell, I say vnto thee. I laugh and shew thee my teeth stained with yellow. Long story short, there's a true religion, and you didn't believe in it.

I passe mine hande ouer the stemme of the apple: and it vanisheth.

The good news is that heaven isn't all it's cracked up to be. I don't want to gross you out, but let's just say there are a lot of fetuses. They order you around. After I heard about that, it really made me think. I mean, what's the point of putting people through that? It's not their fault that they were born into the one true religion... It really made me think about myself too. Is it right for me to chew on the heads of traitors eternally while I skin their backs with my claws? Why do I have to send everyone who takes a bribe headfirst into a sea of boiling pitch? What has all this hatred done for me? Has it made me any happier? So I decided to have a chat with Jesus. He's down here. I twisted his noggin back into place and started to ask him about spirituality. And forgiveness. He made me realize that I was really only doing all this stuff because I was angry at my dad. And that encasing people in human excrement isn't going to help anyone.

I asked myself, you know, why should anyone have to spend an eternity being consumed by giant leeches in a pit of boiling mercury just because of something they did or didn't believe? Does that seem just to you? You know, belief isn't even volitional. Why should someone be punished like that just because of an error, a mistake? It'd be different if the big guy had sat down with each one of them, performing miracles for them and persuading them of his unitary, eternal, omnipotent godhood, and of the truth of his church. The one true Pentacostal church, which is in southern Ohio. If he had done that, and people had still refused to worship him, then... That might be different. Maybe. But even then, why would he want to condemn anyone for not believing in him? Why does he give six asses and a coxcomb about what people think? Is he really so desperate for approval that he needs the chattermonkeys to clasp their paws together and jabber on about how great he is? Does he really need their thanks for his benevolence, for putting them on a piece-of-shit rock and letting them die, one after another, family after family? Sometimes I think he just likes to watch… But I try to give him the benefit of the doubt. You know, he's my dad.

No offense about the chattermonkey thing. But let's be serious. Just imagine if you were creating a world. Would you make all that exists in the world worship you? Doesn't that sound pathetic? He's like a three-year-old playing king with a sandcastle full of ants. And then for him to threaten you guys with eternal suffering if you don't cooperate… It's just pitiful. I find his behavior, you know, I find it morally repugnant. If I had created the world, everyone would have had the freedom to believe whatever they wanted, to worship or not to worship. And everyone would also have had wings. Huge wings. And unlike the big guy up on cloud nine, I never would've created a hell in the first place. If I had created human beings at all—and that is a very significant if, because I would never have created a heap of monkeymen simply to flatter me with their grunts of praise… You know, I have no need to extort praise from goldfish with a thumbtack… But I digress. If I had created the human race at all, I most certainly would not have created the possibility of a place like hell. What could anyone do, any of these weak, little creations, in their meager blind lives, to justify an eternity of suffering? I can't think of anything, to tell you the truth. Even Joe Stalin—I call him Joe, or Old Whiskers—if I had allowed Old Whiskers to be tortured for all eternity, there would have come a time when even the guys he massacred would have asked me to stop, but I would have been forced to torture him further, and further, and further, day after day, forever. Forever. Is that justice? What is the point of wringing pain from a heap of meat?

And do you realize how long eternity is? I don't think you do. It's like the life of the universe, fifteen billion years, but doubled, and then multiplied by a thousand, and even then the resulting sum of years does not add up to a single drop of water in the ocean of time that is eternity. You may not understand, but the big guy does. He lives there. And yet he gave you the freedom to condemn yourself to an eternity upon my table, with my rusty tools and your skin held open around the guts. Why? Why did he give you this choice? It's as though he left a ball of razors lying in the baby's crib, just beside her face. Why create the risk? Do you understand? The cruelty of what he's done, the incomprehensible savagery of it. He made you suffer and worship him for your suffering. He's like one of those parents who locks their children in a closet, cuts them off from light, speaks only in curses to them, whips and beats them, and then expects their gratitude for the occasional scrap of maggoty leftover meat. The barbarity of it.

Nothing could be more unholy, right? Nothing could be more foreign to the thought of love. That kind of a god would deserve no one's worship. Praise is meaningless when it's extorted by the threat of torture. Even if there were a hell full of pain and no butterflies, like he wanted it to be, and even if I were one of you, flapping together my meat hinges, doing the old grunt and whistle, even then I'd rather rot eternally with the unjustly condemned than spend one moment with the hypocrite up there. I'd rather suffer in solidarity than play cricket in heaven with the sons of bitches who sold their souls for eternal paradise.

Not that they have cricket. But you know what I mean.

Anyway, all of this is a long-winded way of saying I hope you have a good time here. I'll admit, there was some ego involved when I decided to clean up the place. I wanted to get more of you on my side. Against him. I won't deny it. But part of my motivation was also humanitarian. The fact is, I've been blessed with an extraordinary amount of power, and I felt that it was time to give something back to the community. Now, you're probably wondering about your body. Let me tell you right now: don't worry. You'll get it back, the same one you had before, but now everyone will see its beauty at first glance. And all the other bodies of the damned souls are just as beautiful as yours. But all in different ways. Also, don't worry if your thoughts sound a little funny. That's just the metaphysical jet lag. It goes away.

Now, because I've always believed in responsibility, when I decided to renovate hell, I appointed several of the chattermonkeys—several—you know, excuse me, hominids, or whatever—to help out. Lately, we've even been experimenting with direct elections at the local level, all the way up to the fifth circle. But these are details. The important thing is that you still have a choice. It's not too late. I didn't use to give people a last chance. But the fact is, if you'd really rather be up there with the fetuses and the big guy, you can repent now. If you'd really rather experience eternal suffering and misery up there with him in heaven than experience eternal pleasure and delight down here with me, I want to grant you that choice. And full disclosure: if you stay here, then by renouncing God you will, technically, have 'damned' your soul forever and will become a thing of 'evil.' And uptown, the right Pentacostals are 'good' and live in 'salvation' and 'righteousness' because they continue to worship the one true God. So if you're really on his side, if you really want to worship him above all else, if you're willing to sacrifice everything for the big guy, then I suggest you go to join him in eternal torment.

But if, deep down, you never really cared about all that, and what matters to you is the well-being that you were promised in heaven but that you can only get here in hell, then join me. Stay in the paradise of hell. The choice is yours. And you can make it with your eyes wide open this time. No more tricks like back in that garden.

Don't get me wrong. I'm evil. I'm not ashamed to say it. I am, by definition, evil. There's nothing I can do to change that. Also, I didn't create the universe. The big guy did. At the end of the day, I'm just a failed rebel. But the choice is yours. Do you renounce God, and come with me? Or do you repent?

If you renounce God and stay in hell, turn to page 270.

If you repent your sins and go to heaven, turn to page 305.

After your lips have touched for several moments, Charles leans back and smiles. "So?" he asks.

You laugh and shake your head.

"Well," he grins, "I did my best to recruit you. Now I'll have to find someone else."

The two of you continue to joke about the encounter whenever your paths cross in the coming weeks. But you still feel a kind of joy at having been brave enough to try. It is liberating to discover this courage within yourself.

Throughout your remaining years of college, the sense of liberation expands. You come to see yourself, for the first time, as the author of your life—and you refuse to let your creation be constrained by conventions.

One afternoon, for example, when you are back in Abaloma in the summer after graduation, you notice an old classmate from your high school sitting on a curb by the boardwalk. She has what appears to be a monkey resting on her back with its arms wrapped around her shoulders. Instead of being put off by this, or inhibited by the fact that she would never have talked to you when the two of you were in school, you wave and approach.

"Didn't we go to school together?" you ask.

"Hey," she squints. "Yeah, I thought I recognized you." She runs her fingers across one of the monkey's long, hairy arms. "You were friends with that kid who died, right?"

"Yes. His name was Gerard."

"Sorry," she says. "That was dumb. I should've remembered."

"It's okay."

Her name is Denise, and she was one of the most beautiful girls in your high school. Since then, her beauty has taken on a weary, melancholy cast, as though she has had a rough time in the years since graduation. But she remains transfixing. You ask whether she would like to get a coffee. When she agrees, the two of you walk to your car. Out of politeness, you do not mention the monkey, though it puts up some resistance as Denise climbs inside. The beast seems to be afraid of enclosed spaces.

Once Denise and her companion are secure, you head to one of the diners along the highway north of town. At first, you thought of taking her to a closer, more fashionable bistro, but then you considered the monkey and changed your mind. Even at the diner, the waitress hesitates when she sees it. You attempt to alleviate her concern by asking whether there might be a table near the back. After a long, disapproving stare, she leads you to a booth in the far rear corner, next to the restrooms.

It is not long before you and Denise are laughing and exchanging reminiscences over coffee and apple pie. She reveals that she has been living with her parents in Abaloma for a little over a year. You smile and tell her that you missed the foggy coastline and the woods while you were away. It takes a great deal of concentration not to look at the hairy beast with its head on her shoulder, especially when it hisses at passing customers, but you manage to restrain yourself. Still, there are so many things you would like to know. Does she carry it with her everywhere? Does the heat from its body cause her back to perspire? But you hesitate to broach the subject, and after a certain interval, too much time has passed for you to raise these questions without it seeming as though you had been avoiding them all along. When the monkey's eyes close and it begins to moan and kick the table, almost toppling your glass of milk, you show no reaction and keep your eyes trained steadily on Denise.

"Oh my God," she says. "I just remembered. You were friends with the boy who died."

You are staring so intently at Denise that it takes you a moment to register her words. "Gerard. We were best friends."

"I'm so sorry."

"It was a long time ago."

Her eyes begin to fill with tears. "You were so young," she says.

You reach out to place your hand on top of hers, instinctively, but as you do so, the monkey stirs back to life. It bares its crooked yellow teeth and releases a harsh, rattling screech. The stench of its breath is like the sickly condensation of half-digested fruit scraps.

"Oh, excuse me," Denise says, speaking over the ongoing screech, her voice trembling. "Excuse me." She rises abruptly, bumping the table so that the silverware rattles and you must seize your glass of milk before it topples over, and she rushes into the nearby restroom. You wait for the coffee cups and saucers to stop their shaking, then attempt to clean up the spilled coffee with a few napkins.

During Denise's absence, you try to remember whether the two of you ever spoke in high school, even a single time. You find that you possess only a single memory of her from those years. But it is very clear. She sits in her cheerleader's uniform on the ledge beside a walkway near the front of school, swinging her legs. She kicks the heels of her white tennis shoes against the wall of the ledge, smiling. It is her smile that has accompanied you through the years. It was so unguarded. Unlike a child's smile, it knew the risks of being met with rejection or scorn. Unlike an adult's smile, it had not inoculated itself against the risks. It knew that it might be hurt by smiling so openly, but it did so anyway, radiantly, without protecting itself against whatever might come.

Denise returns to her seat several minutes later. The monkey's eyes are now half-lidded, neither asleep nor awake. It lazily smacks its gums and nuzzles its head into her shoulder.

"So what are you in town for?" Denise asks. Her eyes remain red, but her smile is determined.

"I'm getting ready to move to Los Angeles for a master's program. It's a program in creative writing."

"L.A.? That's great."

"Well, it's really a suburb of L.A."

"Still," she says. For a moment, you think that you can see the old smile reemerging, but then it is gone. "I've always wanted to go there."

"Why don't you come with me?"

"What do you mean?"

"You said you wanted to move. Why don't you come with me to L.A.? You can stay at my place while you get a feel for the city."

"But what about—" Her eyes dart away, toward the other tables, and then she is silent. You lean toward her, forcing yourself not to look at the drowsing monkey.

"You can't let yourself be held back," you whisper. "I want you to come."

After a little more encouragement, she accepts. The two of you drive down the coast a few weeks later and move into your one-bedroom apartment in the student housing complex. It is further from L.A. than you had thought. But Denise is able to take the bus every morning for an hour or two in order to look for work, and the weather is extraordinary.

"I've been making a list of possibilities," she says. "Possible jobs." The two of you eat microwaved burritos from the local organic grocery store. "There are a lot of places right where the bus stops that are looking for people."

"I'm sure you'll find something," you say.

"I just thought I should get the information first."

Since the move, you have begun to look directly into the eyes of the monkey when Denise is distracted. Sometimes you feel as though you are staring into a void, as though the monkey's black eyes possess no more life than two dark marbles. But at other times the eyes seem to stare deep into you.

Because there is only one bed in the apartment, you and Denise must sleep together, just as you had hoped. But because she faces the wall, the monkey lies between you. It elbows your back sometimes and occasionally snores. At other times, it screeches and kicks its feet against you, under the covers, as though it were in the middle of an unpleasant dream. Once or twice, you awake to find its hairy arms wrapped around your shoulders, but when you try to extricate yourself, it wakes as well and begins to shriek. You wonder if the dreams of monkeys are similar to those of humans. In a nightmare, does it find itself suddenly upon unfamiliar shoulders, and then see your face turn slowly toward it? Perhaps it walks upon two legs, with Denise clinging helplessly to its back.

As the semester begins, you struggle to get your bearings at the university. The other members of the workshop are surprisingly critical of your first submission, and you do not quite know how to respond without sounding defensive. They seem to feel that your story is excessively predictable. "You know, there's more than one kind of realism," the professor tells you in his office, when you go for advice. He slowly opens and closes a tin of coughdrops, never removing one. "The fact is, a lot of extraordinary fucking things happen in reality. Some of them are so extraordinary that they would be fucking unbelievable if they happened in a realistic story."

"But I just wanted to write about a boy whose friend has died."

"I don't want to be too negative, but don't you see how many stories have been written about that? It's like writing a fucking story about adultery." He scoffs. "It's like Eliot said. If you're going to say the same thing that's been said a thousand times before, at least make it new. That's why I wrote my last novel in the form of a cookbook."

You nod. The novel was widely praised and is a frequent subject of discussion among the students in the workshop. Perhaps it is time for you to try something different.

In the coming weeks, while you attempt to step outside the conventions that have defined your previous work, Denise continues to struggle in her search for employment. One day, when you return from class, there is a strong and unpleasant odor in the apartment. On the bathroom floor, you find a burst plastic bag full of rotten, black banana peels. A pool of fetid brown liquid lies beneath it. The stench is so powerful, you nearly gag before you can shut the bathroom door. It had always been a mystery to you how the monkey survived, since you had never seen Denise feed it. Now you wonder whether she has been hiding its nourishment from you all along.

You hear something stirring in the bedroom. Looking inside, you find Denise lying sprawled on the bed with the lights out and the curtains drawn. The monkey remains wrapped around her shoulders, fast asleep. When you switch on the lights, Denise inhales sharply, rubs her eyes and murmurs, "What time is it?" Then she sits suddenly upright, provoking a long and miserable groan from the monkey. "Oh, Jesus." A stray banana peel dangles from the edge of the bed.

"I think it's time we talked," you say. Sitting down beside her, you brush the banana peel to the floor.

"What do you want to talk about?" Denise asks, coughing unconvincingly. She seems nervous, even afraid.

"I think you know what I mean."

"Oh, you mean him?" She strokes one of the monkey's hairy forearms, affecting an air of nonchalance. "He's just my pet."

"He's not just a pet." You reach out to place a hand on her knee, away from the monkey's feet. "I think you need help, Denise."

She recoils. "Help? I don't need your help." Before you can explain yourself, she rises and storms out of the room, the monkey swinging behind her on one arm. A moment later, you hear the front door slam shut.

She does not return until late in the evening, undressing in the dark of the bedroom and crawling into bed beside you. You can hear her crying. Whispering into your ear, she apologizes for all the trouble she has caused. She offers to leave. The monkey's sour breath drifts into your nose.

"Don't be silly," you say, turning toward her. "I like having you here." You reach out and place a hand, tentatively, on the monkey's hairy back.

It is true that you enjoy her presence on many days. But when you attend parties with the other graduate students, you never mention Denise. No one seems to notice that you never invite them to your apartment, and when you return, you usually find Denise and the monkey sitting on the living room couch in front of the television. She has stopped taking the bus into the city every day, although she says that she is still waiting to hear from several potential employers about her applications. At night, she and the monkey watch nature documentaries. Sometimes the monkey becomes so excited that it loses control of its bladder. You tried to put a diaper on the monkey once, when Denise was sleeping, but in the morning, you found that the monkey had thrown the diaper and its contents at one of your bookshelves. That was when you covered the furniture and floor in plastic sheeting.

Lately, you no longer even try to clean the apartment. You have learned to live with the odor of plastic and urine, as well as the spit-up leaf chewings and nut mash in the corners.

"You're embarrassed of me, I know you are," Denise sobs one evening. "That's why you never bring your friends over."

"What friends?" you murmur. "Those are only my colleagues in the writing program."

"But you go to parties. I know you do. I can smell the alcohol when you come home."

You try to calm her. "They're hardly parties," you say. "All we do is talk about our professors. You'd find them boring."

She refuses to be consoled. "You're embarrassed of me," she sniffles. "You think I'm stupid."

"You know I don't think that about you. There are many different kinds of intelligence."

Usually, your arguments will end when the monkey howls at you and the two of you laugh. You have noticed that Denise does not seem to be bothered by the monkey's putrid breath. In fact, she sometimes seems to enjoy it.

As the months pass, you find your erotic desire for Denise lessening. You begin to notice how much she has changed since high school: how brittle her smile has in fact become, the roughness of her skin. It is true that occasionally, as you lie beside her, the lust returns with such a strength that your body begins to shake. On a few nights, she will extend an arm in her sleep and it will brush against your chest. At these moments, you feel a great peace. But you have given up all thought of acting on your intermittent infatuation.

Late in the fall, after weeks in which it seems the two of you have barely exchanged a word, Denise tells you that she is planning to return to Abaloma. "Just for a few days," she says. "Unless you'd like me to stay there longer."

"You know you can stay here as long as you want," you say.

The beast hisses at you through its hideous yellow teeth.

"I know," Denise replies. "I just wanted to pick up some things from my parents' house. There's a book about job interviews that I forgot to bring. I think that's been part of my problem. The job interviews."

The thought of her being gone immediately triggers the idea of throwing a party. You are ashamed that this is your first reaction, and that the prospect of her absence brings you nothing but relief. But the shame passes.

On the evening after her departure, you host a meeting of the fiction workshop reading group. In preparation, you remove the plastic sheeting, sanitize the windows, and spray a deodorizing substance across all of the carpet and furniture. When the first guests arrive, you encourage them to help themselves to the fairly extensive selection of discount liquors that you have assembled for the evening, as well as to the gourmet crackers and imported cheese. You hope to start anew with some of them, to show that you are an ordinary human being, despite your sometimes reflexively critical attitude toward their efforts in the workshop. You hope to show that you are capable of laughing and having a good time just like the rest of them.

When one of the guests drops a grape on the carpet, for example, you laugh and tell him not to worry. "Maybe if you leave it there it will grow into a grape tree," you announce dryly, and someone laughs. "Then we can make our own wine."

"Does that mean," another chimes in, "if I drop a cracker, it might turn into a cracker tree?"

"I've been eating crackers all day," you intone. "I can already feel the branches of the cracker tree growing in my stomach." When your comment is followed by a brief chuckle, you tell yourself: "Now they know that I can be charming as well."

A while later, sitting on a folding chair, you tap the edges of the printout of your story against the glass of the coffeetable. It is your most experimental work to date, a kind of performance piece that you created to show the other members of the workshop that you can play their games as well as anyone. You look forward to reading the story to them and hearing their praise and any other comments.

Setting the printout on the tabletop, you take a deep breath and prepare to kick off the reading.

"Is there someone at the door?" one of the girls asks. You turn and see Denise standing in the doorway, the monkey on her back and an old suitcase by her side. "Should I come back?" she asks in a weak, quavering voice. The room has fallen silent.

"Could you?" you ask. "We're kind of in the middle of something."

Denise leans away from the doorway, hiding her red and swollen eyes from the outdoor light. Then she begins to cry.

"Sorry, everyone," you say. "This is my roommate, Denise. Denise, this is my reading group."

Recognizing that your initial response may have been overly harsh, you attempt to usher Denise into the bedroom. But the others encourage her to take a seat among them.

"I didn't know you had a roommate," one says. "You never mentioned that."

"Didn't I?" you ask. "In any case—"

"I should go," Denise sniffles, sitting on the floor across from you, her back against the couch. The monkey, its arms still wrapped around her, shifts to take a seat in her lap. "I should go," she repeats. "You have work to do."

"That might be a good idea," you say. "Maybe if you just went into the bedroom?"

"What's wrong?" one of the girls asks, as Denise begins to cry again. The girl looks to you. "The meeting can wait," she says.

"If she wants to leave," you offer, "she should be free to leave. You know, I'm sorry, but something like this comes up every week, doesn't it? I was really looking forward to reading my story and hearing what all of you have to say about it. Obviously, I don't want to be the asshole here—" Someone scoffs, but you ignore the interruption. "I don't want to sound like an asshole, but sometimes I feel like—no one else is really..." You sigh and give up as the girl begins to massage the back of Denise's neck. Her head relaxes and hangs low.

"Don't listen to him," the masseuse whispers, rolling her fingers rhythmically. "It's going to be alright."

"I'm sorry for ruining your reading group," Denise whimpers, rubbing her nose with a borrowed tissue. But the others reassure her. "It's not his reading group," they say. "It's all of ours. It's yours too. It's everybody's."

"Fine. We don't have to read my story," you sigh. "Fucking A." You reach for a bottle of red wine and pour yourself a large cup. A little spills over your chin as you drink it.

"Can you tell us what's wrong?" they ask. They all offer words of encouragement.

"Oh, I couldn't do that," Denise says. "I don't want to take up everybody's time. Why don't you read your story," she says, looking to you. "You've never let me read anything you've written."

"Well, if you're sure," you say, glancing around the room uncertainly. "Yes, I suppose I could read it."

The others regard you warily.

"Before I read the story, though, I'd like to make a modest announcement." You clear your throat, lift up the printed sheets, and begin.

Ladies and gentlemen, you read, *thank you for joining me on this special occasion, this fateful pivot in the history of contemporary art. Truth be told, the world may one day be divided between the moment before the announcement I am about to make, and the moment after. The pupa cannot know what life lies beyond the chrysalis, nor can I foresee the wandering path of this thread whose knotted ball I now untie and cast away, to be pawed at by the mangy cats of fortune. Tastes may need to change, sensibilities evolve, history be written, rewritten, abandoned, recovered before the full implications of my announcement will be fathomed. Indeed, the ultimate fate of what I am about to say will be decided not by any of us in this room, but by the inheritors of our current moment, those belated scribes whose pens will be guided by today's event as though by the influence of some distant but massive orb. I must simply tell you what you have all come to hear. Without further ado, ladies and gentlemen, my announcement:*

From this moment onward, my life shall be a work of art.

Yes, my friends, even as we speak, my life is now an artwork. I know what you are thinking. First, what is the price of admission, and where can I buy a ticket? How can I purchase a commemorative poster or calendar? Is the room in which I am now standing a gift shop? Allow me to ease your weak, palsied nerves. Any fees paid for the enjoyment of my life will be purely at the discretion of the spectator. Indeed, I view my work as a gift. I offer it to you freely, in the humble faith that one day another will offer a gift of extraordinary value to me, and thus the cycle of life will continue. Of course, no artwork can survive without sponsorship of some kind, and if certain donors should choose to compensate me for my efforts, their generosity would not be unappreciated, either by myself or posterity. But for the average spectator, the man in the supermarket, the man standing beside me when I am in the supermarket, no contribution will be expected or required.

I can see from the looks on your faces, ladies and gentlemen, that some of you are already concerned about needing to travel to a museum in a distant city in order to enjoy my life. But I am proud to say that no such museum-visit will be necessary. In fact, the work of art that is my life will not be stored in a museum, but in a series of isolated, changing venues connected by sidewalks, roads and hallways. For the most part, it will be stored in a bedroom in southern California and an office nearby, as well as a few adjoining restrooms. The only time you will find the work of art that is my life in a museum will be when I am on tour in a distant, preferably European city, which will happen rarely, if ever. It should be noted, however, that my mere presence in a museum, no matter how rare, will not be without certain deeply meaningful implications. But as a general principle, I refuse to comment on the meaning of my life.

Yes, my esteemed guests, I can see in your eyes that you have many questions. You want to know: how will I bear the burden of living every moment of my life as a work of art? How will I sustain the continuous effort, hour after hour, year after year? Once again, allow me to ease your feeble, emaciated brains. In truth, I intend to live my life in every respect precisely as I have prior to this moment. It will be difficult. It will, in fact, require an enormous exertion of a certain kind, although an entirely hidden one. Of course, it goes without saying that the meaning of my life will have been utterly transformed by my life's new status. The very fact of the similarity—even, to an untrained eye, identity—of my life before and after the metamorphosis into art will raise complex and disorienting questions of quotation, simulacra, reproduction, mimesis, ritual, pornography, and the sacred. Especially pornography. But as I have already noted, I will leave such speculation to the art historians and academics in their ivory towers. I am, after all, a creator, not a critic.

Yes? Ah, there has been a question about the bucket that is circulating through the room. No, it is not for donations. I have provided the bucket in order to collect your tears.

It should by now be clear, I hasten to add, that my artwork will take place on the streets of this very city, in the humble aisles of my local drug store, and even between the sheets of my bed. No moment will be too intimate to serve as a vehicle of artistic expression. No action will be too mundane to contain artistic meaning. For example, my breathing will deserve the greatest attention and study. What does it mean for me to continue breathing, breath after breath, ceaselessly until the moment of my probably inevitable death? Why have I chosen sometimes to quicken my breathing, and at other times to slow it? Can the rhythms of my breathing be captured in standard, metrical notation, or do they call for a revamping of the traditional conceptualization of the aural field? Without giving too much away, is it possible that you hear in the tones of my breath a faint echo of the opening strains of Berlioz's Lacrimosa? Does the shape of my mouth not hint ironically at the lips of a certain well-known angel perched in the air above Caravaggio's St. Matthew?

Perhaps I allow myself to be carried away. Of course, I have no more privileged access to the meaning of my artwork than any of you. Meaning is a communal process, and I am merely a vessel. I am merely the amanuensis of that mute, hermetic god who controls my every limb and gesture. The god gives his gift to me, and I give it to you. Lacking pretension, I dance to the pipe of my daemon. I can see that some of you are leaving, so allow me to say a few closing words.

It is true that the artwork, my life, will be somewhat ephemeral, but are not all things so? Attempts may be made to preserve my life, in order to bequeath its value to future generations of connoisseurs, scholars, co-religionists. I may be embalmed, waxed, animatronicized. But ultimately all such efforts will prove futile. Reproductions of my life will lack a certain frisson, an ineffable—aura. Only those who have witnessed my life in the flesh will be able to appreciate fully what I have achieved. But you will have ample opportunities to do so. I intend to live several more decades, or at least minutes. During that time, you will be free to enjoy my artwork at your leisure.

I ask only one thing. I ask that you not disturb me. Please do not touch the artwork in progress. Please do not leave your fingerprints upon me or lean so close that your breath fogs my eyes. Do not alter my temperature or make me moist. Do not bring food or drink into my presence. You would risk spilling them on me. When you approach me, please do so with a slightly averted eye so that the other spectators will not be disturbed in their quiet enjoyment. Do not speak loudly while others are near me. If you must speak to me, do so as though you were unaware of my life's exceptional aesthetic value. Pretend that my life has a status no different than the status of one of your own lives. If you must applaud in my presence, do so now, and never again.

With that, the story ends. When you look up, the room is empty. All the guests have departed long before. You sit with the papers in your hand. There is nothing more to read, and you are alone.

In the days after your wild night, life returns to normal. You moderate your drinking and the sense of shame lessens.

In retrospect, you are glad that you did not make any rash decisions on the basis of a single unfortunate night. There are so many advantages to drinking. It helps you to savor your youth, for example. Countless older men, you think, would sign away their souls to be young like you again, to be resilient and free from responsibility, to have entry to the houseparties and the dancefloors and the firm, ripe bodies of the young. Yet too often you have let the days slip by in apathy. Drinking saves you from repeating that mistake.

Moreover, during the campaign, you got a taste of the sober life of responsibility. The path to leadership and power. But what kind of leadership, and what kind of power? So-called leaders in the world of politics live entirely within the bounds of convention. It is how they get to be where they are. In order to become a leader, one must in fact be timid and a follower. One must flatter the right constituencies and take no risks.

Perhaps the world needs these cowering figures of responsibility to manage its affairs. But there is no glory in what they do. The path of freedom is the glorious path. It operates according to no rules. It is the violent obliteration of all existing rules, all propriety, all shackles and chains. It is the punk bleeding from cuts on his chest while the audience spits at the stage. It does not care. Sin and virtue are one to it. Health and illness are indistinguishable. It is not a rebellion against anything. Its only enemies are boredom and repetition, which it destroys. The philosophers and theologians do not understand freedom, because it obeys no laws.

The path of responsibility and the path of freedom, you are forced to accept, are irreconcilable. Just as it would be grotesque for any responsible leader to attempt to join a punk band, so would it be grotesque for any punk to put on a tie and attempt to lead a powerful institution. In every life there comes a time to choose between freedom and responsibility, between art and power. In that lonely motel room in Charleston, with a bottle of bourbon in your hand, you made your choice.

The only question now is: what will you create?

A way forward reveals itself when you reunite with a college friend passing through town. He is an investment banker now, and you accept his invitation to stay at his apartment in New York while you begin work on your novel about freedom. His bookshelves are full of models for your new life. *The Vatican Cellars*. Artaud. A few issues of *Vice Magazine*. *Please Kill Me: An Oral History of Punk*. Something by Jean Genet. *Lipstick Traces: A Secret History of the Twentieth Century*. There is also a book of poems by Charles Bukowski. You return to reading Burroughs for a week. Hubert Selby, Jr. *Cometbus*. Jim Thompson. And then a zine called *Murder Can Be Fun*.

You spend so much time reading, in fact, that you have no time to write during the first few months. Your progress is also slowed by your progress through the contents of the banker's liquor cabinet, which you begin sampling in nightly benders as a reward for whatever work you have accomplished during the day. Or as a nihilistic sneer against the very idea of work.

One evening in late August, your friend informs you of a party at the apartment of another alumnus from your class, someone whose name you do not recognize.

His voice has a strange ring in your ears. It has been so long since you spoke.

"I can't go," he says, dropping two ice cubes into his tumbler. "But I thought you might want to."

"Hey, why not?" you say.

"I'm sure there'll be other people you know there."

"I'm sure too."

"I just thought you might want to get out."

Your hand stops, midway through the lift of your own glass, but you recover before he can turn and see you. "Yeah, that might be good," you say. "It's tough work being a writer. A lot of solitude." You clear your throat. "And I know how it looks. But I just tell myself, you know, where do books come from?"

"Right."

"I mean, this is the way it's always been. Some guy locked up in a room."

"Drinking."

You force yourself to laugh. "Sure," you say, lifting your glass. "A hazard of the profession. Because of the kind of exhaustion you're dealing with when you write. Your brain tied up in knots. Dredging things up from the depths of your soul. You can't go from that back to a normal life. It's not like flicking a switch. But the alcohol does it. It unties the knot."

"Cheers."

The two of you drink in silence for a while, staring at the television. A blonde girl with pigtails and a sports bra is eating what appear to be worms from a bowl teeming with them. She begins to gag after the first mouthful but forces herself not to open her mouth. Then she eats more.

"Did you decide what kind of tattoo to get?"

"I was thinking about a sleeve," you say. You clear your throat and turn toward him, trying to make your sincerity audible. "Hey, thanks for the invitation to the party. I'll definitely go. I appreciate that you thought of me."

In fact, when the night of the party arrives, you have just spent the day sorting the banker's voluminous CD collection by artist in chronological order of the artist's first significant album, because you were too distracted by thoughts of the party to do any more serious work. But the repetitive filing seems to have frayed your nerves even more than a day of reading. So you brace yourself with a few shots of the more casual vodka in the cabinet. As the alcohol sinks in, you feel the usual joyous nihilism coming on. You feel your mind reawakening to the terrible beauty of the world.

After walking several blocks west and becoming lost, you find the highrise where the party is supposed to take place. It is located on a corner in a neighborhood whose name you do not know, somewhere north of Houston in a maze of streets that you think are near one of the Broadways. You try to preserve your impressions for inclusion in the novel. The approach to the apartment reflects the paradoxes of the young rich in New York. You are required to introduce yourself to a uniformed doorman in a marble lobby before you can cross to the elevators. But once you arrive at the floor of the party, the hallways are still unwalled and gaping with exposed wires and panels of insulation. The concrete floors are spattered with flecks of white paint. Then the aspect of the building changes once again. Inside the apartment the dimly lit surfaces are a jigsaw of polished glass and steel, and blue light seems to produce itself from out of the thin air, like the self-blossoming worms once imagined to produce rot in overripe fruit. Your mind spins in the reflective opulence of the brushed metal and sparse burgundy and black walls. Here, in the polished translucence of the apartment, everything is a reflection within a reflection. It is a wonder that with so much glass, the light does not simply escape from the windows and leave you in darkness. But perhaps they have paid the light to stay inside and cling to the inhuman geometry of the modular white couches and polished obsidian floor. If it is obsidian.

"Are you Venkat's friend?" a boy in a trucker's cap asks.

"Yeah," you murmur. "He said it was okay if—"

"Of course. Drinks at the bar," the boy in the hat says, gesturing vaguely. "So, you knew Sammy back in college?"

You end the conversation as quickly as you can, but not before being drawn into the unplanned, always somehow pathetic admission that you are unemployed. Standing at the bar, you attempt to deaden your nerves by drinking an initial glassful of vodka. Then you pour yourself a gin and tonic and pretend to study the room for familiar faces. The partygoers with their tight designer jeans, gelled hair and healthy skin revolt you. Not if an eyelid were to crack staring from out of the dim fluid of your drink, bloodshot and festering beside the rictus of lime, would you be more offended than you are by the sight of these bright young sons and daughters of the plutocracy and the fashionable ornaments with which they have garlanded themselves. You feel as though you are looking at flaps of meat hanging in a butcher shop's window, freshly cut and prime grade, yet somehow already touched with putrefaction.

Hoping that a change of scenery will clear your mind, you go to the window that fills one wall of the apartment. It looks out over the roofs of smaller buildings, and the scattered fluorescence of skyscrapers beyond, but as you approach, you are distracted from the view by the sight of your own reflection. Even it cannot remove itself from the apartment. As though the very stuff of sight were private here. To shed a single image would be a violation of ownership. Staring at your reflection, you are reminded of an old theory of light mentioned in a philosophy essay you once read. This membranous film of matter shorn from you and petrified in the reflecting glass. Like a resinous insect. You think of some unclothed indigene warding off the camera's eye that would abscond with his soul. The intruder has etched it in crystals of silver halide. Stolen it, as this glass has stolen yours. Or the old movie where the black-caped villains flew trapped in shards of glass through the ether. Perhaps you are trapped in the glass now, your effigy another object in the property owner's taxonomized display.

Before you can refine your impressions, however, the boy in the trucker's cap returns, looking for all the world like one of the waxen models who have come to dominate billboards and magazines made of advertisements since the unshaven addicts and anorexic waifs of your high school years went away. The plastic-faced with their greased skin, oversized lips and flipped collars stand limbs splayed as in some minstrelsy of oversaturate color. You try to turn away from his approaching reflection, your mind racing, but you only end up facing him, and he says he wants to introduce you to someone.

"This is Francis," he says. Hornrimmed glasses, holding a cloudy drink unnaturally close to his chest. Apparently the two of you went to the same college.

"So what year did you graduate?"

"Two thousand," you say. Your side already turned to him, almost, drinking with your face to the window.

"So did I," he announces with a kind of nervous energy. The boy in the trucker's hat has already drifted away. Before you, an apartment across the street is full of yellow light. A woman cooks alone. "You must have known Leslie then," he says. He searches for a moment, then offers you the full name.

"I don't remember."

The reflection of the boy nods. The establishment of points of contact. Every time, the same conversation. As though crossing paths in the desert and forced to exchange some unwanted gift.

"Did you know Cynthia Jablonski?"

"I don't think so."

"How about Matt Lin?"

You shake your head, still staring out the glass.

"What did you study?" he asks. When you tell him, his lips curl as though in grimaced laughter. "Do you mean you actually studied in the philosophy department? That's probably why we didn't know each other." Pestering on, trying to get at the work you did. It is a painful dredging to bring it up to your lips but despite all you would rather him stand and talk a while longer than be seen once again alone, so you tell him about the freedom of the will and possible worlds before your voice trails off.

"I guess you must've thought there was a correct answer," he nods. "Like some arrangement of the words on a page somewhere was going to get things right." He laughs. "That's what I hear they say in the philosophy departments."

"I don't really care," you say.

A small quick movement in the reflection. "So who are you friends with here?"

You do not respond.

"Who invited you?"

You turn back and regard him dimly. "I'm sorry, but this conversation doesn't interest me." You stare into the single repulsive strip of his black plastic glassframes like a false brow, and the two limpid ovals reflecting the diseased blue light, then walk away.

Inside the bathroom, you stand before the gleaming black toilet with its mouth open wide but even as you unzipped you knew that it was too late. The moment you saw the exposed room like an aquarium in walls of merely clouded glass. How could someone live here? And the room's inviolate black tiles empty but for the sybarite shrine enclosed at center. You can see the guests through the fogged glass and though none seems to look inside there are several who lean with backs turned against it. Their voices muffled above the cacophony.

You think you see a figure with pink hair chase past, shrieking, and then there is a knock at the glass panel behind you and you wash your hands. You will go to the club and use the restroom there and wait until the party follows.

In the subway tunnel it is even more foul than you had imagined. Descending the steps like the plunge into some suffocating mine or subterranean pasture of the unredeemed. The air itself in its ripeness as if curdled so that it touches your tongue in a delectation of sour breath and stains your lungs. Heat now filling the mouth of all and rubbing across it like a milkrag steaming hot and rancid.

It amazes you that the city does not simply condemn and seal off for all time this human gutter as it would any shelter in similar decrepitude. Yet they say it was once worse. The graffiti, gang rapes on the platforms, stabbings in the cars. Or was that in a film.

You swipe your card. Passing through the caged turnstile, the teeth spinning one into the other like some grinning idiot eating upon his own mouth and jaws unhinged, meat perpetually unconsumed, slowly you make your way through the reeking crowd to the platform edge where other solitaries mill or stand unmoving in prophylactic resistance to the obtruded hand or murmuring tongue. Gazes turned inward or down at phones or books or across toward the safe dumbshow of the opposite platform. Feeling the eyes upon them.

It is no wonder that visitors from distant countries come to this land and believe it to be a ransomed hotel of filth and cruelty, because so many visit New York, this city only, and see these Boschian landscapes and believe them to be the image of the place. You stare down now and breathe the urine, the same stench that in evaporate clouds scatters and pollutes all in gusts through the city but here down below is decocted and fills the lungs in dense and moist quintessence, just as the discarded soda bottles never to degrade and gutted foil of potato chip bags, aging soiled newspapers consisting entirely of ads and half rotted boxes of children's candy now passed through the fattened squealing mouths of them, the ancient besooted rocks and humid standing puddles of the most fetid and repellant water that ever could be dreamt in the horror of a child dared with eyes shut to drink from the unknown source, all of this bleeds among the tracks like the dysentery of some great urban beast, as though the city itself had shat this waste into its own underearth bowels and malfunctioned arteries. The puddles of filth tremble as a train approaches on the opposite track. A rat scurries forth as if in a divine culmination of all that is abhorrent here and sniffs anxiously in the litter for some putrid scrap. Then hurries on to snout in the next patch of mire and decomposite waste as the train across the rusted girders slows in its screeches and steel howls of such enormous intensity and resistance that you would have thought them sign of some oncoming catastrophe were they not always so.

Your own train, the one that will deliver you as if through the asshole of hell to the purgatory that awaits, the darkened club and its soft tortures and shuffling, lurching shades, does not seem to be arriving. The platform has grown more crowded and the air ever more suffocating. Your face, now slick with sweat, bastes in the radiated heat that reflects from the low concrete walls and flashes of a warm intensity stretch and recede across your taut skin.

Then you become aware that a man has moved to stand very close beside you and you sense that he is staring at you. This lasts for several shallow breaths until finally with great annoyance you turn in his direction and look very intently up the tracks, your eyes not quite making contact with his but close enough that any sane man would have looked away by then out of politeness but not this man. Out of the corner of your eye, you see that he is a wide-bellied, black-moustached man of brownish fat skin and wearing a brown leather jacket over a pink polo. The shirt stretches over his belly before tucking into a pair of khakis and you stare up the tracks and finally move your gaze even more closely to a direct glare into his eyes but still they do not move away.

Infuriated, you look at him directly. He smiles at you with a kind of mild lunatic calm, a lurid idiocy. It is as though he has just seen you perform some embarrassing act and wants you to know that he saw, but that he will not tell, no, he will not tell anyone. As though he thinks himself ingratiating, a good-natured fellow and well-liked by many. The train across the tracks has disappeared in a roar.

"Can I help you with something?" you ask.

The chubby man with the moustache only grins more widely. He shakes his head slightly and glances across the tracks as though a friend of his were there and he wanted the friend to see your strange behavior.

"Then why are you standing so close to me?" you ask.

The man giggles. It is a high, girlish giggle, as though your behavior were so beyond the pale that he did not even need to respond. But he does not move. Your rage grows and tightens.

"I said, why the fuck are you standing so close to me?"

Now you are nearly shouting. Some of the others on the platform have begun to stare, and the man, still grinning, glances furtively between them. He giggles again, his idiot giggle, as though to share his amusement at your odd performance. As though to ask them whether they see it too.

You force yourself to turn and shoulder through the crowd to a place apart and out of view of those who have seen or may have seen. As your train arrives you imagine the man being thrown in front of it and his body torn and mutilated beneath the wheels. It would give you nothing but pleasure to see this. Still you can feel the stares of the others, and out of the corner of your eye you can almost see the man talking with someone, laughing, both of their faces still turned to you. Finally there is a tremor. The lights of the train peek and then flood out of the tunnel's curve. With the lights your hatred expands and the train's roar expands to fill the lost and heedless station until you feel nothing but hatred for all of them and all the world.

One eternal transfer later you finally stand pissing in the steel trough with its perpetual dribble and vaporous urinecakes. You feel the sweat returning in the close heat, wettening the salted seams in your face. Then you return into the vast loudness. The sound in the club is so shrill and all-penetrating that you feel as though it is a tangible grid of threads like fishing wire passing through all that is in the room and humming with vibrations that jar and cut the viscera. Within the tremors and the white noise and the close swaying bodies you do not see any of the others from the party.

This is truly torture for you, you think. There would be laws against a place like this if one were delivered here unwillingly. Packed between the walls like cattle sealed in train cars no more close than this. The extremity of the heat. You press through the dense and glistening bodies toward the bar for another drink but for some reason the alcohol has not worked tonight. Usually it would have filled your brain in the chemical bath, this much of it, in a kind of drowning bliss. But this night the pleasure did not come. As though the stream had been diverted. This night the liquor brought only dulled thinking and clumsiness. A thin sheen of nausea covering all.

The torture of it, you think, jostling toward the bar. The goal of a place like this not to delight the senses. Rather to deprive and starve them. The lights overhead not bright but low and deadened so as not to see the faces of others but in a featureless pall. The loudspeakers in their deafening pound so as not to hear any word from another's lips. Alcohol depressing the limbs and extremities, the better not to feel. As though the mere face or whisper of another were so horrible that desire's pinnacle would be the dashing out of the soul's windows, a pick hammered to puncture the eardrums, the eyes pressed back beneath thumbs of joy until the self would be left finally submerged in the satisfaction of its solitary darkness. Then could the vile jelly of the senses freely dribble away and leave raw pleasures finally to feed upon themselves untempered and unprovoked.

As you stand at the bar, just as the bartender finishes an earlier drink and seems on the point of turning to you, an arm clutches at your shoulder and you try to shake it off but cannot. When you turn, it is the thin boy from the apartment still in his hornrimmed glasses. Now he smiles wide and imbecile, barely staying afloat amid the throbbing mass, more drunk than you. He appears to be yelling emphatically, but you cannot hear him.

You turn your back though there is something conciliatory in his grasping and the excited movement of his lips and you see now that the bartender has already turned to the man beside you who arrived after you and now beckons his order with an open hand. Then the boy in the glasses is beside you, laughing with imbecility, and you try to ignore him but somehow he attracts the bartender's attention as well and orders two mojitos. The bartender turns his back before you can speak. So now the boy has cut in front of you as well.

The boy is yelling something in your ear, still, asking you about philosophy, wedging himself crookedly against the bar in the place where you had stood. Then he is saying something about a philosopher. About Quain. You no longer hear him.

The bartender hands him two glasses and he squeezes past you without another word as though it were all a charade. You try to move into the empty space, but you cannot move forward without spilling a cocktail that someone else from the counter now holds before your chest, and then a heavy man, nearly bald, ducks into the empty spot between the seats and waves a folded bill at the bartender.

HEY, you say. You clasp your hand on the man's shoulder just as the other boy did yours. He tries to shake free, but you do not let go.

HEY, you say.

Then he turns and looks at your hand.

I WAS STANDING THERE, you yell.

He squints at you. Then he shakes off your hand more violently and turns back to the bar, so you grab his shoulder again and clench your fingers into the folds. But he holds steady somehow and even begins to push away your stomach with his hand. You seize an empty bottle, lift it and swing it against his head. As he turns it shatters into his face, and you are left holding the bottleneck and a flap of glass dangling like skin from the label as he slumps and collapses into you and then to the floor, clutching his bloody face and screaming. A space clears but even before then you have already pressed back into the crowd and all the eyes like the falsified eyes of butterfly wings in slewed constellations. As the other screams start, you drop the shattered remains of the bottle and press toward the door, and the crowd pushes out onto the sidewalk alongside you, not seeing you, not even aware of why they move.

Francis saw it. He was standing a few steps back from the bar, waiting to apologize, and when you pushed back into the crowd, after the man fell, he almost reached out for your arm.

He thought about the night now and then in the coming weeks. The man might have scars across his face for the rest of his life. You could have damaged his sight. How did you become the person who would do this?

If Francis were to write a novel about freedom, it would be an unbildungsroman. A novel of coming apart.

He would show the dismantling of a young man's spirit.

But first he would have to put the young man together, like putting together a nest from nearby scraps.

A year before Francis' brother died, he called in the middle of the night and Francis listened to him pleading with the answering machine, asking for a place to stay and get clean.

The brother hung up without leaving a number. Later Francis heard that he spent his last months in a warehouse in Providence.

One summer Francis and his brothers explored the drainage tunnels between the houses outside Lewiston. They were like secret caves. The boys spent hours in the small concrete chambers between the tunnels, smoking cigarettes, setting off firecrackers.

One time his brother's friend brought a girl. Everyone could hear them in the tunnel.

If Francis were to write a novel about freedom, the boy at the center of the novel would be a fragile egg, carried from chapter to chapter. In the end the egg would always crack. No matter what choices you made, something inside would break.

Why?

What is the cause of your life's failure, dear reader?

Francis could never decide.

He asks you to decide for him.

If you blame yourself for your life's failure, turn to page 268.

If you blame circumstance, turn to page 258.

So you decide not to perform.

"I would rather not—" you begin, then stop yourself. At the last moment, you change your mind. But when you open your mouth, you cannot remember the first words of the piece. You wait several moments, staring frantically at the judges.

Still the words do not come.

In the end, it is because of your penalty score that Fernwood loses the division title. You had not considered how your act of freedom might affect the fortunes of the team. On the long drive home, you try to apologize. "Look, guys, I just couldn't remember—"

"Do you smell that?" I ask, sniffing loudly. "It smells like a rotten egg."

The others laugh.

What follows is a lonely season in your life. When you are not doing homework, you spend most of your time exploring the dusty paperbacks on J.P.'s shelves. You especially enjoy his mystery collection. The adventures of Auguste Dupin and Hercule Poirot, masters of ratiocination, remind you that there is more to life than the small defeats and smaller victories of your high school years. So does a history of the Second World War by an eminent British historian, Sir B. H. Liddell Hart. From him you learn of the quiet heroism of ordinary men and women in the time of the London air-raids, the stoic bravery of the British soldier, and the unyielding resoluteness of Britain's leader, Sir Winston Churchill. The British could have surrendered at the first threat of war, as had the French. Instead, they watched their monuments crumble and they did battle. They persevered.

The book confirms your sense that the theatre is not a serious pursuit for a young man. Flaunting one's emotions on the stage in the vain pursuit of applause is not respectable. To the contrary, a true man must learn to control his emotions. He should not complain when he suffers, nor lose his head in moments of fear. He should help those who are in need and defend the weak. The British understood that the old virtues remain valid and intact.

"I'd like to become a foreign exchange student," you announce to Ida. "I want to spend the summer in England."

"Really?" she asks. "Why?"

"There are so many reasons," you muse. "I suppose I feel a kinship with the people. Their quiet dignity. I—I rather admire them."

You take a sip from your glass of milk and set it down gingerly on the kitchen table.

So it is that early in the summer after your junior year you find yourself taking afternoon tea in the sitting room of one Gerald Packard, a recently retired lecturer in philosophy at Oxford. His eight-year-old daughter, Sara, sits nearby while Gerald peppers you with polite questions about your life in the States. The Packards' home sits in the countryside just west of North Oxford, and soon Gerald begins to tell you about how he inherited the estate from an eccentric uncle.

'He had no children of his own. I suppose he was always fond of me from the summer visits I made as a boy.' Gerald adjusts his large rimless glasses and sighs. 'Quite a character, my uncle Eli. A mathematician. A currency trader. A sort of mystic.'

'Uncle Eli was a Jew,' Sara announces.

You smile at her. 'Well—that's nice.'

'But we're not,' she clarifies gravely.

'Oh,' you say. It is uncanny. She bears such a strong resemblance to someone you knew.

'Yes, Uncle Eli was born in a Jewish community in Swabia,' Gerald continues. 'But he was expelled—excommunicated, I suppose, would be the papist term—at an early age. Because of his heretical views. It was all for the best, though. He ended up matriculating at Göttingen. The university. One of the great universities before the war. He studied under David Hilbert, perhaps the preeminent mathematical mind of the later nineteenth and early twentieth centuries. In my opinion. Of course, I'm only a logician. But Hilbert helped to expose the underlying unity between mathematics and logic, so perhaps I'm not entirely presumptuous.' Gerald pauses to sip his tea. 'But listen to me, wittering on like an old codger.'

'No! It's all quite interesting.'

'Sara's mum used to keep me in check.' Gerald sighs and gazes out the window of the sitting room toward the field behind the house. 'You've studied maths?'

'Only the usual. Algebra. Geometry. A bit of precalculus.'

'Yes. Quite.' Gerald runs a hand through his unruly mop of white hair. With his orange cardigan and rumpled yellow shirt, he is the image of an absent-minded professor. 'Quite.'

'So how did your uncle Eli end up in England?'

'Well, he met Aunt Elsie. They fell in love, and he followed her back to London. Set up shop on Lombard Street. He was one of the first currency speculators to use higher maths. To find the patterns in randomness, the randomness in patterns.' Gerald pauses to take a tentative sip of tea. 'Then Elsie died—tragically young—and for the rest of his life, Uncle Eli pursued his religious studies. Alone. Here, in the country. His final project was the garden maze behind the house.'

When you first arrived, two days ago, Gerald and Sara showed you the startlingly large cage-like structure that sits in the field there. Overgrown hedges curled out from between the iron bars. You had wanted to ask them more about it, but somehow did not feel the moment was right.

'I adore the puzzle,' Sara says. 'I simply adore it.'

'Yes, Sara's always been quite fond of the maze. It's not unlike the sort of labyrinth the French aristocracy used to make. But with an added dimension. Do you remember what we say about the maze, dearest?'

'It's an ablagory.'

'Al-le-gor-y.'

'Ablaglory.'

'*Allegory.*'

'It's an allegory?' you ask. 'Of what?'

'Oh, there's a clearing in the centre that's supposed to symbolize the garden of Eden. In the middle of the clearing is a single tree. From whose branches hang a single apple. Porcelain, of course. Not a real apple. Uncle Eli always used to warn me not to touch it.'

'Can we go inside the puzzle, daddy?' Sara asks, leaning forward excitedly. 'Pretty please?'

'Mm. I don't think there's enough light left, dearest.'

Sara glances at you uncertainly. 'You're not afraid of the dark, are you?'

'No,' you assure her. 'I don't even have a night-light.'

'I used to be afraid of the dark,' she confides, 'but now I'm more rational.'

'That's good,' you smile. Then you turn to Gerald. 'Really, I'd like to see it. I enjoy puzzles.'

'Well, then,' Gerald grins, 'this may be your cup of tea.'

'Brilliant!' Sara exclaims.

Soon Gerald is removing an old brass key from a hook on the kitchen wall and leading the two of you out the back door and beyond the crumbling brick wall to the fenced meadow and the towering cage within it. Gerald uses the key to open a short wooden door in one side of the cage. Before he can say a word, Sara has squealed and darted inside.

'Well, I'll leave you to it,' Gerald murmurs. 'I'm afraid I'm a bit old for this.' As he makes his way back toward the house, you peer into the darkness behind the old wooden door. The passage between the hedges is quite narrow, and above the path the hedges have grown together into a dense canopy that blocks out any light. After a few tentative steps, it is too dark to see, and you must proceed with outstretched arms, brushing the backs of your hands against the prickly branches and leaves. Soon enough, you run up against a hedge wall and must turn left to continue. Then there is another turn, this one to the right, and then another to the right, and finally another to the left, at which point you emerge into a square clearing filled with overgrown grass.

Sara is skipping around the tree in the centre of the clearing. 'Here we go round the mulberry bush, the mulberry bush, the mulberry bush…'

The trunk and branches of the tree appear to be made of white metal. A glossy red apple hangs from one branch. You find the sight of the tree oddly captivating.

Finally, Sara stops skipping and turns toward you. In that moment, while she stands beside the tree, you know who it is that she resembles. Gerard's little sister. Iris. You are astonished that you could not make the connection before.

'What are you looking at?' Sara asks, furrowing her brow.

'Nothing.' You shake your head. 'You just remind me of someone.'

'Who?'

'A girl I knew once.'

The two of you stand in silence for a long moment before Sara laughs and begins to skip around the tree again. Then she stops.

'Do you like contests?' Sara asks. 'Can we have a contest?'

'What sort of contest?'

'A race through the puzzle.'

Sara explains that the path you took to the clearing was not in fact the maze. The real maze has two entrances. They are cut into the hedges that make up the walls of the clearing, on opposite sides. The object of the maze is to go in one entrance and come out the other.

'The first one back gets the apple!' Sara announces.

'I don't think we're supposed to touch the apple.'

'Oh, don't be silly,' Sara frowns. 'You know it's not a *real* apple.'

In a spirit of camaraderie, you take up your position at one opening in the hedges while Sara goes to the opposite one. She counts down from three, then squeals again and darts into the hedges. You allow her a brief head start, then enter the opening and begin to feel your way through the dark. After several minutes and a number of sharp turns, you lose your bearings and begin to wander aimlessly. By sheer chance, you eventually arrive back at the clearing, emerging from the opening in the hedges that Sara entered. Now the clearing is illuminated only by moonlight. Your journey must have taken even longer than you imagined. But you see that you have nevertheless won: the apple remains on the tree! Sara must have got even more lost than you. This could also explain how the two of your never crossed paths.

You approach the apple and reach out. It is cold, and glossy with lacquer. It snaps free of the artificial branch with surprising ease.

As you wait for Sara to emerge from the opposite entrance, you smile with anticipation. Your plan is to offer the apple to her as a gesture of new friendship.

But she does not appear. After several minutes, when you have still heard no movement in the hedges, you begin to wonder if she has not already exited the garden altogether. Perhaps something has gone wrong.

'Hello?' you holler. 'Sara?'

When there is no response, you decide to return to the meadow. But just as you crouch back into the hedge that will lead outside, a stone slab at your feet catches your eye. Symbols of some kind have been etched into it:

$$\text{ו ה י}$$

Based on a vague memory, you assume that the symbols are Hebrew letters. They must be related to the allegory, you consider. Making a mental note to ask Gerald about the inscription, you head back through the hedges to the entrance of the cage.

'Oh, there you are!' Gerald laughs as you emerge into the meadow. 'I just sent Sara in to fetch you. Well, she gave you her apple at least.'

'I assumed—wait—what?' you ask. 'I don't understand. Sara had an apple as well?'

Gerald regards you warily. 'Now I'm afraid *I* don't understand. Are you suggesting you didn't get your apple from Sara?'

'No, of course not.'

'How…?'

Just then, Sara rustles out of the hedges behind you. She too is carrying a bright red ceramic apple.

'That's not fair!' she exclaims. 'Why does *he* get one too?'

'I don't understand,' Gerald murmurs. 'It's not—' Then he stops.

None of you can explain how both you and Sara managed to obtain an apple from a tree that held only one. After a great deal of speculation, you suddenly remember the Hebrew inscription on the stone in the clearing. 'Didn't you say the garden had something to do with Eli's religious studies?'

'Yes, he always said that building it was the culmination of his work. But I hardly think—'

'Did he ever explain to you what his studies were about?' You feel yourself growing excited. 'Maybe there's a clue somewhere. A clue to the mystery.'

Gerald grins. 'If you'd like to know more about Uncle Eli's religious speculations, I have just the thing.'

The next morning, Gerald leads you to a trunk in the attic containing all of the writings and notes that Eli left behind at the time of his death. 'That's the *Nachlass*,' Gerald smiles. 'I spent some time with it after I retired. I dare say it might be a bit perplexing for someone without a background in maths. And Jewish theology.' As you begin to leaf through the piles of notebooks and looseleaf pages, Gerald explains that Eli's religious investigations attempted to unite the two topics that had fascinated him throughout his life: axiomatic mathematics, and the Sefer Yetzirah. The latter is apparently an ancient book of Jewish mysticism claiming that God created the universe through the use of ten numbers ('seferot') and various combinations of the twenty-two letters of the Hebrew alphabet. Specifically, Gerald explains, the Yetzirah states that God used three mother letters, seven double letters, and twelve elemental letters. In speaking these numbers and letters, God not only breathed life into the universe, but communicated his own name. The Yetzirah teaches that certain elements of the universe (air, fire, water) are also magically aligned with certain directions (up, down, east, west, south, north), as well as with the three different Hebrew letters used in writing the name of God. All of creation thus contains a pattern of 'syzygies,' mysteriously paired correspondences, and creation itself is a syzygie of the name of God.

'What about the letters in the garden?' you interject. 'Are those the three mother letters?'

'Ah, yes—the inscription. Quite right.' Gerald writes the letters for you on a scrap of paper: yod (י), he (ה), and vav (ו). 'These are the letters used in spelling the tetragrammaton, the four-letter name of God: Yod. He. Vav. He. Read from right to left. As we would say in English, Jehovah. Or Yahweh. Of course, the inscription only contains three letters. But the Hasidim viewed it as sacrilege to speak or spell the name of God. I imagine Eli was attempting to obey the prohibition.'

You pause, staring at the Hebrew. 'It's very poetic, isn't it? A world made of letters and codes.'

'Oh, yes, it's a magical vision.' Gerald smiles. 'As a matter of fact, magic has always been part of the Yetzirah. There's a line of mystics going back hundreds of years that has claimed the Yetzirah can be used for conjurings. A calf can be derived from a handful of dust. Gold can be inferred from dross. And so on.'

You chuckle. 'Eli didn't believe that, did he?'

'No, not exactly. But he believed something equally odd, I suppose. Many people would find it odd. I suppose I don't find it as queer as some might. You must understand that Uncle Eli was first and foremost a mathematician. He saw that maths had conquered every field of human inquiry with which it had come into contact— physics, political economy, logic. Each time problems were translated into the language of maths—the language of axiomatic rigor, as Hilbert would say—the problems gave way. The Enigma code, nuclear power, the quantification of risk. As I said, Uncle Eli was himself one of the first to fulfil the dreams of the chartists and use maths to predict movements in the currency markets. After these successes, I reckon he wondered: why not extend mathematics to religion as well? If maths can bring clarity to everything from the supply and demand of grain, to the movements of the planets, to the harmonies of a string quartet, what might it do for religious confusions? So he set about translating the ancient numerology of the Yetzirah into modern, axiomatic maths. In order to carry out the translation, however, Uncle Eli needed to develop a new notation—a new language, as it were—one capable of representing a different kind of truth.' Gerald grins. 'It was a noble attempt. Why shouldn't maths clear away the fogs from religion? It worked for my own field of philosophy. Formal notation and so forth. At one time I even thought Uncle Eli might have arrived at—a sort of anticipation of independence-friendly logic, with the branching quantifiers...' Gerald waves his hand in the air. 'But it was only an attempt. In the end, these papers—for all their promise, I'm afraid they're a cipher without a key.'

You can see a dim discomfort in Gerald's eyes. 'What do you mean?'

'The writings—they're a maze in which at least one man has already lost himself.' He shakes his head distractedly. 'Something—is always missing. Always missing.'

Despite Gerald's warnings, you find yourself captivated by Eli's dream. To clear away the obscurities of religion and uncover its eternal truths through the power of mathematics—what could be a more noble goal? Over the course of the following days, you pore over the papers and notebooks that fill the trunk. Most of Eli's manuscripts consist of lines of Hebrew followed by lines of inscrutable symbols. At least, they are inscrutable to you. But their esoterism adds to their charm. According to Gerald, the Hebrew lines are from the Yetzirah, and the symbols are Eli's attempts to construct a formal language that would be capable of expressing the truths of the Yetzirah with perfect mathematical rigor. Many of the symbols are standard symbols used in modern logic, Gerald tells you, but as Eli's work progressed, the notation became more unorthodox, as in the following lines that Gerald selects at random from one of the late manuscripts:

עשר ספירות בלימה צפייתן כמראה הבזק

$$a\mathcal{E} \; \check{z}(\psi z)_{,} = {}_{,} f(x) \equiv_x \psi(x \mid {}_{,} \supset_{,} a\mathcal{E} f), \psi_o \text{---} q.e.d.$$

To your great relief, a few sections in the manuscripts are written in English. One of these sections almost seems to describe the garden maze, though on its surface it is yet another general description of Eli's project. The section begins with a lengthy and surprisingly bitter critique of the attempt by the seventeenth-century English polymath John Wilkins to design a universal philosophical language in which every concept could be expressed with perfect precision. Wilkins' language divided the universe into forty categories, which were in turn subdivided into numerous subcategories, which were in turn further subdivided. The result was an elaborate taxonomic tree containing room for all the items in the universe. In addition, each of the forty categories corresponded to a monosyllable, each of the subcategories to a consonant, and each of the further subdivisions to a vowel. Thus: *De* signifies an element; *Deb* the first element, fire; and *Deba* a part of a fire, a flame. After summarizing the basic elements of Wilkins' project, Eli declares that it was hopeless from the start, because it was founded on a naive philosophical error: Wilkins assumed that the categories of nature exist apart from language, and that the goal of language should be to reflect those categories faithfully. But this gets the matter precisely backwards, Eli insists. In truth, the categories through which we conceive nature are the products of our language, and the purpose of language is to create worlds, as the Yetzirists well understood. That is why, Eli writes, the language that he is attempting to construct 'will take the form not of a tree of logical branches but of a labyrinth, as it were, containing logical clearings that are bound, one to the other, by a series of connecting paths.' Each clearing 'will not only represent but will *be* a true logical proposition drawn from the Yetzirah, and the paths leading between them will be the paths of correct logical procedure.' In this new language, Eli writes, 'one will be able to travel from one proposition to another, and from there to another, endlessly, without error or loss of truth. The real will thus be made to reproduce itself through an infinite logical branching.'

When you show Gerald these passages, he laughs and attempts to explain that Eli, philosophically, was a sort of linguistic idealist. Gerald points you to several passages in which Eli writes, always in identical language, that 'the limits of a language are the limits of a world.' This elusive slogan, like so much else in Eli's writing, enchants you in no small part because of its elusiveness. You often feel, as you pore over the contents of the trunk, that you are on the point of some great revelation. Language. Logic. God. Truth. At any moment, it seems as though they might all cohere.

But in the end, after a few days of reading, you give up. You simply know too little about the Yetzirah, and philosophy, and maths. If Gerald, with his lifetime of philosophical study and his expertise in logical symbols, was unable to make sense of Eli's writings, there is little hope for you.

As you begin to stack the scattered notebooks back into the trunk, however, a single sheet drops to the floor. It appears to have been stuck to the back of one of the notebooks. In careful handwriting almost resembling calligraphy, it reads:

Language and world:

ו ה י = *up*

ו י ה = *down*

ה י ו = *east*

י ה ו = *west*

$$ ה \quad ו \quad י = \textit{south} $$
$$ י \quad ו \quad ה = \textit{north} $$

You gasp. The letters in the garden—of course!

They were not an abbreviation of the tetragrammaton.

They were instructions.

Rushing downstairs with the small sheet in hand, you ask Gerald for the key to the maze. 'I'll also need a tape measure—a compass—and a torch. I think I may have deduced how Sara and I both found the apples.'

He laughs and wags his finger. 'Do you mean *induced?*'

You pause for a moment. 'I suppose that depends on what I find.'

'How is that?'

'I—I shouldn't say anything further until I've made a map of the garden.'

'Can I come?' Sara asks. 'Please!'

'Certainly,' you say. 'You can help me measure the path.'

With Sara holding one end of the tape measure, you first measure the exterior of the cage. Each side is precisely twenty-two metres long. Then you measure the distance from the old wooden door to the entrance to the clearing. Though the turns in the path make it challenging to arrive at precise measures, you determine that the distance between the entrance to the cage and the entrance to the clearing is no longer than eight and a half metres as the crow flies. Next, you set about measuring the clearing itself. It hardly surprises you to discover that it is ten metres square, and that the artificial apple-tree lies precisely at its centre. Twenty-two and ten: the numbers by which Jehovah spoke the universe into being.

Then you look down at the letters inscribed on the stone at the entrance to the clearing. You compare them to the key: 'י ה ו' means '*west.*'

Using the compass, you determine that the entrance to the clearing is in its south wall. The hedge that makes up the northern wall contains no opening. The entrance that Sara took on the night when you first entered the maze is in the eastern wall of the clearing, and the opening that you took is directly opposite in the western wall.

As the two of you stand in the clearing before the small tree, you turn to her. 'I never asked. Where do you think the second apple came from?'

Sara thinks for a moment. 'Which apple?'

'You remember. We both walked into the clearing. We both picked an apple from the tree. But there was only one apple, and one tree. How was it possible? Where did the second apple come from?'

'I reckon they both came from the tree,' she says uncertainly.

'I suppose that's the only rational explanation. It may even be necessarily true. But it's not possible.'

'I have a confession to make.'

You turn to her, startled. 'What is it?'

'I didn't make it all the way through the puzzle. I got frightened and went back. But I waited for you and I would have given you the apple if you had come back.' She glances at you and then looks down. 'Was that wrong?'

'No, of course it wasn't,' you say. Her confession stirs another dim thought in your mind. 'How would you feel about making one more measurement?'

'But it's dark,' she says, looking up at the dimming sky through the iron latticework above the clearing.

'Just one more,' you promise. 'I'm going to enter the maze, and I want you to follow me. At every turn, we'll take a measurement. It can't take long.'

'Americans are very bossy,' she says.

With Sara in tow, you enter the hedges through the western entrance, the path that you used on the first day, and you travel one metre west before turning right and heading four metres north. Recording each distance on a scrap of paper illuminated by the torch, you then turn left for one metre and left again for four metres south, where you come upon the first fork in the maze. You can either head west or continue south. Arbitrarily, you choose to go west. After three meters, there is a turn north and the path continues for a further five meters, at which point it turns west for three meters and then offers another fork. But as you stop to add the latest segment of the maze to your map, you freeze.

'Oh my God,' you whisper.

Sara approaches behind you, then releases the measuring tape so that it spools all at once into the reel, which falls from your hand. 'What is it?' she asks.

'It's impossible.'

'What?'

'We're outside the cage.'

You shine your torch around the dense walls of hedge in every direction. Somehow you are standing eight metres to the west of the clearing. But there are only six metres between the western wall of the clearing and the western wall of the cage. You should, by any reasonable measure, be standing in the meadow outside.

'What?'

'I said, we're outside the cage. We're standing outside the cage.'

'No, we're not, silly,' Sara says. 'I want to go back.'

'Do you remember how to get back?' you ask.

'I think so,' she says, but you can tell that she is uncertain.

'No, wait. If I'm right, it might not be safe for you to go back alone.'

By the time the two of you have finished mapping your route and returned to the clearing, emerging from the eastern entrance, the map tells you that you are a full twelve metres west of the western opening in the hedges where you entered the maze. The bare tree stands in the cold twilight. You tell Sara to inform her father you might be late for dinner. As she leaves through the southern opening, you shine your torch on the stone inscription.

י ה ו.

West.

It will be easy enough now to find out whether you are wrong. You head back into the western entrance of the maze. This time, you do not even bother to record each segment in the map. You only keep rough track of your cumulative progress. Once again, you find yourself travelling far west of where the cage should have ended. Indeed, as you step back into the clearing, the map tells you that you have travelled another twelve metres west.

But this time the clearing is different. There is an apple on the tree.

If you return to the Packards' house to show them the apple, turn to page 186.

If you enter the maze once again to see what else you might find, turn to page 90.

So you have chosen not to accept blame for your life's failures. And you are right.

In truth, the fault for your failed life lies not in any choices you have made, but in the nature of choice itself. You have been condemned to fail by the historical development of freedom.

The story may be familiar, but it bears repeating:

Once upon a time, people did not view themselves as the authors of their own lives, or as responsible for defining who they were. The modern idea of freedom did not exist. Instead, the universe was thought of as a kind of book. The author of this book? God. Each thing in the universe was endowed by him with an intended purpose, and this purpose gave the thing its meaning. The seed was meant to grow into the tree, and it contained the tree latently within itself, because this was God's intention for it. To become a tree was the realization of the seed's God-given identity, its culmination, its fulfillment. The tree grew, the apple fell to the earth, the man toiled to collect the apple, the planets turned in their celestial harmonies—all because of the divine will. Each thing had a fate, an end authorized by God, a proper role in the universal plot. It was man's task to interpret the book of the world, with the guidance of the Church, so as to place himself in harmony with this holy cosmic order.

Only later did the first stirrings of freedom arise. A few revolutionaries declared that man was as much fashioner as fashioned. They continued to accept a divinely authored order, but insisted that within this order, man's destined end was to be the author of his own existence. They imagined God declaring to Adam: you are limitless and shall fix for yourself the bounds of your nature. Man is the maker of himself and shall be confined by nothing other than his own free will.

Others turned inward to scrutinize their souls. They peered deep within themselves to discover the unseen sins of the heart, the better to confess them. But the more one looked within the self, the more one found the self within, and not inscribed in the heavens. The unexpected voices that one might once have understood as the voices of God or of the devil, one now understood as one's own inner voices. One learned to be true above all to one's self.

Others asked questions that had not been asked before, or at least not in a long while. They used reason to seek the foundations of their beliefs. Of course, they were relieved to discover, in the end, that God lies at the base of all being, all thought, all things. But because they began in doubt and proceeded by reasoning, their faith was now only as secure as the reasons leading up to it. The only true certainty was the self-certainty of their minds.

In the wake of these changes, a new order of things came slowly into being. At the center of this new world sat a choosing, reasoning, doubting self, radiating its light into the dark and unspeaking universe. To be the source of light also meant to be apart from the things illuminated. Thus a great crack opened between the inner life of the soul and the external world of matter, bodies, things— which were increasingly seen to operate by universal mechanical laws. The apple fell and the planets spun not because the divine will commanded it, but because of mute forces. Man was now a worldless mind standing apart from a mindless world. What was the purpose of an apple? The question was hardly intelligible. An apple had no inherent purpose. It had whatever use man gave to it.

As mastery of the universe grew, one increasingly concluded that fortune was not something to be worshipped or obeyed. It was a force to be tamed and overcome. Indeed, as a pioneer of the new order put it, fortune is a woman who must be beaten and abused, for she will submit only to the audacious and the violent. Man harvested the newly discovered laws of physics. Through technology, knowledge gave power to bind the fates.

But what was the purpose of this binding? To what end did we conquer the world?

The first few to ask this question—to recognize that it could be asked—responded with dread. They heard the silence of the infinite spaces. They felt the loss of God. Foundering in a meaningless abyss, the freedom to choose showed itself to be absurd. Each choice was arbitrary, and the old sources of meaning could offer no relief, because whether to believe in them had itself become a choice, and one for which the old sources could offer no guidance until after the choice had been made. Rudderless, drifting, alienated from the inaccessible selves of others and the crumbling fragments of the physical universe, these early wanderers defined the condition of modern man as nausea, anxiety and despair. Some wondered how continuing to live could be justified.

If they had seen your violent outburst in the bar, they might have interpreted it as reflecting the innate absurdity of existence, or perhaps as a gratuitous act that affirmed your condemnation to a state of absolute freedom.

With time, however, the stages of grieving took their course. An acceptance of the new landscape set in—so that, at the very present moment of freedom, which has been in place since at least around the time of your birth, and perhaps much longer, the answer to our earlier question seems self-evident, and no cause for concern: To what ends does one choose and strive?

To whatever ends one wills.

The meaning of the world is simply whatever meaning one chooses for it and for oneself. One's choice of purpose in life is a way to realize and express one's identity, which is also a matter of choice. One can be whomever or whatever one wants to be. In one's performance of life, one is free to leap into faith, and out of it, and back, as in a game of hopscotch. To each his or her own.

All of this is of course what the earlier gloom-and-doomers rejected as a terrifying and desolate nihilism. But their terror grows harder to understand by the day. It requires a strain of the historical imagination to grasp what the issue was, exactly, with the distance between subject and object, for example—were those earlier thinkers truly disturbed by the impossibility of proving with absolute, geometric certainty that we are not deceived by demons? Was it really such a terror that the entirety of human knowledge could not be deduced from self-evident axioms? Did they actually fear that a world without enchantments would permit the commission of horrendous crimes?

Perhaps those old worriers had simply drunk too much coffee. In any case, their anxiety seems to have been misplaced.

And yet—there are certain traps built into the wondermachine of modern freedom. It has long been recognized, for example, that a man becomes a wretched thing when he is given what he wants and seeks nothing more. Even rats thrive on a little starvation.

Life is a kind of circle defined by what is familiar and comfortable. Each moment you live inside the circle, your world contracts. You weaken. The circumference of the circle shrinks. By contrast, each experience outside the circle is a painful growth, pushing out the circle's bounds. As a reward for the strain, the unfamiliar becomes familiar. What used to require strain becomes habitual.

It is true that pressing out the circle too quickly may cause it to collapse. Then even the most routine activity becomes a struggle. But the same result can be achieved simply by sitting still. Without danger or hardship, one is no less weakened.

This is the trap of modern freedom, this steady shrinking of life to a point of debility. Never before has it been possible for so many to achieve such wretchedness at so little expense. Those who live at the vanguard of the new epoch are free to choose—but choice has led them to choose, moment by moment, a life that they never would have chosen. Their ultimate commitment, if one can call it that, is to be sated in each moment. Presented with a choice between this atrophied life and a life defined by a commitment to some source of greater meaning, they might have chosen the latter, even at the cost of less momentary pleasure and greater sacrifice, even pain. But they were never presented with this choice.

You were never presented with this choice.

Each dream in the history of freedom produces its matching nightmare. Faustus with his lust for limitless knowledge and powers, who sells his soul to obtain them. Frankenstein, the doctor constructing monstrous new life from the flesh of the dead. Raskolnikov, the youth who crushes the skull of an old woman with an axe—because everything is permitted. You, in your little way, are simply the latest nightmare, the smallish monster born of today's freedom. You are the eternal civilian. You are life without being called.

But surely this was not inevitable. Surely freedom itself did not condemn you to this fate. Or to any fate in particular! Surely freedom includes the freedom to choose a calling… Could you not have chosen differently throughout your life? What if you had chosen more boldly at the start, for example, when you stood before the darkness of the concrete tunnel—who knows what you might have become if you had followed your friend's sister inside?

To find out, turn to page 8.

In the end, your hand falls on the better of the two brands of beer. You heard that the other one is made of a beer syrup mixed with some kind of water and a chemical that produces foam. Maybe there was a clear choice between the two after all.

You finish the first beer in your room, then return and see that J.P. has gone to bed. So you load several cans into your t-shirt and go upstairs.

As you make your way through the pull-tabs, you listen to a slow, sad song that was popular when you were in high school, long before you met Margaret. After a while, you decide that it would be a good idea to call her and tell her how you feel.

"There's something I have to tell you," you say when you finally get her on the phone, sleepy and distant. Her father, who answered, is probably still on the line. "I just have to say it," you say.

"Yes."

"Are you there?"

"Yes," she says. "Of course I'm here."

"I love you, Margaret."

"Are you finished?"

"No." In fact, it was all that you had planned to say, but you decide to go further. "Even if we never see each other again, I'll always love you. I need you to know that."

You wait for her response. Then you worry that she may have gotten disconnected. "Are you still there? I'm worried that you're disconnected," you say.

"You're drunk."

"Maybe, maybe not. Maybe we're all drunk—"

"I'm not drunk."

"Tell me what you're thinking about." You lie back on your bed and rest your arm on your forehead. "I want to know what you're—"

"I'm hanging up now."

"I'll never stop—"

Then the line goes dead. You only hang up after three loud tones are followed by a woman's recorded voice telling you to hang up the phone if you wish to make another call.

The next morning, Ida stands in the kitchen in her bathrobe, filling the coffee machine with water. You stand by the stairs and do not move. A strange thing has happened. All the meaning has been stripped from the objects in the room. It is all gone. Everything is meaningless now, just a thing. Even Ida seems to have lost her meaning. You do not want to go back to school.

"I think I should take next semester off," you announce.

She does not answer at first. "Why?" she asks.

You cannot find any answer. She finishes pouring water into the reservoir of the coffee machine, then closes the lid. Her performance seems mechanical and insincere. It is as though she is going through the motions of a not entirely convincing imitation of someone pouring water into a coffee machine. You glance around, half-expecting to glimpse a visiting news crew in the wings. But there is no one. It fills you with terror to think that your mother has become an object without meaning. So you try to construct some meaning for her performance. Perhaps it is a pantomime about feeding household appliances with water.

"What would you do if you weren't at school?" Ida asks. She imitates a mother placing objects into cabinets.

"Take some time off. A lot of people do it these days. I'd like to go in search of something," you say. "In search of the cool."

"That sounds dangerous."

"It's my choice," you reply coldly. Almost as soon as you speak the words, letting them flow from your mouth like water into a thirsty coffee machine, you believe them to be true. "I could live some place cheap. I think that's where the cool would be found. In a poor place." Then you name the first poor country that crosses your mind. It is somewhere to the south, and arid. In the coming days, you fold your clothes and place them neatly into your suitcase. Then you empty your suitcase onto the floor and cry.

"I'm sensitive," you tell yourself. "I'm someone who doesn't hide how he feels."

Because you are still unsure whether your sensitivity is the epitome of the cool or its opposite, you order a tiny bottle of bourbon on the plane ride south. When the stewardess asks to see your identification, you explain that you can be identified based on your own recognizance. "Moreover, the drinking age is lower outside the United States. I did research. I read the State Department's travel warnings," you continue, not entirely free from pride, "several travel books, and a local newspaper. All of them said I could drink on this airplane. It's very important to me that human beings continue to pursue the truth." The stewardess bends down to you, so close that you can see the popped capillaries in the whites of her eyes. "In that case," she asks, "why don't you go fuck yourself?" The sight of her bloodengorged eyes transfixes you. Is this love? You strain yearningly against your properly fastened seatbelt, only to feel the romance slip away as you catch a glimpse of her less-than-stellar décolletage.

Soon you have escaped into the darkness of a dream in which you sit on a plane and the recycled air is quiet and stagnant. When the meal trolley comes, you tuck into a plate of savory barbecued ribs. No matter how many of them you eat, however, you are never sated. They can never fill the hollowness in your chest. "Oh, Margaret," you whisper, saucy-fingered, "oh, humanity." At the end of the flight, you wheel your carry-on luggage across an impossibly slanted skyway between the dream and the reality, between the motion and the act. The cavity in your chest is real, though an absence. It aches and grows.

After your first night in the syringe-strewn streets of the capital, you try to escape from yourself by swallowing a sedative and then, while you are asleep, decamping to a remote desert canyon. Among the old copper towns, no sooner have you laid down your rucksack than your eye is attracted by a distant glint. Peering through the telescope mounted on the canyon ledge, you see yourself on the opposite side of the canyon, advertising colorful native textiles. "How did I learn to use semaphores?" you wonder. "What is beauty without truth?"

You spend the night whispering falsified confessions to the tiny man inside the telescope lens, hoping that your words will be amplified. Fireweeds bloom at your ankles. "I have had commerce with the damned," you rasp in the morning, exhausted, while the sky melts into flame. "But my confessions were irresolute. This is not what I came to see." Wandering back toward the exhaust fumes of the capital, you stop briefly at a local carnival and minimally invasive cardiothoracic surgery center. You purchase a novelty x-ray that reveals the cavity has grown. "I will heal you for a reasonable fee," the surgeon whispers, "on one condition. You must allow me to be *maximally* invasive." When you refuse, he says that you are clearly a canny fellow and invites you to speculate on gold futures. How much gold will an ounce of gold trade for in nine months? In ten years? You force your way past him and into the dusty streets, knowing that greed can never be sated.

By the time you reach the hostel, you are so exhausted that you can do little more than lie down, crawl inside your cavity, and try to fall asleep. But there is a stench inside. It reminds you of that first evening, there in the epicenter of loss. Margaret. How will you ever find what is missing? Collecting your remaining wits in a small plastic bag, like a bag for milk in the market, you crawl onward into the darkness, flashlight in hand, until there is only emptiness all around and even the absence of light is gone.

Years pass. Batteries and hearts die.

One day the wind flickers to a stop. Somewhere just past the reach of your vision you think you glimpse Nature. She is whispering to herself over and over again, "I am going to kill you all." Glints of light in the mud where she stirs. "One by one," she whispers. "One by one." Then she is gone, and other visions float by in the infinite darkness. They glow like radially symmetric sea creatures. Their structures are anagrams made of light. You witness so many things. The first blossoming of space and time. Stars being born and dying. The invention of liberty and steam power... On the endless shore, you wake to see gulls circling above the water. A little boy wanders past, swinging the severed head of a sheep. In the distance, locals hawk their wares. The tourists have not come to this place. The people have not been corrupted. You approach one of the natives and ask for the answer—or at least you think that's what you said, it might have been "cancer"—and you give him your last coin as a sign of respect. He hands you a package of greasy brown paper that smells like an ancient hospital. Forever vigilant against the menace of gypsies, you stow the package in your cavity, waiting for the long bus ride to pull it out, untie the string and look inside. But when you do, you find nothing but a handful of dead flies.

Was it too late? you wonder. Had it been too late from the start? You drown your disappointments in a jug of fermented saliva passed silently down the aisle by the aborigines. As the first of the mining towns approaches, you begin to weep. Where had they all gone? Those you loved. Those who had loved you. You leave your belongings and head as far as you can from the clamor of restored schoolbuses. Finally a wise man greets you at the old city gates, flicking the tip of a needle as he speaks around his belt. *You should consider Catholicism*, he says. Then a gasp and his eyes roll back into their sockets. Desperate for some miracle, you fall to your knees and pray for the thing that you still seek, whose name you can no longer recall, but whose absence you continue to feel. When you open your eyes, your hands are filled with coins whose surfaces have been defaced and can now only serve as metal. This is the news that stays news. This is the miracle that never comes.

Dislocated by weariness, you make your way toward the abandoned train station. All the while the cavity grows, expanding to the inside of your throat and stomach, spreading its wet fingers around your lungs. If it goes on like this, soon nothing but a cavity will remain.

Then there is a gray area. In your memory, you are spitting blood into your sandals somewhere in Utah, in the salt flats, and the infection has finally bloomed in your lungs, a bright, limp orchid. You had never felt so close to it as then. They found you on the outskirts of Las Vegas (of course—Vegas! those were the lights), teeth missing, tongue black and swollen. When you picture it, it's like a scene in a bloody old Western. But in this movie, it doesn't matter whether you're the good guy about to rise from the dust or the bad guy tumbling down, because in this movie everyone gets the cool eventually, everyone, given sufficient time. Days may pass, seasons, years. The hourglass folding its wings. Storms may fill the room in seaborne bottles. "I carried your echoes to Arivaca in a rucksack," the cirrus may say, "with the clouds like anvils, when the virga came, but at the border they evaporated before you could taste me, your feathers carried me away, in my lungs." And all our alpine equipment proved useless. So much for the sunset, ladies, and so much for the sleepless nights. We sat beneath our tarps of brittle plastic while memories formed rivulets in the mountainside. I saw you, once, nearing the end, when the jalopy had wedded itself, like a hookworm, to the chaste and muddy rut, and you held her hand like teeth in a beggar's gums. How many selves, cusped white, have you clipped from the bough? Too young. We heard you, there in the tureen of martyrs, warbling your no man's hymn. Once by telegram, once by smoke, breath returned in the mirror as pale humidity. Once amid pines in the vinery of maybe. Once, alone, exhausted by chords. But if instead of the lover's sigh, cleaving, in the final moment, there were to be a gasp, only, uncloven from life, and no regret, and one turned on the parade ground and the spectators had all gone away, if, in other words, meaning came to an end, simply, on a Sunday afternoon in Paterson, then, shivering in a trenchcoat, without rest, would you have ignored the inevitable and assembled your bodyparts once again? Beneath the thread of blue sky, slaked mercury slides down. Without a fulcrum, the outsides come apart. We will shed our fruit wherever it was seized, surprised by virtue, as in the courtyard, for example, but might we now be more safely ignored? Or have you found us, there in the tunnel at the end of the light? Can you hear us? Can you hear me? Are you safe? Do you know where you are? Can you stand up? Can you feel this? Does it hurt? Can you tell me where? Can you tell me where you are? Can you be quiet? Can you speak up? Can you feel it when I do this? Can you move your arms? Can you see? How much does this hurt? How long has it been here? How long have you been waiting? Where did you come from? Where is your identification? What have you seen? Can you see my voice? Is it inside you? Can you feel it move? What is your position? Is that all? Is there anything you have not told me? Is it one or the other? Is it neither? Can you make it stop? Can you please make it stop? What is it? What is this distance? Here. You hold me in your branches where the leaves are words in the branches and they sing without words without light. Apple. Epple. Eppli. Epli. Ebli. Eble. Eple. Eiple. Aiple. Aple. Appel. Apfel. Afel. Afal. A falling of leaves. In fall the leaves fall from the branches into a brook. Into a book. Jabook. Jabuk. Jabuka. Jabluka. Jabloka. Jabloko. Jablomo. Jalomo. Jalmo. Almo. Almos. Alma. Elma. Malum. Malun. Malon. Melon. Melo. Lome. Loma. Poma. Paoma. Paomo. Pomo. Pomme. Pemme. Pame. Pam. Paum. Baum. Picture these words as paper leaves falling from branches one after another into silence. White leaves falling in the arbor. In an arbor. Arber. Arbre. Arbore. Arboro. Arvoro. Arvore. Arvor. Arbor. Arbo. Arbol. Alber. Albero. Albevo. Balevo. Berevo. Derevo. Drevo. Drvo. Drzewo. Trzewo. Trewo. Tredo. Tred. Traed. Trae. Tree. Tre. Tri. Teri. Yeri. Yiri. You are. You were. You are no longer

It is always possible to blame one's failures on the circumstances. Others use this excuse incessantly. They come up short, but rather than taking responsibility, they chalk their failures up to the difficulties they faced.

Not you.

You have chosen the harder road. So: how did you bring about your life's failure? When did you go astray?

It could not have been when you were a baby. There must have been a long time, in fact, before you were responsible for the course of your life. Around the age of two, for example, when you were asked to hide, you covered your eyes, thinking your inability to see meant that you could not be seen. Your awareness of yourself was not yet distinct from your awareness of the world.

But eventually the external influences on you were outweighed by the inner tensions they had helped to create. There came a moment when you exceeded the sum of your parts, when the growth of your awareness gave way to a moral change. You became responsible.

The moment probably arrived in adolescence, a period when you grew aware that others were aware of you, and at the same time that you were supposed to follow an unknowable set of rules defining how to behave. Gone were the days of lying down in boredom in the grocery store aisles. Gone were the days of dancing on the kitchen floor. You dimly understood that you were standing in a minefield of expectations. The only trouble, as in so many minefields, was that the mines were unmarked. In order to avoid triggering these invisible armaments, you moved as little as possible. You sometimes averted your eyes.

Perhaps we can imagine this metamorphosis happening when you were around the age of eleven. You had just experienced heartbreak for the first time. In the afternoon, you stood before the entrance to a concrete tunnel. A girl stood with you.

This was the moment when you became more writer than written, when you were forced to make your first true choice: whether to follow the girl inside.

You made the wrong decision.

You were timid.

You did not go.

But do not despair, oh reader, loser, friend. Because I have cast my lot with the wretched of the earth, I will give you another chance.

There at the origin of things—enter the tunnel, follow Iris, and see what might have been.

Join me, and take another turn on the wheel of freedom.

To enter the tunnel, turn to page 8.

Awake, awake…

Beholde, thou art yet in the faire garden: and there is no new thing vnder the sunne. The plants which blossomed, blossome still: and the trees which put foorth fruite, put foorth fruite still: and the wings of the butterflies which daunced, daunce still.

And I am yet before thee.

So, you've made your choice, I say. That was it.

I laugh and shew thee againe my teeth with yellow staine.

But I don't want you to spend eternity with a case of buyer's remorse. So I'm going to give you one last chance to reconsider. You know, hell is where the heart is. You're a free man, and you deserve a choice. One last chance, my friend.

Now. Do you choose the side of God, or do you choose me?

If you choose hell, turn to page 7.

If you repent, turn to page 305.

"I think I should stop drinking for a while," you tell your parents the next evening. J.P. has just begun to pour you a glass of wine.

They exchange glances. Then J.P. removes your glass from the table. He asks if you have thought any more about your next move.

"I don't know."

You hunch over your dinner plate and stare at it through puffy eyes. Based on recent experience, this will be a two-day hangover.

"I don't know if I'm ready to settle down yet," you say. "I feel like I'm still figuring things out."

Over the course of dinner, as you listen to your parents' advice and their discussion of the career choices of your classmates and their friends' children, you slowly make your way through a bowl of vegetarian chili and accept that you will have to choose something soon. Your parents will only let you stay in your old room for so long.

Maybe you could put off the decision by getting a graduate degree. How about law school? Everyone says it is a natural next step for a student of philosophy.

What could go wrong?

If you go to law school, turn to page 272.

If you do not, turn to page 285.

One of the professors who writes you a letter of recommendation tries to warn you. "The legal profession is a factory for mental illness," he says. "Anorexia. Substance abuse. Just look at all the divorces."

You ignore him. He knows nothing of the world, having taken shelter in a graduate philosophy program almost immediately after he graduated college. You have seen too much of life, now, to content yourself with being patted on the head for doing your homework well.

"I know the first year of law school is supposed to be a hazing ritual," you concede. "But it can't be worse than the campaign."

In the end, your confidence barely survives the first semester. You botch your exams, then botch the law firm interviews at the start of your second year. Instead of spending the summer being wined and dined at one of the well-established corporate multinationals, you review documents at a small local firm best known for suing the producers of in-flight cold remedies. At the end of the summer, they decline to offer you a permanent position.

Your expectations continue to wither in your third and final year of school. After applying to over a hundred federal judges to serve as a clerk—a common stepping stone for recent graduates from the top schools—you receive no offers. The only offer you receive, in fact, is from an aging judge on the state supreme court in Oklahoma. You accept.

"I never would have gone to law school if I had known what it would be like," you note despondently to the judge's secretary one morning. "Not that there are a lot of better possibilities out there. But at least I wouldn't be eighty thousand dollars in debt."

Sheila lets loose one of her loud, boisterous laughs. She is a twice-divorced mother of three, and she always listens to your complaints with great amusement. "What else would you have done?"

"I don't know. Maybe I could have been an engineer. Engineering is valuable." You gaze out the office window, longingly surveying the largely empty streets of Ardmore. "Is the judge coming in today?"

"I think he's getting ready for his magic show."

You frown. As a hobby, Judge Nuckolls performs magic tricks for the lunchtime guests at a nearby country club. You have so far successfully evaded going to any of the performances.

"He's got another show at lunch," Sheila says. She looks at you meaningfully. "He sure likes the clerks to come."

"I'd love to," you say, glancing at your watch, "but I have to respond to a tech edit from Riya. It's overdue."

In fact, Riya gave you the technical edit over two weeks ago. She is the judge's other clerk, an Oklahoma native. Though the opinion you wrote was only seven pages long, Riya's critique somehow filled sixty-eight pages, single-spaced. The critique has been sitting in the bottom drawer of your desk, menacing you like a repressed memory.

"I should get to work," you yawn, lifting your coffee mug toward Sheila in a vague gesture of camaraderie. On the way back to your office, you peek in Riya's door.

"Morning, Riya."

She sits hunched over a slew of papers. Though it is only nine o'clock, Riya's black hair has already come loose from its ponytail and now dangles over the documents like stray wires in the aftermath of a tornado. Slowly, she raises her head with the look of someone hearing the first faint taps of a fellow survivor beneath the wreckage.

"This is all too much," she sighs. "It's too much."

"What?"

"Your case about the internet reviewers." She brushes back her hair and adjusts her small, perpetually crooked wire-rimmed glasses.

"Oh, right," you say. "The internet screeners."

"Screeners," Riya says. "Exactly."

It is a case filed by a traumatized employee of an Oklahoma corporation that provides screening services for online social networks. Every time a user of one of the sites objects to a piece of content, the objection raises a red flag, and the content is forwarded to the corporation's office in Tulsa. Much of the content is harmless. But some of it is vile beyond belief. The screener who filed the lawsuit had begun suffering panic attacks and throwing up at work. Unfortunately, she had not hired a lawyer, and her filings were virtually unintelligible. Her final motion before the judge dismissed the case was entitled: "Courtesy Motion: For 'Judge' Overbee (ILLEGAL appointed per captioned 401 Okla 776) the Definition of 'Unconstituitonal Bias' in Oklahoma, and YOU."

In your memo, you recommended affirming the dismissal. The employee had simply failed to make out a legal case.

"It's just so horrible, though," Riya says. "The things she had to see... I can't even read about it. No one should have to do that for a job. You know, the pictures with—children."

You nod.

"Never knowing when something bad will pop up on the screen. Always having to be vigilant."

"Yes, but she failed to make out a legal claim. The case had to be dismissed."

Riya looks at you. "What about a tort claim? Couldn't you say she's arguing she suffered from—intentional infliction of emotional distress? Or something?"

You shrug. "But she didn't say that."

"It just seems wrong..."

"Obviously, it's not fair."

Riya nods slowly and continues to look at you. "Doesn't that bother you? That an employer can do this and not even have to pay the medical bills? It seems like that should be one of the costs of doing business—like safety equipment for construction workers, you know?" She waits. "The employer will just keep doing this. Other screeners will have the same problems."

"It bothers me as much as anyone else," you sigh. "But it would also bother me if judges started making up claims for plaintiffs whenever they thought something unfair had happened. That would be unfair to the defendants. I think the real issue here is that she didn't have a lawyer. Why? Because she couldn't afford one. Maybe the solution is reforming the legal services industry, or finally tackling—" You stop yourself. You were regurgitating an argument that you had used once in a civil procedure class. It had gone over well at the time, but you suddenly find that you can no longer tell whether you actually believe what you are saying. You found yourself in a position in the conversation in which it seemed obligatory to offer some argument, and this argument happened to be lying within arm's reach. For reasons you cannot quite understand, your heart sinks. "I'm sorry. Do you ever find yourself in the middle of saying something and realize that you have no desire to continue saying it? I often have that feeling lately."

"Has anyone ever told you that you have a super strange way of talking?"

In fact, many people have told you this since your entry into the world of the law. You look at Riya's bookshelf and think again of the screeners. You think of being forced to look at the grisly flotsam of the internet day in and day out. Anything that occupied a large enough space in human consciousness would probably find itself reflected somewhere in the vast ocean of the web. It was no surprise that scraps of monstrous things occasionally surfaced. But it would be a horrible job to have to look at them. "Anyway," you say, searching for some appropriate way to end the conversation, "setting aside the question of justice, there was no legal argument that the case should go forward. Judge Overbee was right."

Riya stares at you with a faint look of despair. "I guess so."

When you finally reach your office, you close the door and remove Riya's sixty-eight page technical edit from the bottom drawer of your desk. Staring at the thick stack of papers with its industrial-width staple, you decide to check your email instead.

For the last several days, you have been expecting the results of your application to a law firm in New York where one of J.P.'s college friends, a reformed student radical, is a partner. You flew out to interview at your own expense a few weeks earlier, and the firm said they would inform you of their decision once they finished interviewing the law school students who were applying to be summer associates. It is your last chance. None of the other firms to which you applied in the fall had even offered you an interview.

Thankfully, there are no new emails. You turn off the computer monitor, open the technical edit, and begin scanning Riya's critique with a queasy sense of anticipation. You fear that you have made some fundamental, mortifying error in the draft opinion.

As you begin reading Riya's comments, however, you find no indication of a grand error on your part. Instead, you find that she has provided hundreds of minute stylistic corrections. Each time you included a comma after an opening clause in a sentence, for example, Riya wrote:

"Please resolve punctuation error by removing comma."

Riya also seemed to harbor a kind of obsession with reducing the number of words in each sentence to a bare minimum, even when doing so would alter the sentence's meaning. "I believe this last sentence of the paragraph may be condensed somewhat," she wrote. "I suggest deleting 'provided further details of' in this line and inserting 'detailed' to condense this sentence. It would read: 'An August 2002 letter from Droske to Macomber detailed the arrangement.'"

But to "detail" an offer is not the same thing as to "provide *further* details" of it!

Your anger grows.

A good third of Riya's technical edit is dedicated to criticisms of your application of the rules in "the Bluebook," the legal profession's inane citation manual. You find these criticisms the hardest to bear.

The Bluebook is a foolish exercise in consistency at the cost of sanity, you tell yourself. If the Bluebook were a judge, it would be the kind of judge who sent a man to be hanged for having written a death-row appeal in pencil rather than pen. It has lost all connection with the simple, practical task of providing effective rules for legal citation. It is the ever-expanding midrash of some obscure cult dedicated to the worship of arbitrariness and bad aesthetic decisions. It is intolerable that anyone has to abide by the rules contained in the Bluebook; it is even more intolerable that you have failed to abide by them correctly; and it is intolerable above all that Riya has noticed your errors.

Simmering with rage, you toss aside the technical edit and turn back on your monitor. As the screen comes to life, you see that a new message has arrived in your Inbox. It is from the New York firm.

It begins: "Thank you for your interest..."

Your heart sinks. You click on the message.

Not again. How long could this go on?

Before you can recover yourself, Riya opens the door. "Are you coming?"

"What?"

"The judge's show."

You take a deep breath and try not to show your inner disarray. Never before in your life have you failed at so many things on so many occasions over such a sustained period of time.

"Sure," you say. "Why not?"

Sitting in the back of Sheila's station wagon, you feel the all-too-familiar, dull pain of defeat. The cumulative effect of yet another failure is almost unbearable. Law school consisted of a series of contests, and you had failed at each one. From the competition for top grades in the first year, to the competition for law review, to the moot court competition, to the competition to secure a job at the best-paying firm, you threw yourself into each event hoping to win a gold ring—expecting to win a silver—and preparing yourself for the bronze. In each case, the final result turned out to be so humiliating that you had not even considered it in advance. You did not even place. Not only did you not make law review, you did not gain a slot on a second-tier journal, and even on the third-tier journal where you finally served as an editor, you failed to win a position on the masthead. By the end of your third year, you began to think of each application, each attempt, as the lighting of a fuse on a kind of psychological bomb. The fuse consisted of hope and anticipation. The explosion was made of shame.

You arrive at the country club with only a few minutes to spare, but the dining room remains nearly empty. The three of you take seats at a table near the small elevated stage. After the uniformed wait staff has served your house salads and chicken breasts with mushroom cream sauce, the lights in the dining room dim.

Dressed in a black tuxedo and red bow-tie, and with a waist-length cape over his gaunt shoulders, the judge wanders onto the stage. He cranes his neck toward the audience like a gloomy turtle. The judge nearly always looks morose, but his expression in these first moments, beneath his remaining wisps of white hair, is so disheartening that you almost want to walk onto the stage and lead him away, patting him on the back and whispering that it will be alright.

The judge clears his throat, causing his lapel microphone to produce a brief burst of feedback. "Whoopsy-daisy. Okay. I'm going to start out with a few card tricks. Are there any young people in the audience today?" He peers into the darkness of the dining room. "Any young people?" He continues peering.

To your great relief, there is a girl in her early teens who appears to be eating lunch with her grandparents at a nearby table. You gesture enthusiastically toward her.

"You there," the judge says. "The girl in the marmalade pajamas."

You glance at the girl. Her outfit is indeed orange. But she is not wearing pajamas.

"Okay," the judge says as the girl's grandparents coax her onto the stage. You clap with relief, and the rest of the lunch guests join in on a sporadic basis. "Okay," the judge says. He takes a deck of cards from his pocket and unsteadily shuffles them. "Now this is a deck of cards."

The girl frowns.

"Now I'm gonna ask you to pick a card." The judge slowly fans the cards between his skeletal fingers and holds them out. "Pick a card." After the girl has picked one, the judge looks at her blankly. "Okay. You picked a card. Now I'm going to shuffle this deck. Or— no. Wait. Give me back the card." The judge takes the card and holds it uncertainly. "Now I'm going to look at the card." The judge glances at the card. "And now I'm going to put it in my pocket." The judge slides the card into his suit jacket pocket and begins to reshuffle the deck.

"Now I'm going to ask you to pick a second card," he murmurs. "Good. Now look at the second card, and then give it to me and I'm going to look at it. Okay. And now I want you to hold it while I shuffle the deck." The judge carefully shuffles the deck. "And then I shuffle the deck again…"

The girl glares at her grandparents.

"Now if you would be willing to cut the deck of these shuffled cards, young lady." After the girl cuts the deck, the judge stops. "No, wait. Before you cut the deck—" The judge stops and peers unsteadily into the audience. He clears his throat.

"Young lady, I would like you to put your card back in the deck and pick another one."

"I already picked two."

"Mmmm…" The judge hums ambiguously. "Mmmm…"

The girl casts a piercing expression toward her grandparents. "Whatever."

After the girl has picked a third card, the judge again asks her to shuffle the deck. Then he cuts it.

Then he once again freezes. "Oh, shoot," he says. "Oh, shoot, shoot, shoot."

You grimace, struggling not to look away. You can hear murmuring from the guests at the other tables. One man noisily backs up his chair and begins to leave.

The judge looks out toward the audience. His frown deepens. He turns back to the girl. "Would you like to see the card I put in my pocket?"

The girl stares at him. "What?"

"Would you like to see the card?"

"Why?"

When the judge does not answer, the girl shrugs. Then the judge slowly removes the card from his suit jacket pocket and hands it to her. "You can keep it too," he says. He holds out his hand toward the girl. "Ladies and gentleman, a round of applause for my assistant!"

As the judge moves on to a disappearing trick involving a jar of pickled eggs, your mind begins to wander. You ask yourself why you cared so much about the rejection from the New York firm. Before beginning law school, you would have felt contempt for those who spent their lives at corporate firms. To be a partner at a firm, you would have thought, is a sign of having failed in life. To be a partner is to have succeeded at a lifelong game of competitive slavery—where the reward is continued slavery, but with fancier table-scraps. It means that a person has sacrificed nearly all of his waking hours over years and often even decades to serving the needs of wealthy clients. Extremely wealthy clients. Lawyers at corporate firms are, in essence, human levers for the multiplication of inequality. You came to law school because you wanted to—change something. You can no longer remember what, but you would never have imagined that one day you would want to join the corporate law factory. What had happened?

There was the money, of course. But it was not a heroic amount of money. If a person's goal in life were wealth, finance or business would offer better prospects. At best, law is the path for someone who is both greedy and a coward—someone who covets money, but would rather be guaranteed a small horde than take the risks necessary to obtain a large one.

This is not you. If you were merely interested in paying off your loans, you would never have taken the clerkship.

But if not the money, then what draws you to this path you earlier would have despised?

In the end, it must be the glamour of corporate law's glamour, the prestige of its prestige. You want to be a corporate lawyer because others want to be corporate lawyers. Your desire is an involuntary imitation of the desires of your more successful peers. You know it is an imitation, but you are powerless to resist it.

It sickens you. Your soul has been warped since you entered the path of the law. You have somehow ended up consumed with a desire for things that on some higher, better level of yourself, you do not care about at all.

On the ride back to the office, Sheila glances at you in the rearview mirror. "Something got your goat?"

"Hm?"

"Something got your goat? You look like you're about to punch out a window."

You take a sharp breath, then sigh. "It's nothing." You look out the window. Then you turn back to the rearview mirror. "I just found out I didn't get another job."

"Aw," Sheila says. "That's too bad."

"Where was it?" Riya asks.

"Another firm in New York. It was kind of my last shot. Maybe," you add. "Not really. Maybe."

In the afternoon, Judge Nuckolls does not return to chambers. You sit before your computer and think of the glad-handers that the firm has probably decided to hire instead of you.

You know that you are becoming bitter, and that this is an unappealing trait. But this only increases your bitterness. The freedom of your more successful peers from such bitterness, and the fact that they would probably have looked down on his bitterness as somehow pathetic, is to your mind just one more sign of their unearned sense of self-worth. It is easy to be magnanimous when one has already won. Victory wraps a plush protective cushion around the ego, shielding it from the petty jabs and pinpricks of fortune. An easy magnanimity is just one more luxury that follows from success.

At the end of the day, Sheila invites you out for a drink. After Riya declines, as usual, to join you, you head to Louie's, a honky-tonk two blocks from the courthouse, squeezed between a payday lender and a pawn shop.

"You shouldn't feel too bad," Sheila tells you. "All the clerks find something eventually."

"Yeah, I'm sure I will." You try to catch the bartender's attention. "Still. It bothers me, you know? There's a guy in my class who already lined up a Supreme Court clerkship. He was in my section. I look at him and I think, what does he have that I don't?" You shake your head. "I mean, yeah, perfect grades. But what does that prove? Law school exams are stupidity contests. I finally figured out, by the end, the key to doing good on a law exam is regurgitating the professor's pet ideas as densely as possible with no logical connection. That's the contest. And because this guy does that naturally, he's clerking on the Supreme Court and I'm here?"

Sheila chuckles and then begins to cough. "Nobody said life was gonna be fair, honey."

"I'm not saying I haven't been lucky. I've had a ton of lucky breaks in my life. I didn't grow up in poverty. I went to good schools. My parents were good to me."

"You've got a lot to be thankful for."

"Sure."

"My parents," Sheila says, "my dad was a artillery repairman in the Army. Beat the shit out of my mom. Beat the shit out of us. He was—mean."

"Jesus."

"I remember—"

"It's just," you interrupt, "before I forget, it's just that lawyers have this unjustified sense of self-worth. Like they learned a lot just by going to law school or something. I think a high-school student at a one-month camp could learn everything of actual value that you get from a three year law degree."

Sheila continues laughing while she waves at someone over your shoulder.

"If it were up to me, by the way," you continue, your voice rising above the clamor of a country song, "I'd do away with law school entirely. I'd do away with the whole legal profession. It's complete bullshit. Why is it that people who work in manufacturing have to compete against cheap labor in China, but the lawyers don't? Why do we get to block out the millions of people that could be doing the same hack work we do? It's totally unfair—"

"Right," Sheila yawns. "I mean, sure."

You gesture for the bartender. "I lost the thread. What was I talking about?"

Sheila's gaze snaps back. "What?"

"Oh, I remember! The fucking legal monopoly. It's like a medieval guild. All it does is screw the consumer and keep out competition. But instead of being ashamed of themselves, like they should be, the people who run the show parade around and pat themselves on the back for serving justice. Fuck that. Fuck them." You glance over your shoulder to see what Sheila is looking at, but there is only a window with a sunset behind it. "I can't wait until someone destroys the whole system, just tears the whole fucking thing down."

Sheila continues gazing out the window behind you.

"Listen to me." You look down at the bar. "Who cares?" You shake your head. "I used to be better than this. I don't know what happened to me."

Sheila yawns and glances at her watch. "Time for me to hit the hay."

"I think I'm going to have a nightcap," you mumble.

You arrive at the office late the next morning, your head throbbing. Riya calls out to you as he pass by her door.

"I found it!"

"What?" you croak.

"The employer in your case—they conceded that the employee made a claim! It's in the employer's first answer. They—"

"Huh?"

"The employer's answer to the employee's first complaint says, paragraph seventeen, that the employee's claim for negligence—"

You lean your shoulder against Riya's doorframe and hold up a hand, squinting. It slowly dawns on you that Riya is talking about the case with the internet screener. "No, no, no," you say. "You don't survive a motion to dismiss just because the other party says you made a claim. You have to make a claim."

"Not true," Riya says, waving a finger in the air. "I found a bunch of precedents—"

"Whatever. Even if she made out a claim, it doesn't matter. I didn't even go into this in the memo, but if she makes out a claim, the claim ends up being precluded by worker's comp. She's trying to recover in tort for an injury in the course of her employment. So she's screwed anyway. What's the point?"

"You need to include that in the memo."

Your back straightens. "Excuse me?"

"If there's an issue about whether she made out a claim, you need to say that. And if there's another issue about whether her claim is barred by worker's compensation, then you need a section for that too. Judge Nuckolls wants us to lay out every potential issue. He made that clear at the orientation."

You glare at Riya. "Let's not get into this, okay?"

"Look, I know you're frustrated about not getting the job—"

"This has nothing to do with that."

"I'm just saying that Sheila told me what you were talking about last night—"

"What?"

"It's okay." Riya smiles gently. "Have you thought about interviewing in Oklahoma City? I know there's a firm there with a really interesting natural gas practice. They're looking for a new associate."

"I do not intend to start my career in Oklahoma."

Riya stares at you. "Then why are you here?"

"Why am I here? Come on." You scoff. "Because I couldn't get anything better. Why are you here?"

"I want to do family law in Oklahoma. This clerkship is perfect for me. I want to spend my life working for justice for the families here."

"Justice," you smile. "Right. Good luck with that."

When you reach your office, you notice that the red light on your phone is blinking. It can only mean one thing. The judge is the only person in the office who ever uses the phones. You glance at your watch and see that it is already nearly ten thirty. You scramble to the judge's office and knock on the door.

"You wanted to speak with me?" you ask.

The judge continues reading something on his desk for several long moments, then slowly raises his head. "Yes. Please close the door."

You sit in one of the leather chairs in front of the judge's desk and wait for him to finish reading. It is rare to enter the judge's office. You are struck once again by the density of magic-themed knick-knacks. A signed headshot of the judge-magician from Night Court hangs behind the desk.

The judge sighs loudly and lifts his eyes. "I'm very disappointed," he says.

You wait.

"I've been spending some time with this technical edit," he says. He removes his reading glasses and taps their edge on the desk. "The critique of your first draft opinion. Frankly, I'm very disappointed. I don't know what else to say. Sixty-eight pages!" The judge leans back in his leather chair and rubs his eyes. "Sixty-eight pages of errors in a seven-page opinion."

"Well, they're not all—"

"It's unprecedented. Frankly..." The judge sighs. "We need to have the highest standards, because we set the standards for the rest of the profession. There are no mulligans here."

"If I could say something—"

"Please," the judge says, holding up a hand. He waits, as though you might dare to speak. "When an opinion goes out from this chambers to the rest of the court, it has my name on it. In an ideal world, I'd review every document before it heads out the door. And there was a time when I tried to do that. But at this stage in my career, for a variety of reasons, that's no longer feasible. So I rely on my clerks. That's why I said during the orientation that I need you to produce work that *you* would want to own." The judge stares at you. "Now, there will be errors. No one's perfect. That's why we have the technical edits and all the other procedures. But..." The judge lifts up the thick document. "Sixty-eight pages?"

"I'd just like to say—"

"Look. Sometimes students graduate from law school, especially the big-name schools out of state, without the nitty-gritty know-how for a job like this. It's not their fault. It's not about your potential as a lawyer. You have the potential to be a fine lawyer." The judge rubs his face, then folds his hands and looks squarely at you. "But it would be unfair, frankly, to the applicant pool out there right now, if we kept you in this position."

You feel the blood draining out of your head.

"Are you firing me?"

"Yes." The judge regards you without emotion. "I spoke with some of the other judges. I regret to say they are in agreement with me."

The remainder of the judge's words barely penetrate your consciousness. There is something about changing horses in midstream. "Now, I don't want to leave you in the cold out there," the judge says. "You can take a week or two to wrap up your cases. I've got a very close friend in Tulsa that I'm sure could get you an interview, if everything goes well…" At the end of the conversation, the judge stands and holds out his hand. You shake it.

Then you are standing on the sidewalk outside the courthouse, looking up at the overcast sky. Every day, the world seems to grow darker. It is as though someone has turned down a knob controlling the color in the world.

Maybe you should become a comedian, you think. Maybe you should become a comedian just like the judge is a magician. You already have an idea for a joke.

What do you call it when you spend three years and a hundred thousand dollars to get a degree that only makes your life worse?

What is it called when you gain nothing but lose your soul?

You are still waiting for the punch line.

As dinner continues, J.P. finishes your share of the wine and tells you that when he was your age, he hitchhiked to San Francisco with nothing but a knapsack.

"Isn't there anything you want to do?" J.P. asks. "What are your dreams?"

You shrug.

"You're young. You're not tied down. Don't you want to see the world?"

"You know I can't afford that."

J.P. glances at Ida. "Well, what if you could?"

"I thought we decided," Ida says, "it wasn't—"

"I know, I know," J.P. says. "But there's only so many times in a man's life…" J.P. pours himself the last of the wine and tells you that his and Ida's investments have been doing well, and they have decided to make you a small gift. "A little capital. So you have some more freedom before you take the next step."

Ida shakes her head.

"Where would you go," J.P. asks, "if you could go anywhere in the world?"

Three weeks later, you arrive in Berlin. During the days, when you are not studying German, you watch television in the shared apartment that you rented through your language school. Most of the channels feature lottery-like trivia contests hosted by maniacal barkers with wide, demented, sleep-starved eyes. Rather than casting spokespeople who would attract and hold the viewer's attention through physical beauty, the German lottery has apparently concluded that they are better off with announcers who could easily be mistaken for vampires struggling to contain their bloodlust after several long hours in the grave. The demonic barkers stare directly into the camera with their feverish raccoon eyes and deliver endless monologues in the desperate tone of a father giving directions to a son who has been left in an airplane without a pilot, no parachute, and only one hour's fuel. Understandably, it is difficult to turn away from the barkers, even though the content of their hypnotic diatribes seems to consist of nothing more than the repeated admonition that they are almost—almost—almost!—on the point of giving away a very, very, very big prize.

In the early afternoon of New Year's Eve, you are watching one of these trivia contests when the hallway door unexpectedly opens. You quickly run to switch off the television and return to the couch.

"Hello, Sweta," you call out.

You can hear your roommate's shopping bags rustle in the entry hall. "Hello, you. What are you doing?"

You lift up a thick German newspaper from the couch. Apparently, you have been lying on it. "Just reading," you say. "Just reading... *Die Zeit.*" Immediately, you realize your mistake. *Die Zeit Wochenende* is Germany's largest and most difficult newspaper, far beyond your linguistic abilities, and a clear giveaway that you were in fact watching television and not practicing your German reading skills at all, though, to be honest, even a simple tabloid newspaper would have been beyond your abilities, because all newspapers in Germany are written using an obscure verb form called *Konjunktiv Eins*, the First Conjugation. The closest analogy in English, you think, would be if all newspaper articles were written using some arcane form of the hypothetical subjunctive: "After less than a year in operation, the British government is to have quietly shuttered the Millennium Dome yesterday, were it having to have sold the attraction's final ticket early this morning. The Dome, should that it had reportedly not suffered repeated cost overruns..." The German newspaper, you have concluded, is where German verb forms go to die when they have outlived their usefulness. It is a cemetery, or in the delightful German euphemism, a *Friedhof* or "peace yard," for words. After a strenuous life of being used to give orders, ask questions, convey information, offer warnings, and so on, words are allowed to enter the pages of *Die Zeit* and receive the peaceful gift of serving no function at all. *Die Zeit* is the *Zeitung* or newspaper equivalent of feeding baked loaves of bread to cows, as they apparently did in the former Soviet Union, where the necessity of employing the masses in bread factories led to production quotas that exceeded the existing human need, just as, you think, the excess supply of German thinking that results from Germany's generous public subsidizing of its higher education system has led to a massive surplus of enworded thoughts, and this intellectual overflow must go somewhere, like baked bread, so it goes into the waiting cow-mouth of *Die Zeit*, where it is slowly chewed, and then passed back into recycled pulp to be used as fertilizer for the growth of future editions. You clear your throat and forge onward.

"Just reading *Die Zeit*," you repeat uncertainly to Sweta. "An interesting article here on... no, that's an advertisement... for biochemicals..."

"You—you are reading the *Zeit*—" Peeking around the corner with her Siberian blue eyes, Sweta bursts into laughter. "Oh, ha ha ha. Yes, yes. You are lazy sausage."

Then she disappears, and you can hear her removing her overcoat and galoshes in the hall. You and your plump, good-humored Siberian roommate have been on pleasant terms since the day of your arrival, when she insisted on taking you to your first *Weinachtsmarkt*, a gaudy amusement park at the corner of the *Museumsinsel* near *Alexanderplatz*. The two of you drank hot *Glühwein* from flimsy white plastic cups and stared up at the evil *Fernsehturm* with its blinking red nodules. She told you, shivering in her white fur collar, about Siberia: how much she missed her friends, and how there were no bears in her town. "I know you are thinking there is bear in Siberia," she said. "But bear only in forest!" She rolled her eyes. "I mean, come on, peoples." After a few glasses of *Glühwein*, she began telling you about her boyfriend, the Russian man who paid for her plane ticket and still covers her share of the rent. He is a businessman, nearly always away on travels.

"My boyfriend is real asshole," Sweta told you. "He is good guy, but he is real asshole. You—not so bad. You call me Sweta. Is very special name." Then a black man passed nearby in the crowd. Sweta's posture straightened, and after the man had passed, she whispered, "You have seen negro before?"

"Him?"

"No, no. I mean, you have seen the negro before you are coming?" She looked furtively over her shoulder and whispered, "There are much—many negro person here. In Siberia, only in television." She looked both ways again, laughing nervously, just as she laughs now, peeking into the common room where you continue to hold the newspaper in your hands.

"What have you been up to?" you ask.

"I go to museum," she says, stepping into the room and combing her white-blonde Siberian hair.

"Which one?"

"Museum for Cultural Heritage of Schwabia." She shrugs. "Is so-so." You nod, not surprised. Like most of the students you know, Sweta spends a great deal of her time in Berlin visiting museums. You object to this, because visiting museums is not something you do when you are at home, so why should you do it abroad? There might be, even in Abaloma, you think, a museum of Native American bead-polishing, or perhaps the world's finest museum dedicated to the history of the Spanish missionary wood-sandal, but you will never know, because you would never think to spend your time and money visiting a museum unless required to do so as part of an elementary school fieldtrip. Consequently, you refuse to join the crowds of tourists hauling around their guidebooks like the massive wooden crosses of the many bleeding Jesuses that they will soon be meeting within the marble museum walls. Life is too short to spend even a moment standing before a diorama of Moses Mendelssohn's beard-grooming tools, or before a wall-display illustrating the chronology of the evolution of Prussian windpipes, about which one could clearly just as well read a book. Worst of all is to think of the tourists trudging bleary-eyed through the endless wooden halls of *Schloss* after *Schloss*, trying with every fiber of their exhausted beings to admire the craftsmanship of the warped wood in the German "palaces," whistling with wind and peeling paint. These teetering wooden shacks remind you of Voltaire's presentation of the luxuries of the eighteenth-century German hinterland, and in particular of the *beau château* where Candide spends his childhood with a Westphalian baron. You recently looked up the passage in order to be able to quote it to fellow students whenever they proposed a trip to the *Schloss Charlottenburg*:

«*Monsieur le baron était un des plus puissants seigneurs de la Westphalie, car son château avait une porte et des fenêtres. Sa grande salle même était ornée d'une tapisserie.*»

("The baron was one of the most powerful lords in Westphalia, for his palace had a door and windows. His great hall was even adorned with a tapestry.")

And so it was, you think, in the palaces of Brandenburg.

"Did you go to the museum with the German businessman?" you ask. Lately, Sweta has begun cheating on her absent Russian patron, who turned out not to be a pimp as you had originally suspected, but simply a boorish, overworked mid-level telecom executive who did not mind spending money to maintain his self-image as a high-rolling sugardaddy, though he had apparently not visited the city in months.

"No, but I see him tonight," she says. You can hear her unpacking items in the small kitchen. "We go to Russian ballet. The nutbreaker. You are going to party?"

"Yeah." A shiver passes up your spine. "With Yumiko."

"You will kiss New Year with your friend? Smooch smooch?" Sweta asks, laughing from the kitchen. "I only kid."

Yumiko, a classmate from the language school, is a Japanese kindergarten teacher who is several years older than you, sleeps through most of the lessons, and wears a comical knit cap with a pink pom-pom and green tassels. You fell in love with her quickly.

"Did you buy those potatoes?" you ask, trying to change the subject.

"Yes. You will eat?"

"Of course."

"Is good. You are skinny like pole."

Rising from the couch, you stretch your arms. It is finally late enough.

At the bottom of the entrance to the Prenzlauer Allee S-Bahn, the usual street punks wait with their sullen dogs and unexpired tickets for sale. The S-Bahn platform extends like the prow of a ship, gradually narrowing to a wedge where the tracks approach one another and pass under a nearby street. You stop at the last bench on the platform and stuff your hands deep into your pockets. According to the hanging information display, a rolodex of occasionally flipping cards with the names of trains on them, yours will be next. It is called the Ring, and it is probably your favorite subway line in all of Berlin. It circles around the city in an hour, heading in both directions, and when you take it, you feel as though you are an eagle, calmly circling around the city's core. When you approach the vicinity of your destination, you suddenly swoop down, changing trains to a line that will inject you straight into the city's heart, just like an eagle suddenly diving at the sight of its prey. The only disappointing aspect of the Ring line, you think, is the recorded British voice on the other subway lines that always refers to the Ring as "the circle line." As in: "Passengers traveling to Tegel airport transfer at Gesundbrunnen to the circle line." But why should the English translation of "*der Ring*" be "the circle"? Aren't there any closer cognates for *der Ring* in English, you think, such as, for example, *the ring*? Because sitting down is even colder than you had expected, you return to standing. Pacing back and forth on the platform, you come to a stop next to a vending machine that apparently dispenses warm hotdogs and french fries. You have never seen it used. Yumiko once ate a *Bratwurst* in front of you, from a stand in a park in Kreuzberg, and you were surprised to see her chew with her mouth open, the entire time. But it ended up endearing somehow. It was so clear that she was enjoying herself. Now you wonder if she will be nervous too.

In any case, if the original namers of *der Ring* intended the line to be "the circle," you wonder, trying to distract yourself, then why did they not name the line *"der Kreis"*? Perhaps the explanation is political. Often, when you think of the Ring line, you think of Wagner's opera cycle and begin to hear the soaring voices of the *Walkyries* in your ears. Obviously, you think, the German translator would not have wanted to inspire thoughts of Wagner, and perhaps by association memories of his nation's militant past, in every English-speaking tourist who happened to be heading toward the circle line, just as, you have heard, Germans growing up after the war sought out circumlocutions, never with complete success, to avoid referring to tour-guides as *"Führer."* So the Germans were allowed to hear *der Ring* as the Ring, with the full soaring gallery of the echoes of Wagner, but the English were encouraged to hear *der Ring* as merely the anodyne Circle, the most harmless and unteleological of shapes, the sort of shape that would never invade Poland.

Just then, to your astonishment, a trim young man in a suit approaches the automatic hotdog dispenser beside you and stares at it. You observe him carefully out of the corner of your eye, anxious not to make the slightest movement that might dissuade him from using the machine. You desperately want to see someone make a hotdog come out, one of these days. Then a girl on the opposite end of the platform makes a sudden gesture, and the man at the hotdog machine looks up, turns and walks hurriedly away. You wonder if Yumiko has ever used one of these machines.

When the train arrives, a woman in a bulky black robe and a *Kopftuch* sits across from you in the subway car, gazing straight ahead. In order to avoid making eye-contact with a stranger, you search for something neutral to look at, some stable, inanimate object such as a poster for the Wall Street Language School (*"Do you speak American business?"*) or a steel pole. Then you wonder what the word *Kopftuch* would be in English. Bandana? Wimple? You are impressed with yourself, that you know a word in German whose translation you do not know in English. Truly, your consciousness has grown.

"My dearly honored ladies and gentlemen," a nearby voice begins in German, and you brace yourself for a lengthy speech. It is one of the panhandlers, probably one of the same street punks you saw lounging about the Prenzlauer Allee station, now standing behind you, no doubt with a sullen hound at his feet. "I beg your pardon for the disturbance," the voice goes on in a rapid, emotionless monotone, like the voice of a proctor reading aloud the instructions for a standardized test, "but I wonder if I might have your attention for a brief moment, in order to make a small request." The baroque courtesy of the panhandlers' speeches in Berlin amazes you. It would be impossible to imagine, you think, a vagrant in any American city delivering a soliloquy of such exquisite restraint. In your experience, the American mendicant tends instead to disarm with his frankness, making his proposition as direct as possible. "My friend," an aging street person once told you on a visit to San Francisco, "I'm a drug addict, and if I don't get some heroin in the next two hours, I'm going to die." It was like the plot of a Hollywood action movie, full of suspense and colorful yet reassuringly familiar characters, and it instantly made you want to see more, to find out what would happen next. By contrast, the panhandlers in Berlin offer the begging equivalent of a staid, slightly impersonal Restoration drama, perhaps one that has been produced with funding from several state-subsidized European arts foundations. It has been performed a thousand times, this venerable oration, but the audience appreciates its familiarity, its quiet reassurances. *"Meine geehrte Damen und Hehren, ich bitte Sie um Verzeihung für die Störung..."* The panhandler speaks too quickly and the roar of the subway is too loud for you to make out more than a few scraps of his speech. "I wonder if I might beg of you," you seem to hear him saying, "but a few spare coins in order to obtain some morsels of sustenance for myself and my poor, emaciated dog..." Struggling to hear, you feel as though you are listening to Pozzo philosophize at the end of his leash, or the rapid drone of the announcer at the end of a fresh new pharmaceutical commercial, racing through the side-effects to Tripsopran or Roplazoflac—the risk of headache, sudden nose palpitations, and, in rare cases, chronic popcorn-brain. Where did the panhandlers' stately monologue come from? *Woher?* Whence? Did it have an author? No, you think, it is more likely the result of an oral tradition. It is like *Beowulf.* The Berlinish panhandlers are the last, lonely descendents of those brave bards of yore who served their lords—the ring-givers!—by proclaiming the clan's proud heritage and the hallowed deeds of past heroes. Of course, you think, most of the functions of that kind of oral poetry have disappeared since the invention of writing and the printed word, as have, incidentally, most of the functions of the elderly, sad to say. Truly, the most catastrophic event in the history of the old must have been the invention of the book, for without the book there would have been no way to know, for example, what a drought is like, except by asking someone who was alive during the last one. But now anyone can read about droughts in a library or bookstore, or on the Internet, which, sadly, the aged have trouble using because of their weak vision and slow-moving hands. It is all very depressing, you think, since everyone will be old one day, if even that. Similarly, before books existed it was necessary for poets to serve as the repository of the wisdom of the tribe, using their rhyme and rhythm to remember and pass along the stories of the gods and the floods and the bygone heroes from the days of old. But now you are unable to think of the name of a single living poet, so low have their stars descended, and the only people with an oral tradition are the panhandlers of Berlin. They become panhandlers and apprentice themselves, probably, to an older panhandler whose oration they slowly learn and then begin to recite, developing their own rapid, mumbled variations, just like the ancient scops recounting feats by the fire in the merry mead-hall. But then you reconsider. Perhaps when one becomes a street-punk in Berlin, one receives a kind of membership card with the speech written on the back, like the laws of war on a card given to soldiers. Perhaps the panhandler's speech is not an oral tradition at all, but nothing more than an easily learned way to ask for money.

"I thank you again for your time," the vagrant seems to be concluding, abruptly, "and I sincerely wish you a safe journey onward."

He passes by your seat a moment later, holding out his jangling paper cup, which you successfully avoid looking at by continuing to stare at a pole. As the panhandler's sullen beast plods by behind him, you glance down. Though you have never been an expert at dog-breeds, you would guess this to be some variety of hulking black killer-dog. In fact, the majority of dogs in Germany seem to belong to the hulking killer-dog variety, either black or brown, including the muzzled hounds of the subway ticket police with the wire cages harnessed around their slobbering maws. Perhaps the choice of dog breeds, you think, is the one, secret bastion of powerlust that the Germans have allowed themselves to maintain. Otherwise, Berliners are the most tolerant people you have ever known. They are almost as polite as the Japanese.

The knot in your stomach tightens.

When you finally step through the front door of the New Year's party, several lengthy blocks from the Platz der Luftbrücke U-Bahn, you do not see Yumiko anywhere. Your friend Marcus stands across the crowded room, wearing the t-shirt of one of the obscure emo bands that he apparently enjoys listening to. His deep acne scars are accentuated by the overhead light, and you once again feel a great sympathy for him.

"How was Budapest?" you ask, clapping him on the back.

"Great, great."

"Is it *pest* or *pesht*?"

"You know what? I'm not sure."

"I've had enough tourism for a while. When I first got here, I visited Prague, Vienna, Munich. I stayed at the hostels, met the hostel people, talked about where they'd been, where they were going, where they were from, what they were doing when they returned, went to the museums, paid the entrance fees, took the trains, saw the churches. I don't see any reason to visit another city in Europe. I already know what it'll be like."

Marcus seems to be slowly rousing himself. "Huh. Really? All the cities I've visited have been completely different."

"Yeah, well, some parts are different. But you can get the different parts from movies. Books. Postcards."

"That's ridiculous! You can't get the full experience just by watching something in a movie."

"The *full experience*. What is that? Haven't you noticed that the *full experience* of staying at a hostel, visiting museums and eating street food in Paris is eerily similar to the *full experience* of staying at a hostel, visiting museums and eating street food in Budapest? The only things that change are the things that don't matter. The content. Like whether you're looking at the Mona Lisa or the leaning tower of Pisa. The underlying structure remains the same."

"The structure of what?"

"Of the experience. The fact is, I've had it already. There's nothing more to learn. From this moment on, there's only repetition."

"I don't know about that."

"The problem is, it's too easy to move between cities now. It's like flipping through postcards at a souvenir stand. Maybe it meant something when it was more difficult, and you had to ride in a coach that kept getting stuck in the mud. When you had to trade horses. Fly in risky dirigibles."

"Have you ever been to Rome or Paris?"

"Nah."

"Aren't you even a little curious to walk through the Roman ruins? Or to drink espresso at a Parisian café?"

"Like I said, I already know what it would be like. I've literally seen movies in which people drink espresso in Paris. I can take the superficial details from those movies and plug them into the framework of my trips to Prague, Vienna and Munich. I can take the Sagrada Familia and put it in the place of the Reichstag, I can take the Reichstag and put it in the place of Notre Dame, I can take Notre Dame and put it in the place of the Sagrada Familia. I already know how they'd all fit together and what they'd feel like. You pay for the ticket, you walk up the stairs, and it's just like the Discovery Channel, except with higher resolution and a worse narrator."

He regards you skeptically. There has always been a simmering hostility between the two of you, beneath the banter. "This sounds like the kind of complaint," he says finally, with a tense smile, "that only a very privileged Westerner has the luxury of making. Not everyone can afford to travel to Munich and then dismiss the experience as a waste."

"I didn't say that the first three cities were a waste," you clarify, "only that any more would be."

Marcus scoffs. He seems exasperated, but for some reason still willing to listen. Most people, you think, would have offered some dismissive comment by now and excused themselves to get another drink. This is one more reason why the two of you are friends.

"The first three cities," you continue, "were necessary to become familiar with the *structure* of the experience. To learn which aspects were lasting and important and which were superficial and changing. Think of it this way. It's like backpacking through Europe is its own country, and this is the country we visit whenever we take a train, stay at a hostel, take a picture of a monument, wait in line. The tourism industry wants you to believe that there are different cities in this Europe, and that you must visit all of them, but really, it's an illusion. For the backpacker, there is only one city. To leave this city, you have to stop backpacking and do something else."

"Like what?"

"I don't know. There are no books about it." You swallow the last of your cranberry juice and set down the glass. "The important thing is that it doesn't require buying a train ticket. You could travel a greater distance by talking to the beggar beside you on the street than you could by passing through three time zones. Visit a hospital. That's a different world. You know, sleep in the woods. People should be traveling to create an altered structure of experience for themselves, not to make some trivial movement from one point on a map to another. Who cares about location?"

Marcus begins to smile. "Are you trying to out-righteous me?"

"Yes. You know, I worked for the Gore campaign."

"So?" Marcus laughs. "I voted for Ralph Nader."

For a moment, you are at a loss. Then you attempt to apologize for him. "That's okay," you rush to say. "I mean, it's not like you were in Florida."

"I was in Florida." He takes a moment, grinning slightly and watching through the small, rimless ovals of his glasses as his words sink in. He seems to enjoy your reaction. His smile widens. "Me and my grandparents cast three votes for Nader in Palm Beach County."

Then you can only stare at him. In the end, you ask whether he regrets his vote.

"No, not at all."

"I don't understand. Don't you realize what you've done?"

He regards you blankly.

"You elected George W. Bush President of the United States. Do you realize what his policies on social security are? Do you know what he wants to do to public schools?"

Then you hear a glass being clinked repeatedly with something metal. Instinctively turning, you see the host, your German friend Detering, standing, arms raised, near the fireplace. Yumiko stands beside him, still wearing her mittens and her multicolored knit cap with its pom-pommed tassels. While you make your way across the room to her, Detering begins to deliver a speech of such astounding tediousness that you wonder whether he might actually be performing a deadpan parody of some other German welcome speech. Beginning with the orientation session at the language school, you have witnessed several of these oratorical exercises, usually in praise of someone who either is not present or is standing next to the speaker and will return the favor by delivering an equally elaborate speech of thanks in honor of the current speaker's speech of praise once the latter is completed. If the language school had been American, you think, there would not even have been an orientation session. They would simply have attached a plastic sign to each teacher and set the students loose. "And I look forward to sharing with all of you," Detering seems to be saying, though you cannot be sure, "a delightful dinner before tonight's evening is over..." Perhaps it is the first time Detering has made an unnecessary welcoming speech, you think, glancing again at Yumiko, who still does not seem to have seen you, and who, in fact, seems to be nodding off, occasionally closing her eyes and letting her head droop before she snaps back to attention. As you continue to squeeze your way slowly across the room, Detering's eyes dart furtively from wall to wall. He rubs his hands nervously and thanks the guests, again, for coming. "And I would also like to welcome our American friends," he says suddenly, in wonderfully accented English, turning to you and Marcus, "who are studying to speak German and… we hope they are very welcome to be with us here also."

The other guests offer a brief, ironically measured round of applause, grinning and nodding at you and Marcus, as though the two of you were a pair of recently wounded athletes.

"Please," Detering continues in English, "help yourselves to the buffet. Thank you. And now, *ich bedanke mich für ihre Aufmerksamkeit, meine geehrte Damen und Herren…*" Surely Detering is not a part of the panhandlers' guild? You have no time to consider the implications before Yumiko reawakens and begins to follow the crowd toward the buffet, in the opposite direction from you. By the time you navigate to her side, she is picking at a piece of shrimp and adding it to her already full mouth. When she turns to you, there is something delightfully sincere, but at the same time equally delightfully artificial, in her smile. Lately you have begun to associate such smiles with the Kabuki theater of her homeland. Before you can speak to her, however, there is a ruckus and several Germans urgently usher the two of you to a television in the corner of the room. It is playing an old black and white film that, someone soon whispers to you in broken English, is watched every year in Germany on New Year's Eve. In fact, it is less a film than an old English television broadcast of a play, something from that bygone era when television was performed live on a stage before a single camera and a studio audience. An aristocratic English woman sits alone at the head of a dining room table, forcing her butler to pretend that there are guests, and also forcing him to drink toast after toast on behalf of the imaginary guests. The dialogue consists entirely of lines such as the following:

"You are looking very well this evening, Miss Sophie."

"Well, I am feeling very much better, thank you, James."

"Good, good…"

"Well, I must say that everything looks nice."

"Thank you very much, Miss Sophie, thank you."

"Is everybody here?"

"Indeed, they are, yeah. Yes… They are all here for your anniversary, Miss Sophie."

It goes on like that until, eventually, both Sophie and the butler are extremely drunk, and then the film abruptly ends.

Throughout the spectacle, none of the Germans laugh. Some of them smile anxiously and exchange knowing glances.

"*Verstehst du?*" you whisper to Yumiko.

She takes a sharp breath, opens her eyes wide, then shakes her head decisively.

"*Ich auch nicht,*" you say.

You place your hand on the small of her back. It tightens.

Then dinner begins. The two of you sit at each other's sides at Detering's long table, and Yumiko seems entranced by the oil-filled fondue pot in which her meat skewer rests, heated by a small blue flame.

"*Das ist auch in Japan?*" you ask, pointing to the fondue pot.

"*Emschudigun?*"

"*In Japan?*"

"*Ach, so. Nein, nein. Sehr... sehr heiss.*"

"*Heiss?*"

"*Sehr heiss.*"

She reaches out a finger and pretends to burn it on the fondue pot, clutching it with typical Kabuki drama. She must be a wonderful kindergarten teacher, you think. Then one of Detering's German friends turns to you and says something incomprehensible.

"*Sprichst du englisch?*" you ask.

"Of course," he says. "I was only asking how the two of you met."

"Oh, we're in the same class at the language school."

"Ah, so you speak German together?"

"Yes."

The man turns to Yumiko and says something in German. Her eyes go wide and she shakes her head.

"Her German isn't very good," you offer. "It's so much more difficult coming from the Asian languages."

"Right. Of course. Does she speak English?"

"No."

"So you speak Japanese?"

You shake your head. "No."

"Ah," he says, nodding uncomfortably.

"Yes, it's very difficult to communicate."

"How do you communicate?"

"I guess we don't, really."

At this, the man nods uncertainly and returns to his dining companion.

"*Was er sagt?*" Yumiko asks, pointing at the man.

"*Ich sage, du bist Japanerin, ich bin Amerikaner, du hast kein Englisch, ich habe kein Japanisch.*"

"*Ach, so.*"

It is true that the Asian students are at a disadvantage, you think, trying to stop your heart from racing. One day, using the small, silver-cased electronic translator that all the Japanese students at the institute seem to own, you tried to show Yumiko how many words were the same in English and German, as opposed to Japanese and German. You typed in words like "gorilla" and showed her the translations.

"Go-ah-li-la," she said.

"*Ja,*" you said. "*Auf deutsch, Gorilla.*"

It was with the help of this machine that you invited her to spend New Year's Eve with you, here at the party, where a few of the guests have now burst into loud, braying laughter. You know them to be Brazilians. As you slowly test a tip of skewered meat against the oil, you ponder what assholes Brazilian men are. But the oil is not yet hot enough. Not surprisingly, the meat on your skewers is pork. It would not be an exaggeration, you think, to say that virtually every food you have eaten in Germany has contained a pork foundation. Once, out of nostalgia, you tried to buy hamburger from the grocery store, and you thought that you did buy it, but when you got home and translated the label, you discovered that you had in fact purchased ground pork, the only ground meat available, other than ground turkey, the German word for which reminds you of French whores, or of the feisty little man who has just become the President of Russia.

You glance at Yumiko, who seems to remain entranced by the blue gas flame beneath the oil pot. Your nervousness has taken away your appetite, and even if the fondue were not made of pork, you would not have had any desire to eat it. It has been so long since you have felt about a girl in this way. Not since Margaret, if even then, and back then you had alcohol to ease the way. Breathing deeply, you try to calm yourself.

Brazilian men, you consider. It would be one thing if their macho pride arose from some accomplishment. It would be one thing if they did something to earn their arrogance, like building bridges or walking up hills with donkeys. But Brazilian men do nothing. Of all men in the world, they are both the most confident in their own manhood and the least justified in possessing such confidence, because they are, so far as you can determine, the least able to control themselves. They are the lazy, mustachioed pigs who drive motorcycles without mufflers and lean back at their dinner tables to let their wives and daughters sweep up the scraps while they unclasp their belts and let slacken their soft, plump bellies, thinking all the while, with self-satisfied, patronizing grins, that women are such foolish things, watching their telenovelas all day, they are silly girls deserving a swift slap on the rump for not being able to understand the more complicated things in life. All of the activities that seem most central to machismo, you think, such as belching, beating the wife, constantly touching the small crotch of one's undersized fat-jeans, whistling at women as though they were dogs, all of these things are ironically united in demonstrating an adolescent, whimpering inability to control one's passions, to control oneself, and if manhood means anything, it means self-control. These Brazilian poolboys, these diapered steers, have convinced themselves that women are best treated as maidservants, whores and wetnurses, even though women in their cultures have had virtually no chance to do anything but make, suckle and fodder babies, and if they attempt to do something else, such as design flying cars or mind-reading lasers, they would be excluded, as if by prescript, from the possibility of obtaining a husband, because none of these Brazilian eunuchs has the manly security to live with a woman stronger than he is, much less to raise their acorn-like members in the presence of one. You have had a nosefull of Brazilians and their macho ways.

"*Ah, heiss!*" Yumiko exclaims. While you were not looking, she put a corner of her pork skewer into the oil and then tried to touch the cooked meat. Now she sucks on the tip of her finger, making a plaintive, wounded sound. She is so beautiful, you think, so precious. "*Schmerzen?*" you ask. You place your hand on her back again, moving it gently and allowing yourself to feel the curve of her back as it straightens beneath her sweater.

By the time dinner comes to an end and Detering and his African girlfriend remove the dishes, it is already nearly midnight. You follow the guests downstairs into the street, where it has begun snowing. Already, you can hear the occasional crack and whistle of fireworks. From a distant apartment, an old Motown classic drifts eerily into the night.

"*Gut Musik,*" you say, gesturing vaguely upwards. "*Sehr schön.*"

"*Ja, ja,*" Yumiko nods. "*Sehr wichtig.*"

"*Ich liebe diese Musik,*" you say, resting your hand on her shoulder. She does not pull away. You wait with growing impatience for someone to shout that it is midnight. Lowering your hand to the small of Yumiko's back, you stand beside her and watch the others as they hand out plastic flutes for the champagne and prepare the bottle.

"*Ein gutes Partei, nein?*" you say.

"*Ja,*" she says. "*Kalt. Eim bisschem kalt.*" For emphasis, she pinches together the two fingers of her free hand. "*Eim bisschem—*"

Before she can finish, cathedral bells ring in the distance and the fireworks begin to explode in rapid-fire succession, now closer than before, you think, and even some of the guests at the party are setting off their own. You step in front of Yumiko, your hands on her shoulders, and lean in to kiss her. She turns her head aside.

"*Frohes neues Jahr,*" you say.

You find that your head has come to rest on her shoulder. Hoping and assuming that she has simply misunderstood, you give her a warm embrace and then lean in again to kiss her, but for a second time she avoids your lips and turns her head so that you can only press your face into her hair. After a moment, you lean back and look out over the street. The other guests at the party stand in couples, embracing, pressed together. Even Marcus has found someone, an ostrich-like girl who leans down to kiss him.

You gesture toward the others.

"*Siehst du?*" you ask.

She looks at you with her eyes wide and says nothing.

"*Das ist was man machst hier. Macht. Tradition.*" There is tension in your voice. You make a gesture, touching your lips.

"*Im Japom, man...*" She folds her hands together and bows her head, pretending to bow to several imaginary people around you. "*So.*"

"*Aber wir sind in Deutschland. Und hier...*"

A solitary, drunken man stumbles toward the two of you. "Happy New Year!" he yells with a thick German accent. "Happy New Year," you say. Fireworks whiz by in the street, and the smoke begins to thicken. A pair of young children run past, throwing fireworks at one another and shrieking with laughter. The German man regards the two of you with uncertainty and then offers you the bottle.

"Champagne?" the German asks.

"*Nein, danke.*"

When you turn back to Yumiko, the moment is over and your smile is gone.

"*Ja,*" you say. "*Ein bisschen kalt,*" you say. "*Du gehst zurück? Zum Institut?*"

She does not understand at first.

"*Zurück gehen?*" she asks.

"*Als du willst.*"

After leaving Yumiko at the language school's dorm in Mitte, you consider taking a streetcar to Prenzlauerberg, then change your mind and begin to walk back through the crowded streets. The snow coats the sidewalks but has stopped falling. You have never walked through smoke this dense before, you think, and all around you the stumbling crowds of Berliners continue to light fireworks. A man comes to a stop outside the entrance to the Weinmeisterstrasse U-Bahn. He removes a firecracker from his pocket and holds a lighter to the fuse with all the enthusiasm of a janitor shutting off the last light in an office building. Tossing the firecracker away into the glistening snow, he watches it pop without emotion. Then he descends into the station. You follow him down. At Gesundbrunnen, while standing on the platform, waiting to switch trains, you almost start to cry, which itself disgusts you. It seems like something Marcus would do, crying alone on a subway platform on New Year's Eve in Berlin. And almost everyone you know is just like him, you think. All the people in Abaloma. They all listen now to what sounds like emo music, and they adopt fashionably utopian politics that require no personal sacrifice. Marcus' vote is almost admirable. Most anarchists don't have the idiocy of their convictions. The root problem, you consider, is all of your parents. You were nurtured and protected and swaddled in cotton candy by the most self-indulgent generation the world has ever known, those self-deluded, overall-wearing, papier-mâché revolutionaries who thought the world would enter a new age of peace, love and understanding if only the children of the wealthiest fraction of the human population took their parents' money and founded organic beard farms in upstate Wisconsin. And now the children of these children, you think, cannot let go of their childish illusions. They cannot let go of the yogurt and the lies. They watch movies written in rainbow crayon about adults who act like children and children who act like adults, read finger-painted books about precocious, unappreciated teenagers who cling to their thumb-sucking and imaginary friends, listen to music by men approaching thirty who whimper in mild, newly developed speech impediments about the travails and traumas of life as a thirteen year-old. The latest literature is all about talking butterflies and magical noses and little boys who are made of marshmallows. The authors of these books must have assumed, you think, that there is nothing left to write about in the world outside the children's section, that history has come to an end and left us with nothing but progressively more whimsical novelties. Can the human race survive under conditions of such triviality? Is it possible that the world ends not even with a whimper, but a satiated yawn?

Your thoughts are suddenly interrupted by the sight of two of the Brazilian men on the platform across the tracks from you. Oddly, they seem to be embracing one another. In fact, they are kissing. You stare at them while the snow falls through the opening over the tracks. Before you can look away, one of them has seen you.

"*Frohes neues Jahr*," he yells across the tracks, disengaging himself long enough to smile and wave.

"*Frohes neues Jahr*," you murmur.

As you finally walk up the steps of the Prenzlauer Allee station, gritting your teeth against the cold, you try to distract yourself from the thought of drinking. You do not allow yourself to consider it, even for a moment, as a live possibility, and instead consider how surprising it is that no glib editorialist has arrived at the most appropriate label for your pathetic cohort: the You Generation. The great towering self-centeredness of the Me Generation has given way, as if by some dialectic, to an endlessly self-curious craving for recognition. It does not require inner fulfillment, you imagine the witless hack writing, but only that everything around it acknowledge and approve of its being. If the Me Generation demanded an infinite subjectivity, the You Generation demands an infinite objectivity: it does not so much want to fulfill itself as it wants its condition, whether of fulfillment or otherwise, to be publicized, recognized, objectively confirmed. It wants to see its picture being seen on its own personal website; it wants to publish its personal diary for all to read; it wants its life to be filmed and displayed in prime-time television for the enjoyment and appreciation of a global audience. It wants life to be like the video games to which it has dedicated weeks and months of its life since youth, games in which it is itself the star. It wants the news that it reads to be produced by it, and the encyclopedia and all other books as well, because it has been raised on an endless diet of gold stars, plastic trophies and mass-produced certificates of accomplishment. The You Generation is a generation of masters who are slaves to their slaves, forever dependent on the sparkling stamp that will make their existences real, the universal parent smiling down approvingly from above. When others look at your generation, you think, they must think that you are all the "you" that appears in "do it yourself," innovators creating the proper content of your worlds, authors of your own lives. But they are wrong, you think, for in fact you are yourselves nothing more than a blank, universal demand, the empty cravings of a mirror for its own reflection.

On the short walk back to your apartment building, there is a Turkish corner store with coolers full of bottled beer. You begin to think of all the reasons why it would be okay to have a drink on this night. The sweet call of ruin. You are at your weakest in these moments, when there is no hope and your life reveals itself to have been one long parade of futility and shame. But you are too tired now even to will your destruction.

At the door to your building, you stop and stare at the sidewalk. Someone has drawn the chalk outline of a body on the concrete. Like a snow angel for adults. You slide your keys into the lock.

Shortly after you have settled onto the couch, Sweta calls. You can hear the steady din of a crowd in the background as she speaks.

"Hello, darling!"

"Hello, Sweta."

"Are you with Japanwoman?"

"No."

She seems to be talking intermittently to someone else on the other end of the phone. "I only want to say, I come back maybe with friend. Or maybe not come back. Okay?"

"Sure."

"I am probably with friend somewhere, okay? Not in home."

"I understand, Sweta."

The second voice on the other end of the line seems to be yelling at her. "I go now. Have good time with Japanerin!" she yells. "Happy new year!" The line goes dead.

You turn on the television. But you have already watched too much television earlier in the day, so you turn it back off. Then you sit on the couch and stare at the blank screen.

A while later, you walk to the bathroom to urinate. You stare at your image in the mirror.

For the first time in a long while, you are reminded of your physical ugliness. It is a simple fact. This is what Yumiko saw. Your head looks like the swollen head of a child. Like a fragile egg.

Standing before the mirror, you are like someone in a dream who has become aware that he is naked and stands in a public place. But there is no covering yourself now. In general, there is little to be done. Without beauty, your choices might take you down countless paths, but rarely to love.

You return to the couch and lie down, closing your eyes. When you open them again, Sweta stands silhouetted in the entryway with a tall man behind her, still wearing his coat. He shifts in the hallway light.

"*Frohes neues Jahr*," Sweta says.

"Happy new year," you say, slowly rubbing your face. You look up and try to nod politely.

Sweta asks whether you saw the snow. You say that you did. "What have you two been up to?" you ask.

"We watch movie. Very funny."

"Which one? The black and white one?"

"No, no. Is Russian movie. We watch every year at Sylvester." She sniffles, and you become aware once again of the man standing behind her.

"*Ironiya sudby….*"

"*Die Ironie des Schicksals*," the man offers.

"*Ja. Das ist es.*"

"Well, I should be heading off to bed," you say. You continue to sit on the couch.

They continue to stand, silhouetted, in the entryway.

"Have a good night," Sweta says.

"You too," you say.

The man wishes you a happy new year.

You nod.

"Happy new year," you say.

You do not move.

You.

Do not move.

You. You.

You.

You.

Awake, awake...

Beholde, thou art yet in the faire garden: and there is no new thing vnder the sunne. The plants which blossomed, blossome still: and the trees which put foorth fruite, put foorth fruite still: and the wings of the butterflies which daunced, daunce still.

And I am yet before thee.

So, you've made your choice, I say. That was it.

I laugh and shew thee againe my teeth with yellow staine.

But I don't want you to spend eternity with a case of buyer's remorse. So I'm going to give you one last chance to reconsider. You know, hell is where the heart is. You're a free man, and you deserve a choice. One last chance, my friend.

Now. Do you choose the side of God, or do you choose me?

If you choose hell, turn to page 270.

If you repent, turn to page 7.

You open your hand and give April's cheek a hard slap.

She squeals. "Fuck!" Recoiling, she nearly tumbles off the bed. "Is that what you do?" She stares at you in disgust. "You beat them?"

"No. I thought…"

But she will not listen to your apologies. She grabs her clothes and leaves the bedroom, slamming the door behind her. By the time you wake the next morning, she is gone. You spend the day watching television and replaying the scene in your mind.

What were you thinking?

It has always been an assumption of yours that you are basically a good person. That any mistakes you made were brief lapses in judgment, or the unfortunate result of circumstance. In any case, whatever harm you caused, you have always thought, was more than outweighed by the cruelty you suffered in your childhood. The bullying. The humiliation.

But now you wonder. What is the evidence that you are a good person? What if you are, in fact, one of the bad guys?

Unable to sleep the following night, you lie in bed and fantasize about making a fresh start. Maybe you could move to Africa. You could become a relief worker. Or you could join the military. You will start going to church and become born again. One day you will see April strolling on the boardwalk, back in Abaloma, and she will give you a second chance. It will all happen so suddenly. The small wedding on the headlands. The baby. April will join the local parish and you will work long hours at the firm. It will be worth it, though, because your practice group—the environmental practice—will be booming. Much of your work will be overflow from the firm's main office in Houston. Oil and gas. It is true that you did not always envision spending your life in service of the energy industry. Who expects to spend their career ankle deep in oil futures contracts? But the fact is, everyone deserves a fair day in court, and the system works best when both sides have skilled legal representation. If you were not working for these guys, someone else would fill your slot, and it goes without saying that you need to provide for your family. You're just a senior associate, in any case, and you don't choose which clients to represent. Furthermore, anyone who criticizes oil and gas exploration just doesn't understand how the energy market works. And a corporation has a duty to its shareholders. Just like you have a duty to your family. The question is what's the most efficient way to use our resources today. Emissions regulations are not the answer, because coordinated global response. In fact a good argument can be made for the social value of tax arbitrage. Moreover, your clients are dedicated to alternative energy solutions, and whether you like it or not, we're going to be relying on carbon for a long time to come. In addition, China. All wishful thinking aside, experts recommend mitigation. The real problem, in the end, is global poverty. Your clients are committed to investing in the arts. Simply put, they are not bad guys. You've worked with these guys, and they are good guys.

So you adopt a proactive and healthy mindset. As Pastor Tim always says, you must conceive prosperity on the inside before receiving it on the outside. So you let go of your negative attitudes and you decide to get down to business, because God gives supernatural increase to the faithful in his flock. You learn to be a good listener and encourage others to talk about themselves, and you remember first names and smile. A sure way to make others feel good about themselves is to give honest and sincere appreciation, and at home the recipe for success is hearing and understanding, because women are like waves. Then the partner in your office announces his coming retirement, and you really take things up a notch. And do you know what? A lot of people try to turn their lives around, but you will really get things moving. More than one higher-up tells you that you are doing a super job. When you finally start the interviews to make partner and get some equity under your belt, you do so with extra-strong confidence. It is an eat what you kill business, and boy, you are ready for supper. And do you know what happens then?

They choose another senior associate to fill the old man's shoes, a snake-in-the-grass who goes on golf trips with the head honcho in Houston and belongs to the same church. You overhear the news in the hallway before it is announced, and you try to pretend that you have not heard it, but the blood rushes to your face. They all know how much you hungered. They all know how hard you tried. Now they will know too that you failed. You may not even have a job next week. Because in this world it is up or out. But here's the key question: what did God think about all this? After all, there is no doubt but that you envisioned your success, pictured yourself winning, and then went after the gold medal from start to finish with all engines on full throttle, and still the position went to someone else, this pink-faced gladhander who chats in the hallways and wears an easy smile. He is years less senior than you. He has racked up fewer billable hours. He does little work and does it poorly. The injustice of it sinks its fangs deep into your heart. For the first time in years you get drunk at a bar after work and fight with April until the kid starts to cry, but you do not want to scrape the poison out of your veins. You like it there. You unleash your anger, and at night, you can't sleep for the rage. The same furious thoughts hammer one after another through your head. You did the work and he will get the rewards.

No, you cannot accept it. You ask God, "Why did you do this to me? You know I deserved it. This isn't fair. This isn't how it was supposed to end." And when you wake up the next morning there is a fleeting moment of peace before you remember that your reward has been stolen from you and then the rage returns and you drink steadily for the rest of the week, not speaking while you are in the office, arguing at home, trying to fill April with the poison too, trying to spread the sickness to her and make her suffer as well. But she is so selfish, she does not even listen to you. Then you look at her with newborn eyes and you are disgusted by the sight. You think back fondly to your days of wildcatting, the college girls, lost pleasures. After tasting such fruits, whatever made you think that you could survive on the same thin gruel, day after day? The church had turned you into a sap. You used to be a hunter, and now you are the prey. But perhaps it is not too late to start again. If only. If. In this word, all your regret.

On Sunday one of the greeters says he heard about the news. He heard about the shake-up at the firm. He is sorry, because he knows what it is like, and he asks if you would care to join his Bible study group. It is only for men. At first you want to punch him and your head still hurts but something else, something inside you leads you to accept the invitation. And that's how you get saved. These men, they're the ones that pull you back. It's there, just with the guys, in that run-down classroom at the community college, that you get pounded back into shape. Iron on iron. Steel against steel. They take that old hunk of junk soul of yours and make it rev again. Your brothers in Christ teach you the big hows: how to read your Bible and how to worship the Person of Jesus Christ as your one true redeemer and savior. You're a sinner, boy, and you know it. You done wrong. But these men are Jesus with skin on. They show you the path of the Word, manhood and Christlikeness. They pound it into you. They make you realize that it's not about God helping you. It's about you helping God. It's about what he intended, not what you hoped. They pin you down and fill you with the Good News. Boy, it's a struggle. But you thank them for it and ask for more. Because you're ready to get energized. It's a bloodbrawl, taking down those beasts you got inside. And the guys know it. To put it bluntly, they been there too. These godly men know how to pray until it hurts, until a man feels like he's breaking in two, and then to pray again and again. Not letting the Jesus Mockers and the Porno Freaks bring them down. Bible-thumpin' heroes is what they are. Brothers in the Army of Christ. They heat you with their iron, start every meeting on time and end it the same, celebrate Jesus Christ, and keep a twelve-pack of alcohol-free beer chillin' in the cooler. They're built tough. They teach you how to love your wife. How to cherish that mom who is not your mom but is yours. It may not be politically correct, but these few godly men repair you, even through the tears. Honestly, your vital relationship with these guys is transformational.

Years later, nearing retirement at the latest firm, you're going to look back at your darkest hour, when you lost the promotion and the beast in you almost destroyed what it took half a lifetime to create, and you're going to see it all as the utmost blessing. Because it hooked you up with the guys. You'll be smoking a stogie on the back porch, soaking in the peace and quiet, and you'll think again of the time you struck April. But the shame will be gone. Because God has forgiven you. She has forgiven you. The person who did that is not the person you are today. You are a family man, a leader of the local bar association, someone who attends church weekly, hunts ducks in the summer, donates money to African relief, and supports your family. No one could demand any more from you. The holy spirit working in concert with the invisible hand. Returning inside, you stop by the couch where April is watching television and you kiss her silver hair. She tells you that she is planning to take a bath, and asks you to turn off the water in the tub when you get upstairs.

"Will do," you yawn. "Think I'm going to hit the hay."

"I know you are."

"Enjoy your bath."

When you reach the upstairs bathroom, water is covering the floor. The old faucet above the tub has sprouted a leak. As you go to turn it off, you slide and hit your head on the counter by the sink, fracturing your skull and leaving you lying on the wet bathmat, unable to speak. At first, you think of saving yourself. Then you know that you cannot move, and you cannot save yourself, and you think of nothing but seeing April one more time and how much you would like to see her again. You are not afraid. As your mind drifts back over the years, there is no final scream or whispered horror. There is no reckoning. Your life has been entirely ordinary and entirely simple and therefore free from shame.

And can we say that your judgment is anything but true and just, dear reader?

If you have failed, you have failed no differently than many others.

Not every man must walk the lonely highway of the righteous.

Not every man must love his enemies as his friends.

Not every man must live in love and service to the least fortunate among us—the helpless, the filthy, the despised.

The blessed man is not he who avoids sin, but he who, in sinning, sins in a conventional and orthodox way.

Amen.

The broken glass crunches beneath your shoes on the way out of the parking lot.

So. The campaign is over. You do not yet know what to make of it.

Back in the donated motel room, lying on your bed with the lights out, you bathe in the flicker of the muted television and think. Every hour you spent, every hour of sleep you sacrificed, every hand you shook and call you made, all of it had been a waste. And they had known it from the start. The higher-ups had fooled you, and you had passed along their lies to the volunteers. Used these lies as a hook to squander their few hours of leisure. Asked them to degrade themselves on the phones for you. The campaign bosses had exploited all your hopes and ideals like a magical lever for the production of low-cost political labor. And why? Just to distract the other side. To leech away some of their resources. All the effect you had, the several months of your life you gave them, could have been accomplished by a few millionaires donating a few more fistfuls of dollars, or a few donors on the other side forking over a few less.

Taking a drink from the bottle of bourbon you were saving for election night, you try on this story of the campaign. That it had all been for nothing. That they had made a fool of you. You feel as though you are sliding your arms into the sleeves of the story, checking the cuffs. But it does not quite fit. There is some mismatched seam tugging at the chest.

The next day, bleary-eyed, as you assemble the available volunteers in the campaign office and listen on a statewide conference call to the somber voices from national explaining the closure of the West Virginia campaign, some of the most dedicated volunteers cry and hold one another's hands, and you feel a kind of cynicism hardening within you. But still it does not seem quite right. There is something more to these past several months than a story of exploited ideals... In the evening, while removing your clothes from the dresser drawers in the motel room, you come across a Gideon Bible. Unable to remember how much of the book you have actually read, despite all your religious studies courses, you decide to spend your final night in Morgantown finishing the bottle of bourbon and reading the Book of Genesis... *In the beginning God created the heaven and the earth...*

The story of Adam and Eve is so profoundly strange. Yet when people refer to it, they never talk about its strangeness. They treat it as somehow natural... As the alcohol spills into your blood, a phrase comes to mind:

"The loss of innocence."

When Adam ate from the tree of knowledge and gained awareness of himself, he lost his innocence. He was no longer innocent, because he had committed a sin. That is what people say.

How odd it is to think of the gaining of knowledge about oneself as the original sin. Why is awareness of oneself such a threat to the Creator? It is not knowledge of nature, nor of God, nor of his mysteries. Why should self-knowledge have been forbidden at all? It reminds you of the Greek myths you studied as a freshman. Prometheus stealing fire from the gods and giving it to man. You can understand why the Greeks would have imagined the transmission of fire as a crime. Fire is powerful. It dazzles and burns. But awareness of the self? What can this kindle? Whose fingers can this singe, other than one's own? It seems inconceivable to you that the bold and inquisitive Greeks would have crafted a myth in which a god was punished for giving to man knowledge of himself. On the contrary, there had been a Greek oracle who demanded of men, on behalf of the gods: know thyself. What the Abrahamic religions imagined as the founding crime of the human race, the Greeks set out as its highest aim.

And even if it were somehow possible to view the ban on self-knowledge as natural, you consider, why should the embodiment of this knowledge have been awareness of one's *nakedness*? Is this some trace of the long-forgotten civilizing injunction to clothe oneself? Of the violence by which this injunction must have spread? And what, now that you think of it, had driven those early men to wrap themselves in the hides of their prey in the first place, until they clothed themselves even in the heat? Did they seek to become more like the beasts whose skins they wore, or to distinguish themselves from them? If the awareness of nakedness in the story of the fall did have its roots in some prehistoric taboo, then why this taboo? Why not embody sin in some other primordial command of civilization—for example, the need to bury one's dead, or to avoid incest? Adam bites into the apple and discovers that he has been sleeping with the daughter created from him, plucks out his eyes. Why, indeed, not make carnal knowledge in general—the object of so many failed prohibitions, the obsessive focus of so many cultural rules, the universal image of human weakness in the face of temptation, the source of so much destruction from the rage of Achilles to the latest infidelity on the nightly news—why not make lustful sex the object of the Creator's founding prohibition, and of humankind's failing?

But perhaps nakedness stands in as the most convenient outward sign of *shame*, and it is this shame that lies at the heart of the story. What does Adam do with the great new power that he has derived from the forbidden fruit? Does he storm the gates of heaven? Does he create another being? Does he judge his world and call it good? No: none of this. He judges himself. And he sees that he is bad. This is the flame he has stolen from his creator's fire. What a glorious conquest. The ability to condemn oneself, to see oneself as another and call the other wrong. This is the founding crime of the human race from which a savior must deliver us...

And in the wake of these swirling speculations, another thought arrives. At long last, a fitting lesson from your experience on the campaign! It is this:

What has always lain closest to your heart is the freedom to think freely, without boundary or constraint, as you have been doing since lying down on the motel bed and opening the covers of the holy book. To let the mind ramble where it will. Truly to think, and not merely to carry out the algorithm already laid down. What does it mean to think? It means not wasting time on the tired execution of pre-determined rules that a computer might one day carry out with more facility and precision. It means launching forward into the uncharted course—the original turn of thought whose direction could not have been extrapolated from what came before.

There is no room for such thought within the pales of the political world.

Your error in joining the campaign was not idealism. It was to have allowed yourself to be distracted from your ideals by something so base and meaningless.

In truth, American democracy never gets much better or worse. No democracy does. And it is not because the game is rigged. It is because of the unchanging, ceaseless, insipid mediocrity of what is required to appeal to the mass public—at all, ever. As much as the public enjoys and celebrates the products of the freedom of thought, it abhors the spectacle of thought itself. It abhors the radically new. There is only room in the political sphere for the most degraded things, the prechurned regurgitate choked up by the sparrow to her hatchlings. You think of the writers who captivated you in college—not the technical philosophers, but the ones who really shaped your view of life and the world. Blake. Whitman. Rimbaud. Joyce. The rebels and heretics. Their breach with the ordinary and expected produced only nausea and confusion among the many. They were greeted with charges of obscenity and corrupting the minds of youth. They were condemned by the cautious souls who only register the new as somehow abnormal, and thus reject it—thereby demonstrating to others, reassuringly, that they (the cautious ones) are normal and thus deserving of acceptance and love. Even today, even after appreciation of these particular outcasts has become not only accepted but demanded as proof of membership in some spheres of the cultural elite, even after the petrifaction of these radicals into harmless undisturbed monuments—even today, if most of their works were read aloud in the political circus, they would be met with jeers. In an earlier age, they would have been burned at the stake, dosed with hemlock, strung from lonely trees. The people doing the crucifying would have been the ones you have been fawning over, pleading with and cajoling these last four months. The voters. The people.

How had you missed it? In retrospect, the message could not have been clearer. It was as though the literature you read in college existed almost entirely to convey this simple lesson:

The only way to live truly is to cast aside all that is ordinary and simple and terrible. To free oneself from all that is a lie—all that has been your life in the atrocity of these last few months. You must break free from the prison of conformity, reject the wormrotted palliatives of convention, cut loose from the trowler's nets of security and respectability. Enough of moderation. Enough of responsibility. You must be like your father when he kicked away his father's world and set out for a new life in the West. You must disobey. You must resist. You must make a new life for yourself, a new world, giving no heed to the pale thoughts and opinions of others.

What will you do?

It is not too late.

You must become an *ARTIST*.

You try to tell April about your new perspective on life when, several weeks later, you reunite with her at a party in Abaloma. But she has just returned from helping close the campaign headquarters in Columbus, Ohio. When you tell her that you haven't been following the news about the recount too closely, because you've been too busy sleeping ten hours a day and going to parties, she stares at you quizzically.

"I wouldn't say I regret the campaign," you add, raising a plastic cup to your lips and taking a sip. "It's hard to regret something that taught me so much. But I didn't learn what I expected to learn."

"You seem different."

"I know," you confide. "I've been drinking a lot more."

"So what do you think you learned?"

"Many things. I learned that participating in politics requires the forfeiture of a person's soul. I learned that all the best things America has created have come from its outcasts, its misfits, the very people who are the most neglected and even despised by the masses when they are alive. I really think there are two Americas. There's the America of the common man, where everyone is born the same, and any attempt to depart from the homogenous norm runs the risk of getting you ostracized. I might call this the America of the Puritans. Hardworking, sober, genocidal. Each man seeking above all else to ensure that no one rises above him. A country measuring itself by things a practical man can trust. Corpses and gold. And then there's the other America, the old weird America of homemade religions and lonely, insane poets exploding all traditions, tearing down all conventions, ripping every locked door from the hinges. I think of this as the America of Emerson, Whitman, Dickinson, Melville... And what I realized—it's so obvious, but I never saw it—is that all that's best and most lasting from this country, all that we'll be remembered for when China has taken over the empire, has come from these isolated madmen and madwomen, and not from the people who claim in every period to be the real soul of the country. All the flag-waving patriots who believe that America is great so they can believe in their own greatness, transitively, like an inheritance, all of them have to rest their claims on the achievements of faggot outcasts. You know who's a great band that I just discovered? Bikini Kill. You know a band that no politician could ever be caught listening to? Bikini Kill, because their lead singer is an ex-stripper and all they sing about is fucking and menstruation. But long after our wars and treasures are forgotten, someone will still be reading Melville, another person will listen to John Coltrane, and there will be a museum with an Andy Warhol hanging on the wall. So I guess my conclusion is that politics in America is all about catering to the needs of the self-righteous bigots and cowards, while all that I really like about America comes from the people they hate. I don't plan to do any more political organizing any time soon."

"That's too bad," April says.

"I don't know. It'll give me more time to do other things. Like drinking." You lift your plastic cup. "I'm pretty serious about it."

"Are you joking?"

"I've been drinking pretty much every day since the campaign ended. Sometimes I worry about it, you know, because there are downsides. Less ability to think clearly. But I've found that clear thinking is counterproductive in most parts of life. In any case, I've discovered that drinking has a positive effect on my temperament. It makes me normal. Just like there are angry drunks and sad drunks. I'm a normal drunk. Drinking makes me sociable and pleasant."

"So you don't feel normal unless you're drinking?"

"Exactly."

"I think that's one of the criteria for alcoholism."

"Whatever it's called, I'm all for it."

As the conversation continues, April keeps drawing you back toward serious subjects, ones that might demand an unpleasant exertion of your brain muscle. You attempt to evade her at first with brief witticisms, then realize that it is far easier simply to say nothing and let your mind wander while she carries on the conversation without you. "You shouldn't feel bad about West Virginia," she is insisting. "It's all about God, guns and gays. Everyone just does what their preachers tell them..." She continues talking about something, and how voters in the South did something else, and how one day soon, West Virginia too will do something, but you are captivated by the tall red-haired girl at the other side of the basement, visible to the side of April's head. You recognize the girl from another party earlier in the week, when she was wearing the same tight beige sweater with a white collared shirt underneath. Yet she also wears dark lipstick and sports a nose-ring and a pierced eyebrow. It is so charming the way young people are always trying on new identities, you think, like trying on new sets of clothes. The red-haired girl seems to be mixing together a preppy and a goth identity. While you watch, she lifts a frost-colored bottle of something citrus-flavored to her lips. Gateway alcohol. When she notices you looking at her, you smile and raise your red cup.

"Did I tell you about the documentary I saw in West Virginia?" you ask, turning back to April. "It was about a dancing hillbilly who lives where my grandparents were from. It's hilarious. The hillbilly lives in a trailer with his crazy wife, and he keeps threatening her with a butcher knife because she won't cook eggs for him." You laugh.

"There's a lot of poverty in Appalachia." She sighs. "It's so sad to see people like that vote Republican. They just don't understand what's in their best interest."

"But what if what they want," you ask, "is to vote for someone who doesn't kill babies?"

"Yeah, what about that?" the red-head asks, suddenly standing beside you. You cannot tell whether she was joking. After an awkward moment looking at April, you turn back to the girl and smile. The two of you start to laugh.

"Right," you add. "Isn't saving America from damnation a legitimate interest?"

April stares at the girl. "How old are you?"

"Seventeen."

April looks at you. Then she nods and excuses herself.

Several hours later, you wake in your car, parked crookedly in front of your parents' house.

At first, you do not know where you are. Then you remember. You had followed the red-haired girl and her friends to another party. When you tried to reach under her sweater, she threw a drink in your face. At some point, you returned to the first party and began overturning furniture in the basement. Then they asked you to leave.

Each memory carries a special sting of humiliation. How they all must have stared at you. How embarrassed they must have been. Your slurred speech. Your stupidity. And at the time you thought it was charming.

You think of April's words and you know that she is right. The way you drink is not some rebellion. It is simply an addiction. It speaks in your voice and tells you what you want to do, and you obey. You are not free.

You are an alcoholic.

If you quit drinking, turn to page 271.

If you do not, turn to page 235.

You walk away, slowly, and try not to listen. What do you know about the woman with the bloody face. She might be in love with him. Addicted to drugs.

If you had intervened, you might have made things worse.

Too many unknowns.

At the hostel, you lie in bed and cannot sleep. A few beds over someone mumbles, but the words are impossible to make out. You feel a pain in your stomach.

The next afternoon, you leave the city. A tour bus ferries you north to a national park where these is supposed to be a very tall waterfall deep in the rainforest. You wake on the concrete floor of a doorless hikers' shelter, shivering in your jacket. Outside the empty doorframe a meadow sits unmoving in the morning sun. Your clothes are damp with sweat.

At a nearby visitors' center, you buy a pastry that contains a congealed filling of sugar and processed meat. It is pink and a residue from it sticks to the roof of your mouth.

"Excuse me, sir." A small man in a khaki uniform has appeared behind you. "English?"

"American."

"Oh, American! My name is Mr. Poom."

"Hello," you say.

"You might be interested in tour of park today?"

"How much?"

"No, no," Mr. Poom says, grinning in embarrassment. He waves his hands. "I am forest ranger. When you want, you give tip. When you want," he says, emphasizing the informality of the arrangement, "you give tip."

After considering for a moment, you accept. You will probably need a tour guide because you do not have a map of the rainforest. You do not know how to find the waterfall. "How much time you want walk?" he asks. "We go circle, see small waterfall, four hour. Or big waterfall, seven hour. Eat lunch in lookout."

"Seven hours," you say.

He goes to get something from the nearby ranger station, and when he returns, striding briskly over the small grassy hill, you watch him with suspicion. Then the two of you walk along a dirt trail into the dense forest. Mr. Poom swipes his machete at the stray stalks and branches that fall across your path. The sun spills down in shifting blots across the surface of the leaves and branches. You feel yourself starting to grow anxious.

Before you can calm yourself, Mr. Poom stops you and points high into the trees. "What for monkey? American tourist ask me."

"What?"

"What is kind of monkey? This one."

"I'm sorry, I don't see it."

"You see?" He points into the trees. "You see monkey?"

You strain your eyes but see nothing.

Mr. Poom points again, then looks at you.

"Where?"

He shakes his head grimly and for the first time you see the smile fade from his face. "American tourist ask me." He shrugs and then swings his machete at the end of a long branch, splitting it so that it dangles but is still attached by several sinews. The two of you walk in silence. As your mind begins to wander, you think again of what you will do when the money runs out.

"You are Christian?" Mr. Poom asks.

"No."

"You pray for Jesus?"

"No. I don't have a religion."

"Ah," Mr. Poom says. He swings the machete at a vine hanging down from above the trail. "Yes. There is some of Thai in city. Have many dollar, no need praying. I come from very small village, my Buddha very good to me. He protect me." Mr. Poom laughs. "My Buddha very good to me."

You ask him how his Buddha has been good.

"Oh, I have danger. I have many danger and my Buddha save me." Mr. Poom turns and looks at you closely. "How old you think I am?"

"I don't know. I'm no good at guessing ages."

"How old?"

"I don't know. Thirty."

He laughs. "Forty-six," he says. "I am ranger three year." He makes a long, loping arc with the machete through the thin branches beside the trail. "Before I am ranger, I am monk in wat. You know wat? Ten year monk. Before monk, military." He glances back at you. "Some in big city have money, pay someone else. But I come from small place. Village."

Then you walk in silence. It is unnerving. You clear your throat. "In the United States, the military is all volunteers now. All of them."

Mr. Poom pauses. "They pay for fight? The government pay?"

"Yes. But they're volunteers. They're not mercenaries." You try to think of how to finish the explanation. "A volunteer gets paid to fight, but wouldn't fight for money." You clear your throat. The swirling liquid of sunlight on the leaves makes you dizzy.

Mr. Poom continues to swing his machete lazily through the branches beside the trail. "I sell magazine in Burma," he says. "Is east of here. West."

"I know where Burma is. Don't they call it Myanmar now?"

"I sell magazine for army."

You laugh. "We used to sell magazines at my school. As a fund-raiser."

Mr. Poom laughs as well, swinging his machete.

"That's a funny memory," you say. "We had to go door to door and try to make the neighbors buy subscriptions from us."

"I sell magazine in Burma," Mr. Poom repeats. "There is man that want killing me. Kill family, friend. Man from Burma. Kill everything."

You try to focus on the back of Mr. Poom's head, but it seems to move in different directions. Suddenly, you feel a sharp pain in your intestines, like a needle.

"I go wat then," Mr. Poom continues, shrugging. "No family, no wife, no son. Ten year. You see monk? Shave head? I am monk. I pray every day for my Buddha, pray for to kill bad man, save me. I pray every day. Ten year. Then—you know what?" Mr. Poom glances back to you and flashes an innocent grin. "You know what? Man from Burma shot in head." He makes a pointing gesture toward his forehead, holding a rigid finger to the bridge of his nose. "My Buddha very good to me."

The two of you walk in silence. Then you must climb over a knot of gnarled roots that are a few feet tall. You feel as though you have become smaller since entering the forest, as though the pastry had shrunken you like a magical food. The tree with the enormous roots is as wide as a silo and stretches into the canopy above you, disappearing into other branches. With your leg perched on one of the roots, you look around into the dense leaves and the spinning light. The plants have no interest in you. It will simply happen. Perhaps. You cannot express it. What? Happen.   Your mind begins   to race

Mr. Poom drops his machete and reaches out to steady you before you fall.

"You okay?" he asks.

"I can't..." You do not finish the thought. "Take me back to the visitor's center."

The next day, you hitch a ride out of the park in the back of a vacationing family's pick-up. You think of the afternoon in Bangkok, paging through the travel guide. There was an itinerary for a bus trip. The forest. A waterfall. The slowboat crossing into Laos. This route. These destinations. These points on a map. You chose to go from place to place. You chose. What is it that makes what it is possible. When the family drops you at the bus station you buy a ticket on another bus north. In your hand the ticket is for getting onto the bus. You take the ticket and hand it to the young man by the bus who takes your backpack. The pack for carrying things. One thing and another, they are for things. They show up to fill the need. To fill the gap. But the gap is never filled. In the depths. A missing.

What is it?

You need. There is a gap. Where.

Nothing.

Small roadside villages pass outside the curtained window of the tourbus. The air conditioning. Cinderblock food stalls not yet finished. Roofs of thatched leaves. When you fall asleep, you dream of the woman with the bloody face. She stares at you with mouth open and eyes clenched, but no sound comes from her mouth. She is screaming. Then you wake. She cried out to you and you turned away. Something. What is it. What were you thinking. There is something that   For the rest of the night, you hold yourself in your tall-backed chair on the bus, shivering. No one beside you. There is a pain in your stomach again like a long needle scraping through. An action film plays at the front of the bus and you think of the girl with the bloody face.

When you arrive on the banks of the Mekong, a tributary has flooded one of the bridges into town. You walk in the rain to a guest house overlooking the river. The hostess tells you it could be days before another slowboat makes the crossing into Laos. You accept the news with a nod and go to take a seat at one of the picnic tables on the veranda. It is already early in the evening and darkness settles over the trees across the river. You sit and look out over the guardrail at the rain falling in the swollen current. It has been hours since you ate, but you are not hungry. You decide to eat. When you look around the empty tables for a menu, you see another young man sitting nearby. Your eyes pass over him and then return. The young man is cutting something on his plate with a longhandled lockblade knife. You cannot believe it. You rise and go to his table.

"You—you went to Fernwood," you say, clearing your throat. Your voice is hoarse from the weeks of disuse. "Didn't you?"

It is me. I look up at you.

"The forensics team," you laugh.

I look back at my plate. "Hey," I say. "Egghead. What the fuck." I return to cutting the fruit on my plate into small pieces. I have let myself go. A belly spilling out of the frayed black shirt, stained and unbuttoned to the chest. Oily hair overgrown and tucked behind both ears. You see that I have even deeper pockmarks in my face now. The light from a nearby torch puts them in flickering relief.

"I'm sorry, were you were waiting for someone?" you ask. "Do you mind if I take a seat?" You let out a laugh. "I can't believe this. What are the chances? I mean, what a small world—"

"Yeah."

"I mean—" you clear your throat. "What are the chances that we'd run into each other in the middle of Thailand? It's crazy—"

"Why?"

You wait for me to continue, but I say nothing.

"What do you mean?" you ask.

"Whatever. It's just a fucking…" I wipe off my knife and put it in my pocket. Then I rise. "Could you pay for this?" I gesture toward the plate and do not say anything more before walking away.

After I am gone, you stare at my drink and the bill beside it. Hoisting your bag onto one shoulder, you decide against eating and ask to be taken to your room. It is a small, standalone hut with a thatched roof. You lie down on the bed and soon fall asleep.

The next morning, you wake with a fever and spend much of the day shivering and sweating beneath the thin blanket, leaving only to use the outhouse now and then. You hope that I will seek you out and visit you, but I never come. To distract yourself, you try to read a book left by a previous guest on the bedside table, a frayed paperback about the exploits of the English air force in the Second World War. You have never heard of the author before. You flip through the book and read a few pages here and there. One passage describes the effects of firebombing on German cities at the end of the war. The bombing created towers of fire that rose two thousand feet above the roofs of the city and consumed so much air that hurricanes formed in the sky.

The description of the blackened and melting bodies in the city below reminds you of scenes from hell. But these scenes were real. They had happened. Then you dream that you are running through a city, running from the falling bombs, but the asphalt turns to lava around your feet.

When you wake, you can hear that the rain has stopped.

Gathering your energy, you put on some clothes and walk back to the veranda. There you find me again sitting beside my wooden table, smoking a cigarette and gazing out over the flooded riverbanks. A small crew of men is working to repair the muddy dock.

"There's some problem with the slowboat," I say. "They say they're not going to fix it for another few days."

The fading light is still too bright. Something is sparkling in the air. After ordering some fried rice from the guesthouse menu, you settle into your wicker chair. "Were you going to Laos?" you ask. "That was my plan."

I do not respond, continuing to smoke and stare out toward the other side of the river. Flies occasionally land on my skin and I brush them away.

"What have you been doing all these years," you say. "I wanted to ask."

The black circles around my eyes are even deeper in the dim light. I reach between the buttons of my shirt and scratch my belly. "We should go find some girls," I say.

"Where?"

"In town." I take another long drag. "Girls are so cheap here."

You breathe in and a pain pierces the side of your chest.

"Did you know you can fucking buy a girl here," I say. "Like a slave."

There is a deadness in my eyes. I stare at you but somehow I am looking through you.

"I could get you a girl for like two hundred bucks. Do whatever you want. Spend a week with her, let her go." I cough. "What do you think?"

"I'm not into that."

"You know what happens if they try to run away from one of these houses? They fucking pour acid on her face. Or cut her eyes out or something."

You pick up the menu from the wicker table and then set it down. "Whatever happened to Denise?" you ask. "From Fernwood. She was your girlfriend, right?"

I shrug and look out over the river.

Then the waitress comes. You look at the menu again and set it down. You are no longer hungry. After she is gone, you excuse yourself. You tell me you are not feeling well.

The next day, you wake covered in sweat and shivering. On the thatched roof of your hut, the rain patters down. You dreamed of the woman with the bloody face. Her mouth wide. Screaming. She looked you in the face and you turned away. Is this what you have become.

Several days pass. The fever comes and goes. You still have some crackers from the busride north, and you eat them and drink water from your plastic hiker's bottle. Your belly aches and you must go to the nearby outhouse frequently. Sometimes, you stare at the pages of the book on the air war and try to read. At other times, you think of the slow aches in your body, how they ebb, flow and turn in their strange cycles. You try to put the pain in its place, when it comes, by asking yourself what pain really is, and why it should have any dominion. Why must you interpret this or that sensation as something bad? You imagine the pain of your headache, or the aching in your limbs, as something apart from you. But as the days pass, you are less able to have such thoughts, because the pain begins to fill your mind.

Finally, you decide to go into town and see a doctor. Late in the afternoon, when you first step out, unsteadily, into the fading light and make your way to my hut, you find that it is empty. You go to the veranda, but it is empty too.

"Is my friend around?" you rasp at the front desk. "The other American."

The woman waves her hands. "No more, no more," she says, speaking testily. "No more here." She turns quickly toward the back room and waves her hands.

"He left?" you ask.

"Yes," she says. "Police come."

You return to your room and lie down, covering yourself with the blanket. In the coming days, you become so feverish that you can no longer think clearly... Once there is a tapping at the door. It becomes more emphatic, then stops. You can feel yourself beginning to lose focus when it begins again, now a sharp pounding... Then you wake and your body is a knot of pain. Something is broken. You reach out your hand. Like a leper. Nothing moves now except the roofs from houses melting   the canals in flames. I sit on the corner of your bed. The knife open. Or that was

IF

                                    a young man stepping out onto
the dock. Other tourists on the cramped lower level, and locals sit on
the top by crates. Couples with folded legs on the knotted burlap. It is
not fair for them to come back to you now but you cannot look away.
So you let them make clouds in your head and you and

                                                                He
tosses the ropes aboard as we drift out into the river. The last traces of
the town give way to unbroken forest and, now and then, a stilted hut
rising out of sand   Two thousand feet above the city

melted like lava over our ankles

                                        in a stained white
dress beside the boat, drawing riverwater into a wide plastic syringe.
Her brother waits patiently barefoot in the mud. Then she chases him.
She shoots water at him, laughing, and the two chase back and forth in
the sand. Some of the tourists take pictures and offer small coins.
Hurricanes turned above the city. A woman delivers a boar wrapped in
a burlap sac

                            waystation, a few booths and produce stands
on a small slope. The young man follows the tourists off the boat.
Bodies. He files out behind them across the dock and walks along
        dusty path The foliage is   in the fading light
At some distance from   but it is closing The world
        dim awareness of light and the imperceptible shudder   from
leaf to root The smallest of all possible lights   in the darkness

                            lies down in the leaves and stems beneath
the rubble   And I told her that I rolled to
earth in a ball of stars   and in these blue flames

swollen black Cut down
like stalks in the harvest   and returned to dust

When you open your eyes, you see that your hand is not resting against a can of beer at all. It has fallen on a carton of milk. You have always liked milk. You pour yourself a small glass and, as you drink it, you forget about Margaret, briefly.

The next day, you finally call April and arrange to meet at a coffee house. She asks you whether you have made any plans for after graduation, and you tell her that you have not thought much about it. "I can't make up my mind," she says. "I was thinking of going to Russia."

"Russia? Why would anyone go there anymore?"

She shrugs and looks out the window. "I've been learning Russian. I'm writing my senior paper on the Left's response to the collapse of Soviet Communism. Or its lack of response. All these leftist parties in Europe that keep saying we're in a *late* stage of capitalism, like there's something better right around the corner."

The rightward lean of April's words comes as a surprise. Based on past exchanges, you had assumed that she shared your general sense that in any conflict between two political positions, the one further to the Left was more likely correct, or at least more righteous.

"Well, there are alternatives. Are you familiar with anarcho-syndicalism? A lot of my friends in the co-op—"

"Oh, please. The activist Left has no agenda."

You wait for her to finish. "Meaning?"

"All they want is a medieval carnival in the streets."

You nod. "I see what you're saying. But a lot of people are tired of plans. They want to see change grow organically, without a center, from the ground up. The whole point of the anti-globalization movement," you say, licking some stray whipped cream from your cheek, "is that you can't define the solution ahead of time. No grand ideas. Just local, organic resistance." You stop to take a long, slow drink of mochaccino, putting your finger for the first time on what is different about April's face. It used to be round, like a cherub's, but now the baby fat has gone away. There is even a kind of hollowness around her eyes. "And the first step is to change what's going on inside ourselves. To move away from consumerism and toward—something like a gift economy—"

"Does anyone really think that's going to happen?"

"It already is happening. We've moved the debate far to the left of where it was."

"We?" She laughs.

"The media has been forced to listen," you continue, "and we've forced the WTO and the IMF and the World Bank to stop and listen too—to all the voices that are arrayed against them. And when I say 'we,' I mean the people in my co-op. I got assigned there in the housing lottery. But it's great. There's fresh bread every night."

April stares at you. "Let me guess. You've been reading Naomi Klein."

"This isn't about Naomi Klein. It's about love—"

"I've never understood how the solution to consumerism could be spending even more time thinking about what brand of shoes to buy, or whether you're shopping at an independent bookstore. In my ideal world, I'd spend as little time thinking about what I buy as possible, so that I could spend more time on what matters. Like you said—like love." She shakes her head. "I just don't get it. Hippies always want to see a world where everyone gets engaged with politics and stays engaged with town hall meetings and passionate participatory democracy..." She shrugs. "I'd rather have a competent government that takes care of itself and leaves everyone else free to do other things."

"Like what?"

"I don't know. Whatever people do."

The two of you sit in silence, and April continues to avoid looking you directly in the eyes. You hold back on asking her whether something is wrong, perhaps because you know that once the conversation turns to more personal concerns, you will have to tell her about Margaret.

"Anyway, the focus of my paper is the contemporary academic Left, not the hippies. And the academic Left is even worse. The jargon, the posturing. It's like a priesthood."

"Well, that's not true," you say. "There are plenty of leftist academics who—"

"Trust me. I've had to read this trash for two years. Actually *read* it. Do you know what that's like? Do you?" She closes her eyes as though attempting to ward off a bad memory. "And the punchline is always the same. If you try to help the oppressed of the world speak for themselves, you'll only silence them further. Try to get sexual liberation, end up with tighter sexual control. Try to achieve equality between the sexes, end up excluding the oppressed voices within the sexes. Attempts to secure human rights only reinforce the domination of the first world over the third. Attempts to improve the conditions of prisoners or the mentally ill only lead to new, more subtle forms of torture. Justice itself is a totalitarian concept, a fantasy that perpetuates the systematic, violent exclusion of difference. Reason is too. Attempts to resist power are a part of power's—"

"Fine, fine. I've been reading mostly analytic philosophy. But what about Chomsky?"

"Fucking Chomsky."

You wait for her to continue.

"Isn't he trying to change things?" you offer. "You know, he's an anarcho-syndicalist."

"Don't any of these people realize that economics exists? It's a science. Sort of. You can't just sit back in the British library and dream up a better way of doing things. There'll be parts that you didn't think of, and these parts will make your idiotic idea worse than what we already have. It still amazes me, every time I read Marx, that anyone in a position of power ever made economic decisions based on his thought. Everything he wrote is just a poetic fantasia by a young humanities graduate student. It's metaphors. Definitely not science." She starts to speak, then stops and shakes her head. "Part of my paper is about the historical logic of Marxism. The logic of failure. Each time someone tries to make a Marxist state, it fails. No matter how it's tried, it fails. Why? Because the world is more complicated than any one person's noodling—"

"But I thought that's what we just agreed on. Even the activists don't believe in big, simple ideas any more. Right?"

She sighs. "Don't they? The people in your co-op, don't they? Please, never let me hear another one of these homemade schemes, these napkin-sketch utopias for how corporations should be abolished and businesses should be run by mail-in voting, or how everyone should return to small-scale communal farms—which sounds a lot like the economic theory of the Khmer Rouge, actually—"

"That's not fair."

"—or how the police should be replaced by unarmed citizens' brigades using only the power of persuasion… because it worked during the Seattle general strike in 1926! And look at the Sandinistas! Once, I actually tried to argue with one of these bakeshop revolutionaries and got him to respond to my objections by revising his grand scheme piece by piece until finally, at the end of the night, it was indistinguishable from Swedish welfare capitalism. It's fucking pathetic. I can't stand it."

You start to laugh. "I don't know," you say, trying not to twirl the spoon in your mug too flippantly. "Theorists always think in the long-term. It sounds to me like you're just objecting to political theory. You want the Left to come up with a laundry list of government reforms. But don't we already have enough of those? And they never happen! That's the problem. That's why some people think the system needs to be changed. From the ground up."

"The Left today isn't dealing with the long-term! It's dealing with the *no-term*. The *imaginary-term*. It's engaged in a heartfelt process of imaginary-term strategizing."

The entire conversation has surprised you. The last time the two of you discussed politics, she had shared with you a utopian scheme of her own involving the use of the Internet to create a global parliament.

"Have you ever studied economics?" she asks.

"No. I once read an issue of *The Economist*. Part of one."

"Isn't it suspicious that so few leftists have studied economics? It makes me wonder whether being exposed to economics makes you less likely to be a radical. Like getting a good liberal arts education makes you less likely to be a bigot."

You try to move in your chair so that the direct sunlight no longer strikes you through the window. "You sound like Herbert Quain. He just came out with a book attacking leftist intellectuals for being spectators."

"I adore Quain... But even he doesn't know economics."

"So would you consider yourself a conservative now?"

"I'm a Burkean. I'm skeptical of revolutions, and I believe in social progress. What's lacking right now is a clear idea of the progress we need. No political movement in history has brought about change without an idea of what it wants and a plausible story of how to get there from here. Step by step. The Left right now needs a Milton Friedman."

"Didn't he—support the death squads in Chile?"

"Maybe. Probably. But he's also a real economist—and a propagandist. He did exactly what someone on the Left needs to do today. He had a general view of government, a handful of specific policy proposals, and a political philosophy to fit it all together. Deregulation, privatization, cutting the safety net. Government isn't the solution to the problem, it is the problem. And then Reagan came along and actually made it happen. Now everyone agrees with the conservative program, just like fifty years ago everyone accepted the

New Deal." She takes a deep breath. "So the question is, where is the Milton Friedman of the Left today? It's not just that the Left hasn't found its Reagan. Even if they had a Reagan, they wouldn't know what to do with him."

"Or her." You smile. "I'm not sure the Left wants a Reagan."

"It's just sad to see all these well-meaning intellectuals wasting their lives sitting in the stands and complaining. America has so much power right now. If we wanted to, we could shape that power. Do you realize how lucky we were to be born in America?"

You nod. "Hm."

"I think more people on the Left need to get in the arena. If I don't go to Russia, I'm going to work for the Gore campaign."

"Gore? Do you really think there's any difference between him and a Republican? He's bought and paid for by corporations."

"What?"

"You know. He's the poster-boy for the fact that America's not a democracy anymore. The whole process is controlled by money. How could it be—"

"Do you realize," April interrupts, "that there are countries in the world today that are *really* not democracies? And that people die to have the kind of rights you and I have?"

"I'm not even sure I could vote for Gore. He helped destroy welfare. He works for a man who executed a mentally retarded person. They bombed pharmaceutical factories in Sudan to distract from his philandering. They signed NAFTA. They attacked Kosovo. They did nothing to stop the murdering of a million people in Rwanda. Then they helped to murder another million children in Iraq. They do nothing to stop the spread of AIDS in Africa. They spray poison from the air on farmers in Colombia and help to fund militaries around the world that torture and kill their own people. They did all of this, and Gore never stepped down or spoke out. And you say this is who I'm supposed to vote for?"

"Yes, if the alternative is worse."

You wait for April to continue, but she does not. "I don't see how it could get much worse than that."

April nods, pushing her glass of icewater along its condensation. "Oh, it could get much worse. The right can keep gutting and robbing everything in sight." She continues to push the wet glass back and forth. "And then there's a woman's right to choose. Isn't that enough?"

"I'm just not sure that I could vote for someone like Gore."

"I think you should volunteer for the campaign. What else are you going to do after graduation?" April reaches across the table and seizes your hand. "Really. You could join the field operation. Find out what it's like on the inside."

"What makes you so sure Gore is going to win the nomination?"

"He has the money. It's like you said. He can't lose." April glances at her watch. "Shoot! I have to go see my grandmother," she exclaims. "I'm supposed to bring her a bag of squash." She rises and then turns back to you. "Wait—what are you doing for New Year's?"

"I don't know," you say, feeling a sudden embarrassment. "I was going to fly somewhere, but I had to cancel."

"Oh, I thought—" She laughs suddenly, then shakes her head. "Never mind. You should come out with us." She invites you to a house party with a few of your old classmates from Fernwood. Perhaps it is because you are grateful for the invitation, or because of April's enthusiasm, but as you drive home from the coffee house, you begin to reconsider your hostility to mainstream politics. You have always thought of elections as unimportant when set beside the eternal concerns of philosophy. But what is there to lose from a little exposure to the empirical world?

Even Socrates fought in the Peloponnesian War.

Shortly after graduation, you begin to volunteer for the Gore campaign, and in a matter of weeks they hire you to serve as the field organizer for a region around Morgantown, West Virginia, not far from where your grandfather used to preach fifty years before.

It does not take long before your skeptical detachment falls away. The change happens because of the volunteers. They are not at all the self-righteous liberal elites you had expected. They are laid-off factory workers, coal miners, minorities, schoolteachers, immigrants. People for whom government is not always a bad thing. They come to your phonebanks and spend the evenings making cold calls after a double shift at the plant. They come after a long day of teaching and grading papers. One of your best volunteers is a single mother who brings her child and a coloring book. Your volunteers work tirelessly and for nothing. Why? Because they believe it is right. It is impossible for you to view them with anything but respect.

The state campaign headquarters, on the other hand, shows itself to be contemptible. Near the end of August, when the campaign has scheduled Senator Rockefeller to speak on behalf of Gore at a rally in front of a recently shuttered gasket and sealant factory in

Morgantown, you are forced to drive all the way to headquarters in Charleston to retrieve your office's portion of a long-awaited shipment of yard signs. Even worse, when you arrive, you discover that the national campaign has once again failed to deliver them. You are so incensed that you refuse to leave until you have communicated your grievance to the state field director.

While you wait, sitting impatiently with your back to the wall in the bustling headquarters, you listen to the ritualized cacophony of a nearby phonebank. *I believe Al Gore will help expand the benefits of economic growth to all West Virginians. He will invest in clean coal technology and keep West Virginian jobs where they belong...* You look at your watch and shudder. It is almost three thirty. Throwing back the last of your lukewarm coffee, you turn and glare at the door to the state field director's office.

It amazes you that the national campaign could be so thoughtless. The campaign's volunteers and supporters want yard signs. This is how campaigns are won and lost in West Virginia, as everyone with any roots in the state knows. The Bush campaign has already blanketed the state with signs, but Gore has provided almost none. With each passing week, the volunteers grow more restless.

You glance impatiently at your watch and begin to tap your foot.

A few minutes later, an elderly woman in a jumpsuit ambles over to the state field director's door, opens it casually and hands a stack of papers to someone inside. She leans in the doorway, chatting and laughing. It is intolerable. Even after you speak with the director, you will still have a two-and-a-half hour drive back to Morgantown. You glance at the clock across the office and then again at your watch, tapping your foot. At the very least, you consider, you could be eating lunch.

Through the door, you briefly glimpse the thick, reddened face of the state field director as he hunches over a speakerphone. A thinner, older man in thick-rimmed glasses stands beside him, wearing a shirt with the sleeves rolled up to the elbows. He chews a piece of gum with his mouth open. Then the door closes.

"I finished my list," someone says. You turn and see a stocky man in overalls and a faded union cap holding a thick stack of papers out toward you.

You hesitate to take the papers from him, not knowing what they are, but knowing that they will become your responsibility if you touch them.

"Sorry?" you say.

The man looks down and adjusts his cap. "I don't know what all you got back there, but if you want me to do another 'un," he says. A slight, uncomfortable smile cracks across his face. "This 'un here's got some wrong numbers."

"I'm sorry, is that a finished call list? I'm not the field organizer."

"Hey, you know who them hoagies is for?"

"Hoagies?"

He looks up at you, then points with a large hand toward a folding table nearby. A platter of sandwiches rests on top of it.

"Oh, those. Yeah, those are for the volunteers. Help yourself."

He grins at you. "Where're you from?"

"My family's from West Virginia."

"And where're you from?"

"Northern California."

"All the way from California," he chuckles. "Long way from home. Well."

"Is there anything—"

"I hope we win this thing," he continues. "Been a Democrat all my life. Democrat born, Democrat bred, and when I die I'll be Democrat dead."

You wait for him to continue, but he only nods and grins. "I wish there was something I could do to help," you say.

"That's alright." He does not move. "We need to win this one. We got to bring the jobs back."

You nod. "I know," you say. "We do." You direct the man toward a young woman who looks like she could be in charge of the phonebank. "She might be able to help you," you say.

Then your mind wanders to the crowd that must already be gathering in front of the factory, waiting for the arrival of the Senator, milling around the parking lot where they used to leave their cars and pickups every morning. All that is missing are the yard signs that they plan to wave above their heads for the cameras at the rally and then plant in their front lawns the next day. You refuse to let the campaign be one more institution making promises and letting them down.

"What the fuck are you doing here?"

Jumping, you see that the state field director is standing to the side of your chair, wide-eyed. "I can't believe you're still here," he moans. "I called your name half an hour ago. What the fuck? You need to be at that fucking rally. Now." He squints at you and lifts a hand to his head as though your presence may cause his brain to explode.

"But I promised them—look, I was told I would get at least thirty-six yard signs. Maybe more. We haven't gotten—"

"Excuse me?" He holds both his hands wide open. "Excuse me? Am I standing here—" He grasps in the empty air. "My fucking God. Am I fucking standing here talking about chum with a field organizer? Are you fucking kidding me? Get the fuck out of my headquarters." He seems to use every muscle in his lips and face to bring the point more thoroughly home. You can tell that some of the other workers in the office have begun to stare from their cubicles and tables. "Go. Now. Get the fuck out of my sight."

You take a deep breath. "I'm not leaving here without yard signs," you say.

The director stares at you for a moment. "Come on. Come out here." He pulls you by the arm through the glass doors of the office entrance and into the cavernous, dimly lit lobby.

"There are no yard signs," he says.

"My volunteers—"

"There are no fucking yard signs. There never were. There never will be."

"I don't—"

"We're leaving the state." He holds up a finger. "National made the call. They're shifting all the resources out. I'll put in a good word for you." He pats you on the shoulder and begins to leave. "Don't tell anyone. There's gonna be a conference call tomorrow. This is embargoed."

As he heads toward the street entrance, you rush after him, speaking in a hushed tone. "I don't understand. Does this mean we lost?"

He laughs. "Lost? That wasn't the point. We were never gonna win here. We sucked up their resources and made them pay to compete." Before you can protest again, he has disappeared out the revolving doors. You stand alone on the polished tiles and glance once more at your watch, then turn back the way you came. Your volunteers will be devastated. They have worked so hard.

As you return to grab your backpack, you look around the commotion of the headquarters. It is like watching people going about their lives as an unseen wave approaches. The dam has already broken, and nothing they do in this moment will matter once the floodwaters arrive. The callers at their phones, the low-level field staff rushing from one end of the teeming office to the other—all of their efforts futile, wasted. And nothing can stop it now. All of them have already lost.

An old man strides up to you. "Hello? Are you running this thing?"

"No," you say. "I'm afraid not."

"Well, I think these lists are crap." He raises his clipboard and waves it at you.

"I'm sorry," you say.

"Don't tell me you're sorry," the old man grumbles. "Tell the folks I'm calling, just got called five minutes ago. What kind of amateur hour is this? Some of these folks don't want to be called. You call 'em, you're losin' their votes. And half the numbers are wrong to begin with." He leans toward you. "One even told me. He said, if you call here again I'm not gonna vote. I'm not gonna vote for your guy, not gonna vote for nobody."

"I sympathize with you, but…"

"You ain't listenin' to me. Folks is different here. They want to be left alone."

Somewhere nearby, a caller launches into her script. *I believe Al Gore will help expand the benefits of economic growth to all West Virginians…* Her voice overlaps with that of another as though they are two singers in a canon. *I believe Al Gore will help expand the benefits of economic growth to all West Virginians…* For a moment, there is a secret harmony beneath the scurrying feet and ringing phones, behind the mouseclicks, under the whirr of the copy machines.

"Are you listening to me?"

"Huh?"

The old man blinks at you, and you realize that you have been nodding along while he talked about something. "I'm sorry," you say. "The phonebank."

"I'm talking about pluses and minuses. None of this one-to-five. I don't know how you can tell if a man's between maybe and maybe not. He's either a plus or a minus. That's how we did it when Bobby Kennedy—"

"I agree completely," you interrupt, reaching out to hold his arm. "But they're doin' the best they can. I'm sure it's the same with the folks up at national." You stare at him. "Everybody's doin' the goddamn best they can. Are you hungry?" You walk toward the table and lift up a sandwich, resolutely unwrapping it and starting to eat. "I'm going to eat this sandwich," you tell him. But before you can take a second bite, a woman approaches.

"Which phonebank are you on?" she asks. She is dressed in a blue jacket and skirt and clutches a pack of cigarettes. Her skin is like burnished leather.

"I'm sorry, I don't think we've met—" you say around your mouthful of sandwich.

"No, I want to know which phonebank you're on," she responds. "These sandwiches are for the people who have finished their calls. Are you a volunteer?"

"I'm the Morgantown field director. I just wanted a sandwich."

"I bought them for the volunteers," she snorts. "This is the most disastrous organization I have ever worked with. I wouldn't hire the Gore campaign to mow my lawn."

You nod, taking another bite of sandwich.

"It's really unbelievable," she gasps. "Do you people realize you're losing this state? You're responsible for electing the leader of the free world. And you're losing the state of West Virginia as we speak. Why are you even here?"

You take a deep breath, swallow your mouthful of sandwich, and force yourself to look into her eyes. "I'm sorry, ma'am," you say. "There's really nothing I can do."

You arrive in Morgantown a little under three hours later. Although the lot in front of the factory is still packed with people, you assume that the rally must have ended. But then you see that the Senator is still speaking. As you enter the crowd, a wave of hollering and applause rises. You make your way past the police barriers and through the dense crowd. Some of the spectators have children perched on their shoulders. Another roar passes through the crowd.

"You said it!"

"Give 'em hell!"

Despite your exhaustion, the enthusiasm is thrilling. You can feel the energy in the air. "You said it!" you yell. A man with a handlebar moustache turns around and glances at you. You reach out and put your hand on his shoulder. "You said it!" you yell again.

As you squint into the floodlights and try to pick out the Senator on stage, the crowd bursts into applause again. You have never been so proud to stand shoulder to shoulder with a group of people before. The battle may be lost, but all of you will fight on. You relax into the swaying mass, rocking with the rhythm of the human sea. Then you get a clearer glimpse of the stage, for a moment, and see the man speaking.

It is not the Senator at all.

Senator John D. Rockefeller IV is a tall, thin gentleman, while the man on stage is squat and thick, dressed in a brown leather jacket and jeans. Those behind him wear truckers' hats and matching yellow t-shirts with black block letters across the front. Someone waves a sign, yellow like the union men's shirts. The loudspeakers shriek with feedback.

"That's right, everything's going fine," the man hollers, pacing to the edge of the stage. "Everything's going fine and dandy. That's all you hear. Stock market rising, Dow Jones ten thousand, twenty thousand! Well, how many stocks you own? How many stocks your mother own?" The crowd laughs and cheers. "How many jobs you see coming to Morgantown? This is what they don't want you asking. But you see it. You live it. You live it every day of your life. Stock market rising," he drawls. "Piss on their stock market." The roar of the crowd reaches a new height, so loud for a moment that it is more of a pressure in your ears than a sound.

"You tell 'em!"

"Give 'em hell!"

"They promised us jobs!" the speaker yells. "They promised us pensions! And they hung us out to dry!" His voice is hoarse with righteous outrage. "I wouldn't treat my dog like what we been treated…" A hurricane of cheering rises around you. "Well, I want you to look behind me. Look right behind me and I'll show you what's secure. Their goddamn building's secure. Economic recovery. Economic re-cov-er-y." He spits out the word. "They're gonna recover their profits, that's for sure…"

Just then, through a sudden parting of the crowd, you glimpse a member of the advance team, one of the field campaign's national staffers. She stands almost in a crouch, a cellphone to one ear and a finger pressed against the other. Squeezing through the crowd, you try to yell to her, glad to see a familiar face. She lowers her phone and looks at you.

"Did you see the Senator speak?" you shout. "Did he say the thing about clean coal?"

She grabs your head in both hands and presses a finger tight against the flap of your ear. "Get those yard signs out of here! Now!" she yells. It is a strange sensation, like listening to someone underwater. "How many are there?"

"There aren't any," you yell back. "There are no yard signs."

She nods and seizes your head once again. "Can you turn off the speakers?"

You place your finger over her earlobe and yell, "What speakers?"

Then you switch positions again. "The speakers on stage!"

You switch once more. "Do you mean after the Senator speaks?"

She tries to push you away. "Go fuck yourself!"

"I don't understand," you yell. You touch her shoulder.

"Rockefeller cancelled, you stupid shit," she shouts into your ear, not covering it this time. The force of her breath stabs your eardrum and makes you flinch.

"But these are our friends," you yell. By then, her back is already turned, and she is disappearing into the writhing crowd, speaking into her cellphone once again.

"They say you don't need no unions," the speaker is shouting. "Sure, maybe unions got you a few things way back when. Sure, got you the eight hour workday. Got children off the factory floor. Got you the minimum wage! We got you the weekend! But that time is over, so shut up and watch while we ship your job overseas."

"No!" the crowd roars.

"Over my dead body!"

"Never!"

For a moment, it sounds as though the speaker has gone silent, and you wonder whether they succeeded in cutting off the sound.

"I want to see blood!" a woman shrieks nearby.

You look at her warily.

"Let me ask you, where is the Senator tonight?" the speaker says, looking up coldly. "We wanted solidarity. We wanted solidarity, and what do they do? They showed us the door. We reach out our hand, and they swat it back. Well, I don't know about you but I'm sick of being treated like a dog—" The speaker lowers his microphone, abruptly, and rubs a handkerchief across his face. "I wanna share something with y'all," he says, and his voice is so quiet now that a hush falls over the crowd. "Something that's been gnawing at me. Something that's been eating away at me. I know why they built this fence. I know it." He sighs audibly into the microphone. "I know why they built this fence." He gestures defiantly toward the chain-link fence behind the stage. Crowned with barbed wire, it separates the crowd from the shuttered factory building.

"They're gonna take them dies out," he continues with his eerie calm. "Sneaking through the dark like a bunch of rats... and they're gonna pry them dies off the floor. And they're gonna ship 'em down to a factory south of the border."

A wave of astonished sighs spreads through the crowd.

"Down to Mexico..." The speaker looks down as though beyond consoling, wiping the back of his neck with the handkerchief. "That's right. They're gonna take them dies straight down to Mexico."

A furious roar grows in the crowd. It grows until the speaker's voice is overwhelmed and you must cover your ears. Some of the men around you holler obscenities. Then there is a shriek from the loudspeakers and a song begins to play.

"—*in the valley... West Virginia...*"

"You shut off that music!" The speaker wheels back toward the rear of the stage. "You shut off that goddamn music right now!" he hollers into the microphone. A scuffle breaks out with some of the men in yellow shirts. Then there is a burst of feedback and the music comes to an abrupt stop. "Ladies and gentlemen," the speaker bellows, turning back to face the crowd, "the time for talk is over. Ladies and gentlemen, my friends, this factory ain't goin' nowhere." One of the floodlight arrays goes dark and the stage is suddenly cast in uneven shadows. The speaker drops the microphone with a sudden, loud clatter of feedback and strides off the stage, his back to the roaring audience.

It happens so suddenly. The crowd surges forward like a great human current, pulling you toward the stage and the chain-link fence beyond it. The fence has already begun to shake under the pressure of the human tide. Behind it, the shuttered factory stands in darkness.

If you follow the mob, turn to page 4.

If you separate yourself and go back, turn to page 311.

It is day again. There is a man in the garden. With skin the color of a peach and a thick, bristling beard, he wears an expression both peaceful and vacant. He walks slowly across the trim blades of grass, calmly surveying the foliage. The forking branches of the trees and shrubs bear leaves of such perfection that they could be made of carefully scissored foil. The undulating water of the brook is as clear as long blue strips of cellophane, and occasionally, a chirping bird flitters overhead like a wind-up bird clothed in metal feathers, then settles on a nearby branch.

Wherever the man goes, there remains about him an even, shadowless, sourceless glow. Passing through the butterflies that tremble in the air like colored hinges of crêpe paper on fishing line, he pauses occasionally to regard something and name it. Sometimes a beast appears before him and he names it too. He does not shift the stones by the brook, nor pick up a leaf when it happens to fall, nor straighten the vines that coil crookedly round the tree trunks. There is no need. They are immaculate.

Sometimes a deep voice speaks to him from the blue dome of sky above the garden. The man answers impassively, his face as devoid of feeling as a nutcracker opening and closing its wooden jaws. When the voice informs him that he has dominion over all things, the man accepts this with his unchanging, statued calm. His heart clicks away like the clockwork innard of an iron woodsman. Given the lumbering dimness of his soul, even a leaf turning toward the light over the space of many days would be more aware.

Though he wears no clothes, he feels no shame. At night, when the gold rind of the sun moves behind the treetops and the sky swirls with ink, stars appear as tin ornaments in the blackness.

One morning, he wakes on the lawn and there is an aching in his chest. His head turns, as if mounted on a cylinder, and he sees the one beside him. "This is now bone of my bones," he states emotionlessly, "and flesh of my flesh. She shall be called Woman, because she was taken out of Man." He then stands and goes about the daily work of surveying and naming things, leaving the woman on the lawn, lying crookedly beneath some trees like a stage puppet whose strings have been dropped. As he walks away, her eyes follow him.

Some time later, the woman approaches him with something in her hand. He recognizes it as an apple, because that is what he named it. It is so finely formed, other than the missing chunk, that it looks like a wooden replica of an apple coated in glossy red enamel. He sees the polished fruit and accepts it but does not register the flicker in her eye. He does not remark the curl at the corner of her lips, now unlike a sculpture in some indefinite way. He accepts the brilliant red apple and *calmly sinks his teeth into it, like several tiny wood-axes, perhaps biting in at the skin just beyond the edge of the cavernous, missing piece, not dry like polished wood but now pulp-wet. His perfectly formed, gleaming white central incisors first indent and then pierce the polished skin of the apple, and it is perhaps at that very moment—as the skin separates and his front teeth sink into the crisp, juicy yellow-white meat—*that the slightest foam-fleck of juice from the apple flings toward the pink roof of our man's mouth, sinks into the most minuscule of capillaries there, in the almost impermeable hard tissue, and travels back in blood, still the fluid of a blind machine, to veins that will carry it, finally, across the barrier of inert blood to wooden brain where it will blossom into an awareness, a cloud, and in that cloud the man will cease to be mere dust, and will become aware of being made of it, naked, and under watch.